Heston

In the Company of Snipers

Book 25

Irish Winters

COPYRIGHT

Heston; In the Company of Snipers, Book 25

Cover design: Kelli Ann Morgan, Inspire Creative Services
Cover image: Paul Henry Serres Photography, www.paulhenryserres.com
Interior book design: Bob Houston eBook Formatting
Editor: Linda Clarkson, Black Opal Editing

ISBN Paperback: 978-1-942895-12-1
ISBN eBook: 978-1-942895-14-5
Library of Congress Control Number: 2022922388

In the Company of Snipers

You can find Irish Winters

On Facebook:
https://www.facebook.com/author.irishwinters

On Twitter:
https://twitter.com/irishwinters1

For news on upcoming releases, sign up for
Irish Winters' Newsletter at IrishWinters.com.

For more information about all my books, visit
IrishWinters.com.

IN THE COMPANY OF SNIPERS

This series revolves around former Marine scout sniper, Alex Stewart, and his covert surveillance company, The TEAM, home-based out of Alexandria, Virginia. An obsessive patriot and workaholic, he created the company to give former military snipers like him, a chance at returning to civilian life with a decent job, security, and a future.

This is not a serial with each book ending at a cliffhanger. *In the Company of Snipers* is a collection of passionate love stories involving strong women and men who are tough enough to take on the world alone. Each is a stand-alone read, complete in itself.

Spoiler alert: Every story contains adult scenes including sexual situations (some explicit), language, and violence. I don't write sweet romance, so be forewarned.

Book 1, *ALEX*, reveals how The TEAM came to be, as well as how Alex met Kelsey, how they fell in love and fought all odds to stay together. Each of the following books is a complete romance in itself, where, in the course of an active TEAM operation, one agent comes face to face with his or her demons. The men and women I write about are all patriots and warriors, dealing with what they've lived through or mistakes they've made.

It's my hope that you will come to realize along with my heroes...

Love changes everything.

Chapter One

The White River's water was running cold. Damned cold. The frosty fog hovering over it like a thick quilt was colder, making it hard to inhale without the half-balaclava Alex had tucked over his nose and mouth to warm his breath. He took hold of Kelsey's shoulders and turned her around to face him. She'd been awestruck as the splendid glory of Mount Rainier's northeast flank unfolded. Mountains stretched as far as she could see, some snowcapped and grander than others, some covered in the verdant greens of stately Douglas Firs, Sitka Spruce, Western Cedar, the ever-persistent Balsam, and Mountain Hemlock. Lush valleys overflowing with vine maple, mock orange, sword fern, and the occasional Madrone, divided the peaks into protective canyons that sheltered a wealth of wildlife. Among them, Washington state's unique Roosevelt Elk, the largest of the surviving subspecies of elk. While the majestic creature's geographic range extended to the temperate rain forests in Oregon and Northern California, it was Theodore Roosevelt the animal was named for, and Roosevelt who'd created Olympic National Park to protect his noble namesake.

First and foremost, this hike was Kelsey's idea of a getaway, and Alex's job was to make sure she got what she wanted from what might be their last retreat from the world for a long while. An enormously tough decision lay ahead for both of them. He'd been approached by the President of the United States, President Adams to serve as his Vice President, an onerous calling Alex knew damned well he hadn't the skills, tact, or patience for. Yes, he was dedicated to his Commander-in-Chief, and yes, despite being former military, or maybe because of it, he still lived to serve.

Alex's problem with accepting the offer was simply that the VP role was all about diplomacy, white-wash bullshit, and propaganda, essentially kissing the President's and Congress's asses. Becoming an obedient, subservient yes-man wasn't a skill Alex was known for. His modus operandi could be summed up in ten bolded words: **Lead. Follow. Or get the hell out of my way.** Hell being an interchangeable word, depending on the circumstances or the fool dumb enough to stand in his way.

The challenge to Kelsey, if Alex accepted his president's invitation, would be just as arduous, maybe more so. Arduous because she'd be instantly cast into a hostile spotlight along with him, and he was already considered a pariah by the very biased press. They hated him. He hated them more, especially if they ever attacked Kelsey again like they had in the past.

So when she'd suggested hiking the Wonderland Trail that circled Washington's Mount Rainier, Alex had jumped at the chance. He needed alone time with the woman who had never, not even once, let him down. The faithful woman who'd always had his back. Who'd defended him to his enemies, nursed him when he'd been stupid and got hurt on the job, and loved him through his darkest nights and his bleakest moments. Hell, she'd baked more treats for the people in his office than the local bakery did for their daily customers. Kelsey was simply *it* for him. He'd hike to the moon and back for her, if it were possible.

The day began sunny, and the sky was still a crystal blue bowl over their heads. Not for long, though. A frigid storm front had piled mile-high, dark and ominous clouds to the north behind their backs. They needed to be off Mount Rainier's famous Wonderland Trail and safe inside the bed-and-breakfast Alex had reserved for the last three nights of their getaway before that storm hit.

For the moment, they were standing high on the southern bank of the upper White River, just short of the Emmons Glacier icefield. Because of recent severe summer temperatures, previously unknown in Washington's history, the glaciers above were melting at record speeds, and all of Rainier's rivers and streams were running inordinately high. The White was no different. Its granite banks had been cut sharp by the fierce erosion of this year's spring runoff. There was no shoreline, just dark gray granite edges, wet from the splashing river for perhaps the first time in its history.

The previous night, they'd pitched their tent at White River campgrounds. At zero-dark-thirty, they'd broken camp, then hiked higher up the mountain than they probably should've. But Kelsey wanted to watch the sun rise on the last morning of their getaway, and Alex lived to serve her more than he did President Adams. So they'd packed their gear, slung their onerous, overladen backpacks onto their shoulders, and crossed the footbridge over the noisy White River to Goat Island Mountain, before any other campers stirred.

They'd climbed in the dark as high onto Emmons Glacier as they'd dared, and made it just in time to watch the sun spread its first pink rays across the magnificent landscape below. Alex had to admit the view was breathtaking and worth every step of the climb. The dark purple horizon had turned the softest pink before it had shattered into hues of orange juice, then lemonade. While Kelsey oohed and aahed, he'd held her back against his front, his nose in the top of her head. More than any sunrise or sunset, Alex was thankful for the woman in his arms. The sunrise was just another sunrise to him, but Kelsey was his miracle. The real deal.

After the sun rose, they'd deliberated climbing farther west to the peak of Mount Ruth, an elevation of eight thousand six hundred and ninety-some feet. But that would've been foolish, considering the ice fields between here and there, and Alex was opposed to putting his diminutive wife at peril. They hadn't brought ice axes or crampons along to facilitate hiking the glacier. So together they'd decided against besting Mount Ruth and opted to save that adventure for the day when their children, Lexie and Bradley, could join them.

Slinging his gear off his shoulders and stowing it at his feet, Alex tugged the balaclava from his mouth and pointed south. "See that one? Do you know which peak it is?"

Still facing him, Kelsey glanced sideways, the delighted grin splitting her pretty face and making her rosy cheeks glow. Yup, this cocky Washington native knew the Cascade Range like the back of her hand. Reaching one hand up, she slipped her balaclava down under her chin and replied, "Sure, I see it, and of course I know which peak it is. That, my dear, is Mount Adams and to the right is Mount Hood in Oregon. We can't see Mount Saint Helens from here because it blew its top, and now it's a National Volcanic Memorial. But it's still" —she pointed a finger west of Mount Hood— "r-r-right about there. Maybe we'll see it on the flight home."

"And that?" he quizzed her, pointing due east.

You wouldn't think a woman could smile wider, but Kelsey did. The best thing about her was that smile. It was what hooked him all those years ago, the way she faced every day with positivity and her just-as-big heart, the way she forgave easily and loved deeply. Even some folks who never deserved it. Like him. He'd been a selfish, mean bastard when they'd first met, and he wasn't sure he'd changed much since. Even if he had, he'd never measure up to the gentle person she was. He'd never be that good or that kind.

She cocked her head at him, her brown eyes full of sparkles and love. "Aww, that's home, Alex," she breathed into his face. "Our home."

He closed his eyes, and… Yeah. His tough heart melted and his usually unbending knees wobbled. Just knowing he was loved by Kelsey made him a better man. Hell, she made him a better human being.

She leaned into him, wrapping her arms around his neck and pressing her breasts against his chest. Both covered in too much padding. Not like he didn't already know precisely what was beneath the cute winter jacket she was wearing and the padded flannel shirt beneath it. Alex knew and he licked his lips at the thought of spending three more nights with her without interruption. Without clothes. They deserved every pleasurable second of this mini-vacation, and he was going to make sure she got that, too.

Pulling back just enough to look down at her, Alex planted a kiss on her forehead. "Yes, sweetheart, that's home. Do you miss it?"

She shrugged, her gaze locked on his eyes. "Yes and no. Sure I miss Lexie and Baby Bradley, but we needed this break,

Alex. It's been a long time since it's been just you and me. And if getting you up on this mountain is the only way I can get you away from your phones, office, your helicopter, and"—she shook her head, still encased in a black woolen cap with a bright pink pompom on top— "all that work, then from now on we're hiking the world."

Her voice pitched higher as she spoke. Damn, he loved her enthusiasm. Kelsey was too beautiful for words.

"All you ever have to do is say the word, sweetheart, and I'll never go back to my office again. I'm retired. You know that." He'd told her that many times before.

She had the nerve to giggle. "Yeah, right. I know how much you love what you do, and that you're not ready to retire, even though you said you would. I'm no dummy. I can see how you snap into command mode whenever your phone rings. They still need you and you need them. Right?"

He opened his mouth to protest, but she beat him to it with, "Admit it. You'll never be content to sit home, watching TV, changing diapers, or running your dad to his appointments. Mr. Mom is not who you are, Alex. Besides, that's my job."

She almost sounded offended, but he knew better. "You're Mr. Mom?" he teased.

Kelsey turned toward where Mount Saint Helens had once stood, tall and proud. "I'm…" She took a deep breath, then let it go on a sigh. "I'm what I've always wanted to be, Alex. I'm Lexie's and Bradley's mom. I'm your wife, the keeper of your castle, your heart, and your—"

Suddenly, her skull jerked viciously to the right. Her stocking cap with its bright pink pompom hung suspended in the air behind her. *Mist? Mist!* A gawddamned red mist puffed off the left side of her face. Above her ear. Her big brown eyes closed, as if she'd been… as if she'd been…

She'd been shot! Up here in the middle of no-gawddamned-where!

"Kelsey!" Alex bellowed, reaching to pull her in tight before she fell, before he lost her. But her body had twisted to her left. Precisely as the son of bitchin laws of physics demanded when kinetic energy impacted flesh and bone. The body rotated away from the impact. Like a damned top.

His fingers caught a tenuous hold of the edge of her coat sleeve. He'd no more than gripped it when a wicked pain pierced his shoulder. The energy from that hit knocked him away from Kelsey and flat on his ass. The nerve! Not a solid hit, but who the hell was shooting at them?

'*Too high,*' Alex thought as he pushed back to his knees, breathing hard, his eyes watering at the impact. That badly spaced second hit meant a single sniper had taken both shots. The first, the steadier, more accurate shot that hit Kelsey, the second taken in haste. Too quickly. Before the sniper could regain his calm space, slow his breathing, move his rifle to reacquire the crosshairs on his scope, clear his vision enough to refocus on his second target, and fire. The son of a bitch had sacrificed accuracy for speed.

But he'd hit Kelsey! And worse, Alex had lost hold of her. In the few seconds it took him to get back to his feet, her slack body tilted backward, toward the icy snow field they'd climbed earlier. Where she would too soon slide into the creek fed by that snow field. And from there—God, no!—into the churning white water rapids of the White River.

Alex scrambled to get her back into his arms. He stretched both hands out to her, but the tips of his boots failed to dig in. Her slack weight slid too quickly from his reach. The momentum created by the steep terrain took her away and—

Splash. She fell into the White River. Face first without struggling. Without even knowing she'd been shot. Was she dead?

"Son of a bitch!" Alex ran, heart-pounding panic driving him into the river, his arms stretched over his head in a dive to intercept her limp body before she disappeared. Both of them bounced over lava smoothed slick by eons of ice and erosion, but—

He couldn't reach her!

"Kelsey!" he roared above the noisy torrent, the frigid wind in his eyes, blurring the path forward, making it harder to differentiate her jacket from the froth and shadows of the rapids. At last, he got close enough to snag the heel of her boot. Just the heel. But he had her, by God! He'd saved her and he could fix this. He still had the sat phone she hated so much in his inner jacket pocket. He knew people, damn it, and he would call every last one of them for help. This was not the end. But no, no, no! Her tiny boot slipped off her foot and—

"Kelsey!"

Alex didn't feel the cold. Not the harsh smack of boulders, trapped logs, and branches pummeling his injured shoulder, his thighs, chest or glutes. Not the sting of silt in his eyes. Like a madman, he stabbed through the raging water with powerful, forward thrusts of arms and legs. His sodden boots, now heavy with ice water, held him back. He went under. The White River roared around him in a punishing maelstrom as he sank beneath it. The sky turned black, and—

Like hell!

He fought the river with all he had. He would not die until he saved Kelsey. He refused! But by the time his head broke the surface, she was nowhere in sight. No trace of her anywhere.

Son of a bitch!

He wasn't giving up, just needed a way to slow this damned river. He couldn't catch his breath, much less his footing long enough to be able to spot where she'd gone. No way to project his bleary sight forward or backward. No way to grab anything strong enough to stop himself from being pulled along. No way to know if she were still alive and struggling or if—or if—

The wicked current forced his head under yet again, gawddamnit! Shaking it off, he came up spitting mad, but still no sign of the woman he'd gladly die for. No sign of that damned pink pompom because it wasn't on her pretty head where it should've been.

He powered on, blinking against the foamy, blistering river that would sand his corneas into milky blindness if he didn't get his ass to dry land. Abject misery poured into Alex as he faced reality and let his body slam against one of many fallen logs, itself trapped under the raging river, between two boulders the size of Volkswagens. He had two choices: save himself and run the riverbank searching for his wife, or keep fighting the white water and see nothing, find nothing.

Alex clung to the massive log the river kept him pressed against. There was no other way. No choice. To save Kelsey, he had to save himself first. Tears came unbidden, rolling down his face in a hot stream the river snatched away as quickly as it had Kelsey.

But he would find her. He would save her and warm her, and he would serve her to the end of her days. He would. Even if it killed him.

Chapter Two

"Meeting! Sit Room! Now, gawddamnit!" Murphy roared from the hallway into TEAM One's work bay. "And you two…" He stuck a finger at agents Heston Contreras and Asher Downey in their shared workspace. "Get your asses over to the helo pad, and take your gear. You're Oscar Mike and you're already late! Keep your ears on."

It wasn't often Murphy cussed, which Heston interpreted to mean they were headed into a dangerous assignment. Oscar Mike was military speak for On the Move. Fine with him. Since returning from Arkansas and that debacle with agents Shane Hayes and Everlee Yeager, he'd been itching for more action.

Mark Houston's usually calm voice issued the same command just as nasty as Murphy's, across the hall where he faced TEAM Two's workbay. Heston hurried faster. Jerking his already packed go-bag from under his desk, he scrambled for the side exit out of TEAM HQ, tucking his comm link into his ear as he ran. Asher was fast on his six, both men running against the tide of available TEAM agents flooding the hallway and headed for the Sit Room.

The only difference between the two TEAMs was their leaders. Senior Agent Mark Houston handled the Virginia group, TEAM One; Senior Agent Murphy Finnegan and what agents had relocated with him from the Seattle Office, comprised TEAM Two. All former military, some spec ops, but every last one of those men and women dedicated to Alex Stewart.

Soon to be VP Stewart, or so the scuttlebutt went. Which was a shame. Losing Stewart to the grandiose debacle that was Washington DC, would be an extreme waste of talent. Alex should be President, not assigned some dead-weight job as VP, ass-kissing the toxic powers of the press, Hollywood, and Congress.

"Whatever's up, it's big," Asher murmured in Heston's comm link as they slammed through TEAM Headquarters' side exit and headed north, around the entire complex of buildings, to the helo pad situated far south of Harley Mortimer's barns and Maverick's corrals. "Any ideas?"

"Could be anything," Heston replied as he lengthened his stride. The chopper's rotors were already spinning. "The bombing in Paris last Friday. Maybe the freighter stuck in the Suez. Latest intel indicated radicals from Syria planned to bomb it. Create more chaos."

That brought Heston's attention back to Murphy. It wasn't often the Vietnam vet looked like shit, but he did today. What hair he had left was mussed, and his coloring had been damned near gray. His blue eyes usually twinkled. Murphy was good cop to Alex's perpetual bad cop. But there'd been no twinkle today. Murph's eyes were as ashen as his pallor.

Mark didn't look much better, and Heston wanted to know who'd died.

"Alex is in trouble," Murph declared from the Sit Room, his voice clipped and firm in the comm link inside Heston's ear. "Heston and Asher are flying to Washington's Rainier National Forest, his and Kelsey's last known location. A

Forest Service chopper will meet them at SEA-TAC, then fly them up to the Longmire Wilderness Information Center inside the park. You copy, Heston? Asher? You got your ears on and listening, gawddamnit?"

"Copy that," both agents answered simultaneously.

Murphy continued tersely, "Forest Service'll get you up to Glacier Basin and the White River campground, which, according to the permit Alex filed, is where he and Kelsey camped last night. But knowing Alex, he wouldn't pass up the chance to crest either Mount Ruth north of Emmons or K Spire inside Fryingpan Glacier. Both are nearby and both have altitudes around eight thousand. That leaves two rivers you'll need to search: the White and the Fryingpan. Emmons Glacier feeds directly into the White, then joins the Fryingpan before it dumps into the lower White at Owyhigh Lakes. Either Alex called from the eastern most tip of Emmons where it feeds the White, like Mother suspects or he called from Fryingpan before its confluence with the White."

"As of now," Mark Houston interjected, "we have no way to know which way they went or exactly where they are. You'll be spread damned thin. Do your best to find them."

"Where's the White go after the Fryingpan joins it?" Heston asked.

Something cracked in the background before Murphy could answer. Must've been the Sit Room door banging open because Mother called out, "Got his coordinates, Murph. If he's still got his phone. If not, I've got his last known location. Don't have a clue where Kelsey is. Her GPS hasn't pinged all day."

Which meant her cellphone was either turned off or broken.

"Then where the fuck is he?" Murph growled. Another first: the one and only F-bomb Heston had ever heard come out of the Vietnam vet's mouth.

"GPS puts his last location east of Emmons Glacier, Murph," Mother snapped. "North of Baker Point. Forget the Fryingpan. He's in the White because Kelsey's in the White."

"God, no," Heston growled. Kelsey and Alex both in a glacier-fed river? In the middle of no-damned-where on that mountain? What the hell happened?

"At least we won't have to search both rivers," Asher whispered.

"You sure about that wild-assed guess, Mom?" Murphy was in rare form if he dared call her Mom.

"When am I ever not sure about what I tell you, Murph?" Mother bit back at him.

Tempers were frayed thin if these two were already at each other's throats.

"Why were they even up there?" Heston asked Mother, Murphy, and Mark, not wanting to interrupt, but needing to know.

Mark took over. "Sorry TEAM. We're a little stressed. Should've filled you in sooner. Alex and Kelsey were on a much-needed getaway. Kelsey wanted to hike the Wonderland Trail that circles Mount Rainier, but yeah, something went wrong. Only intel we've got so far is from the SOS Alex sent before he went dark. Which wasn't much, just that Kelsey took a headshot and fell in the river. At that time we didn't know which river. Now we do. Bottom line, he couldn't get to her in time and, yeah, he's probably in that same river trying to save her. Thanks, Mother. We really appreciate everything you've done. Anything else you can tell us?"

Sasha Kennedy, affectionately called Mother or Mom, must've been standing closer to Mark, judging by the volume of her voice over Heston's commlink. "I've been on Jed McCormack's geo-synchronous satellite system since Murphy got the call at ten AM our time, people. Which is seven on the Pacific Coast. Which means Alex and Kelsey were up too damned early!"

Heston thumbed his cell phone on. The screen showed East Coast time at eleven fifteen; eight fifteen in the Pacific Northwest. Kelsey had been in the water for more than an hour. Alex, possibly—no, scratch that—make it just as long.

"Too many trees and undergrowth," Mother complained, plenty of irritation in her tone. "I can't see the terrain, but Alex was definitely close to the White when he made the last call. Which tells me he's tracking Kelsey, or trying to. Only the chance he'll find her is damned slim. The White used to be a placid run-off stream, but lately, it's a dangerous stretch of rapids known for white water, underlying boulders, fallen trees, undertow, whirlpools, and—"

"Hypothermia," Ember Dennison's voice spoke up from somewhere in the Sit Room. "Those are all glacier-fed rivers, guys. Ice-cold water might slow down Kelsey's system enough to help her survive, if she was dressed in cold weather gear, and if she was healthy when she fell in. But if she's been shot, she's bleeding from her brain, and—"

"Right. Understood," Mark cut in somberly. "The cold might not help at all, Ember. Got it. Mother, continue. Hurry."

Heston quickened his run. Limp bodies in turbulent waters still bled. Might even bleed faster.

"We believe Alex was shot, too. Can't confirm, but can't deny he was probably the intended target, not" —Mother's voice cracked— "not her. Not poor Kelsey."

Heston gritted his teeth at the nightmare taking place too far away for him to do either Alex or Kelsey any good. He and Asher raced the rest of the way to the helo pad, nodded to the man who would get them to SEA-TAC, former Air Force colonel and A-10 pilot, Decker Edison. Within seconds, their asses were strapped into the rear seats of the latest experimental helo out of McCormack Industries, and their safety headsets were in place.

This helo was a sleek, black, and deadly-quick tiltrotor that could easily transform into an airplane while in flight. Originally engineered for the FBI's SWAT use inside densely populated cities during riots, it came with tiltrotors that allowed it to land vertically with very little engine noise. Because of its flat-black paint, non-reflective bullet-proof windows, and silent approach, it had quickly become the Bureau's prized weapon against the growing mob violence within American cities. It hadn't been designed to transport troops or heavy payloads, and it offered more air speed than other tiltrotors, including the V22 Osprey. To date, McCormack Industries was the only defense contractor to produce a helicopter/tiltrotor that reached MACH 1 air speed.

"Ready to take off, Mark, Murph," Heston advised curtly.

"Thank God you youngsters are quick on your feet," Murphy replied huskily. "Find Alex. Find Kelsey. God…" His voice cracked. "Find those kids as quick as you can. Bring them… bring them home."

"Yes, sir," Heston vowed.

"Safe travels," Mark added hoarsely. "We'll be sending every available agent to assist, but you two are point. Do what you can, as fast as you can. Stay in touch."

"Copy that," both Heston and Asher answered.

"I'll report as soon as we hit SEA-TAC," Heston added. "Again once we're on Rainier."

"Hope you've got warm coats in those gear bags. It's only September," Mark offered, as if Heston didn't know what time of year it was. "Winter starts early at high altitudes."

Decker sent Heston a thumbs-up over his shoulder.

"Don't worry, Boss. Decker's got us covered. Talk to you soon."

"Copy that," Mark said. The connection ended.

Asher growled from the rear-facing seat across from Heston. "I've got a bad feeling. Fuckin' bad."

Heston nodded. He had the same ugly feeling. A limp body floating in a glacier-fed river stood little chance of survival, no matter how warmly that body was dressed. Hypothermia was a silent killer. Once a body lost heat faster than it replaced it, hypothermia didn't take long to do its worst. Normal body temp was ninety-eight point six degrees Fahrenheit. Anything less than ninety-five would be deadly. There were five stages, each more critical than the previous, ranging from mild to moderate to severe, ending at irreversible hypothermia and—death. If Alex and Kelsey were still in that river... *God, help them.*

Heston squeezed his eyes shut to block the blowback from karma that came from throwing negativity into the universe, from even thinking Kelsey might be dead. That he and Asher were too late. Alex and his wife needed all the hope he could send them. So Heston prayed the prayers of his

Mama, Bellisa Contreras, the humblest woman on the planet, the one who'd taught him to trust the Lord when all seemed lost. The lady who'd taught him that, more than anyone else, Christ was able.

Heston bowed his head and begged for Divine intervention. Because this mission was sounding more and more like body recovery than rescue.

The helo dropped Heston and Asher swiftly at Jed McCormack's private terminal at SEA-TAC. A sleek, forest green Forest Service helicopter sat waiting on the tarmac, its rotors spinning. Egress was a quick run across the tarmac, quicker introductions to the pilot, whose name Heston instantly forgot, then lift-off and a sharp veer eastward. The flight from Virginia had burned enough daylight.

Heston continued to refuse the cold, hard logic that shadowed every hopeful prayer and wish he sent heavenward. More than anything, more than The TEAM he'd created, maybe even more than his children, Alex adored Kelsey. One had only to look at the way they treated each other, how their eyes lit up when the other was around, to know that. They were the stuff romance novels were made of. They were genuine. They were everything Heston wanted in his life, but didn't have a clue how to get. Kelsey had to be alive. Somehow. She just had to.

Because Heston knew what heartache was. He knew the opposite of true love. The cold, hard slap of desertion. He knew the death of dreams. The beginning of lonely, empty nights, of too many TV dinners and take-out. Too many fast-food wrappers, empty plastic drink cups, smashed lids, and broken straws littering the floor of his truck. The unending looks of pity from friends and family. He didn't wish that on anyone. Surely not on Alex.

The flight to Rainier took them northbound over I-5 to SR 7. From there, the helo followed a river Heston couldn't identify. The upper Nisqually? The Puyallup? Didn't matter. Mount Rainier's glaciers fed both.

Before long, strong northerly winds from the approaching storm buffeted the elite helo. Damn. Bad weather could officially end the search for Kelsey before it started. Not like Heston cared what officials decreed. He didn't work for them. Just Alex. Just Alex and Kelsey.

An idea struck hard and in seconds, he'd fingered his commlink, hoping his call to Mark Houston could get through at the altitude the helo was flying. It did. Mark had no more than answered, "Houston. Talk to me," when Heston ordered, "Bring the dogs, Mark. Whisper and Smoke. Get Alex's dogs to Washington right damned now. They'll find Kelsey. I know they will."

"I should've thought of that," Mark shouted. "Damn straight. Should've sent them with you and Asher, damn my stupid—"

"Damn your stupid nothing," Heston retorted, watching Asher come to life across from him. This mission had been one bleak clusterfuck after another, but for the first time, something that felt a lot like hope unfurled between him and Asher. Mark needed to send the two former EOD K-9s that adored Alex and Kelsey to Mount Rainier ASAP.

Whisper was a pure black, fierce-as-hell, unpredictable GSD known for his over-protective snarl and his sharp as shit canines. The older he'd gotten, the testier he'd become whenever anyone approached Alex's kids. Smoke was a silver

Malinois and as obedient as the day was long. Both had been utilized as trackers before when others had been lost. They were the answer today, not the two bone-headed agents still too far from Rainier to do Alex and his wife any good.

"Copy that," Mark replied with a little more enthusiasm than before.

"You heard back from the rangers on Rainier yet? Any word on Alex or Kelsey?" *Please say yes.*

"No, nothing," Mark replied. "Hope that means they're too busy searching to get back to us. See you soon."

"God, I hope so," Heston murmured to himself when the call disconnected.

The helo banked a hard left that took them around Mount Rainier's southwestern flank, up to the Northeast side of the mountain and Emmons Glacier. Heston swallowed hard against the hollow pit in his gut, the feeling that this was a suicide mission. He needed to throw up, but swallowed the bile creeping up his throat instead. The men and women on The TEAM were each made of tougher stuff than most soldiers, sailors, Coasties, and guardsmen and women. The TEAM had done good all over the world, some in combat-torn countries, some in clean suburbia. So had he. Heston steeled his heart, denying the strong emotions that linked him with his boss, compartmentalizing the fear of losing the man who should be king, and the wicked pain of not getting to that man's queen in time.

Whisper and Smoke might be what they needed to locate the Stewarts, but the cold hard truth was—the inescapable fact of Nature was—even two highly-trained dogs might not be able to locate Alex and Kelsey. Not if those rivers froze and not in what looked like upcoming blizzard conditions. It might already be too late.

Heston bowed his head and stared at the floor mat between his boots. His feelings didn't matter. He was no different than those dogs. He'd signed on with Alex to be just another resource, another highly-trained machine with a damned hard job to do today. Nothing more. Nothing less. And just like Alex's dogs, if necessary, Heston would give his life to save his boss and Kelsey.

Chapter Three

Thunder rumbled and crashed around her. She was lost inside a giant kettledrum. Wicked vibrations bounced her to the right, then left. The terrific noise inside the kettle pounded her into a ragdoll. There was nothing to grab or hold onto. Nothing to stop the endless battering. Just noise, pain, and mayhem.

Ice slashed the skin on her face and hands with razor-sharp teeth. Her body rolled and dipped on this ghastly, out-of-control carnival ride. What the river couldn't steal, hidden boulders, logs, and relentless grit did. Like tentacled sea monsters, the churning current dragged her down, then shoved her back up, through and into whatever lay in her path. She'd become unwanted flotsam banging against rocks and branches on her way to nowhere. Too warm to keep. Too limp to fight back. Caught in Mother Nature's evil web, the maker of grand canyons and steep, widow-making crevices, the supreme breaker of mountains and stone, she went unwillingly in unwanted directions. Her body was literally being ripped apart, as if the river couldn't decide whether to keep her or throw her back, like a dead fish it had no use for.

There was no way to fight back, no weapons to fight with. No way to stop the assault or keep her head above water. No way to save herself.

Caught in the maelstrom, fighting for the simple miracle of breath, she prayed for the will to live. All she found was an ice-cold grave and the cruel hand of death at her throat. Her burning lungs had already sucked in more ice water than air. Living was not possible. Not anymore.

The frigid river had stolen everything.

Her breath.

Her strength.

Her will to live.

Her mind.

Hers was truly just to suffer and die. Until…

She crashed into the rigid gate of Hell. Water raced around her at breakneck speed, eager to get away from her. By some weird twist of fate, the force of this new obstacle tipped her chin up—just enough—she stole a gasp of air. Then another. Hurriedly. Quickly. Before she lost her one slim chance to survive.

But as quickly as her lungs filled, the water surged over her face and pushed her head below its wicked torrent. Her eyes opened but she only saw the churning, underwater whiteness that would be her death. There was no sense struggling. The river was too strong and too angry, and she was nothing more than a tiny sparrow trapped in its death-grip.

The brute force of it held her fast against the iron gate. Her bones were turning into water. She'd swallowed enough of it. Her mouth and throat were still full of it. Before long, water would saturate her muscles, tissues, her heart, and… her soul. There was no escape. She belonged to the river.

The world turned colder. Meaner. Her eyes were too battered to see, her fingers too weak to flex. Hope no longer mattered. In minutes, she'd be a bloated, water-saturated corpse. An ugly truth, but nonetheless—a truth.

Oblivion beckoned with one long, icy-cold finger. Her heartbeat faded. The contest was over. The river had won. With one last bubble of air from her drowning lungs, she sent her soul to the man who'd helped her find it so long ago.

To Alex.

Chapter Four

Disgusted with himself and mad at the world, Alex sat alone on the east bank of the White River, a short way from the campground where he and Kelsey had spent their last night. *Not their last night. Just last night!* They'd have many more nights together. Alex would make damned sure of it. He just had to find her.

Breathing hard from his fight with the river, he shivered. Not so much because night had fallen, nor because a thin layer of frost now glazed his hair, face, neck, and hands. All were good signs he was still alive. He shivered because, in less than a split second this morning, he'd lost the mother of his children, the woman he adored, and his reason for living. He shivered, not from cowardice or fear, but from an anger so deep, he could barely hold it back.

Once again, the mantra of all his past mistakes whispered, *"You should've been there."*

"I know!" he ground out. Problem was he *had* been there, had been right there when she'd been hit. Had had both hands on Kelsey. *Could've* saved her. *Should've* taken the hit for her. But he hadn't done either, had he? Sure, he'd been hit too, grazed, which still seemed an impossible second shot for anyone to have made. *If* it had been intentional and wasn't the mistake of a harried sniper like he'd first thought. Or if that sniper had been closer than Alex had estimated. He'd had too much time to think, but think, he had.

Until remorse started eating him alive.

Fortunately, a man and his son had been strolling the edge of the White and had run to help him. *Him,* a self-made man. *Him,* the guy in line to be the nation's next gawddamned VP. *Him,* the bastard who couldn't even save his own wife.

Accepting help—charity—was not Alex's strong suit. He was the strong one, the giver, the protector. The generous benefactor. But he hadn't yet been able to catch his breath at that moment. So he'd allowed the kindly hand-up and overbearing concern from a stranger, as well as a steaming cup of soup from the guy's stainless-steel thermos. He'd allowed Tom, whose last name Alex could not recall, to help him crawl up the rocky riverbank and onto dry land. The kindly Good Samaritan had then helped Alex out of his wet clothes, into warm sweats and a pair of sturdy work boots. Thank God, everything fit.

The whole time, Tom's little boy had sat nearby watching. Kid had to have been around five. His big, brown eyes and tousled, curly brown hair—dry hair—had stabbed a dagger into Alex's heart. Kelsey had—*has, damn it! Has!*—brown hair. The same tint. The same lush, dark shine and natural curl. *So does Lexie. Her eyes are just as dark brown. Gawddamnit, Kelsey is still alive. Somewhere. She has to be.* Alex couldn't conceive of a world without her in it. Refused to consider the possibility.

Tom had handed over his cell phone then, and Alex had gotten out the briefest SOS to TEAM HQ. The connection hadn't been clear, but Murphy had answered. He'd heard. Alex was sure of it. At least… he'd thought he was. He'd led with how Kelsey'd been shot, but then the connection went dead. He hadn't clearly heard Murphy's answer, but Murphy'd know what to do. He'd send The TEAM. They might even be on their way now. Alex hoped…

Just as his frantic SOS got cut off, Ranger Bates, his name tag declared, arrived on scene. He left his truck running while he ran to where Alex sat, too weak and tired to fight. "Came as soon as I heard. You okay? Where're you injured?"

For some reason, Tom signaled Alex with a firm headshake, as he and his kid faded into the shadows. Was that a warning? Or was Tom guilty of something? Alex couldn't tell. Tom was gone before he could ask. But that small tell from the man who'd braved the White long enough to drag him to safety, made Alex think twice.

"I'm not injured," he lied to Bates, not admitting weakness until he knew what Tom's unspoken message meant and what kind of man Bates was. "But someone shot my wife. We were up on Emmons Glacier. He hit her left temple." *I think.* The longer Alex thought about what he knew, the more he doubted himself. "She fell in the river. I jumped in after her and—"

"You jumped into the White? On purpose?" Bates' gloved hands splayed over Alex's wide shoulders, attempting to press him flat to the ground. "What are you, stupid? The White's never been this high before and—"

"I had no choice!" Alex shoved this joker's idea of help off.

Glaring, Bates tipped back on his haunches and clenched his thighs. "And you figured drowning would help your dead wife?"

"She's not dead!"

"You Californians are all the same entitled—"

"We're not from California! Never mind. Get out of my way! My TEAM's on the way. They'll be here soon and—"

"Your *team?*"

Pissed at the sarcasm pouring out of this guy's mouth, Alex began to doubt himself and his TEAM. Surely Murphy or Mark would've sent agents to assist by now. Alex had to admit the call he'd made may not have been clear enough. There'd been plenty of static over the connection, and it had failed before he'd gotten a definite reply. Maybe Murphy hadn't understood the call for help. Maybe he hadn't heard… anything.

Even if Alex hadn't made complete sense, Murphy was smart. He'd know what to do. He'd investigate. He'd follow through. He was Alex's right-hand man. Well, one of them. By hell, Murphy'd move heaven and, well, hell, to find Kelsey—

If he'd understood and had actually heard that poor excuse of an SOS. Suddenly, Alex wasn't sure of anything. Was anyone from his TEAM coming? What exactly had Murphy heard?

Truth was, Alex had also been shot, but wouldn't accept aid until Kelsey was found. His heart hurt worse than his shoulder. Not his actual heart, he hoped, but his chest. His ribs. His sternum. They felt broken. Or cracked. Which was concerning. Because beneath that powerful breastbone was his damned heart, and he'd had problems with it before. He didn't need those problems again. Not today. He didn't need Ranger Bates' help, either. Not like he was going to get it. Just a first-aid kit. That was all Alex wanted.

Bates jerked a walkie-talkie out of his parka pocket. "Listen, buddy, you're not going anywhere. I've got the local ambulances on speed-dial. They'll come from Eatonville or Enumclaw and it'll take a while for them to get here, so sit tight and—"

"You're just now calling them?" Alex climbed gingerly to his feet. "They should already be here. You knew my wife was in that river hours. Murphy Finnegan called you guys." *I know damned well he did. He got my message, damn it. He did!* "I'm not leaving without my wife. She's the one who needs help. Not me." *You son of a bitch!* "Where's Search and Rescue?"

"Sorry, mister… Err, what is your name anyway?"

One of many questions Bates should've led with the second he'd arrived on scene—if he honestly hadn't known what happened or what Alex was talking about. If Murph hadn't understood Alex's SOS. If no one from The TEAM was coming. *Shit.* Maybe Bates was the only help around.

"Alex Stewart. My wife's Kelsey," Alex bit out, scrubbing a bruised hand over his wet, aching head, not giving into despair. Not yet. This was one time he wished he were Vice President Stewart. Bet Bates would be jumping through hoops to find Kelsey then.

"Well, Mr. Alex Stewart," Bates replied with plenty of snark. "Stay put. I'm in charge now and I've got—" His walkie-talkie crackled with static. Pressing it to his ear, Bates ordered, "You're cutting out, Wilde. Say again."

Whoever Wilde was, he, make that she, enunciated slowly but loudly, "Search. And. Rescue. Units. Are. On. Their. Way." Which told Alex he'd definitely gotten through to Murphy and someone was already searching for Kelsey. Thank God.

"I'm not deaf!" Bates yelled back at Wilde. "Who told you to contact S and R? That's my call." When no response came back, he yelled, "Answer me, Wilde. Who told you we needed Search and Rescue, gawddamnit?"

Again, Wilde didn't respond. Which was interesting—if Alex had time to care about insubordination within USFS's chain of command. "You're pissed because someone else called Search and Rescue? Who the hell are you? What's going on?"

Bates stuffed the walkie-talkie back into his pocket. "You heard. S-and-R's on their way."

"They should already be here! You knew damned well that my wife was shot, you son of a bitch!" Alex cocked his right hand back, ready to kill this useless excuse of a human being.

Bates turned toward his truck. "I'm outta here."

"You call this help?" Alex spat. He stood there in the dark, watching Bates stomp off. He honestly didn't know where to search anymore. In the river? Along the bank? Was he a fool for believing Kelsey had survived?

"Jesus," he growled at the Lord. "She believes in you, damn it. Don't you dare let her die!"

Remorse hit Alex hard. There he was, back at square one, back to the darkest days in his life, when cursing God was all he'd done. All he'd been smart enough to do. Supposedly he knew better now. Allegedly, he was a better, smarter man because of his wife's faith. Kelsey had shown him a better way. He'd learned to pray, and he actually felt a connection with the Almighty sometimes. But it was easier to believe when Alex wasn't faced with losing her.

Maybe that was what his chest pain was. Regret. Guilt. They hurt like sons of bitches, and they weighed him down like his water-logged boots had. He'd kicked the worthless suckers off the second he was on dry land. They signified everything he'd lost.

Would Kelsey have any doubt that you were alive if that was you in the river?

Alex had no idea his conscience could be so loud. He dropped back to his knees. "She believes in you," he told the Man Upstairs. "With all her heart, she believes in you, and she trusts you. Please don't take her. Take me. Lexie and Bradley need her more than they need me. You know that. Please…"

Alex forced a swallow that hurt all the way to his soul. He was every bit as lost as George Bailey had been, standing on that bridge in a blizzard, wishing he'd never been born, in that black-and-white film from 1946, *"It's a Wonderful Life."*

"Please take me instead of Kelsey, God. Please."

Of course, God didn't answer Alex tonight any more than he'd answered George Bailey then. God was sly like that. Silent when you most needed to hear His voice. When you most needed to believe. If Kelsey were there, she'd say this was what faith was about. Believing in the dark. Never doubting that He cared or that He heard. Trusting in Him when all others turned their backs on you. Which Bates had surely done.

It was damned hard to be humble, but Alex chose to believe Kelsey, and that God was silent because He was working too hard saving Kelsey to waste time answering.

Okay then. Alex lifted to his feet, a fraction of his energy restored. Or maybe that was his faith. Because God had already given him a sign in disobedient Ranger Wilde. She'd activated the Search and Rescue personnel without Bates' permission. Good on her. Hopefully, she'd also ordered all available Forest Service personnel to the scene. Wilde was Alex's miracle, his prayer answered, interestingly, before he'd offered it.

Right on cue, flashlights from other campers pierced the bleak darkness where Alex stood. Holy shit. Strangers were now tramping this side of the White, calling out loud and strong for "Kelsey Stewart!" Beams from their flashlights gleamed across the noisy river, into the late growth of spindly alpine flowers on the opposite bank.

A chill raced up the back of his neck. Every last one of those flowers would freeze in the coming storm. If they lasted the night. If Kelsey lasted the night… She was every bit as fragile as those damned flower petals. A thousand times more precious. And she was in the river—somewhere—not planted safely on some sandy shore. Not warm. Not within reach…

"Son of a bitch!" Alex hissed at the clouds covering Rainier's three peaks. Like a stupid greenhorn, he'd handed Tom What's-His-Name's phone back to him and now had no way to contact his long list of resources. His pack with his gear was on the northern bank of the river. He had nothing but the borrowed clothes on his back.

His lashes fell at the awful truth. He'd saved his life, not Kelsey's. What kind of man did that make him? A bastard. A low down, sniveling—

"You the bloke what's looking for his wife?"

Alex glared at the guy asking the stupid question. *Bloke?* Interesting word choice. Interesting Irish brogue, too. The guy was slender enough to be called athletic and sported a neatly trimmed salt-and-pepper beard, which made him look older, but Alex pegged him at thirty-five, maybe forty. Dressed in spit-polished black boots, black jeans, a black L.L. Bean down-jacket, and a light-gray ballcap, the guy stayed a good ten yards uphill from Alex. Away from the river and behind the nearest pine. Half-hidden in shadow.

"I am," Alex answered as civilly as his growing despair allowed.

The man reached inside his jacket and pulled out a rolled package, then tossed it to Alex. He caught it one-handed, pissed that he wasn't even armed. But that was what happened when you were so stricken with your wife's absence that you lost all track of operational security.

His two pistols were somewhere in the river, swept away in the icy torrent along with his holster rig. Kelsey's was probably still in her backpack. Which was why she'd sunk out of sight so quickly. Why she'd sunk at all. If she had. He wasn't sure of anything. The entire disaster, everything that contributed to her death, pointed at Alex. He would carry this new shitload of guilt until the day he died.

"Open it," the almost friendly, probably not friendly at all, stranger encouraged. "The next step's up to you."

A chill ran up the back of Alex's neck. "What's going on?" he growled, even as he kept an eye on the guy and let his fingertips slide into the package's seam. The cloth separated and an embroidered black rose the size of his palm fell out.

Shit. This was why Kelsey'd been shot? The Black Irish Rose Tavern in Boston? The one Lucy Delaney had blown to hell when she'd cleaned house of her criminal father's faithful henchmen? Sure, she'd wined and dined them first, got them drunk and mellow, made them believe her takeover of Pops Delaney's illicit business would go down peacefully. But she'd killed them just the same.

Alex thought of his sickly, conniving father, Mel Stewart, and Mel's continual lies about his relationship with Pops Delaney, Godfather of the Irish Mafia in Boston. Lucy Delaney's old man. Pops had been a thug and gunrunner straight out of Ireland to terrorize America. In a jolt of pure luck, Alex's protocol officer, Maddie Bannister ended Pops during a gunfight a year ago. Shortly after, Lucy had died a hard death, courtesy of TEAM Agent Jameson Tenney's sharpshooting, on that same dock in Boston the same day she'd killed her father's men. Problem was, Mel had then revealed that Pops was his brother, making the boss of the Irish Mafia in America Alex's uncle and good old Lucy his gawddamned cousin. Come to find out Pops had changed his name from Stewart to Delaney when he'd run away from home and fled back to Ireland. God, the swamp of lies Mel Stewart had fabricated to excuse the illegal side of his family. Alex's flesh and blood, damn them.

And to think that old fart now lived on Alex's dime. In his house. With his children! But only because Mel had Alzheimer's. He should damned well thank Kelsey for his more than generous circumstances today. Because Alex would've turned his back on the son of a bitch, not invited him in to stay and live out his remaining days in comfort. Not after the shit ton of crap Mel had dumped on his one and only son since the day he'd been born.

Thank God Lexie and Bradley were with trusted neighbors for the duration of this damned getaway. Double thank God that Alex had put Mel in an assisted living home before he and Kelsey left on this disastrous adventure. But if Mel's past was behind what happened to Kelsey today? Mel could rot in that nursing home for the rest of his worthless life. He could and he would. Alex swore it. He never should've let the bastard back into his life.

Still fingering the embroidered rose, he lifted it high enough for the stranger to see. Not saying a word. Not admitting anything. Not giving anything away. If this had to do with the Irish Mafia, like it appeared, things could go south in a blistering second. All Alex gave this *bloke* was his chin.

The man cleared his throat. He was nervous.

He damned well should be.

"D-don't worry, she's alive. F-for now," he stuttered, then cleared his throat again and lifted both palms to Alex, as if warding off an attack. Which he damned well had coming. "You got a decision to make, son, and it'd better be the right one. Understand what I'm saying?"

"I'm not your son! Where is she? What have you done to her?" His body assumed a fighting stance. His borrowed boots spread far enough to balance his weight if he needed to attack this asshat, to strike first. To hit hard. His fists curled into hammers that could and would bludgeon the Irishman to death. All his past agony boiled to the surface. He wasn't a successful businessman tonight. He was only Kelsey's husband. Which made him Armageddon.

His body grew taut and hard with a rage so fierce, it hurt to hold it inside. Without her in his arms, his heart was a scorching cauldron, bubbling with revenge. His blood pumped hot and heavy. Maybe that explained the thumping behind his ribs. Maybe his heart had known all along she was gone. That she needed to be avenged. The thought, the merest hint of her being dead, killed, just killed!

When the Irishman didn't answer, Alex bellowed, "Have you seen her? Did you hurt her? If you—!"

"Wha'd'ya think I am? A bloody wanker who hurts defenseless women?" the imbecile hissed, like he was the offended one.

"Yesssss! You're a bloody bastard!" Alex hissed back, taking a step forward, needing to choke the shit out of this Irish moron to get the answers Kelsey needed to live. "Where is she?"

"I didn't shoot her. If you hurt me, she dies. Stay back," the blithering idiot proclaimed, his hands still up like the coward he was, his clean shiny boots moving him farther into the shadows and away from Alex and the beatdown he had coming.

Alex froze. How'd this guy know Kelsey'd been shot? Alex hadn't told anyone but Bates. The urge to attack lifted Alex's hackles, but logic prevailed. No sense driving this moron away. He wasn't the mastermind behind this new development. Definitely not the shooter. He hadn't the nerve or the intellect. Now was not the time to lose his temper. Kelsey deserved better, and if this guy was to be believed—*if* being the key word—she was, at least, alive.

"Where. Is. She?" Alex asked again.

The Irishman dug into his jacket again and pulled out a cell phone. With a toss, he sent it flying in an arc over Alex's head, high enough he had to stretch to catch it. When at last he had it in his hand, he looked back at the man. The bastard was gone.

Alex bolted forward, pissed he'd lost his one link to Kelsey. The damned phone in his hand rang. By then, he was on the trail that, at his left led to camp, at his right led into the darkening forest. No sound of a vehicle. No sound of anyone running away. Which meant the Irishman might not be as stupid as he appeared. Which made sense. Whoever was behind this attack had planned well. Maybe all they wanted was ransom. Too bad. All they'd get from Alex was dead.

He hit the answer button, lifted the phone to his ear, and spat, "What?"

"Ah, Alex. Alex Stewart. So good to finally hear your voice," a cultured but definitely male voice purred. His Irish brogue wasn't thick, just enough to be noticeable. Hell, it might've been fake. Alex was too angry to care. "Hope that little love tap I gave you hasn't caused much trouble. You are still alive, aren't you? You can breathe well enough to converse, right?"

"You shot my wife!"

"Tsk, tsk. Such hostility in the face of infinite wealth and power."

"Where is she? Where's my wife?"

"All in good time, my chap. All in—"

"Where. Is. She?" Alex boomed. "I'll kill you both! Bring her to me. That's the only way you and that chicken shit errand boy you sent get to live!"

A sinister chuckle was his only answer before the connection went dead. Because that was all the caller intended, to rub salt in the cuts he'd created. Alex cocked his throwing arm behind his head, hearkening back to the day when fast-balling his cell phone into the nearest wall brought some measure of relief from the rage he'd carried then.

But today was different. He was different. At least, he was a work-in-progress, trying to be different, to be a better man. His arm lowered slowly as he held onto the only link he had with Kelsey, this untraceable burner phone and some nameless Irishman. If he could be believed, she was alive. And if she was, he and that other bastard had somehow orchestrated the entire fiasco. Which meant the Irishman was either an excellent sniper to have hit both marks like he had or that he'd employed one. Or that his cocky boss was the sniper. That he'd tracked Alex and Kelsey early this morning, that he'd planned to drop her into that precise spot along the river. That he'd purposefully put her life at further risk by letting her drown, then recovering her. Saving her. Which he wanted Alex to believe he had. That she was—somehow—still alive.

For an instant, Alex was thankful. But only because he needed to believe that this jerk would keep her alive until he achieved his goal. The temporary rush of gratitude didn't last. Whoever the guy behind this was, he was using Kelsey to get at Alex. Alex would have to manipulate him, go along with his demands long enough to get her back. Unwittingly, the mastermind behind her attempted murder had just given Alex what he needed. The thinnest shred of hope.

Chapter Five

The Forest Service helo couldn't land where the pilot wanted. Too much gusting wind and snow. To reach the clearing below, Heston and Asher had to fast-rope down. While it snowed. No problem. All TEAM agents were trained in everything military, including long-distance shooting, skydiving, fast-roping, even rappelling. So stepping off the edge of a perfectly safe helicopter wasn't unusual. The first step was a little breathtaking, but it was the simplest way to get to the northern shore of the river below.

Overall, it was a short drop. Heston flexed his knees to absorb the shock as he landed. Visibility was poor to zero. "Contreras touchdown," he reported to the Forest Service pilot in the helo above via their shared radio communication link.

"Copy that," came back the steady reply just as Asher dropped to all fours beside Heston.

"Splashdown," Asher sent upward.

"Stay safe, guys. Let me know when you need a lift out of here," the pilot advised as the helo lifted into the clouds. "You've got my number."

The rotor slap had barely ended when Deck growled over the same channel, "And you've got my number, boys. I'll be close by for the duration of this clusterfuck."

"Copy that, Colonel Edison," the Forest Service pilot replied respectfully. "Good luck finding your people, sir."

"Thanks. Now get off this channel and let me talk to my guys."

Heston grinned at the fierce man in the black ops tiltrotor above. "Good to hear you again, Deck. Thought you might've stayed in Seattle."

"Doesn't take me long to refuel. Comm check in sixty. Don't be late," was all the reply Heston received. Made him smile. Deck might sound like a troll who lived under a bridge and ate children for breakfast, but he was by far the best pilot Heston had ever flown with.

They humped onward. The temperature was fairly warm, unusual for this altitude Heston guessed. He'd spent time in Washington before, courtesy of the 2nd Battalion, 75th Ranger Regiment's combat-focused training years ago. He knew the Ranger code and he'd damned well-earned the privilege of wearing the coveted tan beret. He'd never made it to Delta, though. Stopped short of selling his soul to the Devil. His parents had never wanted him to join the Army in the first place. He figured, out of respect and love for them, he'd return home with most of his soul intact.

Weather sure sucked though. With heavy, wet snow falling, the chance of finding the Stewarts alive turned from barely possible to damned grim. Only good thing was that most of the storm remained high on the mountain peaks behind him. He took that as the slimmest sign of good luck.

Thank heavens, Decker had provided them with cold weather versions of TEAMwear, the rugged, lightweight, tactical clothing conceived by Alex and designed by Mother. Incorporated in the winter version was a wealth of pockets in both jacket and pants (always a good thing); thick but lightweight liners that wicked away excess sweat and body heat, as well as protected an agent from outside temps; and lighter-than-air, barely noticeable, built-in tactical plating. The outfits were heavier than normal military wear, but more appreciated.

There was a time a few years back when both summer and winter versions of TEAMwear had also packed a butt-load of sensors to monitor an agent's physical status, as well as document every step of his mission via live video and audio links back to TEAM HQ. Those futuristic advancements didn't last long. Scuttlebutt was that Mother threatened to quit when Alex pulled the plug on her over-the-top improvements to his concept. Alex called her bluff. Told her fine, then do it.

For the life of him, Heston wasn't sure why Mother hadn't taken Alex up on that offer, nor why Alex hadn't fired her long ago. Theirs was a love/hate employer/employee relationship if ever Heston saw one. The things they said to each other could be so direct and spoken so sharply, it was like being in a knife fight if you found yourself caught between them. They were downright mean to each other. Fortunately, Mother hadn't quit, and for now, she was working as feverishly as everyone else to locate her missing boss and his wife.

He and Asher headed due east alongside the White River to the campground where they were to meet Forest Service Rangers Bates and Wilde. They both carried two gear bags, one a heavy backpack loaded with bottled water, tasteless MREs, a change of clothes, and other necessities. The other bag was smaller, loaded with ammo, extra pistols, NVGs, blow-out kits, and other survival items.

The closer they came to the campground, the more the snow turned to rain. Another chopper, this one marked with the green and yellow United States Forest Service logo, came into view. Parked dead center of an empty clearing surrounded by spindly alpine pines, it looked like a forlorn mosquito waiting for warm weather. Hopefully that bird had brought an army of volunteers ready to search for Alex and Kelsey when it landed.

Heston radioed his USFS counterparts to let them know he and Asher had arrived.

"Roger," a calm female voice replied. "It's about time."

"Yes, ma'am. Where's Bates and Wilde? Are they here yet?"

"They're at our Incident Command Center at the White River campground, yes, sir, but I'm in dispatch at Snoqualmie Pass. I'll turn on its perimeter lights to help you spot it. Go on in, guys. They'll be glad to have you aboard."

A line of soft yellow lights blossomed ahead, lining the roof, windows, and doors of a large, ruggedized RV marked in bold yellow with: Incident Command Center, ICC.

"Thank you, dispatch," Heston told the lady at Snoqualmie, then sent a quick report to Deck. "Making contact. Will advise as needed."

"I don't hear from you in thirty minutes, I'm hunting you down."

"Copy that," Heston answered, another smile curling the corners of his mouth. There was nothing like the steady kindness of the older, wiser, crustier generation of combat vets.

He and Asher jogged the rest of the distance to the RV, aka the USFC Incident Command Center. Its door swung outward before Heston could knock, and a stalwart man jumped down from the rig's metal steps. His boots hit the muddy ground with a smack.

"You must be Agents Heston Contreras and Asher Downey," the ranger said as he stuck out a gloved hand. "'Bout damned time you lazy bastards showed up. I'm United States Forest Service Captain Devon Bates. Behind me's Lieutenant Wilde." Bates stabbed a thumb over his shoulder, not even looking at his partner. Which struck Heston as just plain disrespectful.

Wilde didn't say anything, but the tops of his cheeks were red and his jacket was zipped up tight under his chin. Looked like he, at least, had been outside searching. That helped.

"Good to meet you, Captain Bates, Lieutenant Wilde." Heston nodded at the silent LT. "We appreciate the assist. I'm Heston. My companion's Asher. I'm sure you appreciate what we're up against."

"Yeah. You guys don't think we can get the job done."

"We're here to locate our people, sir," Asher clarified politely. "Has anyone heard from Mr. Stewart since his distress call this morning?"

"Yeah. I already found him. Dragged him to shore and tried to help, but he fought me. Dumb shit's stubborn. Wouldn't listen and wouldn't let me call him an ambulance, either," Bates shrugged one of those big shoulders.

"You found him?! Where was he?" Heston demanded to know. "Take us to him? Is he okay? Any sign of his wife?" Why the hell wasn't Alex inside the Incident Command Center being treated?

Bates waved into the dark. "He was over there when I left, on this side of the river. Not sure why some office in far-off Virginia sent you guys all the way out here. We don't need your kind of help."

"You left him? Why? Is he injured? Is anyone looking for his wife?" Heston couldn't believe the nonchalance of this guy, or how often Bates dodged answering questions.

"Our kind?" Asher asked. "What kind would that be?"

"You know. Military. We work better alone. Right, Wilde?"

Heston cut Wilde off before he could answer. "Focus, gawddamnit! Captain Bates, where exactly did you leave Mr. Stewart? Has anyone located his wife yet?" Temperatures had dropped since Heston and Asher touched down. Anyone who'd been in that river would be a frozen corpse by now.

"I told you he didn't want help." Bates' brows slammed into an ugly V. "Jesus Christ, what was I supposed to do? Drag him to Enumclaw and make him be good?"

Heston ran a hand up the back of his neck, shocked at the lack of interagency support they were receiving. What the hell was up with this guy? "Just to be clear, we're *former military*. Tell me exactly what Mr. Stewart said. How bad is he hurt? Did you find his wife? For God's sake, answer me!"

Wilde climbed down the steps and stood behind his superior, stiff, as if he didn't dare speak up.

"Let me be frank," Bates groaned, scrubbing a big hand over his salt-and-pepper crewcut. "You guys are too late. The Forest Service officially called off all Search and Rescue efforts hours ago. Weather's nasty. Going to get worse. No sense looking for folks we won't be able to see in this storm, not if your buddy Stewart went back into the river after his wife like he said. Ain't no sense getting ourselves killed. Know what I mean?"

Heston jerked his chin at Asher. "We're done here." They needed assistance, not interference. No sense arguing. Alex and Kelsey didn't have time to waste. "Let's make camp, drop our gear, and get to work."

"You'd be smart to listen to someone who knows, *Contreras*," Bates grumbled. Did he just put that nasty twist into Heston's name on purpose? "I said visibility's poor, and I don't need two more idiots lost on these mountains."

Two more idiots? Them were fighting words. The fingers of tension knotting the muscles in Heston's neck exploded into bone-crushing rage. But Asher beat him to it.

"You want to try that again, *Cap'n Crunch?*" Asher bit out, his right elbow cocked slightly behind his hip, and his right hand balled into a fist that looked like a boxing glove. Asher stood a hefty six-foot-five-inches tall. His shoulders were thicker and wider than Bates', and those shoulders were pure muscle. He was meaner than most men Heston had ever worked with, and this ranger was a dick.

Bates slapped his hands to his hips and tipped forward into Asher's face with a belligerent, "This is *my* mountain, and you don't know shit about the weather up here. You think you can walk into *my* park and take over *my* operation? I said the search is called off, got it? While you're on Forest Service land, you'll do as I say. Understood?"

Heston rolled his shoulder one more time to keep his temper under control—which wasn't easy. There was nothing to be gained by stooping to Bates' level. Pigs and mud and all that. He'd seen plenty of Bates' ilk before. Some men were born leaders; others were power-hungry, small-minded assholes who stomped their subordinates into the dirt. Not tonight.

Heston slapped a steadying hand to Asher's beefy shoulder before Asher exercised that right hook and knocked *Cap'n Crunch* into orbit. Wilde had yet to speak up, but maybe he knew arguing with his supervisor was futile.

"No problem. We'll pitch our tent and—"

"Why do you think I brought that rig up here?" Bates' arm snapped out behind him like a railroad semaphore, his finger pointed at the cumbersome ICC vehicle. "Sure wasn't for the fun of driving all them hairpin turns. You'll sleep inside. With us. Where it's warm and dry. Where I can keep an eye on—"

"No," Heston shot back, then quickly recovered his cool before this turned into a brawl. Wilde was a loud-and-clear no contest, but if push came to shove, Asher could clean Bates' plow without breaking a sweat. "We'll pitch camp where we choose, and we'll wait for the weather to clear. That much makes sense. But come morning, we're searching with or without you." Heston lied through his teeth. They might set up camp, but waiting until morning was pure bullshit.

Bates' nose wrinkled with disgust. Like the leader he wasn't, he climbed back into the RV, slammed the door behind him, and immediately, ICC running lights went dark.

Good riddance.

Wilde, on the other hand, jerked his head toward the riverbank and said, "Let me show you what I found."

Heston's neck damned nearly snapped off the top of his spine with a vicious double-take. *That cool, calm, collected, and very feminine, voice.* Definitely not the woman who'd invited them to the RV. Who'd turned the running lights on. Either Wilde was a very gentle kind of a man or he—

Wilde dragged the black knit cap off his head with one hand and tugged his face covering down with the other. Sure enough. The light turquoise hair Heston remembered so well spilled over his head and flopped into his eyes. Eyes Heston knew were the same intriguing color. Wilde was no guy. He was—

"Hot damn," Asher murmured under his breath. "Will ya look at that? Wilde's not a chicken shit. He's a woman."

"Yes, she is," Heston whispered, more to himself than to his buddy. *Hot damn, indeed.*

"You guys know each other?"

"You could say that. London?" Heston asked, like the dolt her sudden appearance always turned him into.

"Yes, Hes. It's me," she answered brightly, ruffling her long slender fingers through those soft as silk bangs. "Let's get you guys set up for the night. There's a clearing close by that'll suit your needs. Follow me."

Well, duh. Like the love-smitten moron he'd been once before, Heston followed London down a meandering deer trail. A thick line of alpine pines marched between the water's stony bank and the trail, deadening the roar of the White. Sloppy snowflakes, laden with moisture the Northwest was known for, splattered through the branches, marking the trail in wintery white that turned to water as quickly as it landed.

They walked a good half-mile before London turned to face them. "I know you guys aren't going to hang around, but it'd be smart to set up camp. Bates'll think you're sticking around that way. You got a tent?"

"What are you doing here?" Heston asked instead of answering.

She shrugged. "Like you. My job. But trust me, once Bates realizes that you ignored his authority, he'll—"

"Piss on Bates," Asher growled. "Didn't come all this way to let some shithead stop us. If you're not going to help, get outta our way."

London let out a measured huff. "You guys are all the same. Ready to fight before you know what or who you're fighting."

"I knew who I was fighting," Heston said quietly. *Back then.* At least, he'd thought he'd known. Now he wasn't so sure.

"No, Heston, you didn't know squat. Still don't." London shook her head and her long bangs fell back over her forehead and into her eyes. Like before, she brushed them away, and he wished he could, just once, reach out like he had so long ago, before everything went wrong, and touch her again. Let the coolness of her hair drip between his fingers. Soak in the warmth of her satin skin.

She pointed at a flat patch of damp dirt under more pines, itself nearly white with snow. "Get your tent up. The people you came to rescue can't wait."

"You know where Alex and Kelsey are?" Heston asked.

"No, but Bates knew Mr. and Mrs. Stewart were in trouble earlier today. I heard the call come in, but he told me it was just an exercise. That our underwater recovery teams were testing underwater drones and to ignore it. That made me suspicious. Drones are worthless in whitewater. I made some calls and…" She shook her head. "I don't know why he did it, but Bates lied. And he didn't pull Mr. Stewart from the river. Another camper, Tom Landry, did. He got Stewart into warm, dry clothes and boots, gave him food and gear before Bates ever arrived on the scene. Problem is, Bates has been hassling Landry about him carrying concealed weapons, and Tom had his little boy with him. So he backed off and let Bates take over. Only now..." London looked past Heston to the ICC rig. "Bates knew your friends were in trouble and he never called Search and Rescue. So I did. Protocol for any lost hiker, especially someone in the river, is all hands on deck. We should've alerted the sheriff's department, the nearest hospital and ambulance service, and all available Search and Rescue teams the moment that first call came in. We should've spearheaded the search, guys. That's our primary job, to protect and serve. I'm sorry. This is my fault a much as his."

"You're afraid of him," Asher declared.

London blinked. "Am now. He's out of control and" — she ran her fingers through her hair— "he's scaring me."

"Has he hurt you?" Heston damned well needed to know.

"No. But I'm done giving him chances."

"Do you think Kelsey Stewart's still alive?" Heston asked.

London bit her bottom lip. "Anything's possible, but I'm fairly new on this job, and Bates is working against me. Not like I care. Are *you* with me?"

The way she emphasized *'you'* told Heston everything he needed to hear.

"Yes, ma'am," Asher answered quickly.

"Abso-fuckin'-lutely," Heston added.

In less than minutes, the tent was up. Asher tossed a glow stick inside to make it look like someone was home. They stowed their heaviest packs in the tent and stood with London.

"Now what?" Heston asked the woman he'd once pledged his heart and soul to.

She nodded farther down the deer trail. "Come with me. There's something you need to see."

"What?" Heston asked, as he and Asher grabbed their smaller bags and fell in behind her.

"You'll see," she tossed over her shoulder. Even in winter gear, London was all woman.

God, what a lovely view.

Chapter Six

Alex took a step into the dense, unforgiving primeval forest the Pacific Northwest was known for. Didn't it figure? Instead of that damned Irishman, he ran into the guy who'd pulled him to shore earlier, Tom What's-His-Name. Alex should've been suspicious, given the timing of Tom's arrival and the Irishman's departure. But what sort of killer brought his son along with him?

"Hi, Mister," the kid said brightly. As dark as it was in the trees, he looked a lot like Lexie. Sparkly brown-eyed with the same dark undertones in his chocolate hair. He wasn't as stocky as Lexie, but he had her wide-open smile. He had… *Kelsey's smile.*

Alex's heart pinched tighter. His breath caught in his chest. Felt like he'd swallowed a rock. How could he ever tell his little girl that her Mom was… that Kelsey was…?

No. Just no.

The little guy rattled on, "Daddy and me is still looking all over for your wife, Mister, and Mommy said maybe you could use some coffee and some hotdogs, and maybe you'd like to come sleep with us in our camper tonight, too, cuz" — he sucked in a belly full of air, then blew a hearty puff into the chilly night— "it's warmer in there than it is out here, and I can even see my breafff! See?" His cheeks puffed with a very big *'breafff'* indeed.

It wasn't lost on Alex how the boy's mitten-encased hand wrapped tightly around his father's gloved fingers, or how his father smiled lovingly down at his son. Or that the little guy liked to talk. "And you can even sleep in my sleepin' bag if you—"

"Hush, Jackie," Tom interrupted gently, his gaze keen on Alex. "Mr. Stewart, you don't know me, and I wouldn't be offended if you told me where to go, but you can't trust Bates."

"Never did. He's lying. Acted like he had no idea my wife's in trouble, but I know damned well my TEAM alerted the Forest Service. He should've done something. Anything!"

"Yeah, he's worthless. Gave me trouble when he saw I was carrying. Showed him my conceal carry permit, but he still threatened me. Said if anything happened while we were camped here, he'd see me hang."

"Hang what, Daddy?"

Tom winked at his son. "A Christmas wreath, Jackie. Now zip your lips and let me and Mr. Stewart finish talking, okay?"

Jackie mimed zipping his lips—just like Lexie would've done if she'd been there. Alex's heart broke all over again.

"Anyway, here," Tom said, pulling a hefty pistol from his inside jacket pocket and handing it over, grip first. Next came a twenty-count box of nine-millimeter rounds along with a preloaded magazine. "Take these. They're not much but they're yours now. I know you won't rest until you get your wife back and… Oh hell, here." Tom shrugged out of his jacket and handed that over, as well as the backpack he'd previously dropped on the ground. "There are protein bars in the outside pockets, handwarmers and bottled waters inside.

My cell phone's in there, too. Password's *JackieNTommy*, all one word, all lower case except capital J, N, and T. If you need anything else—"

Alex finally heard what Tom was saying. The planet tilted on its axis. His knees nearly buckled at the joining of Kelsey's murdered sons' names. *Jackie and Tommy Not Tom but Tommy? Why those names? Why here? Why now?* Black spots swarmed his vision. His focus faltered, zoomed in and out like a camera lens that couldn't keep up with the fast-moving picture it was recording. Because—

Jackie and Tommy? Was it even possible? *Hell, no. Couldn't be.*

"You're kidding me, right?" Alex managed to get out before he slapped his free hand against the scraggly pine beside him to catch his balance. What was God doing? Messing with his heart? His mind? Why those particular names? Was it in any way possible He'd actually sent Kelsey's dead sons, Jackie and Tommy, to help Alex find their mother? Now? When all seemed lost? Was this merely a coincidence or was it an actual, no-kidding sign from God? Or, which was more likely, was it the breakdown Alex deserved? Had he finally lost his mind?

Tom took a quick step into Alex and, stretching forward, settled a hand onto his shoulder. Tom's fingertips dug into the muscle, his tenacious grip the only thing keeping Alex upright. That had to be the problem. The world was no longer solid. He'd finally lost his mind.

Alex looked across the shimmering space between him and Tom, into the same dark eyes as Kelsey's. As her dead sons' eyes. As Jackie's and Tommy's eyes. Those were their names. The boys Kelsey's ex-husband had drowned in frigid

Henderson Bay. It happened years ago, but the similarity in Kelsey's boys' looks, the color of their hair and eyes, with Tom's and his son's, was frightening. Tears for all Kelsey'd lost filled Alex's eyes. *Why those names?!*

"You need help. You're still bleeding, sir," Tom said quietly. "I'd be glad to search with you, Sergeant Stewart, for as long as it takes. All night if you're up for it. But you need medical care for that—"

"Do I know you?" Alex interrupted. He didn't care that he was bleeding. He wasn't the important one here.

"Probably don't remember me, but yeah, a long time ago, I had the privilege of spotting for you. We were in Iraq. It was before you were called home. Before you got the news… just before you lost your family."

Alex had zero recollection of this guy. But the warmth radiating off that sturdy hand on his shoulder reminded him that Kelsey wasn't warm, that he was wasting time she didn't have. That it didn't matter who God sent, they'd better be able to shoot while they ran. He didn't care that he was bleeding. Didn't care at all.

"Thank you," he huffed, straightening his spine, pulling away, once again ready to search all night. Hell, for the rest of his life if needed.

"I'd be glad to go with you, sir. Honest," Tom offered again. "I've got another pistol. It's my wife's, but she won't mind if I take it. She's just as worried for you and your wife as we are."

Alex shook the man's sincerity off. "No, stay with your family. Take care of them. They're your first priority. I'll be… I'll be fine… Tom."

Taking a full step back, Tom nodded reluctantly, then tugged his son in front of him. "We'll be here in the morning if you need anything. That camper over there is ours. The red, white, and blue one. Can't miss it. All you have to do is ask."

"Me and Mommy will say a prayer for you and your wife tonight, Mister," Jackie chirped.

Alex looked down at the little guy who could've passed for Lexie's twin. "Thank you, Jackie. I'd like that. Will you also promise to take good care of your mom for the rest of your life?"

"You betcha!" Jackie squealed, as if Alex had asked if he'd wanted a bag full of candy instead of the responsibility he'd so cheerfully accepted. Which good mothers were, weren't they? The best sort of candy? The perfect blessings. Sweetness and honey wrapped inside kind hands and warm hugs. And now he was waxing poetic? *WTF?*

Stoically, Alex turned away from the friendship radiating from these two unlikely, shaggy-haired strangers—a man and a boy. Who just might be angels sent from heaven. Alex knew better than to discount miracles. Especially when he needed one so badly.

He faced the wall of pines looming around and over the campground, as dark as the powers of Hell that lurked over good and honest families the world over. Alex didn't usually drop F-bombs, but tonight was different. Because of the gentle father and son who'd helped him when another had walked away, he didn't speak it. But he thought it. *Hell had better get the fuck out of my way.*

First task? Search the campground. Whoever had Kelsey might just be hiding her under Alex's nose. That was what he'd do. Hiding her nearby made the most sense in this weather. How else could the Irish bastard have gotten away so quickly?

Alex headed for the circular gravel road that branched off into four separate campsite loops, but went the opposite direction of Tom and his son. Rows of skinny alpine firs blocked the views between campsites and campfires. Cedar shavings covered the pathways. Some hikers had tents. A couple had campers. One had a tear-drop trailer, the damned small things he couldn't abide.

He was well into the second loop when he thought of Murphy and Mark. Son of a bitch! He should've called them. He had a phone now. He should've remembered! Shit, he'd never been this slow-witted before. Lifting Tom's phone out of his pocket, he first made sure it wasn't the Irishman's burner, raised it up to his face to read the damned numbers, and—

An orange glow glittered from far in the shadows at his right. What the hell? Some idiot had backed a small trailer into the trees, not into a numbered campsite. The orange glow flickered brightly from inside its dark windows. Alex's heart stopped. The rig was on fire. Too bad! He didn't have time to care about someone else's nightmare. Not now. He had to find Kelsey, not waste precious time saving someone else's piece-of-trash trailer.

His mind replied with something that sounded like what Kelsey would say if she were there. *There might be kids inside. Or a dog or someone who can't save themselves. Maybe someone's grandmother.*

That did it. Stuffing the phone back into his pocket, Alex cursed a blue streak and aimed for the trailer. God, those things were nothing but toxic, gas-filled tinderboxes on wheels, and if there were kids or dogs inside, they'd be helpless. Might already be overcome by fumes.

But Kelsey would want him to help. So would Lexie and baby Bradley and… and Tommy and Jackie and…

"Son of a bitch!" Alex hissed when the trailer's hot-as-hell door handle fell into his gloved hand. He flung the cheap chunk of metal behind him, then charged inside to rescue—

His heart stopped. He couldn't believe what he was seeing.

"Kelsey?" he asked like a dolt.

It was her. On her back. Inside someone else's burning trailer. On a blanket, not under the damned thing. Her coat was gone. So were her boots. She was dressed in someone else's jeans, t-shirt, and socks. Except for her wet hair that someone had spread out on the floor around her head, she was dry. The same asshat had folded her arms across her chest, like… like she was dead.

Anguish that she was, that he'd arrived too late, swamped Alex. He dropped to his knees beside her, afraid to hope, so damned sick at heart that he was too late. Sticking a gloved finger between his teeth, he jerked his glove off, then rested his bare fingers against her neck.

Poor thing was as cold as ice and pale, no coloring at all. Even the dark brown hair she'd twisted into a braid this morning, so she could stow it inside her woolen cap, seemed faded, fanned out like it was.

But there it was, thank God, there. Right there. Alex found her pulse. Barely registering. Thready at best, but her pulse, damn it. She was alive.

He shot a quick, discerning glance around the one-room trailer. The fire had been deliberately set in the sink below the front window. From there, it had spread to the countertops made of particle board, engineered from wood chips and highly flammable synthetic resin to bind it, then pressed into cheap lumber that would burn hot and quick, given the chance.

As if agreeing with his condemnation, the countertop bubbled, popped, and hissed. Flames licked their way up the copper backsplash to the walls, then—

Alex didn't think twice. Just reached as gently as he could beneath his wife's neck and under her knees, and lifted to his feet. He leaned back on his heels until her head tipped against his chest. There wasn't time to calculate the damage moving her might cause. Saving her life came first.

By the time he was upright, fire was skittering up the walls like tiny blue-flamed aliens. Alex curled his head and shoulders over Kelsey, took a deep breath, and kicked the door open. As expected, oxygen rushed in and fed the flame behind him. Growling like a beast, he squared both shoulders against the door frame. Just in time. With a great, roaring breath, the son of a bitchin' trailer tried to blow him out through its narrow doorway. Alex refused the fury at his back, jolting Kelsey just to save himself. It was only a two-foot drop, but—

He would not hurt her!

Chapter Seven

Heston caught sight of a tiny orange glow up ahead just as it exploded into a bright yellow fireball. "Straight ahead, guys. Run! Faster! People might still be in there!"

"Cripes!" London yelled. "That's the old trailer I wanted you guys to see. Looked abandoned. No, no, no! This can't be happening!"

Heston and Asher ran, but light-footed London beat them to the scene, where a small, old-style trailer was fully engulfed. Flames shot out all three windows that Heston could see. Heavy black smoke curled overhead into already smoking branches, poking at the pine like fingers looking for something to grab.

London disappeared around one side of the trailer. Asher ran the other way. Heston whipped out his sat phone and reported the disaster to Bates. The woman who'd answered before answered again. He told her what he knew. Just as quickly, she confirmed the location, told him help was on the way, and advised him to stay clear of the fire.

Not happening. There was no way to check for survivors. The flames were too hot to breach the door, and the ceiling had collapsed, blocking Heston's entry. He growled at the helpless predicament he was in. The fire was out of control. All it needed was to reach the propane tank these crappy trailers came with, and this part of the campground would cease to exist. All the more reason to catch up to London. To protect her. To keep her safe.

Before he took one step, the trailer's side panel popped off its rivets and curled down onto itself, nearly into him. Heston took a full step back to avoid the blow torch flaming out from the swiftly melting aluminum. The blazing heat proved brutal. He lifted the back of his arm to shield his nose and mouth. It was still hard to breathe. He took another step back, then another, looking past the flaming rig for London. Damn it. Where had she disappeared to so quickly?

Powerful heat forced him to retreat again. He could only hope she hadn't done anything crazy, like crash through one of these burning walls. It'd be just like her, stubborn to the end, even if it meant dying.

The fumes were horrendous. The fire scorched his face until tears ran down his cheeks. In his haste, he stumbled over—

"Son of a bitch! Get the hell off me!" some guy bellowed.

"Boss?" Heston dropped to his knees. "Is that you? My God! It's you!"

A hearty "Shit!" roared back at him. "You stepped on me!"

"Didn't see you. Sorry." Heston turned from where Alex lay cursing. Still looking for London, he yelled into the mic snapped on his jacket collar, "Asher. Found Alex. Bring London to the front of the trailer. We're about twenty feet from it. Hurry!"

"On my way," Asher responded hoarsely.

"I'm already here," London replied just as hoarsely as she dropped alongside Alex, who was still face down on the ground. "Are you okay, sir?" she asked, her gloved hand on his shoulder, her head tipped forward as she leaned over to get him to look at her.

"Not me, damn it." Alex groaned. He was hunched over into a push-up position, his weight on his knees and elbows, protectively shielding—

"Kelsey!" Heston cried out. "You found her. Boss! Thank you, God!" His fingertip snapped the button that would bring Decker back on-line. "Nine-one-one!" he barked into the mic, while digging into his smaller bag and grabbing his IFAK, his Individual First Aid Kit. "Deck, Asher, we've got them. Both Alex and Kelsey!" Then he repeated it because it seemed so extraordinarily rare that this bleak rescue mission had turned successful, "We've got them! Both of them, both Alex and Kelsey!"

But then he froze. Afraid. Just because Alex had Kelsey didn't mean she was alive. How could she be? Heston didn't know if she was breathing. He couldn't tell as closely as Alex guarded his wife. His heart fell.

"Boss?" Heston asked more calmly, his finger off the mic, his joy restrained, all excitement gone from his voice. He peered closer at the still body beneath Alex. Kelsey had yet to move. But he could see she wasn't breathing. Not even a puff of frosty breath whispered out of her partly open mouth. *Shit.*

"How's ... how's your wife, Boss?" Heston asked cautiously.

"How do you think she is?" Alex bit out. He'd leaned sideways onto one hip, off her, still keeping his body between hers and the blazing fire, his back to the flames. "She's hurt damned bad, and I can't get her warm. She's too cold."

"I can take care of that," Heston replied evenly. He pulled a dozen hand and foot warmers from his bag, activated them, gave one for Alex to hold, then placed the rest inside Kelsey's too-big-to-be-her t-shirt, under the shirt on her belly, inside her pants pockets and into her socks. But Alex was right. She was as cold as a corpse.

By then London had her own IFAK laid out alongside Kelsey's head and was expertly flashing a pencil light over her face and into her eyes. Cupping Kelsey's cheek with her free hand, London asked Alex, "Was she breathing before? She's not now. I've got oxygen."

Heston noticed her fingers. No ring in sight. Just black nitrile gloves.

'Not now!' he commanded himself. *'Stay on track. Focus!'*

"Yes, but not nearly enough," Alex answered, "and I had to get her out of there and—"

"Understood. No need to explain. Good job, sir. You saved her life. That was your first priority, saving this pretty lady's life. Well done," London shot back. "And now we'll get her ready to transport. Anything broken that you know?"

Alex was on his butt now, sitting cross-legged, his powerful body shaking with an overload of adrenaline—which had most likely saved his life. "I didn't have time to check. The fire... The river... Everything exploded. I... I should've been there..." His voice trailed off, but his steely gaze remained fixed on his wife.

"Nope." London let the P pop. "You did everything right, sir. Same as I would've done. Now sit back and let us help you both." With an authoritative snap of her free hand, she uncoiled the oxygen tubing included with her portable O_2 tank, adjusted the flow, and secured the unit's full mask over Kelsey's nose and mouth. "If she doesn't start breathing on her own, we may need to begin compressions, Alex. But a breath of O_2 might just be enough to—"

Kelsey's chest lifted the tiniest bit. Then lifted again.

"Hurry!" Alex ordered. "Save her! God, save her!"

London hurried. Heston, too. Peeling out of his work gloves, he donned a set of surgical gloves, not willing to risk causing any infections. The ABCDs of triage came as easily as they had when he was in combat. **Airway. Breathing. Circulation/Coma/Convulsion. Dehydration.**

He opened his kit, grabbed the enclosed penlight, flicked it on, and stuck it between his teeth. "Hook her up to saline, Ash. STAT," he mumbled around the light, finally noticing his buddy. "I'm assessing circulation." Which meant he was looking for open wounds to tourniquet or pack with QuikClot powder and the thick rolls of hemostatic gauze from his kit. Kelsey was already in a coma, but bleeders left unattended led to dehydration which ended with convulsions. Shit, he hoped he didn't find any. He began carefully at the sides of her head, feeling quickly for bumps and—

"Head wound," he reported as clinically neutral as possible. Just as critically assessing. Heston tipped forward on his knees and leaned over Kelsey's prone body to better see what he was dealing with. "Graze. Clean. No clotting. Definite skull impact. No fractures" —at least none he could see— "but I can see bone."

"They shot her," Alex growled. "Gawddamned bastards shot her. In the head! I was there. Saw the gawddamned pink mist!"

Heston wasn't going to argue. The infamous pink mist from a headshot usually meant instant death. Not this time. "Well, they missed. Didn't hit anything vital," he told his boss calmly. The kinetic energy behind the round that grazed her skull had probably been enough to knock her out, but it hadn't shattered the bone, and skull bones were hard. Kelsey might just pull through this nightmare after all. The pink mist Alex was positive he'd seen might be nothing more than the fact that head wounds bled like crazy. Or the panic of seeing his wife shot amplified and distorted what he'd thought he'd seen. That'd be enough to fry a man's logic card.

Heston knew what a headshot looked like, and this wasn't it. This was a graze, pure and simple. No longer bleeding. No blood seeping around it whatsoever. Kelsey's scalp, along the length of the two-inch-long, one-inch-wide burn just above her left ear, was a whitish line of frayed, gray flesh. Not a hint of pink, signifying the wound had been washed clean, maybe too clean, by her time in the river. A damned cold river. For the first time, Heston hoped the river had been frigid enough to work the miracle she desperately needed.

Snow started falling again, dropping like wet, soggy spitballs through the tree branches overhead. Not the least bit pretty. Not here. Not now. Heston wished it'd quit.

"H-heat," Alex stuttered, fumbling through the many flaps and pockets of the bag at his side. "She's not warm enough. I need to get her w-warmer. Help me, damn it!"

Heston shot a cursory glance at Alex just as the hefty 'whump, whump, whump' of Decker's helo sounded overhead. Alex was in shock. His lips were thin and his eyes were bleak. Too bleak. He had to know how bad the odds for Kelsey were. But the last thing Heston needed was Alex giving up on his wife.

"Stats," he asked Asher at the same time Deck's strong voice came through their earbuds. "At your location, boys. Touching down. Keep my kids alive, gawddamn it!"

By then, Asher had an IV line inserted into the back of Kelsey's right hand, an automatically inflating pressure cuff on her right biceps, and a stethoscope plugged into his ears while he listened to her heart.

"Thready heart rate, Heston," he reported quietly. "Damned low BP. Eighty-eight over fifty-one." He tipped back on his haunches and squeezed the bag of saline hanging off the portable metal stand he'd retrieved from his IFAK. "She's dehydrated so I'm pushing more fluids. Okay, Boss?"

"Yeah. Okay. Good," Alex rasped. He'd stopped tearing his bag apart, but the man was clearly losing it, and Heston doubted he had what Kelsey needed in that bag anyway. Didn't even look like his.

"I'm bringing two gurneys. Get my friends ready to travel," Decker advised calmly from the helo's cockpit. "University of Washington Medical Center in Seattle is on stand-by to receive."

Heston's eyes blurred at the steadfast strength and sacrifice of the nation's first responders, men and women like Decker. It never ceased to amaze him how quickly medical professionals jumped to assist complete strangers. How damned loyal they were to people they'd never met. Or how much Decker loved his boss and his boss's pretty little wife.

"I couldn't get her warm," Alex whispered. Which wasn't exactly true, not as close as they still were to the burning rubble. But Kelsey needed blood and a trauma team more than she needed warmth. And Alex was in bad shape, too.

"Copy that. Two patients. Both with gunshot wounds. But Deck…" he murmured as quietly as he could. "Seattle's not going to be close enough."

"Understood. Requesting a facility closer to this LZ, right gawddamned now."

"Copy that. We're ready for evac."

"Yup. I see you now."

Heston looked up as Deck cleared the front end of what was left of the trailer, with two portable gurneys on his shoulder and barking orders into his cell phone. When he caught sight of everyone, he stuffed his cell into a pocket and ran straight for Alex. He dropped the gurneys near Asher, then took careful hold of Alex, and pulled him to his feet. "Boss. I'm here. Let's get you and Kelsey safely out of here."

"Deck? You came? You came for… for Kelsey?"

"You bet I came, Boss. For you and Kels, I'll walk through fire. Wouldn't be anywhere else but here now, would I? Can you walk? I brought gurneys if you're—"

"I don't need your help!" Alex yelled. "Help her! Help my wife, damn it! Save her, not me!"

Gently as all get out, London intervened, grabbed hold of Alex by his elbow, and told him, "Hi, Alex. You don't know me but I'm an old friend of Heston's. Maybe he told you about me, London Wilde? No matter if he didn't. That's not important, but Kelsey is. Listen, I came all this way to rescue you and your wife, and I've done the best I can, but Deck's right. You're bleeding. You, sir, need to be seen by a doctor, same as your wife. Kelsey, right? You love her, don't you?"

Wordless, probably for the first time in his life, or maybe because he was as smitten by London's charm as Heston still was, Alex merely stared at her and nodded.

"Well then, let's get out of these professionals' way, shall we? They know what they're doing, Alex, and I trust them. While they wrap Kelsey in those toasty heated blankets" — she nailed Heston with a damned sharp eyebrow, spurring him to do just what London said he'd do— "and on her way to the nearest hospital, you're coming with me."

"But I… I…"

"But you've done all you can, Alex. Let's watch these guys get her loaded, so we can get Kelsey out of here as quickly as possible, okay?"

"Yeah," he answered more calmly. "That's what I want. Her out of here. Right away. Yeah. That."

"Well good, because that's what these men are doing."

Alex seemed appeased. At least pacified for the moment. Hurriedly, Heston jerked the pre-warmed, aluminum-wrapped blankets from inside the still folded gurneys. He'd never seen his take-charge boss this disoriented or looking so lost before. By the time Heston had a neck brace on Kelsey and had her wrapped up tight in the warm blankets, London had draped another heated blanket over Alex's shoulders. He hadn't taken his eyes off Kelsey, not once, and he was every bit as pale as she was.

"She's ready to move," Heston told Asher and Decker.

"Be careful!" Alex snapped when they crouched in tandem and gently lifted Kelsey off the cold ground and settled her onto the gurney. "Don't you dare hurt her!"

"Never, Boss," Asher replied smoothly as he tucked the blankets around Kelsey, then added the last heated blanket over her. "I'd never hurt Kels, you know that. She brings me cinnamon rolls from that bakery by Heston's place every Tuesday, and I know damned well she's going to bring me another one real soon." For a big guy, he did have a gentle side.

"I know," Alex muttered. "I do. It's just that—"

"It's just that you love her, Boss. Understood. But you've got to share her, because we love Kels, too."

Alex was so damned lost. It was hard seeing him like this.

Deck strapped Kelsey onto the gurney. It took minutes to transport her to the helo, its rotors still whirling. Once there, Heston and Asher jumped inside the rear compartment and guided Kelsey's gurney onto the locking floor stanchions. London climbed in behind Alex, instantly motioning for him to sit in the seat closest to his wife. Heston strapped both his boss and Kelsey in tight, then raised the stanchions until she was at the same level as Alex. Might as well. There was no way Alex would stay seated with Kelsey on the floor.

Decker closed the side door and took his place up front. Asher rode shotgun. Heston grabbed the seat across from London. He'd secured his IFAK inside his gear bag, but left its Velcro binding loose, in case. Kelsey was in bad shape. She had more wrong with her than just the bullet graze on the side of her head. Heston hadn't wanted to panic Alex, but the woman was a mess of broken bones and hematomas, some of them damned serious. The most obvious, her poor fingers were twisted. If she lived—

Heston bowed his head the second his brain uttered that despicable *if.*

When she came to, she'd need Alex, and Alex would need her. She *would* live. Heston refused to throw anything but *'when'* into the universe. *When* she was back on her feet… *When. When. When.*

London pulled a walkie-talkie out of an inside jacket pocket and radioed a hurried, "Lieutenant Wilde checking in. Missing persons Kelsey and Alex Stewart have been located. Both alive, but in critical condition. Transporting to the nearest hospital. Will contact you with more info later."

The guy who answered—had to be Bates—sputtered something about fire or fired, Heston wasn't sure. Fire at the trailer or London was fired?

She didn't give whoever it was time to explain or argue. "Wilde, over and out," she said, then stuffed the device back inside her jacket. "Might be looking for a job after tonight," she said to no one in particular. "Never mind, forget what I said. I just really liked this job. Most of the time."

"He's an ass," Asher muttered.

"You have no idea," London agreed. Releasing her safety harness, she dropped to her knees beside Kelsey. Out came a stethoscope from inside her shirt. But instead of using it, she handed it to Alex and asked, "Would you please monitor her heartbeat for me while we travel?"

Heston could've cried the way Alex grabbed onto that lifeline and fumbled the listening ends of the scope into his ears, while London smoothed the monitor end beneath Kelsey's t-shirt. "Can you hear it?" she asked, so damned kindly and sweetly.

And there she was, the only woman Heston could ever fall in love with. Yet, at the same time, the best part of his life slipped away. The woman he'd driven away.

He couldn't help seeing London as only a former lover saw his woman. Her lips were fuller. So were her hips and chest. Might just be the winter gear she was wearing. Might be she wasn't wearing her usual sports bra to contain her deliciously jiggly girls. A man doesn't forget the plump flesh and pebbled nipples his lips, fingers, tongue, and heart had once enjoyed and memorized. The perky girls he'd assumed he'd always have. The generous lover he'd taken for granted. Separation didn't make the heart grow fonder. It only sharpened the pain of his past mistake.

Many women cried after reaching their orgasm. Not London. She laughed when pleasure shuddered through her exquisitely expressive body. Sometimes, she giggled and writhed in his arms, undone by the magic of their lovemaking. He still recalled how she could purr like a sexy, satisfied kitten even while aftershocks consumed her. And consumed him.

It was clear to see she loved life and lived it to the fullest. Always had, and life, in turn, loved her. She used to dance when she wasn't bogged down with coursework. He'd noticed she still moved with the efficient ease of a dancer. Graceful, yet controlled. So damned beautiful. She looked happy. But then that was London Wilde. His biggest, stupidest mistake.

The second Alex located his wife's heart, his head bobbed and his eyes teared up. "Yeah," he choked. "Got… got her."

"I know a guy," Heston whispered to London. "He's a real hardass, but I think you'd like working for him."

A smile tugged at the corners of her pretty mouth. Her pink nose twitched like it used to when she was happy. "I already like him," she whispered back.

God, he'd missed her.

Chapter Eight

From the helo's side window, London watched the September sun set far in the west. Its last few rays were as pinkish-golden as ever, but today they were squashed like slender fingers beneath the weight of the purpling storm front intent on hiding Mount Rainier from the rest of the world. Which was the norm for this side of the Cascades. Most often heard phrase in the Pacific Northwest? *"Is the mountain out today?"* Most days it wasn't, not in a region prone to heavy rain, drizzle, and blankets of fog nine months of every year.

It was hard to believe that, out of all the covert operators in the world, Heston Contreras was one of two sent to locate Mr. and Mrs. Stewart. On London's mountain. In her newly adopted state. Not like that designation would last through the next few days. London knew better. Women working in male-dominated fields were low-hanging fruit, easily marked as first out the door whenever RIFs, reductions-in-force, came down from above. Just as easily passed over for promotions they'd earned; her, by lack of seniority. Guess one had to stick with a federal agency longer than a couple years to make a solid reputation for herself.

Also guess Captain Bates hadn't liked her leaving with Heston and Asher once they'd located the Stewarts. He hadn't liked her tone when she'd checked in with him the last time. She thought she'd been civil, at least as respectful as he deserved. Which was hard considering she worked for a jerk who wore his rank like it made him a god. Honestly, he wasn't a captain in any army. Sure hadn't ever worked as hard as she had.

She'd never had a problem with Bates until his promotion. He'd changed then, from the laid-back man she'd bandied jokes back and forth with, into a bossy, egotistical tyrant who wanted respect and obedience more than the easy-going comradery they'd once shared. He used to be friendly. Now he snapped orders at her, then snapped again when she didn't respond fast enough. The jerk.

London despised being treated like she was anything less than the intelligent woman she knew she was. Hated it with a purple passion. Hated to be minimized and talked down to. She damned well knew she was second best to—No. Body. Not even Heston. Speaking of which…

She snuck a sideways glance at the man she'd once planned to spend the rest of her life with. *Dayum.* He still looked good, even in all that cold weather gear. Course, he'd been dropped into the middle of frigid nowhere. She didn't blame him for over-dressing. Northwest weather was capricious. It could be bitter cold one minute, pouring balmy torrential rain the next.

He was as long-legged as she remembered. As tan. His body was the perfect balance of lean muscle and sharp angles. He'd unzipped his jacket once he'd taken a seat, revealing a chiseled chest wrapped inside a tight black shirt that showed off his pecs. Those muscled thighs challenged the fabric of the black denim he wore. The younger man she'd known had changed into one helluva mature specimen. She squinted at the gold logo sitting high on that chest. *The TEAM, huh?* That was who he worked for, that hotshot covert surveillance company out of Virginia. Lucky them.

He still moved like a panther, not wasting energy or time. But unlike the yellow-eyed beast of the Everglades, his eyes were a heart-stopping, beautiful liquid brown. As deep as a well, filled to the brim with rich, dark coffee. Still as hot. Still razor-sharp. Enhanced by thick black lashes that drew her attention to them when he blinked. She could've sat there and looked at him forever and never gotten her fill.

He'd doffed his cap, revealing a head nearly shorn of what she knew could be rich, lush black hair if he'd let it grow. Cool to the touch. Soft as a lamb. Its length seemed to dictate his soul. It was longer before he enlisted. He'd been a gentle lover and her best friend then. She'd told him everything. That was how it was for them. They finished each other's sentences. Laughed together. Studied together. Made love together. In the shower. On the couch. The floor. That tiny breakfast table they'd dragged home from a yard sale. Every. Where.

But the day he came home with his hair cut high and tight, everything between them changed. Gone was her sweet, soft-hearted boyfriend. In his stead was a task-driven soldier with no patience. Prone to argue over the smallest things. Moody. Abrupt. Driven to be all he could be. Which was when everything went wrong. Well, not precisely then, but shortly after, as in the day she heard from the FBI.

"Guess what?!" she nearly shrieked the second Heston cleared his front door, she was so excited. She ran to him and jumped into his arms, wrapping her legs around his waist. "Guess who hired me? Today! The FBI! I'm supposed to report for duty as soon as possible, no later than seven days

from today! That's one week, Hes! I'm going to be a bonafide federal agent! Can you believe it? Me? Working for Uncle Sam? I'll be just like you!" Like a little girl at dance class, she performed a silly pirouette with her hands cupped over her head. She was so thrilled her hard work paid off. She was on top of the world!

"Can you believe that?" she asked again.

He just stood there in the doorway. Quiet. His eyes dark and—angry? "Not now, London."

"Not now? Aren't you happy for me?" She had to know. This was an important day for both of them. They'd be leaving Killeen, Texas, at the same time. He on to another deployment. Her to Virginia for months of training and drills and more education. And yes! She'd finally be FBI Special Agent London Wilde. Her dream had come true. Life couldn't get any better.

He shook his head. "Have you thought about the ramifications of you taking off for the East Coast? By yourself? Alone? Without me?"

"But we've talked about this. A lot. This was always my plan, to work for the Bureau. To do something that matters. You know that."

"It's dangerous!" he boomed, slamming the door behind him, then kicking it shut again when it bounced back and hit his rear-end. "I won't have you putting yourself in harm's way. Damn it, London. Not now."

"Excuse me? You won't have me putting myself in harm's way? What about when you deploy? It's okay for you to risk your life, but I'm supposed to sit home and do what? Nothing? Sit on my thumbs? Wait for you to call or come home while I worry myself sick?" Her Irish spiked straight up her spine,

*stiffening her resolve. "Yes, now," she asserted stubbornly.
"We had a plan, and I'm sticking to—"*

*"Plans change. You're not going. Period. The FBI is no
place for a woman. Christ, London, look at you" —he did a
Vanna White sweep of her body like she was a contestant's
prize instead of the only student who'd aced her criminal law
class— "a hundred pounds soaking wet—if you're dressed.
You're too beautiful. Too delicate. Who's going to take you
seriously? Tell me, huh? Who? Some cartel boss with a shiv
up his sleeve? Some shyster who kidnaps little girls, then fucks
them to death, little girls who look just like you? You're a
dreamer, London. You go, you're a loser!"*

*She almost caved, because, well, Heston Contreras was
the man of her dreams. The tall, dark, lean, and handsome
man of her dreams. And he was smart, might even be right.
Working for the FBI would be dangerous. Could be deadly.
Just like his job was. She loved him.*

But he'd gone too far and he'd been too harsh.

*London dug her heels in and crossed her arms over her
chest. "If I'm a dreamer, you're a hairy ape with a brain the
size of a pea. I'm going, Hes. Like we planned. If you—"*

*"No, London. I'm putting my foot down and telling you
no. Should've done it a long time ago. Should never have let
you take those online classes to finish your degree. No more
narrow-minded excuses. Jesus, why can't you stay home like
other wives?"*

That did it.

*"Gee whiz, maybe because I'm not anyone's wife? And
I've worked hard to get this job!" Now she was yelling, out of
sheer exasperation. But damn it, what had gotten into Heston?
Did he think he could boss her like he did the guys who worked*

for him? "They chose me, Hes. Don't you know how big a deal working for the FBI is? I'm one of only a hundred applicants that—"

"I don't care about them. I just care about you!"

And there it was. Total male domination wrapped up in a pretty pink bow of "I care." Like a care package of suffocating guilt that stifled every last one of her dreams. Every last brain cell in her empty head. Made her feel guilty for wanting a career as much as he'd wanted to join the Army. She'd supported him then. Why couldn't he support her now? Well, no more.

London took a deep breath to control her trembling. She swallowed hard to summon enough saliva to talk reasonably. And clearly. "It seems to me everything is always about you," she said calmly. "What you care about. What you decide is best. I know you mean well, Heston, but you use that macho caring to make me feel guilty and to bully me into submission. To get what you want. Don't you understand how that minimizes me? How your need to control me negates my opinions? My dreams? I didn't go to college all these years to back out now. Especially since you're going to Ranger school in a few months. Then maybe Delta, right?" She had him there, and she knew it. Why should she stay safe there in Killeen while he marched out into the world and served the same country she wanted to serve?

"You heard me," he growled threateningly. "I don't have time for this tonight. Where's dinner? I'm tired. I've had a really bad day. Enough."

"But Heston—"

"I said enough!" He stalked for their bedroom.

Where he'd be sleeping alone for a damned long time. She was so, so angry. But she didn't call him on his bullshit. Nope. Not this time. Maybe never again. He wouldn't listen anyway.

She'd—they'd—had a plan. For years. And yes, plans changed, because now she knew she didn't need any male dictating the rest of her life. He'd had enough? Well, she did, too. Quietly, she turned the knob to the door he'd slammed, and she left. Just walked away from the argument she couldn't win, caught the bus to Austin, and from there, the only flight headed to the East Coast. It was time for her to be all she could be, too.

Look out world, here I come.

That was the last thought in her head that night. How London wished she could go back in time, morph into some dutiful, subservient, brainless, and submissive little housewife. Like the old black-and-white sitcom from the 1950s, *"The Donna Reed Show."* Donna was the type of woman all men seemed to admire, and obedience was surely what they wanted in a wife. Someone complacent who sat around all day, dreaming how she could please her man when he got home from the office, like she was a slave or too dumb to do anything else. Someone who loved to clean house in her chiffon dress. While she wore heels and smiled like a lunatic…

All. Day. Long.

Still wired from her latest rash decision that would most likely end with suspension or worse, being fired, London stretched a leg straight forward, fighting the urge to kick something—or someone. When the world came back into focus, Heston's eyes were fixed on her. She swallowed hard, embarrassed he'd caught her watching him.

Tugging his earphones off, he tipped forward and put his elbows on his knees. "How'd Quantico work out for you, London? Was FBI training as tough as they say it is? Did you like it? Why aren't you still working there?"

London shrugged. Might as well rip the band-aid off and get it over with. "I washed out."

"Oh? How'd that happen? Talk to me. I'd like to know. You were so excited that night. So ready to work for the Bureau, and you are smart. I remember how smart."

"You do?" She coughed to get the surprise out of her voice. "But, well, yeah. Training was, ah, brutal. I could run, jump, and shoot, sure. Got high scores in those disciplines, and I passed every other test with flying colors. But" —Damn this was hard— "FBI concussion protocol is strict for trainees. First time I went to the mat, I took a hard hit to my head. Right between the eyes. Knocked me out, and I didn't come to right away." She stuck a finger between her brows to show him where.

He winced. "Ouch. Sounds like illegal contact to me."

"It was, but yeah. That's how they train. You're supposed to be prepared for anything and everything. Anyway, I went stars out and when I woke up, I was already in the Bureau's clinic. Didn't come to during transport. Didn't wake up for almost a solid hour after they got me there. That's when my handler warned me, *'That's one strike. Two more and you're out.'*"

She scratched that spot between her brows, not because there was a scar there or that it itched. She just needed something to do. "Second strike came twenty days later during my first live case. I'd been cleared for active duty. Someone robbed a bank in downtown Arlington. I had him dead to rights, but he had a partner. A woman. Only I thought she was an innocent bystander because she was watching from a crowd of spectators, you know? I didn't see her in time."

"Tough break." He almost sounded like pre-Army Heston. Her Heston. The man she'd fallen in love with. The man who used to care about them, not just about the Army.

"Yeah, tough break," London admitted. "My fault. Should've kept better track of my surroundings. Didn't see her coming. She got too close and nailed me with an elbow. Knocked me down. I landed hard and my head hit the curb. Got a hairline skull fracture out of that one. It was permanent desk duty from then on or give up my dream of active service, so I bailed. I didn't train hard to end up a desk jockey. Been a LEO for the Forest Service since then." *Until now.* Whatever Bates told the disciplinary board could end her career—if three wasted years could be called a career.

"We'll be landing soon," Heston said. "You ever think about us?"

"Nope," she replied, popping the P for all it was worth, not going down that rabbit hole again. Might as well piss off Heston now, before he started telling her what to do, how to think, and who to dream of. He might've been right about her not being able to physically fight off aggressors, though. And, yes, the Bureau hadn't been a good fit for her. She knew that now. But he'd been so mean about it. Insulting. And he'd called her a dreamer.

Well, duh. Guess what. People who accomplish things have big dreams. Like me!

Dreams were what put the first men on the moon and the first women into space. If they could be astronauts, she could be somebody, too. She could! Just had to find the right niche. Might not be working with men, though. That was the common thread in all her failures, men who thought they knew better than she did.

"I do," he said quietly. "I think about us all the time. Never thought I'd see you again, babe. Sure glad I did."

Babe. Why'd he have to say that?

London jerked her gaze back to that damned setting sun. Why'd he have to sound so sincere? And look so good? She could almost taste him on her tongue again. Her stupid heart hadn't slowed down since she'd come to the door behind Captain Bates. Since the first word out of Heston's mouth. God, he had soft lips that could melt a girl's heart. And that man could kiss.

He'd looked so damned hot the way he'd handled Bates with deliberate calmness, and she'd nearly broken out in a fever at the take-no-prisoners vehemence in his declaration that he'd find the Stewarts. Heston had always been that guy, the one who wouldn't back down. She knew he'd been in plenty of fights as a kid defending other classmates or neighborhood kids from bullies. He had scars to prove it. His determination to advocate for weaker kids drove his sweet mother crazy, but he'd never walked away from a fight, not even when he'd been outnumbered. Yeah, he was—that guy. That crazy, hot-as-hell guy who even now had more courage than brains and who still set her stupid heart atwitter.

She scrubbed a quick hand over her jacket zipper, aiming for her poor aching nipples that were obviously happy, happy, joy, joy to see him. So happy, they were hard as tiny, sensitive rocks inside her sports bra. Which was all the more reason to keep her distance from Heston Contreras. If she didn't, she'd end up back where she'd started. Minimized and bullied by his dominant male version of "caring."

Yet she couldn't help but be amazed at how he'd taken command of the situation with Bates. Hadn't backed down. How tender he'd been with Kelsey Stewart. How caring with Alex. He'd kept calling Alex, boss. Did that mean Alex owned The TEAM? Working for Mr. Stewart sounded like a good idea, except... That might mean working with Heston.

No. Way. Problem was, the more reasons she found to keep her distance, the more her heart called for him. She needed to set that straight. "I don't think of us. Been too busy. Got too much to do. There is no us." *Lies. All lies.*

Damned if he didn't fall forward to one knee on the floor between them. She tipped back, but not far enough. He almost crashed onto her lap, his arms stiff, his hands on both sides of her shoulders. Close enough to kiss. But he didn't gather her lying ass into his strong, broad chest like she suddenly wished he would. There was no hugging or holding. No physical contact at all. He was doing it again. Being a man. Stealing her breath. Making her hyperventilate and her heart pound. Killing her gently. And surely.

"That's too bad," he whispered into her ear. "Have a good life, London. No matter where you go, I'll always love you. Hope you still believe that."

Her heart jumped into her throat, and her nostrils flared at the musky scent of this man. Her man. Like every time he'd gotten this close before, that feral, masculine scent came to her mixed with pine, smoke, and clean sweat. The perfect trifecta of smells.

"Huh?" was all her frazzled mind could come up with. Her answer would've sounded more absolute if the scruff on his chin hadn't brushed her cheek when he pulled back and returned to his seat. "Yeah, okay. Yeah," she sputtered like an imbecile. "Okay. Back off. Leave me alone."

The second he did, she jerked her gaze back outside the helo. The storm had finally squeezed the life out of those last gorgeous fingers of sunshine, and the light at the edge of the world went out. Just like the light in her heart. *Shit, shit, shit.* Why had she packed so much indifference into that goodbye? She'd sounded heartless, when that was the last thing she was.

With her boundaries so cruelly declared, all London had left was darkness and the big, fat tear glimmering in the corner of her eye. *Men!* Why'd they all have to be so… so…

No satisfying descriptor came to her flustered mind. She pressed a hand on her chest to get her heart to stop pounding. Damned thing seemed to want to leap out of her chest and straight into Heston's big, warm hands. Too bad. He'd had his chance at happily-ever-after and he'd blown it. Big time. London refused to give up on her dreams just because of this chance meeting.

Fate did not rule her, damn it. This was just—and only— a freaking coincidence.

Chapter Nine

Three days later.

Kelsey Stewart had taken an awful beating by the White
River. She was in Intensive Care, with a broken hip, wrist, two
ribs, one clavicle, and three fingers. As well as pneumonia and
a severe concussion that Heston was afraid might end in
irreparable brain injury. The neurosurgeon Alex had flown in
from the East Coast had already removed a piece of her skull
to reduce brain swelling. From what Mark said, Kelsey's
condition improved after that, but from head to toe she'd been
bruised, battered, and broken. How she'd survived and who'd
pulled her from the river remained the mysteries of the day.
As did the identity of who'd shot her, the guy Alex called *'that
gawddamned Irishman!'*

He'd turned into a raging bull when she'd finally come
out of the ten-hour surgery. By then, the bullet hole high on
his chest, not the graze he'd vehemently claimed it was, had
been treated. So had the burns on the back of his head and
neck he'd gotten when the trailer exploded. For a few hours—
thank God!—he'd slept due to whatever pain meds he'd been
given. Which gave everyone a short reprieve.

But once he'd come to, Alex had showered, dressed in
the clean clothes Murphy had brought, then had demanded—
and gotten—the Cadillac of hospital beds for Kelsey and a
simple cot for him so he could stay at her side. He'd flown

most TEAM members to Washington. Everywhere Heston looked, he saw agents and their wives, as well as enough high-tech medical equipment to outfit an entire hospital ward. Maybe two. While the hospital's staff handled her meds and stats, TEAM physicians Libby Houston and McKenna Villanueva, as well as Harley's wife, Judy, attended to Kelsey's personal needs. Things like washing her hair, talking and reading to her, reminding her that she was surrounded by family and friends. That everyone was praying for her recovery.

The same day Alex and Kelsey arrived in this hospital, London was ordered to a Forest Service disciplinary hearing, where, Heston had no idea. He hadn't gotten any time alone with her after they'd landed, hadn't asked the questions he needed answered, hadn't had a chance to tell her goodbye. She'd walked away, just like last time. Without saying goodbye, I love you, or go to hell. Heston couldn't blame her, not since he'd rejected her first.

But watching the way she'd worked so hard to save Kelsey and how she'd expertly handled Alex up on that mountain, knowing she'd willingly put her career on the line by helping Heston and Asher find the Stewarts, had been damned insightful. Told Heston he'd been wrong all those years ago. He'd been stupid. Arrogant for sure.

Because London *was* stronger than he'd thought. She *had* known what she was doing then, and she'd proved it now. She'd been leading them to that suspicious trailer before it exploded. Alex had London to thank for Kelsey's rescue. London *was* efficient and skilled. She *was* brave. Damned brave. She'd trusted her gut up there on that mountain, had known something was odd with the trailer, and she'd stood up to Bates. Outright defied the son of a bitch when she'd gone with Heston and Asher to keep searching.

Heston ducked into the family conference room across the hall from Kelsey's hospital room for a break. He needed a shower and shave, had been on high alert since he'd gotten the assignment to locate Alex and Kelsey. More than that a shower, he needed sleep. A short combat nap was in order.

He pulled two chairs together, one for his butt, the other for his boots. Tipping his head back, he stretched his legs and stared at the ceiling. Then closed his eyes. But all he saw was London's pretty face. Her light turquoise hair. Her jewel-toned eyes. The quirky smile she used to get before she kissed him. The way she'd breathed life back into him, just by being on the same mountain.

Problem was, once London dug her heels in, there was no reasoning with her. Which on Mount Rainier had been a good thing. Not so much in Killeen, Texas, the night they broke up. Her dream of working for the FBI, whether he'd liked it or not, was what ended them. Not because he doubted she could do it. Heston knew damned well London could do anything she set her mind to do. But because she'd left him, just walked out of their apartment and didn't look back. Hadn't called to tell him she'd made it safely to the East Coast. Hadn't answered any of the dozens of letters he'd written.

Correction: Her dream of working for the FBI wasn't the root of their breakup. He'd made his share of mistakes that night, too. Heston knew he'd pushed her too hard and too far the night they'd fought. He'd been stationed at Fort Hood then. She'd just finished her degree in criminal justice. Probably would've helped if he hadn't put his foot down like a moron and asked *'why can't you stay home like other wives?'* He cringed recalling how nasty he'd been—nasty enough she'd primly reminded him she wasn't anybody's wife. Which was true. He hadn't asked to marry him yet. Sure as hell should have.

She'd been so offended at his lack of empathy that she called him a hairy ape with a brain the size of a pea, and she'd walked out on him. Which was just plain bad timing. He'd thought she'd taken off on one of her cooling-off runs, so he'd showered and fixed dinner. But when she hadn't returned, he'd gone looking for her, even ran her usual route thinking he'd spot her and tell her he was sorry. When he didn't find her, he'd panicked. Called her girlfriends. Called her parents, which brought him a shit-ton more disrespect from her father. But not an ounce of real concern. They weren't happy with her *'shacking up with some Hispanic'* to begin with. Their words, not his.

Truly worried, Heston had called the police department then. Another waste of time. London had only been gone hours and she was an adult. Not endangered. Entitled to make her own decisions. He hung up and waited for her to come home. But she didn't.

She could be stubborn. Like the night she'd proudly told her parents that she loved Heston with all her heart, and she didn't care what anyone, including them, thought. They'd made love all night once they'd gotten home. Good times. One of their best. How he'd admired her then.

But how he'd worried the next morning when he'd locked his apartment and had no choice but to board the Air Force C-130 and deploy to Somalia without saying goodbye. Without kissing her. Without knowing where she went or if she was hurt. If she'd been kidnapped.

His gaze dropped to the carpet between the size-twelves he'd stuffed into his big mouth the night of their fight. Which was why she'd walked out. He didn't find out where she'd gone until days later, but he should've known. After enough digging, he'd discovered she'd taken the red-eye out of Austin that night and was in Quantico, Virginia, by the time he left the States. That was what she'd tried to tell him, her good news, that she'd been accepted by the Bureau. One of only a hundred applicants across the nation. That's she'd achieved her dream. She'd been so excited. Bubbly. Effervescent. That was London. Stubborn, but usually happy until—

She wasn't.

He wished he could wind the clock backward and re-do that night. Do it right. Their problem started out simple. London's fantastic news had collided with Heston's butt-ugly day. He should've handled it better. Not been so touchy. So damned rude.

He had been an ass, but only because he'd witnessed an accident with fatalities at Fort Hood, during an exercise that afternoon, and the memory was still fresh. Two privates had destroyed their M1162 Growler, the US Army's light utility, light-strike, and fast-attack vehicle. They'd been off-road, reckless, driving too fast. Weren't wearing seatbelts. Hit a rut. Probably never knew their front left tire had been blown off its rim. Things happened too fast after that. The Growler cartwheeled. The soldier behind the wheel died instantly. The other was ejected and hit a tree. Shattered the front of his skull. It took him a little while, but Heston was with him when he died.

He wiped his hand over his face, as the memories crushed the breath out of him again. There was no getting over it. No forgetting. He swallowed hard, forging ahead like always. He and his LT had been following the Growler. Saw the whole thing. Stayed with those poor guys until the ambulance arrived and took their bodies away. Then he'd gone straight home, thinking only of being in London's arms, of seeking comfort. Of drowning in a bottle of Jack, preferably in bed with her sweet body wrapped around his.

Instead, the moment he'd opened his front door, Heston had been hit by a tsunami of overwhelming enthusiasm. London had been so damned excited. He'd known she'd applied with the FBI. Just hadn't thought all that her acceptance would mean to her. Or to him. He should've realized that, too.

But like some alpha dickhead, instead of listening and offering sincere congratulations to the woman he truly loved, he'd rained shit all over her parade for being selfish and narrow-minded. Had called her a dreamer. A loser. Just that fast, his future changed. She'd wanted—and had gotten—her dream career. He should've been supportive. At least, willing to hear her out. But he'd still been thinking of those two dead privates, their parents and friends. He'd just wanted to spend the night holding her and loving her. Not dealing with one more separation.

She probably thought he hadn't cared at all.

'Wonder why?' Heston thought morosely. Because he had been an ass. Because London was still the same generous, kind, vibrant, and insightful woman she'd been then. Only now...

She wasn't his. She didn't need or want him. There was no *'you complete me'* bullshit to their relationship, like in that

Tom Cruise movie. Heston knew it now. London had been complete before they'd ever met.

He couldn't explain the voracious need to protect her that came over him sometimes, like that night in Killeen or up on the mountain. The moment she'd disappeared around the burning trailer and he'd lost sight of her, he'd panicked. Which was what he'd done in Killeen. *She* could've been in that M1162 Growler. *She* could've been the one who died. Those two men were the same age as London. And honestly, all he'd ever wanted was to keep her safe and protect her and stand beside her and...

Shit. The thought of losing her had choked the life out of him the night they fought. Didn't she know FBI agents were always in the line of fire? Didn't she understand she could be sent into war-torn countries where women were treated no better than cattle? That because she'd be a federal asset, he might never be told the truth of how or where she died? That he might never even be told she had died in the line of duty?

You trust Asher. Mark. Izza Maher. Mother. Why not London?

Because London's different. I love her. I just work with them. They're friends. She's my... everything.

Heston had no qualms working with Asher. Had never worried Asher couldn't do his job. Had no problems trusting his co-workers. So why couldn't he treat London with the same respect and professionalism? The same trust? He'd never been attracted to clingy women who didn't know what they wanted and were afraid to define boundaries or demand respect. London was strong enough for him, and...and every bit as capable and trained as Asher. She was good at her job and she'd proved it.

So why can't you let her be all she can be?

Because the thought of anything happening to London turned Heston into a chest-thumping, testosterone overloaded—what'd she call him? Oh, yeah, a hairy ape with a pea brain. That about summed him up. Heston had no idea why she was the only woman who brought his inner caveman roaring to the surface. Spanish machismo? Possibly. His dad was a Marine. Carter Contreras could be an ass, especially with his sons. Was he that much like his dad?

BLAM! The door behind him slammed open and in came Alex, instantly taking control of the room like a category ten hurricane takes charge of Florida. Had to be a Cat 10 because hurricane ratings only went to five, and Alex's rage was way beyond the requisite 157 mph windspeed for a Cat 5.

"You!" Alex snarled, sticking a long, angry finger in Heston's face. "You and Asher! Get your son of a bitchin' gear. I've got a job for you."

Murphy, Mark, and Asher hustled in on Alex's heels. "Now hold up, Alex," Murphy argued.

Alex whirled on him. "No! You hold up. I want that son of a bitch dead!"

The phrase *son of a bitch* would forever remind Heston of his boss. He looked to Murphy for calmer explanations. "Where am I going and why?"

"Because you work for me and I said so!" Alex roared, pacing around the chairs and tables scattered throughout the room.

Heston inhaled slowly and refused to retaliate. Alex was hurting. That was all this tantrum was about. When he hurt, he took it out on everyone around him. God knew how long he'd be a nightmare to deal with, but deal Heston would. For as long as it took Kelsey to recover. Longer if necessary. If London's best quality was stubbornness, Heston's was loyalty.

"The Irishman has contacted Alex," Mark, instead of Murphy, explained quietly. Mark had grown up somewhere in the Midwest, tossing hay bales, wrestling beef and hogs, and working sunup to sundown on his family's farm. He was wider and thicker muscled than Alex. But Alex was the alpha, and right then Heston could almost see hackles—make that stegosaurus plates—sticking straight up off his pissed-off boss's back.

"That son of a bitch threatened my wife!" Alex spat. "Again!"

Mark said, "He called on the hospital phone in—"

"Because I threw the son of a bitch's burner in the gawddamned White River!"

Deep breath. Count to ten. Let Alex rant and curse all he needed. Wait on Mark.

"He called on the phone in Kelsey's room," Mark continued as if he hadn't been interrupted by the ogre Alex had become. "He told Alex he obviously hadn't learned his lesson. That he could get to Alex or Kelsey anytime he wanted. That he knew which room she was in and next time—
"

"He'll shoot to kill!" Alex roared. "Her! My Kelsey! That bastard's threatened her for the last son of a bitchin' time!"

"What the fuck?" Heston asked, equally offended at the balls this Irish moron thought he had. "Who is this bastard, and what do you want me to do to him when I find him? Because I will find him, Boss." Heston leveled that promise at Alex.

"Damned straight," Asher added from the doorway where he still stood, his arms raised over his head, his hands gripping the overhead jamb. "Heston and me'll hunt the fucker down, Boss. You want him alive or can we just bring back his head on a spike? Or his balls? You'd mount them on your wall, wouldn't you?"

Oddly, Alex calmed at that grisly pronouncement of loyalty. He was shaking. His nostrils flared as if there wasn't enough air in the room. His chest heaved like a blacksmith's bellows. Pursing his lips, he let some of that hot air go. The laser blue ice in his eyes melted the tiniest bit. His Adam's apple ratcheted up, then down. With a hard-won swallow, he finally said, "I want them dead, Heston, Asher. There's at least two of them. The guy who gave me the burner wasn't the shooter. Couldn't've been. He's too weak of a chicken shit to be the only one behind this."

Alex's chest heaved with another deep breath. "Other than that, I've got nothing. No brass left behind to pin those shots to any specific weapon or caliber. Don't know precisely where they fired from anyway. Don't know who the hell they are. Don't even know where to look or who to ask. It happened so fast I couldn't determine trajectory. No fingerprints on Kelsey when I found her, and the fire destroyed all evidence in the trailer, if there even was any. Weather destroyed footprints. I've got nothing!"

Heston watched the man he'd follow into Hell return to a semi-normal version of himself. Still agitated, but calm enough he was breathing better. Hopefully thinking better, too.

"Mother's tracking all cell towers near Mount Rainier, but so far she's found nothing," Murphy added.

"Ember, Beau, and Jameson are running various scenarios with the FBI," Mark said. "The Bureau suspects the Irish Mafia's behind this, but they're not ruling out the Russian or Sicilians."

"No shit," Alex bit out. "If my old man's—"

"Whoa," Heston interrupted, his palms forward for Alex to stop and explain. "Your dad? What's that about?"

Alex turned to Mark and growled, "Tell him."

A pained expression shadowed Mark's face. "Alex recently discovered that his father might've played a part in the Irish Mafia's business out of Boston. But I've investigated every word of Mel Stewart's bragging. He's not a reliable source, but he did run small jobs for Pops Delaney, whose birth name was" —Mark clapped a hand to his mouth and coughed— "Killian Stewart. Pops Delaney, aka Killian Stewart, was Mel's older brother, which makes him Alex's uncle. DNA confirms the lineage. That's the only link I can find, but I haven't found anything that proves Delaney exploited it."

"Don't waste time looking. My dad's a gawddamned liar," Alex said grimly.

"Understood, but Mel and Pops were brothers, and maybe Pops didn't want Mel involved."

Alex snorted. "Wouldn't be surprised. Nobody trusted Mel. Not Mom or Gramps. Sure as hell not me."

Heston's lips pursed at what had to have been a magnitude 9.0 shock when a hard-driven patriot like Alex learned he was related to an Irish crime boss. "How recently did this come to light?"

"Last year," Alex spat. "The bastard showed up the day my son was born. Just walked into Kelsey's hospital room like he owned the place."

"Doesn't your old man have dementia or something?" Asher asked.

"Alzheimer's and a helluva lot of nerve." Alex hadn't stopped pacing the small family conference room where Heston had settled for a few minutes of peace and quiet. Kiss that goodbye.

Someone's cell phone rang. Everyone in the room checked their pockets. Surprisingly, it was Heston's. He palmed it out of his jeans pocket, put it up to his ear, and answered, "Agent Contreras."

"Heston? Oh, good. Hi. London here. I've got something you need to see. Might be the break we're looking for. How long will it take you guys to get back up here?"

We're looking for? "You're back on the mountain? At White River Campground? But I thought—"

"Yup, still working our case, investigating. Watched a couple guys. Took pictures of things and them and, you know, stuff."

"You're still doing your job?" He knew about her disciplinary hearing. Just hadn't expected she'd go back to working the Stewarts' case while she waited on the outcome of that hearing. Wow. London had brass balls, and he wanted to see them.

"Somebody's got to. Bates knew Alex and Kelsey Stewart were missing before you and Asher showed up. He just didn't care. But I did. Still do."

The words were out of his big mouth before he could think. "Don't do anything reckless."

Just that quickly, he lost what little ground he'd made.

"Knock it off, Hes," she snapped. "I'm not your fuck buddy anymore."

He turned and faced the wall. "You never were… that. Honest. You know what we had was—"

"Over. Done. Whatever."

Great. She'd turned surly and it was his fault. Why couldn't he overcome the damned protective instinct that kidnapped his brain and turned him into a Neanderthal over everything that concerned London? The caveman inside of him was ruining everything.

"Copy that, Ranger Wilde," Heston replied more respectfully. "Message received. I'll see what I can do to assist you."

"Ah, yeah. About that. I'm, umm, not Ranger Wilde anymore. You might as well know. They canned me for insubordination. Not like that's a first." She huffed. "Guess the USFS higher-ups don't appreciate it when you make your boss look like an ass because he is one. Meet me south of the footbridge on the other side of the White from where we found the Stewarts. Dress warm. Wind's kicking up and it's bitchin' cold up here."

He looked straight at Alex. "We can be there inside two hours."

"You sure?" London asked. "I'll wait if you mean it."

"I mean it, yes, ma'am." Damn it. Just yes. God, the effect she had on him was embarrassing. "Hold on a sec. Boss? I've got Ranger Wilde on the phone. She's found a solid lead." Heston was willing to extend that bold assumption to redress the way he'd minimized her by telling her not to be reckless. "She needs me and Asher back at the campground."

Alex's answer was sharp. "Good. Go. Find me something I can use to end these bastards."

"We'll be back before dark."

Alex nodded. "I owe you, Hes. You saved Kelsey's life."

"No, Boss, all I did was step on you. London's who led me and Asher to you and Kels. She knew something was going on with that trailer."

"She's a smart woman."

Heston couldn't argue. "She is. We'll find out what else is going on. Promise. And if I catch the rat bastard behind this, I'll kill him."

You could almost hear the angst hiss out of Alex at that bold promise. He licked his lips, like a parched athlete who'd just run the longest marathon of his life. "Make him suffer, Heston. Make it hurt."

"Copy that," was all Heston could answer back. He stuck his chin at Asher. "You ready?"

"I was born ready."

Good enough. He told London, "We're on our way. See you soon..." He almost said 'see you soon, babe.' Instead, he breathed, "Let's roll, Ash."

"Copy that, Hes. Be safe," she answered before the connection went dead.

Heston shook the image of her out of his mind. Safe had nothing to do with London. He wanted her. Just could never have her. Didn't matter. Nothing else mattered but killing the Irishman and his sniper buddy.

Chapter Ten

Alex left Murphy and Mark in the family conference room and walked alone back to Kelsey's room. The hallway was empty. He was down to his last ounce of strength, and she was the only one who could help him. He needed to touch her. Wished he could hold her, but she had so many wires and tubes attached, all he could do was sit at her side and talk to her, remind her that Lexie and Baby Bradley were waiting for her to come home. That they loved her and talked about her every time he called. That he called them every morning and every night. That he missed her so damned much, he felt like he was dying. Which he would if she didn't pull through.

Yes, he'd still have Lexie and Baby Bradley. Alex knew that, and he loved them with his whole soul. But how could he go on without Kelsey's light in his life? How did a man recover from a loss that deep? A pain that lasting? He already felt hollowed out, gutted that his negligence had put her at risk. Take a melon baller to him and you'd find nothing left inside. Just a crusty old shell full of hot air, anger, and self-pity. That was all he had left. All he ran on these miserable days.

He palmed her door open and let himself into the brightly lit room. The nurses kept turning the lights up; he kept turning them down. He dimmed them again. There was no need to blind Kelsey when she came to—and she would—so he erred on the side of hope. Anything else felt like betrayal. Christ, let her wake up slow and easy. Don't jolt her. Everything in this world did not have to be painful and hard.

By the time he was standing at her right, the side with the fewest tubes and wires attached to her, he noticed her right leg was bare. Uncovered. Up to her knee. Somehow, she'd wormed it out from under the blanket. His heart thudded at that seemingly innocuous event. Kelsey hated blankets on her feet, was always kicking them off. She said she was too warm, that she needed one leg exposed. Even if the thermostat at home was set low and the house was cold, at least one foot or leg would be uncovered.

His heart leaped at the possibility that was her first step back to him. Alex took gentle hold of her ankle, circled it with his whole hand. She was so small and petite. "You're still with me, aren't you, sweetheart?" God, he hoped.

She didn't reply. He didn't think she would. But the hope in his heart flamed out of control, and Alex gave in to temptation. He owned this hospital bed, damn it. He'd paid for it; he could damned-well sleep in it with his wife if he wanted to. Who cared if he offended hospital staff? Kelsey needed him. Kicking off his shoes, he stripped down to his boxers. Gingerly, oh, so carefully, he lowered the side rail and put a knee on the mattress alongside his wife. "Mind if I join you, sweetheart?" he whispered.

She was still gray. So pale. The helmet on her poor head was there for protection, but it gave her the air of a spoiled little girl who'd rather be outside biking, than made to go to bed just because it was good for her.

Alex did what he said he'd do and carefully laid down beside her. With infinite tenderness, he eased one arm under her neck and curled her into his side. Under his arm where she belonged. He positioned her helmet against his chest, making sure no wires or tubes were twisted. Making sure she could breathe. Not doing anything that might hurt her. He made sure her exposed leg stayed uncovered. Which meant his feet were, too.

Relief flooded his soul. Just holding her. Just breathing the scent of her back into his broken heart. That was all he wanted. To be with her again. Just this. Which was everything. How does a man quantify the light this woman had brought into his life? The change she'd wrought on his worthless soul? Now words came close to how much he loved Kelsey.

Alex fought his tears, but ended up letting them run down the sides of his head as he held onto all that made his life worth living. For the first time since she'd been shot he had a firm hold on her. She was alive. He could breathe. She *was* going to make it, damn it.

Lying there, with his whole world in his hands, Alex prayed like he'd never prayed before. The Man Upstairs wasn't his enemy anymore. Hadn't been for years. Not the same way Alex had thought He was when Sara and Abby had died. Because of Kelsey, he'd become a believer. Even went to church, just not as often as she did. But he went to please her, and that had made the difference. Because of the insights Kelsey shared—or maybe because of her faith—Alex now knew God wasn't just for faithful followers, the Sunday-go-to-meeting folks who dressed up to be seen, nor the show-up-only-at-Easter-and-Christmas gang. He was for losers and sinners, bastards like Alex. He was for everyone, even atheists, God bless them.

See? Right there? What God had done? Saved a sinner named Alex, saved him good enough that he was now able, maybe smart enough to bless other non-believers without thinking about it. Wasn't too long ago he'd cursed God, the whole human race, and the universe. Not since he'd found Kelsey. Was that the same thing as finding the Lord? Hell, yeah.

She was finally as warm and safe as Alex could make her. He had agents posted around the hospital, others inside the building, all looking for anyone suspicious. His TEAM was made up of damned good women and men, all sworn to protect Kelsey. If the Irishman were within spitting distance, his men and women would intercept and destroy the sucker. At last, Alex closed his eyes and let the simple comfort of his wife's nearness work its magic. If this was as much as she could give him in the future, he'd take it and be thankful for every minute he got to keep her.

"Excuse me…"

Alex ignored the soft voice of the nurse at the door.

"Excuse me, Mr. Stewart, but I need to—"

"I'm not leaving, so go," he hissed into the semi-darkness.

"Shhhhh," she ordered. "Don't wake her. Please, keep your voice down."

"I would if you'd get the hell out of here and let us be," he snarled protectively.

"Don't worry. I'm leaving. Just want you to know that for the first time since she's been with us, your wife's blood pressure is within normal range. Everyone wondered what happened and, well…" The nurse smiled at him like the damned angel of mercy she'd just turned into. "Whatever you're doing, Mr. Stewart, keep doing it. She might not respond to your voice, but she knows you're here. You're helping her. Now go back to sleep. I'll stop in later."

That did it. After the door closed behind the nurse, Alex buried his nose in the crook of Kelsey's warm neck and cried. "I'm here, sweetheart. I'm with you and I'm not letting you go. Never. Come back to me. Please, come all the way back to me."

Chapter Eleven

Decker made good time. Within two hours, Heston and Asher were back at the same LZ they'd landed at days earlier. Only now, they were knee-deep in the wettest, heaviest, moisture-filled snow on Earth and slogging their way to London.

"How do people ski in this crap?" Heston wondered out loud. He'd skied in Utah one winter. Its claim to fame was *"The Greatest Snow on Earth®"*. But this stuff was shit, only good for making fat-bottomed snowmen and droopy snow forts. Not for hiking. Not even for standing up straight in.

"Over here!" A sweet voice yelled from the bank where the White River curved southwest to Owyhigh Lakes. "Hurry! It's gone now. They took it down, but I've got pictures. I can prove it was here. I've got pictures of them, too!"

London wasn't wearing Forest Service green anymore, which was too damned bad. If the Forest Service canned her just because she'd disobeyed Bates, they were dumber than the FBI. She'd dressed in black jeans and a matching jacket today, which made her look sleek and sexy. Like a ski bunny on one of those travel posters for Vale or Lake Tahoe—or the nearest Army recruiting office.

Her cap was bright white, which accentuated her unique hair color, and her boots were bright red, a fashion statement all by themselves. There was the real London, finally. A big cheesy grin lit her pretty face, and she was laughing at them as they trudged along like a couple idiots because… they were. Idiots. At least, Heston was, and he knew it. An idiot for a Wilde woman.

He'd slowed to bask in her laugh, when he noticed the slightest bulge under her left arm. Sure wasn't extra-downy fluff. No, she was carrying. A twinge of pride slithered up Heston's spine. *That's my girl.*

"My bad," the cheeky brat giggled. "I should've warned you guys to bring snowshoes."

"No worries," Asher chuffed once they were at her side. "Walking in crap this heavy builds muscle. It'll keep the fat off Heston's ass."

"My ass isn't as fat as your head," Heston volleyed back. "Show us what you've got, London." Man, it felt good hearing her name roll off his tongue. He wanted to say it again, just for the way it felt.

They were downhill from the footbridge. London was standing between him and Asher. She took her cell phone out of her pants pocket, leaned into Asher and said, "See?"

They put their heads together, her cheek almost against his, she was standing that close. Didn't help that he was taller and had to hunch his big ass down to her level to look at her damned phone. That he'd put a gloved hand on her shoulder, the dog. Heston knew damned well what Asher was doing. Why should Heston care? They weren't kissing. Or hugging. Asher hadn't made a play for her. But he was close enough they were breathing the same air.

"See?" London stuck her phone in Heston's face next. But some butthead had breathed all over it, and condensation fogged the lens, and—

"Can't see a thing," he griped like a petulant child instead of the special operator he was.

London leaned in closer. She was nearly under his arm, where she belonged. Still chuckling, she swiped her thumb over the screen to clear the view. Which Heston still couldn't see, not standing as close as he was to the woman he'd let get away. Not with her flowery scent suddenly in his nose and his brain digging up memories—one after another—of his previous life with this audacious creature. Not with his blood on fire and his stupid heart pounding in his throat.

London hip-checked him to get his attention. Like she used to—a long time ago—back in the days when they'd played around. Teased. Enjoyed each other. Were carefree and—

Time warped, and once again, they were just a couple college kids in love, on their way to fame and glory. So damned happy that being poor hadn't mattered. They'd had each other. Almost made the emptiness of the last few years fade away. Almost...

Except London was no longer the woman he'd known before. The FBI might not have been smart enough to keep her, but she'd gained a butt load of confidence while being on her own. At least, he hoped she'd been on her own. Was still on her own. Might make groveling easier if he knew he stood a chance. Her last name was still Wilde. That had to mean something.

"Do you see it or not?" she asked breathily.

He looked down at her, not at her phone. She was looking up at him. And once again, he fell into the jeweled wells of her eyes. He reached out automatically, rested a hand on her jacket-covered shoulder. Just her shoulder. Might as well have been her bare breast the way electricity sparked between them. Heston felt like he'd grabbed hold of a live wire. The shock was stunning. Tempting. Made him hungry as hell.

"Hes," she growled. "Look. At. The. Picture."

He jerked his mind out of bed, any bed, because that was where it'd gone. Them—naked—under the sheets—in bed—somewhere else. Loving. Holding. Playing. He cleared his throat, nodded 'message received,' and finally studied the damned evidence in her hand. It took a few blinks to get the roaring caveman out of his head, but the moment his eyes focused, he cursed. "What the hell is that? A cattle guard?"

"Finally, *big guy*," Asher teased. *'Big Guy'* was the too-often-heard, cutesy nickname coined by Agent Everlee Yeager, soon to be Mrs. Everlee Yeager-Hayes, for her fiancé Shane Hayes. It had been used so often in the office that it became a joke.

"Stow it, Downey," Heston shot back at the real *'big guy'* on the team, ignoring London so the spike in his pants would stop beating its hairy chest and bellowing, *'Me get girl!'*

There is no way we're getting the girl, bud. We blew it a long time ago, so shut up.

"Yup, a cattle guard," London answered, an unsteady tremor in her voice.

Which did *not* help. Heston was damned if he'd rearrange his junk in public.

She cleared her throat twice, then swallowed hard and asked, "S-see the brackets still attached to the framework below the planks overhanging this side of the bridge? There's two of them. Two brackets. They're what held the cattle guard in place. That's how they caught Kelsey Stewart's body.

That's why she's still alive. They sh-shot her, then waited until she hit this grate and pulled her out of the river."

Yeah, London felt the attraction, too. And she was right. The cattle guard was a sturdy steel device, more or less a massive grate used by farmers the world over, to keep their cattle from crossing a fence line and leaving the farm. It would surely also stop a body traveling downstream. This area of the river was wider and the water less turbulent. The cattle guard was painted USFS green and was nearly invisible, bracketed under the overhang of the bridge and in the shade like it was. Anyone observant enough to notice it would've thought it was Forest Service property. But Heston saw it for what it was: the first clue that would lead him to the man or woman who'd shot Kelsey.

"And the guys?" he asked. "You said you had pictures of some guys. Were they who dismantled it?"

London's head bobbed as she swiftly tapped her cell phone ,then showed him several grainy photos that didn't reveal shit. At least not clear shit. All he could make out was, yes, two shadowy men alongside the river. Both slender and dressed in black. Both holding cell phones to their ears and continually looking over their shoulders. They weren't exactly dismantling anything but they certainly knew about the cattle guard.

"I couldn't get close enough to get better shots, and I know they're pixilated but—"

"They're better than what we've got. Good job, London." Heston gave her Mother's number and ordered her to, "Send these to Sasha Kennedy. She's our technical genius. Maybe she can work her magic and help you identify these guys."

"Oh, okay."

Heston jerked his gaze to the White River. "Did you see them take it apart?" How else could they have gotten something that large out of the river?

"Sorry, no. A couple hikers interrupted me. They'd just found their lost dog and needed my phone to contact their vet because she was hurt and I... I got distracted."

"Nevermind. Show me the brackets." Two men taking a cattle guard apart didn't make sense. Cattle guards were heavy contraptions, not made to be broken down into convenient-to-carry pieces.

"If you're thinking fingerprints, think again," London replied, even as she aimed her snowshoes toward the bridge. "There's no way to know how long it was in place, and there's been a lot of weather up here. It'll be a miracle if you find any evidence on it."

"If *we* find anything. You're part of this investigation. *We'll* see," he said with confidence. Killers and kidnappers were just people, and stupid, eager people made mistakes.

By the time he and Asher struggled through the heavy snow to where London already stood at the bridge in her flat, extra-wide snowshoes, he was winded, and his hamstrings were screaming. But hope kept him going. The underside of that bridge, possibly the entire thing, needed to be dusted for prints. All he needed was one print, but if Mother could clean up those photos, maybe between a couple prints and a clear photo, they'd get the guys behind the shootings. Maybe then Alex could rest.

Heston had barely caught his breath when London took a few steps down the rocky bank to the noisy, splashing water line. It was all he could do to not reach forward and jerk her out of harm's way. To keep her from falling into the river. But this was her world. Her job. And his job today was to respect that she knew precisely what she was doing. Just that.

Respect was all she'd wanted years ago, and by hell, she was going to get it today. Maybe. His fingers still clenched with a desperate need to protect her from herself. His whole body leaned closer in case she slipped or the river grabbed her. He couldn't lose her like Alex had lost Kelsey. He wouldn't survive.

It was a struggle, his better sense against his willful 'I know better than you' ego, but Heston managed to keep it together. At least, he didn't make an ass of himself.

London shot him a smile over her shoulder. A real smile. A daring, teasing smile that told him she knew how hard it was for him to treat her as a highly qualified equal. But she was, wasn't she? She was one of this generation's intelligent, capable, able-bodied women who needed to fly in order to live. And he was the sap who desperately needed London to live—her life, not his. So Heston gulped and swallowed a big mouthful of arrogant male pride. He suppressed his inner caveman and let her be what she was meant to be. In charge.

"There," she said, pointing a finger beneath the left side of the overhang, the side where they'd stopped. "See it? There's two of them. One here, one way over there."

The footbridge was maybe ten-feet-wide, at least a good twenty, maybe twenty-five feet long. Built of sturdy four-by-eight wood planks laid over a sturdier wooden framework that, in turn, was attached to vertical steel beams pounded deep into the volcanic bedrock of the riverbed, at eight-foot intervals. Overall, there were sixteen steel beams. The top planks overhung the supporting framework by a good two feet. The force of white water roaring down the mountain had

had no effect on the steel. They were weathered but tight, and the bridge didn't shudder, which spoke to the strength of its workmanship. Wooden handrails up top kept travelers safe. The safety net stretched beyond the handrail along both sides of the bridge kept debris, slippery cell phones, wayward children, or mischievous teenagers from falling into the river.

Heston peered closer. Industrial-sized lug bolts secured the brackets to the framework. Both brackets and bolts were tucked beneath the overhang, where, until this snow hit, they'd kept fairly dry. Fingerprinting might be the smart thing to do.

But that two feet of extra overhang was a problem. To remove either bracket, some idiot would have to traverse under the overhang by his fingertips, hanging like a monkey from the planks with no safety net. Once he made it to the first bracket, he'd have to hang by one arm while he removed lug bolts, washers, and brackets with the other. Which wasn't a problem if he rigged a bag to catch both brackets and bolts once they were loose. Because, yeah. He was that idiot.

"I'm going in," Heston said to no one in particular, stripping out of his jacket and boots, down to his double holster, his jeans, shirt, and stocking feet. Anxious to get this over with.

London smacked his forearm. Her fingers dug into him, holding him back. "No. That's crazy. You'll be hanging over white water, Hes. It's not safe. Let me call—"

"*You're* calling *me* crazy?" he asked, teasing her while he traded his snow gloves for climbing gloves out of his gear bag and secured the straps tightly at his wrists.

"No. Never," she answered breathlessly. The liar. Her pretty eyes had turned dark turquoise with worry. "I know you're strong and capable, but the net'll be way above your head, Hes. Not under you, and I don't have a safety rope. If you fall—"

"Asher has a rope. London, don't worry. This is my call, my job," he said gently, cocking his head to maintain eye contact with the woman he had never gotten over. "Not yours."

He knew how high her anxiety was. How it was burning a hole in her gut. That her adrenaline level was out of sight. Because he'd been in her shoes the night of their fight. He'd been scared, and he understood now why he'd been an ass to her. Because he had witnessed two men die earlier that same day, and the fear that she could die just as quickly as they had, had been a godawful powerful motivator—just as powerful a manipulator. That was what he'd been running on, the high-octane fear of losing her. Fear of her dying in some distant country without him there to catch her, to hold her, to comfort her while she took her last breath. And enough adrenaline to power that fear, enough to make him say anything to make her stay. To keep her safe.

"But, Hes—"

Damn, he loved it when she used his name. "Trust me, babe. I know what I'm doing. Done crazier stuff than this before. Asher, I need a rope and harness," he ordered, needing to get those brackets bagged before he froze to death.

"You got your Leatherman on you?" Asher asked.

"Yes, but I need to be beneath the overhang before I pull it out. Can't risk dropping it."

"Then use this for the evidence." Asher tossed a small nylon bag with a carabiner attached at one corner. "And this one's" —he sent another bag flying— "for your tools."

Heston caught both bags and snapped the carabiners to his belt loops. "Good thinking."

"And this," Asher tossed a foot-long S-hook.

Heston caught it and threaded one end into his belt loop. "Anything else?"

"Yeah. That harness and rope won't keep you from falling, only from being swept away if you do something stupid. You're taking one hell of a risk, Contreras. The water won't kill you. The rocks will."

True story. The White River was a churning washing machine, and the sharp volcanic rocks sticking through the foam were damned wicked agitators.

"Don't go," London whispered. "Please, Heston. Don't do this."

He winked at her, hoping if he looked cocky enough, she'd understand that there was no way he wasn't doing this. Rangers took chances. Intestinal fortitude was drilled into them. Surrender was not in the Ranger vocabulary. He'd volunteered to be a Ranger, and he'd volunteered to help Alex nail the bastards who'd hurt Kelsey. End of story.

It took a few minutes to strap into the woven harness and rope. By the time Heston was standing at the edge of the overhang, his clothes were chilled and wet, his feet were frozen, and he was breathing frosty vapor. Asher had one end of the rope wrapped around his fist, and Heston was banking that one of those kidnappers had made a mistake. He only needed a partial print. Just one. If they were in the system, Alex would finally have a way forward.

Go time.

Chapter Twelve

Without another word, Heston grabbed the wooden overhang with both hands, wedged his gloved fingertips between the planks, lifted his weight off his feet and swung out over the river. He had the rocky shoreline below him for the first couple feet. After that, he was dangling over rocks as sharp as pikes and Arctic-cold water. He hurried to get under the bridge and out of sight in case the men who'd tried to kill Kelsey were still around.

"Hes, be careful, honey," London called to him.

"Always," he told himself. Her calling him honey was nice, but yelling back cost too much energy, and he'd need every bit to get this job done. At the nearest bracket, Heston discovered how smart the men who'd installed the cattle guard were.

The brackets were fastened to the beams underpinning the planks with hex-capped, half-inch-by-one-and-a-quarter-inch zinc lug bolts. In the center of each bracket, a thick, six-inch steel elbow jutted out at a ninety-degree angle, its receiving end pointed up another six inches. Want to bet there was a corresponding eyelet screw or an eye-nut on each end of the cattle guard, large enough to slide the guard easily over and onto this elbow? Made sense. Rigging a heavy, steel device under this bridge to catch a body would've been damned difficult. It would have taken at least two strong men to lower the guard over the rail and—

Nope. They never could've gotten it over the safety netting. Which meant they'd somehow walked it along the shoreline, one guy on each side of the river, holding the ends of the—

Still nope. A cattle guard long enough to span the river would've weighed too much. Must've used a helicopter. That made sense.

"Shit," Heston hissed. There'd been a USFS helicopter parked not far from the Incident Command Center the day he'd first confronted Bates. Was that how the Irishman had placed, then removed the cattle guard so quickly? Heston assumed the helo had brought in Search and Rescue personnel. Anyone would've made that same leap in logic. But now, knowing what a dick Bates was and that he'd never cared about finding Alex or Kelsey, Heston knew better. Anyone cold-hearted enough to abandon two people to certain death in the White River, certainly wouldn't mind misusing USFS property.

Shivering like crazy, Heston pulled his all-purpose Leatherman tool from the one bag and loosened the lug bolts on the first bracket. Anchoring the S-hook between the planks overhead, he attached the other bag, and bingo. Bracket, bolts, and washer dropped safely into the bag the moment he loosened them entirely. But damn, it was c-c-cold.

He tucked the Leatherman and the brackets into their respective bags, cinched both bags shut, re-secured the S-hook onto his belt loop, and swung over to the other end of the bridge. Collecting evidence. If the brackets and bolts he'd just salvaged were clean of prints, maybe the next wouldn't be.

Finally at the opposite end, Heston took a two second break to breathe and to focus on keeping warm long enough to finish the task. Even inside his gloves, his fingers were numb, and ice crystals had formed on the tips of his eyelashes. He could hear them clatter when he blinked, and he was pretty sure the sweat under his arms had frozen into ice. He crooked his neck, needing to hurry. He was still shivering plenty but his speed and dexterity were gone.

Hypothermia was headed his way.

Nonetheless, he went through the same drill at the second bracket as he had the first, with caution and deliberate slowness. He couldn't get the Leatherman's teeth to grip the first bolt. The tool kept slipping around it, not catching the hex shape like it should. He fumbled and damned near dropped the tool. *Time to regroup. Rethink. Take a deep breath. Try, try again.*

Maybe it was him, maybe these bolts were driven in deeper than the others. They might be frozen into the wood. Whatever the reason, it took him longer to loosen each lug bolt, just as long to situate the evidence bag in the best place to catch the bracket and bolts. By the time he had all twelve bolts and two brackets safely in the bag, he was running on empty.

Heston turned and looked over his shoulder, thinking he'd find London on the far bank. But the bank was empty and—

"Here," she called from the other side.

Dummy. She was smarter than him. She hadn't expected he'd go back the way he'd come when he finished. See? First sign of hypothermia was confusion and an odd sense of peacefulness, when he had no right to feel peaceful. Not hanging like a long-armed orangutan over this deadly river. What he wouldn't give to have his winter jacket back on.

'So hurry, dumbass,' he mentally scolded himself. It took more strength to wedge his fingertips between the planks now. They were stiff and numb. He was swinging dead weight. Heavy dead weight. It was harder to bend his knees and get his body moving with enough force to inch toward London. God, he was cold. Getting colder. Getting weaker. Still had a good ten feet to go. Was starting to wonder if it wouldn't be smarter to just let go and hope he landed on dry land after a good, strong swing. Not like there was dry ground on this mountain. His teeth chattered, sounded like drumsticks inside his skull. Even over the din of the river, he could hear the ice on his lashes clink with every blink.

Heston kept keeping on. Inch by inch. *Quitters never win and winners never quit.* Seemed like hours, but at last, he swung his weight far enough to let go and land safely. He dropped into the wet snowbank at London's feet.

"Stupid shit," Asher cussed the second Heston's frozen stocking feet hit the ground. "Why'd you take your damned boots off but kept your pistols, you ass? They're just as heavy."

"Might've n-n-needed to sh-shoot."

"Get out of those clothes," London ordered. "You're drenched! Now, mister!"

He looked to Asher for assistance in getting undressed or, at least, intervention with London, he wasn't sure which. "Give me a h-hand?"

The *'big guy'* shot Heston an evil glance, then handed London the roll of dry clothes and a towel. "Let me get his holster out of the way first, ma'am. Get his dumb ass dried off. Better hurry. I've got socks and boots, next."

Looked like this was going to be a hands-on adventure with London, though Heston was too tired and cold to care who helped him undress. Still… he couldn't help wishing they were on a tropical island instead of Mount-Damned-Rainier.

The moment Asher lifted Heston's shoulder harness off, London turned into a damned Nazi, ripping his wet shirt over his head, almost taking his ears with it. Growling, she wrapped the towel around his shoulders and draped one corner of it over his wet head. Turning his face, he burrowed into the terry cloth's absorbent warmth. The difference a little heat made.

Still growling, London dragged his wet jeans down his legs while Asher collected everything she tossed out of her way.

Heston really didn't want to bare his ass to London, not like this, not when he was vulnerable and numb and, well, shriveled and shrunken. But she gave him no choice. Didn't even ask. Just yanked that underwear down and off, like she owned him. Which was an entertaining thought—her owning him—for all of about two seconds. Shrinkage was real, and he had nothing to brag about. Nothing. Not like she seemed to notice. But even as he shivered, he noticed her.

London's face was a study of stern, sharp worry. Her long, jewel-toned bangs hung into her face like a tropical waterfall. The harder she rubbed the towel over his legs and thighs, the better his circulation, and the more Heston couldn't stop watching the way the tip of her pink tongue poked over her bottom lip, then disappeared completely when she snared that lip between her teeth, her tell that she was focused. He would know. There was a time she'd been this focused on him in a different way.

Her hands and fingers trembled as she hurried. He was sure he could hear her heart pounding in her veins. Once she stopped toweling him off so roughly, she took firm hold of each of his feet and angled them through the leg holes of his dry jockeys. Embarrassing, yeah. But, despite the cold and fierce urgency with which she worked—tenderly intimate. Made freezing almost worth it, just to have her hands on him again.

There she was, on her knees in wet snow, breathing hard from the effort of getting him into warm clothes and dry—*oh man, they felt good*—socks. Then boots. Maybe she was a little worried, hurrying like she was. Because she cared? He hoped that was her motivation. Anything else would be so much—less. He couldn't deal with the letdown if she were *'just doing her job.'*

Before he had the chance, she'd zipped his pants and fastened the button. Asher took charge of getting him into a dry t-shirt and, over that, a gray sweatshirt with ARMY stenciled on its chest. A black, fluffy down parka followed. But damn, every move hurt. Hanging too long in the cold had done a number on his muscles and shivering wasn't helping his joints. There'd better be a damned partial print on those brackets after all this trouble.

As a finishing touch, London activated several handwarmers and stuffed one in his pants pockets, two more into the mittens she was carefully working over his stiff fingers. By the time she and Asher were done with him, Heston was warmer, but dog-tired. What a day.

London kept rubbing his shoulders and arms. "London, stop," he murmured, shivering so hard his teeth and his lower jaw hurt. "I'm okay, just c-c-cold."

"You scared me to death, damn you," she snapped. "Don't you ever do that—"

Aw, what the hell. He was going to lay down anyway, and thankfully, Asher had spread a tarp to keep everything and everyone drier. Angling his shoulders, Heston tipped over onto his back and jerked London down with him. With full intent, he took hold of her head and mashed her surprised mouth over his stiff lips.

Surprisingly, she gave in, didn't resist, just melted against him. At last. Her breath was as intoxicating as he remembered. Her lips were wet and warm, and her lush body pressing against his was all he'd ever wanted. He could breathe. He was going to live.

The kiss turned steamy for all of sixty seconds, until he felt her tears wetting his cheeks.

"It's okay to be scared," he murmured, shifting her length alongside his, ending their moment of passion with a fast kiss to her forehead and his hand on the small of her back.

"I'm not scared. I'm mad," she growled. "At you. You could've gotten yourself killed, you big dumb ass!"

He rolled his eyes at her. "Man, I love when you cuss."

A sob shuddered out of her. Yes, she was mad, but mostly London was scared. Heston knew the signs. Wasn't long ago, he'd been in her shoes. Scared she'd go off to the East Coast and get herself killed in the line of duty. That the FBI would never tell him when she'd died or which country she'd been in when she'd fallen. That he'd lose her, never see her again, never hold her again, never get the chance to apologize for being a possessive jerk, or—anything.

So, yeah. Holding her now, feeling her heart hammering against his, tasting her lips and tongue—So. Damned. Perfect. Heston blinked, tears melting the icicles on his lashes. He squeezed both eyes shut, needing a minute to compose himself. Men didn't cry, certainly not in front of their companion agent. They bucked up. They carried on.

He fully intended to lighten the mood, maybe crack a joke, make a smart-aleck comment. Instead, "I've missed you so damned much, babe," whispered out of his big mouth. "And I'm sorry. So sorry for everything I said to you that night. I was wrong."

"You were wrong, and you should be sorry," she hissed.

For as angry as she'd been when she'd stormed out on him, she seemed fine lying beside him now. Heston thanked God for the strong-willed woman in his arms and the second chance he'd been given.

But they couldn't stay there. "Come on. Let's get some place dry. We brought a tent—"

"I have a camper. Follow me."

"Yes, ma'am," he told her. *Absolutely. I will follow you forever, if you'll have me.*

Chapter Thirteen

"Where are you taking us?" Heston asked, his head up and his bleary eyes quartering the dreary landscape ahead.

With no sun in the forecast and heavy, moisture-laden clouds hanging like sopping wet blankets over the Cascades, it was important to get him warm. Somewhere London could get some hot soup into him, maybe a cup of coffee. Where she could chew him out and… and…

Love him for the rest of the day and night and—forever? Was that even in the cards for them? Yes, once upon a time, they'd been good together. Make that great. But they were both strong-willed individuals, who had higher purposes in life than just working nine-to-five jobs, owning a rambler with a white picket fence in the 'burbs, and 'two cats in the yard,' like that old Crosby, Stills, Nash, and Young song from the 1970s.

"M-my place. I mean, my camper," she stuttered, her voice so damned meek and weak she wanted to kick her own ass. "The Forest Service retrieved their RV. You guys'll have to bunk with me tonight."

"I need to report in," he answered. "TEAM protocol."

"Understood. You can do that from there. It's got a queen bed and two pull-down bunks. You'll be warm, and you can use my sat phone." *And I need to put my hands on you again, you big jerk.*

London could barely keep her hands off Heston as it was, much less walk calmly beside him while she led them to her camper. He'd risked his life! And for what? A couple stupid brackets and bolts? The impossible notion there were fingerprints on those stupid pieces of hardware? Not likely.

He could've fallen in that white water! Could've been lost forever! Not allegedly lost like Kelsey Stewart had been, but the once and forever, never seen again version of lost. It was all she could do to not scream when he'd jumped under the bridge and muscled his way beneath it. By his fingertips. With his long legs dangling in the wind. One wrong move. One tiny mistake. One rotten plank. That's all it would've taken. He would've fallen and she wouldn't have been able to save him. She would've been sentenced to watching him die. The nerve! The nerve!

Half of her wanted to kick his arrogant, muscular ass. The other fifty-percent wanted to kiss it. Her poor heart hadn't slowed down enough for her to collect her thoughts since he'd taken that first leap, and she was shaking so much her teeth were chattering as much as Heston's. Darn him for always having to be the hero. Not that she wanted Asher to have taken that chance and risked his life. But why'd it always have to be Heston? Why'd he have to be so damned ready to die for everyone else? Why couldn't he be more like the sheep he protected all over the world? Why'd he have to be the damned sheepdog?

He'd kissed her. Finally. A real, wet kiss that had thoroughly stoked the embers she'd been trying to squelch for years. Out in the open. In front of his buddy. London wanted more, but she refused to back down and give in. She was every bit as good as he was, just not as stupid.

London had returned to the mountain early this morning, retraced her steps, trying to recall what she'd thought she'd known. She'd moseyed around the campground and talked to the few diehard campers weathering the storm. She'd run into Tom Landry. He'd filled her in on how he'd known Alex, and how he'd given Alex supplies to tide him over, as well as a pistol. He'd also noticed the derelict trailer and had seen it explode. He had his theory, that some joker had abandoned it, might've rigged the propane tanks to explode for the insurance payout. People did crap like that.

But after London explained her theory, that the trailer exploding with Kelsey Stewart in it was part of the shooter's plan to coerce Alex into working for him, Tom wholeheartedly agreed. Especially once he understood Alex had been tagged to be the next vice president. It made even more sense after London explained that Alex had been particularly vicious with the Irishman when they'd last met. Who could blame Alex? But because of that confrontation, the Irishman might've decided to teach Alex a lesson by killing his wife or that getting Alex to work for him wasn't worth the trouble. Torching the trailer was him cleaning up loose ends. Mafia bosses didn't care who they hurt, especially not the wives of the men they couldn't recruit.

London wished she could've gotten better photos of the men she'd seen earlier, the guys she suspected were the Irishman and his buddy. But she'd been too far away, darn it. And she'd only had her cell phone. The close-ups of the cattle guard were crystal clear, but that alone wouldn't indict anyone. She needed better evidence.

"Hey, you," Tom called out from his camper steps.

"Hey, yourself," London called back. "How's the Landry family?"

"Great!" He headed her way with a foil pan of goodies in his hand. "Here. Suzy thought you could use some hot food. It's going to be another cold one."

"Aw, that's so nice. Please tell her thanks for me," London exclaimed. Thank heavens her gloves were thick. He'd brought piping hot cinnamon rolls over when she'd first pulled in and was leveling her rig with blocks and jacks. "Honest, you don't have to keep feeding me. I do know how to cook."

"Agent Contreras," Heston barked, his hand suddenly stuck in front of London, blocking her progress forward like damned wishbone crossing gates at train tracks, like a barrier between her and Tom. Hes could be such a dick.

Tom didn't seem to notice his grandstanding, just grinned, grabbed Heston's hand, and gave it a good, solid shake. "Agent Contreras, glad to meet you. London told me you'd be back. How's Alex? Kelsey's going to make it, right?"

Heston released Tom's hand, stepped back beside London, and pulled her against his hip. "Alex is as good as can be expected with his wife on life support. We won't know anything until she wakes up."

London stood firm, refusing to acknowledge Heston's territorial display of stupidity.

"So London said." Tom ran a hand over his bare head, ruffling his dark brown, longer than Army hair. "Every day she hangs on is a day closer to full recovery. Hope Alex knows that."

"We all hope," London cut in, elbowing Heston before he did something totally stupid, like pee on her to mark her as his property. He'd do that, too. The oaf!

"Former Delta?" Heston asked.

Tom grinned. "Navy SEAL. Can't let Army have all the fun."

Asher snorted. "SEAL, huh? Knew you looked familiar."

"We do all look alike, don't we?" Tom replied evenly. Which made London smile.

"If you mean you all look like shitheads, yeah." Asher barked out a laugh.

London turned in time to catch the competitive glint in his eyes. "Don't slam my friends, Ash."

"Can't slam a frog, ma'am. They tend to squeak when someone hurts their feelings."

Tom tipped back his head and laughed at the sky. "And everyone knows you can't housetrain Rangers. They pee on everything. Anytime. Anywhere. Come on in, guys. Wife's cooking breakfast, but stow the language. My boy's still sleeping."

"Another time," London intervened, grinning at that very apt description of former Ranger Heston Contreras. "Heston has to report in."

"Door's always open," Tom said as he took a step toward his camper. "Later, London."

"Later, Tom," she agreed sweetly. Honestly, this was why she'd loved working for the Forest Service. Everyone changed into friendly, neighborly people like Tom Landry and his family once they were out of the city and in Mother Nature.

"Later?" Heston hissed as she unlocked her rig.

"Yes, Agent Contreras. Later, you moron. Didn't you know? I always hook up with married men when I'm working." Cold, injured or not, Heston was on his own from now on. She was sick of his macho bullshit.

"I'm doing it again, aren't I?" he asked quietly.

"Yes, Heston, you are," she bit out as she tugged her keys out of an inner pocket. Climbing the three steps to her camper door, she unlocked her rig and swung the door open so quickly, it would've smacked Heston in the face if he hadn't taken a step back.

London pulled herself up into her camper to get away from him. Stepping to the side, she waved them in and pointed to the angled door at their left. "Bathroom's there. My bed's up top over the cab." *And no, you're not joining me, Hes.*

She stabbed a finger at the queen-bed-sized nook over the extended cab of her truck and set the hot food Tom had given her on the counter next to the gas stove. "The high cupboards on the walls are bunks, not storage. Unlatch and use them to sleep. They might not be long enough for you guys, but whatever. I'm fixing soup and toasted cheese sandwiches. Oh, wait."

She'd peeled back the foil on Tom's offering. Hot damn. Chicken enchilada casserole covered with fresh chopped green onions, sliced black olives, and heaps of melted cheese. Yum. "Belay that menu. Chicken enchilada casserole coming right up. Heston, get your call made while I dish up. You guys are doing dishes."

"Yes, ma'am!" Asher exclaimed, his coat and gloves already off and on his way into the tiny restroom. "Washing my hands. Be right out."

Heston had yet to speak.

London turned on him ready to fight for herself, damn it. "You can't keep acting like 'Me Tarzan, you Jane.' Tom's a nice guy. He and his son were part of the Search and Rescue teams that looked for Kelsey. He's the guy who pulled Alex out of that damn river. What is wrong with you?"

"I'm an ass," Heston admitted quietly. "Can't seem to help myself. I get over-protective when I see you with another guy, and I—"

"I'm not with another guy. I'm not with anyone. It's embarrassing. Tom's right. You act like you want to pee on everything you think you own. News flash, Ranger Rick. I don't belong to you anymore. Not sure I ever did. You had your chance and you blew it. Now get out of my way so I can set the table. Go wash your hands!"

London couldn't help herself. As mad as she was at Heston, man, she wanted him. Body and soul. Every kiss. Every breath. Any damned way she could get him. And with Asher in the bathroom—

They were still wearing their jackets and she had a weapon strapped under her left arm, but who cared? She jerked Heston into her face and opened her mouth and kissed the hell out of him. "What am I going to do with you? I can't have you running my life, Hes," she mumbled into his mouth while she devoured his lips and tongue.

"That's the thing," he mumbled back. "I can't seem to breathe without you. I don't want to. Not anymore."

"Oh, Hes," she grumbled, her fingers mapping those rock-hard shoulders, sliding under his parka, needing skin against skin. Body to body. The fire he'd always ignited in her belly roared out of control. She had food on her counter, but she needed more than physical sustenance. She needed this man. It had only ever been Hes, and damn him for ruining her for other guys. Because he had. And now, he was going to ruin her again, and break her heart, and—

"I can't do this," she whined, coming to her senses and pulling away. Out of his arms. Drawing back into herself, to save herself. Yeah, that was why she'd pulled back. Not because she was scared, but because she was smart. She'd learned her lesson. Hadn't she?

But the devastation written all over his face? The bleak pain in his liquid-brown eyes? The way her decision slashed her own heart to ribbons? She hadn't expected to get bitch-slapped for being smart. London clenched her fingers into fists to keep from putting her hands on this handsome, ruthless, terribly kind man again. She'd seen him with Kelsey and Alex. She, more than anyone else, knew the honorable, honest, and too loyal for his own good man Heston was.

But if she faltered now…

If she conceded the fight…

If she gave in and gave up…

Every inch of independence she'd gained would be lost.

"No more. I need to live my life, not yours."

He nodded. "I understand. I do. And I'm trying. But it's hard to walk away."

She saw the shadow flit over his countenance. What he meant to say was, *"Walk away like you did."* Damned if he wasn't right. She had walked away. But she'd done what was best for her, and she'd do it again. "Sometimes a person has to walk away to save themselves. You can't have it both ways. You get to live up to your potential, while I have to stand by and play *Donna Reed*."

"Who?" His expression turned quizzically sad and still so damned sweet.

Instinctively, to comfort him, London cupped his scruffy cheek. The moment she touched him, her senses flared to life. Her nostrils sucked in every male pheromone shimmering in the air between them. Her pupils dilated and her focus sharpened, taking in every last detail of the man who had once been everything to her. The tiny laugh lines at the corners of his dark brown eyes. The thickness and curl of his sooty lashes. The black hairs of his brows, so perfectly curved, they looked like they'd been plucked. The sexy black scruff shadowing his chin and cheeks. Heston had always been lean and trim, and his body was pure marble. He'd always been cleanshaven, his hair, long or short, parted and combed. But the days-old scruff made him look deliciously dangerous.

She knew and loved how dedicated he was to his parents and country. She also knew how physically strong he was, that he'd never had a problem holding her full weight in the shower or against the wall—any wall—whenever the mood hit. There was no better lover than Heston Contreras. He was tactile and generous, always touching her in places she hadn't expected to feel so good, pleasing her before he pleased himself. Understanding when she laughed or giggled through her orgasms. Tenderly cleaning her afterward. Holding her while she jabbered his ears off. Petting her. Whispering the sweetest nothings into her ear, into her hair. Into her heart. Until she fell asleep.

How often had they lain together, just hugging and holding, rubbing up against each other? Loving each other? She couldn't begin to count all of those precious moments.

Which was why she had to let him go now. Before she lost herself in him. Again.

"Nevermind who Donna Reed is. I can't do this again. I won't." Her hand dropped from his face.

He took a full step back and released her, left her standing by the counter, swaying like an untethered kite in the wind. She hadn't expected him to withdraw that easily or so quickly. London smacked a palm to the countertop to keep from falling and making a bigger fool of herself. She was dizzy, breathing hard, and wishing she could trust him again. Wanting to. Loving Heston had never been the problem. Loving herself enough to say no to him, was.

He stood there with his lips pursed, as if he were trying to control his breathing, too.

"You two are the dumbest smart people I've ever seen!" Asher roared from the bathroom doorway, startling London, making her jump. "Get a clue! Look at each other for once, why don't you? Really look!"

London stared at Asher. Either he was uncharacteristically intuitive for a man and could see right through them, or Heston had talked. Which she found hard to believe. Heston was as loyal a man as she'd ever known. He didn't gossip.

"Shut up," Heston growled. He stuck a hand out at London, and she honestly thought he wanted her hand until he snapped, "Phone. Please. Now."

Oh, yeah. Alex. He worked for Alex and… yeah. London stalked around Heston, grabbed the satellite phone and its charger off the end of her bed and handed it over.

With a grumpy huff, he sat at the table, jerked the phone from the charger, and thumbed a number. He didn't look up. Didn't say anything else.

"Stupid ass," Asher hissed. "Stow your gawddamned pride, Contreras, and see what I'm seeing for a change, would you? It's obvious you two have some hot chemistry between you. Damn it, get over your—"

"Mark?" Heston's head came up, his gaze fixed on the paneling across from him. "Yes, Heston here. Did Mother get the photos London sent?" Pause. "Good."

Asher slammed the door on his way out. The camper shook but Heston never blinked. Didn't act like he'd heard Asher at all. "Hoped she could sharpen the clarity... Right." Pause. "I'm glad London didn't take unnecessary chances, too." Heston went on to explain London's theory of how Kelsey had been caught by the cattle guard, then dragged out of the river before she could drown. He told Mark he'd retrieved the brackets and bolts that held the cattle guard in place, and that the entire bridge needed to be fingerprinted. But Heston never said how dangerous retrieving the brackets had been or the risk he'd taken. When he was done speaking, he stuck the phone in London's face and said, "Mark's on the line."

"Hello?" She answered with her heart pounding a zippy salsa beat.

"Excellent job, London. Mark Houston here. Girl, you're one in a million."

"I am?" His earnest praise made her chest swell and her eyes blink. Mark's deep baritone was hot-damned sexy over the phone. He was also married and one of the kindest, most level-headed men she'd ever met.

"I know the Forest Service fired you," he went on. "Sorry about that, but their loss is our gain. Alex wants you on his payroll, possibly as an agent, maybe in a support role, he didn't say. Can I interest you in coming in for an interview when everything settles down?"

"M-me?" she squeaked. "But I…" She cleared her throat and tried again. "But I…" *Aye, aye, aye…*

"Think about it, London." He made thinking sound easy. "No hurry. Just wanted you to know your dedication to locating Kelsey hasn't gone unnoticed. Hell, even now when you're unemployed, you're still working to solve our problem. On your own dime. Aren't you?"

"Yeah, well… yeah." She swallowed hard, lost as how to respond. "I, umm, really like Kelsey and Alex, and anyone can see how much he loves her. How could I not help them? They were in trouble. Helping was the right thing to do."

"Yup. One in a million. Listen, Alex is damned choosy. You'd be one of less than a hundred operators on his payroll. Like I said, think about it. Take your time. Let me know what you decide."

"Okay, um…" Geez, she couldn't think. This was the job Heston had hinted at, working for a hardass. For Alex. With men. Other men, not only Heston. Men like Mark. Wow. "Y-yes, sir, Mr. Houston. I'll get back to you as soon as I can think straight." London cringed. *Did I just say that last part out loud? To the man who might someday be my boss?* Talk about cringe worthy.

A rumbly chuckle came over the connection. "No worries, kiddo. The pictures you took are running through our facial rec program right now. Mother thinks we've got a good chance of nailing the guys who shot Kelsey."

"I sure hope so."

"Put Heston back on. Again, thanks for everything you've done. And please, think seriously about my offer. Okay?" Mark was so, so nice.

"I will. Here's… here's Heston." London's fingers were trembling when she handed the phone back to Heston.

He took it without so much as a touch or a glance. "Hey, Mark…" Pause "He's what? Wow. I guess that's good, but…" He ran a hand over the top of his head. "I'll call Deck for a ride. Yes, tonight. No reason to stay now that I've got what I needed from that cattle guard. Can't check them for prints up here, can I?"

London had to turn away. With a snap of his impatient fingers, he'd changed back into the driven Army Ranger who'd only had room in his life for his CO and his country. Not for her. Not for the real her. He might have room in his heart for a brainless woman who loved cleaning, waiting at home, and chumming around with husband-approved girlfriends. But she refused to live in the stone ages.

"Say again?" Hes barked, then, "You're shitting me? The Irishman wants Alex to accept President Adams' offer? He wants Alex to be Vice President? Why?"

He paused while Mark replied.

"Shit, no. Alex will never do that. Not after what they did to Kelsey. Hell to the no."

"What?" London was dying to know what the Irishman wanted Alex to do.

But Heston ignored her, looked down at his boots, and told Mark, "Copy that. I'll see you as soon as I contact Deck…" Pause. "Sure thing. Three hours, maybe less. Yeah. Thanks." And he hung up the phone.

Chapter Fourteen

Heston stood there in London's camper with her phone in his hand, mad, and not sure where to look or who to look at. She'd done it again, broken his heart when he'd thought he'd stood a chance of getting her back into his life. He flat wasn't going to answer her. Not this time. What Mark told him was TEAM business. Not London's.

Heston wasn't just butt-hurt, but stinging from the teasing that always ended in rejection. Over-exerting himself back at the bridge didn't help his disposition. Every muscle burned and he refused to dig into his bag for his IFAK, to throw back four Motrin in front of London. Neither could he sit around and play house while she dished out lunch. Not with her making future plans to work for Alex. How the hell was that even feasible? Them in the same office, seeing each other during the day, but going home to different houses at night? What if she fell for one of the guys he worked with? His life had turned into one big disaster and his patience was gone. So were his dreams.

"Hes," London murmured from the counter where their lunch waited. "Talk to me. What'd Mark say?"

"TEAM business. Need to know," he replied as evenly as he could.

"He offered me a job."

"I heard."

"I'd be working for that hardass you told me about. We might get to work together. Might even go on missions together. Wouldn't that be nice?"

Nice? Abso-fuckin'-lutely no! "I guess."

"Come on. We were friends once. Can't we be friends again?"

"Is that all we were? Friends? Funny. I thought we were more than that."

"You know what I meant."

"Do I, London? Because it sure seems that you're the one making all the decisions about us. You had enough, you walked out. Hell, you didn't even walk. You flew across the whole damned country. In the middle of the night! Without telling me where you were going or if you'd be back. Without even saying goodbye. Do you have any idea how unhinged I was the night you left? I looked all over Killeen for you! I called your parents! You decide you can't *do this*" —he gestured at the space between them— "whatever's going on between us, and boom! You close down, and off you go. It doesn't matter how hard I chase you, London, you just keep running away. One day you'll leave and there'll be no coming back, do you ever consider that? Second chances aren't guaranteed. You didn't even call to tell me where you were, that you were safe, or that we were through. I can't do… *THIS*" —he whipped his hand through that empty space again— "anymore."

Because it really was an empty space. There was nothing between them, and he wondered if there ever had been. Heston stopped to suck in a breath before he continued in a more measured tone. "You want to know why I was upset the night we fought, babe? I'll tell you. I'd just had the mother of all bad days. The worst day of my life up to that point. But all you did the moment I opened my front door was go on and on about—"

"Enough!" Asher roared as he stomped back into the camper and slammed the door again. "Christ, I can hear you yelling over the gawddamned river. Everyone can. Tell her, damn it. You've talked to me about it before, now tell London what happened. Tell her everything. About those two soldiers. About the M1162 Growler. How one of them was thrown into a tree that day, for fuck sakes. Talk to her, Heston. In English. Because if you don't, I will."

Heston glared at the man who was supposed to have his back, not skewer him like a pork kabob over a blazing grill while he was trying to make a point.

Asher gave him his chin. "Never thought you were chicken shit, Contreras, but please. By all means, keep doing what you're doing and you'll prove me right." With that, he walked out.

"Err, what's a Growler? Isn't it something for beer? Were those two guys… drunk" —London's voice trailed off— "or something?"

Heston looked at her then, really opened his eyes and looked at the woman standing in front of him. The one biting her bottom lip and asking silly questions. The woman who was audacious enough to dye her hair turquoise, smart enough she'd graduated college with honors, and plucky enough to apply, then train with the FBI. The Federal Bureau of Investigation, for hell's sake.

Tiny crystal tears spiked her long lashes, making her look more like a little girl. Turquoise hair and all.

Did she really not know what an M1162 Growler was? Then again, why would she? She'd never been military, had never served the Defense Department in any capacity. She was his age, but she hadn't any of his experiences. Hadn't seen combat or death or—

Shit. He glared at the floor. Pissed at Asher. The snitch. Just as pissed at himself because Asher was right. Heston hadn't shared a single detail of his 'bad day at the office' with London that night. Had just jumped to conclusions, made an ass of himself, and called the woman he adored names. Which, in turn, made her defensive and determined to prove him wrong.

Which… he was.

Which… was why she'd left. Was everything his fault? *Sure feels like it.*

He stuck his fists deep into his jacket pockets, struggling for a way forward. Yeah, he had an ego, and he hated being wrong. Which was why he seldom was. He was that annoying over-achiever, the guy who, despite his eidetic memory, still studied all night before exams because he couldn't accept anything less than perfect grades. He was the sergeant who checked, double-checked, and triple-checked his gear, his squads' gear, their vehicles, the ROEs—ad nauseam. He was the surgeon with a critically ill patient, one of damned few men in the world who couldn't afford to make any mistakes. Because of his extreme over-diligence, no more men had died on Heston's watch. None. Not in any firefight, on any foray or intel gathering mission.

Only those two privates at Fort Hood. *That day.*
Shit.

He lifted his gaze to London. Thank God, Asher had left.

Heston inhaled a long, deep breath and began again. One more time. Trying to fix what he'd broken. Trying like hell to be the man she deserved, not the asshat he was. "An M1162 Growler is" — another deep breath "…an Army Light Strike Vehicle, a beefed-up version of a Jeep. Seats one driver, three passengers. Two privates in my team went off-road during an exercise that same day. They shouldn't have, but they were young and inexperienced, and they were going too fast. Hit a rut hard and lost control. I was in the truck behind them. Watched their front right wheel explode. Saw the rubber disintegrate into ribbons and steel cord. Saw the Growler flip end-over-end…" *Like a damned piece of junk metal.* "Watched them…" *Die.*

Heston stopped talking. He couldn't speak the word. Hated remembering what he'd witnessed. His throat had gone bone-dry, and he wished he could—please—forget those two men dying. Hell, they weren't even old enough to be called men. Certainly weren't old enough to drink, but were considered old enough to die for their country. And die they had—for nothing.

He had carried the weight of their deaths his entire Army career, and he would carry it until the day he died. He'd been their leader. He should've paired each of them with an experienced soldier. But he hadn't. Studying the floor, he swallowed hard and tried again. London needed to understand his reasoning that night. It had never been about her shortcomings, nor her dream to work for the FBI—though he'd surely made it sound that way. He ran a hand up the back of his sweaty neck. She deserved all good things in her life, she truly did. He'd been devastated, had simply struck out at the first person he'd encountered after a day that had sucked boulders.

Anyway…

"I… I stayed with Private DeAngeles. He was the passenger, the soldier ejected from the vehicle." And he'd flown through the air like a damned straw-stuffed scarecrow shot from a cannon, his limbs loose and gangly, no helmet. Damned dumb kid. "He hit a t-tree, the only tree in sight for miles and miles…"

Heston's voice trailed away. Son of a bitchin' live oak. DeAngeles might have lived if he hadn't hit it face first. Not like he could've missed it. The oak's trunk was wider than the one still growing at the Alamo, and that son of a bitch was a damned monster.

It happened without notice. Without sound. Suddenly, London's arms wrapped around Heston's head. Her hand was at the back of his neck, pulling his face into that warm soft spot between her shoulder and neck. Like an opium addict, at the first hint of her sweet, feminine scent, he wrapped his arms around her and sucked every last atom of that unique fragrance into his heart. He was that drowning man gasping in a belly full of his first breath above water. Shaking. Afraid she might shove him away again.

Until a sob shuddered out of her. "I'm so, so sorry," she whispered, her tender arms a welcome shackle around his stiff neck. Around his broken heart. "I didn't know. I didn't think. I was so excited, but then I was just mad, and I reacted, and… I'm sorry I left you that night, Hes. I never thought about what it would do to you. I was selfish."

"No, it's my fault," he finally admitted. "I never gave you a chance. I was mad the minute I opened our front door. They were just a couple green boys from Tennessee. I took it out on you. I lashed out, and I know I hurt you."

She sobbed, "I hurt you back, and you're right. You're more than just my friend. I said that to be mean. But I don't want us to go back to the way we were, Hes. I need my dreams, too. I can't live on just yours."

"I know, I know," he breathed, his eyes squeezed tight against the emotions raging inside. Funny how repentance worked. For the first time in years, his body was in tune with his soul. He could see light at the end of the dark tunnel his life had become. All because he'd confessed his weakness to the woman he adored. Hmmpf. If he kept this up, he'd soon be explaining how that inner caveman of his lost control sometimes. How it took over when he'd lost sight of her when the trailer exploded. Hell, his inner caveman took over at the slightest hint she might be in trouble.

Lifting his head, Heston ran his hands up her biceps to her neck, up until he cupped her jaw. His thumbs landed on her teary cheeks. Slowly, he tipped forward and covered her mouth with his. Heaven. Heaven was London, and he was the devil cast out from heaven, the prodigal lover finally returned to the place of light and stars. The taste of her was pure ambrosia. Overcome by their reconciliation, he devoured everything she gave. Her lips, her mouth, the soft, sweet sigh she breathed into his face.

The fire between them ignited into a scorching blaze, creating its own energy. Its own thunder and lightning. Demanding more. He'd waited so long, hoped so hard for this precise reaction from her. Asher had better stay the hell away for a long time.

Until two popping sounds registered for what they were. Gunfire.

"On the floor!" Heston ordered, pushing London to her knees, away from the windows and below the countertop. Which wasn't much cover for what sounded like a fifty caliber.

The door slammed open. "We gotta go!" Asher bellowed. "One sniper. Maybe two. You with me, Contreras?"

"You bet!" Heston volleyed back. But… "No!" he corrected himself. "I've got to stay with—"

"Go!" London barked. "I'm not helpless, you big, hairy ape. I'm—was—a Forest Service LEO, remember? Go get the bastard who's shooting that cannon before he hurts someone. If it'll make you feel better, I'll stay inside and blow the first sucker who opens my door to hell." She tossed the sat phone at him. "Take this. I've got my cell. Call if you need my help."

Well, okay then. Heston caught the phone and nearly smiled at the belligerent woman staring him down, the one giving him orders. Call *her* if *he* ran into trouble? Not likely. But the armed and dangerous version of London was the sexiest thing he'd ever seen. Look at the sturdy black GLOCK 22 in her right hand, a 40 S&W caliber, standard capacity fifteen rounds. That was what the subtle bulge beneath her jacket was. Damned good choice. This woman was packing, and she knew how to use a GLOCK. Correction. *His woman.* The one with starbursts of green in her pretty, but fierce aqua eyes.

"Yes, ma'am," he told her gruffly. "I'll call out my full name when we return so you'll know it's me." Which was Heston Carter Contreras.

"Copy that," she barked like a damned federal agent. "Now go do what you do best. Protect and serve."

He planted one last, wet kiss on her bossy mouth, then turned and dropped out of the camper where Asher knelt covering him. "How many?" he asked, keeping Asher in his peripheral at his left as he drew one of his two pistols.

"Two, gawddamnit. Not sure they're both trained snipers, though."

"The guy behind that fifty cal is who we want. He's east of us?"

Asher nodded. "Just watch your southern exposure. Pretty sure that's where the second shots came from. Jackass can't shoot for shit. He hit two trees, didn't come close to the camper. The shot that hit it was all fifty cal."

"Alex did say the Irishman was chicken shit," Heston grunted.

"Copy that. Stop Fifty Cal now, nail the Irishman later. Unless you want him taken alive. I wouldn't mind. I need a little practice with my knife."

"We'll see," Heston replied as he took a cautious step eastward. Taking prisoners in Washington state posed a wealth of jurisdictional problems, but hey. That was why Mark Houston and Murphy Finnegan got paid the big bucks. As for that knife comment, time would tell if Asher got the wet practice he wanted.

"Swing right," Ash whispered, nodding to the lush undergrowth. "Away from the camper, straight into those bushes. I'll go left and brush him your way. You take him down."

"Copy that," Heston replied, fading into the shade to avoid being spotted by Fifty Cal.

Like every other mission he'd been on, he'd researched the area surrounding Mount Rainier, as well as the White River campground's layout, while he'd waited for word on Kelsey and Alex. Rainier's highest peak sat at 14,232 feet above sea level. The 112 individual sites were let on a first-come, first-served basis. Most were obscured from each other, for privacy and scenic value, by the mountain's abundant, lush, and oftentimes, dripping-wet greenery.

Sites went for twenty dollars a night. Loops A, B, C, and D lay east of the White. Goat Island Mountain lay to the west, on the other side of the White. No RVs or trailers longer than twenty-five feet were allowed. There were no sewer, water, or electrical hookups. The trailer where Alex had found Kelsey had been stashed at the extreme north end of Loop B, east of site twelve, but not in a site. Two footpaths ran through the campground to the east bank of the White. Glacier Basin Trail went west from the footbridge over the White to Glacier Basin. The Wonderland Trail went east a short while before curving southward in a wide arc around Emmons and Fryingpan glaciers before it continued circling Mount Rainier.

From Alex's description of the events that day, he and Kelsey were up high on the southern bank of the upper White River, just short of Emmons Glacier icefield. He'd been facing downhill. Kelsey had been facing uphill. She'd been standing less than a foot from him when she'd been hit. He'd tried to grab her, but her body had rotated in the direction of the impact, to her left, away from him. Emmons Glacier did the rest. Once she'd collapsed, her unconscious body slid swiftly downhill until the icy glacier dropped her into the White River.

And yet, Alex had completely misdiagnosed the strike that struck her. He'd been adamant he'd seen red mist. Which, in sniper vernacular, meant Kelsey'd suffered a clear and fatal, penetrating brain injury that should've ended in her death. Not a finger-length, raw, oozing abrasion that had only scored the left side of her skull. The physics of a fifty caliber round fired from a distance close enough to remove a person's head dictated instant death, no matter where it struck the skull. It did not ever just injure anyone. The kinetic energy from any sniper rifle was a powerful force to be reckoned with. Ninety percent of all gunshot wounds to the head ended in fatalities, but most of them were caused by much smaller rounds. Most victims succumbed before they made it to the nearest hospital. By all accounts, Kelsey should be dead, and Alex should be planning her funeral.

But she wasn't. Which meant one of two things. Either the sniper had barely missed his target through some minor miscalculation of temperature or air current, or any one of the many factors a decent sniper accounted for before he fired. Or… the sniper hadn't missed Kelsey because he'd never intended to kill her, only wound her. Had in fact waited until she'd moved into his predetermined line of sight, and had unwittingly put herself in the center of his bull's eye. Which brought Heston back full circle to his expert assassin theory. He wanted to meet that guy. Preferably not in a dark alley. And when he did, he'd end the bastard and let Asher decide what body part he wanted to take back as a trophy.

That line of logic led him back to the science behind smart guns and smart munitions. All interesting. All very plausible. But Heston knew of only one man currently working to solve the variables that had made smart guns pipe dreams instead of DoD-approved weaponry carried by United States military members—Jed McCormack of McCormack Industries, Rosslyn, VA.

A smart bullet was simply a miniaturized precision-guided munition fired from a precision-guided firearm. One was not viable without the other, meaning not just any rifle could fire smart bullets. The concept revolved around the three fiber-optic eyes distributed along the circumference of a smart bullet. A laser pointed at the intended victim painted that person as the bullet's target. Once fired, that pre-painted laser designation activated the bullet. As it traveled toward the victim, its laser 'eyes' allowed the bullet to adjust its trajectory as needed to hit the pre-painted target. In theory, the round could be fired well beyond the visual range of the sniper aiming the rifle. Also, in theory, each smart bullet contained a guidance system, powered by a miniature, lightweight, lithium battery.

The farthest distance recorded to date had been well over a mile. In that test performed at the McCormack Industries Lab, the target had been a mass of skin-toned gel molded into a human shape, obscured behind a brick wall, along with three other gel dummies that were not laser painted. The test was designed to prove that a smart bullet would, and could, turn a ninety-degree angle to hit the correct target in the precise, predesignated, laser-painted spot, that being a tiny freckle on the dummy's left hand. Not on its finger or nose. But right in the middle of its palm.

According to McCormack Industry's final report, the smart bullet had performed as expected, just as accurately as a shot taken at a much closer range. It hit the freckle, went clean through the dummy's left hand. Instruments wired inside the gel recorded the precise moment of impact. Nothing mysterious about the science, just a matter of calculating elements any sniper worth his salt was familiar with: bullet weight measured in grains, velocity of bullet at point of impact, and bullet diameter. The biggest problem in developing any smart bullet for today's military was the cost, the convoluted, biased-as-hell Congressional budget cycle, and politics. Jed was known the world over as the US soldier's best friend, which, ironically, also made him the enemy of many politicians. Those people only cared about stuffing yearly appropriation bills with pork barrel initiatives to feed their states' interests. Not national interests. Oftentimes, not even legal interests.

Initially, Heston had guesstimated the sniper's location to be at the west side of the White River, on the north side of neighboring Goat Island Mountain, which sloped northeast from Emmons Glacier. That the shooter had hidden within all that lush Northwest greenery in a sturdy sniper hide, high in one of the majestic Douglas Firs that populated much of Mount Rainier's elevations.

Made the most sense. Goat Island Mountain's altitude of seven thousand plus feet overlooked the precise portion along the White River where Alex and Kelsey had been standing, by more than two thousand feet. If he'd been in any number of trees there with a reasonably decent scope, he would've had a clear shot. The distance less than a mile. An expert sniper could've easily tapped Kelsey without relying on a smart bullet.

But this guy wasn't just an expert, and the bizarre hit he'd made supported Heston's smart bullet theory. The sniper who'd hit Kelsey had made an impossible hit. He'd grazed her skull, not killed her. She'd be dead if he'd wanted her dead, but she wasn't, which meant he hadn't wanted to kill her. Which, if he hadn't used a smart weapon system and there was no smart bullet to be found, put him in a very elite category of sniper. As in he'd be the only one in the category.

Which considerably narrowed down the suspects. One name jumped to the top of the list: Ryan Malloy. Former Irish Ranger, also formerly active duty in Afghanistan as part of the latest failed United Nation's peacekeeping operation. The third son of the most infamous sniper of the IRA, also known as the Irish Provisional Republican Army: Jack Malloy. Jack had been instrumental in organizing Northern Ireland's best sharpshooters into the infamous South Armagh Brigade. The South Armagh Brigade had mercilessly targeted British security forces from 1990 to 1997, as part of the conflict in Northern Ireland. The South Armagh Brigade's weapon of choice? The .50 BMG, the fifty-caliber Browning machine gun, caliber Barrett M82 long-range rifle.

Their motto: *One shot, one kill.*

Hmmm, Heston wondered. Alex had said Kelsey'd wanted to see the sunrise the last morning of their getaway. Exactly who had she shared that wish with? Who'd overheard? Better question, who'd been listening to her conversations and for how long? Situational awareness was hard to maintain within active-duty Army troops, among the most hardened tacticians. How much harder was it to control inside the homes of TEAM agents with kids?

Noiselessly, Heston pulled the sat phone out of his pocket, thumbed Mark's number, and rested the phone between his shoulder and his ear.

"Houston," Mark barked.

"Shit, what's wrong?" Heston asked quietly. Mark was not given to outbursts. Alex, yes, Mark, never.

"The son of a bitchin' Irishman just called. He wants a meeting. Tomorrow morning. Here! In Kelsey's room! He even knew her room number. Alex went ballistic. He's losing it, Heston." *Sounds like you are, too.* "He's spiraling out of control, and… Christ! I don't know what more we can do to keep both of them safe."

Man, that Irish asshat had a lot of nerve. "No worries." Heston kept his voice low and even, his eyes trained overhead on the bottom boards of what had to be the assassin's hide. "He won't be breathing by then."

"God, I hope you're right. Please tell me you're on his trail."

"I am," Heston breathed, "but be forewarned. I think we're dealing with a damned precise sharpshooter who planned to nick Kelsey, not kill her. Who knew right where she and Alex were standing that morning. Who might also have someone inside Stewart's house gathering intel. Ever heard of Ryan Malloy?"

"You're kidding. The Irish sharpshooter? You think he's behind this?"

Heston appreciated the disbelief in Mark's question. It was an unbelievable conclusion given the many awards Malloy had been given. But it sure felt spot-on. "Makes sense if he's using a smart weapon system. I gotta go."

A pursed whistle sounded softly in Heston's ear. "Quite a theory. I'll find out who else might've known Alex's plans. Stay safe."

Heston didn't reply, just disconnected and put his phone away. Whoever was up top in that sniper hide had just kicked the toes of his black boots over the far edge of the platform facing away from London's camper. This guy was lying on his belly, getting comfortable, positioning for another shot. Maybe a kill.

Like hell.

Asher, also crouched low, was looking at Heston.

Heston ducked low behind a stand of dripping wet hemlocks and glanced upward. It took a moment of concentrated listening, but between the drip, drip, drips from the saturated pine needles, came the quiet crackle of a plastic wrapper being crushed. Guess this guy felt confident enough to snack while he waited. Guess he also thought he was invincible, hiding in the trees.

The pines were outstandingly beautiful, verdant green and full, but they were as much a cover for a hunter stalking below as for the asshole stalking above. The problem with a hide built high in a tree-packed forest was the loss of intel from sights and noises below. Pines this dense made excellent soundproofing, leaving the only intel coming to the sniper from beside him or overhead.

Heston saw it then, a thin silver wire studded with tiny drips of moisture strung in a wide circle around the base of this tree. Ryan, if it truly was Ryan Malloy up there, thought a single trip wire would stop two former US Army Rangers?

Guess again, boyo. Heston nodded a go-ahead to Asher, who'd also spotted the wire. Took another step beneath the thick pine branches and—

London's screams from her camper pierced the silence. "Hes, Hes!" And everything went to hell. Should he trust that she could handle herself? Even now? After that terrified scream? Hell, no.

Asher mouthed, 'Go!' and Heston went. Let Asher nab Malloy. Hell, let him carve the guy like a Thanksgiving turkey. Hes had a woman to save.

Chapter Fifteen

London let him in! She'd trusted him! Like a fool, she'd opened her door after checking the peephole. Imagine her surprise seeing Devon Bates standing there in his USFS uniform, staring up at her door like he didn't know if she'd answer or not. She had hesitated. His being there at the same time Heston and Asher were out hunting the guy who'd shot Kelsey was an odd coincidence. But Devon had looked so sincere. Almost like the friendly guy he'd been before his promotion went to his head. Then he'd said he was proud of her for sticking to her guns and finding the Stewarts, that she should get a medal, at least a commendation for that.

And like a sucker fresh out of high school, she'd believed him.

Lies! All lies!

The second she'd unlocked her camper door, he'd shoved his way in, slapped her hard across her face, then punched her belly and disarmed her. Now there she was, draped over his shoulder, trying to catch her breath, on her way to who knew where. And mad as hell!

Bates had taken her pistol. Who was the idiot now? She'd assumed he was a decent human being—her mistake. But he'd assumed she only carried one weapon. Stupid, stupid man.

"Where are you taking me?" she asked, framing the question within weak, feminine, I-am-so-so-helpless bimbo-speak. If she'd been upright, she would've fanned her face and fluttered her eyelashes.

"Where you belong. Where a know-it-all like you will never be found." He slapped her backside and spat, "Bitch!"

Strike two, Bates. Maybe strikes three and four, also.

Her parka was still on, her now empty holster beneath it. He knew she carried, but she'd never told him about the stiletto tucked into the thinnest sheath strapped to the inside of her right forearm. Why would she? Most guys focused on the obvious. Most criminals did, too. Pretty women all had to be brainless. Especially the ones smart enough to master careers and outperform men. Not that all men were shallow, opinionated, or as egotistical as Bates. But guys like him usually overcame those weaker than them by brute force. They name-called and belittled their employees, in this case— her—his soon-to-be victim.

And lastly, but bestly—*gosh, is that even a word?*—they overestimated themselves. Just by the things dangling between their legs, they thought they were better, smarter, and stronger than women, right?

Wrong. Big mistake. She'd practiced hours with that still hidden blade. Throwing it, hitting her paper targets. Trying over and over to hit them just right every time. Slicing and dicing, chipping and stabbing. Parries and thrusts in close quarters. She'd taken a private class taught by a tough old Army major who'd been in the first Desert Storm. Best self-defense class ever. Not even the FBI had taught her what she knew now. To stand up for herself when it counted. To surprise her opponent, not by sheer force, but by cunning. By waiting. By delivering the unseen, unexpected strike. What she didn't have in weight or muscles, she made up for with speed and brains.

Going for a dramatic, girly effect, she let herself go limp. Dangled her arms and let her hands flop against the back of his thighs. She needed him complacent, over-confident, and sure of himself. Bates wasn't stupid. He wouldn't have been promoted if he were. But he was a guy, and she was 'just' a woman. A woman who planned to use that opinionated weakness against him soon. Really soon. Just. Not. Yet…

Heston ran back to London's camper, saw the door swinging open, and froze in his tracks. He quartered the scene behind her rig. Most campsites were empty. The weather was too cold for most to stay. There were no campers in sight. His heart pounded in his ears. Where was she? Who the hell took her? Had Malloy? Was the sniper hide just a decoy? A distraction?

Rolling his neck, Heston measured the facts against his assumptions—and went with his gut. Whoever'd taken London was part of the plan to end the Stewarts. Had to be. The sniper who'd nicked the side of Kelsey's head was in the damned tree that, even now, Asher was targeting. Heston could almost see Asher climbing the pine, hand by hand, toehold by toehold, his knife in his teeth as he dodged those sturdy boughs. Asher preferred wet work. Well, good. Let him carve that Irish bastard to the bone.

Heston inhaled a slow breath through his pursed lips and decided to follow the river. He ran faster. Quieter. Lined with dense undergrowth like it was, no one would notice a body dressed in black winter gear tossing within the rapids. If that was where London had been taken, she'd vanish among the foam and shadows within seconds. It made sense to dispose of a body there. There'd been no shot. Nothing after that single scream.

Which meant hurry, damn it. *Get there now! Save her.* He meant to approach quietly, but quiet be damned. He had to reach her before she died! Before whoever had her killed her! *Faster, Hes! Pump those damned glutes, quads, hamstrings, and calf muscles. Hurry!*

By the time he was at the water's edge, he was sweating, but his senses were wide open, flared to detect her fierce Amazonian spirit and the stink of her chicken shit assailant. *Protect and serve, London,* he whispered. *By God, I know you won't like me protecting you because you think you can handle anything. I know you're a damned strong woman, but there are things you don't know and have never done. I can't live without you!*

There. Farther down the bank. A hefty male. Long stride. Determined stride. Marching away from Heston's position like he was on a mission. A limp body in black slung over his shoulder. Bates! With London! He was headed for Owyhigh Lakes (pronounced O-Y-high). The bastard meant to drown her in one of those two lakes. Which were frozen. Want to bet he'd already cut a hole in the ice?

Heston beelined for the bastard. It was clear London was badly hurt, maybe worse. Her arms slapped helplessly against the back of his legs. The ass! He closed in on the pair, pissed and ready to kill, when inexplicably, London's right arm lifted behind her shoulder. Oh, my hell. She had a small knife. A thin blade and—

Relief puffed out of Heston in a cloud of vapor. He stopped worrying and watched her work some pretty fast magic. With one wicked slash, she stabbed Bates' hamstring. An explosive roar bellowed out of him. Side-stepping and off-balance, he threw her to the ground, grabbed the bloody back of his thigh, and screamed, "You gawddamned bitch! You cut me!"

London landed on her butt, but scrambled quickly to her feet, one palm on the ground, her knife in the other, poised magnificently for battle. Heston couldn't hear her speak, wasn't sure she said anything. Looked more like an Old West stand-off between his silent but bold and beautiful lioness, and the howling hyena thrashing at her feet. Bates might've gotten a few licks in, but she'd drawn first blood, and Heston was proud of his woman.

He cocked his head, not sure if he should assist London in this very personal battle or not. She had everything under control. Damn, look at her. Powerful. Beautiful. Armed and, yeah, dangerous. Also kind of scary that the sweet woman he'd once made love with, the one who giggled and moaned when she'd come all over his fingers and mouth, was now poised like an avenging angel with a blood-stained sword of justice twitching at her fingertips.

Heston walked quietly to her side. She lowered her head and shot him a sideways wink through her jewel-toned locks, the tease. She was enjoying this victory, this moment of comeuppance. And man, did Bates have it coming.

Another highly-pitched, male scream pierced the forest behind Heston, but he didn't turn around, didn't wonder. Guess Asher'd breached the sniper hide and whoever he'd caught by surprise was now being taken care of. Asher promised Alex a trophy. Heston hoped Asher brought a bag for that.

"We need him alive," Heston told London conversationally.

"I know," she agreed easily. "That's why I didn't stab his kidneys. Too messy. I didn't want that shit-heel's blood in my hair."

Made Heston smile. He shrugged at her like what happened with Bates was no big deal. Which it wasn't. This was her kill. A fellow soldier respected that. "None of my business then. Let me know when you're done playing. I'll be—"

"You're not leaving me alone with this bitch!" Bates yelled. "She'll kill me."

"She should," Hes said as he crouched onto the mossy ground, dropped his hands between his knees, and prepared to wait on London's decision. "You started this when you took her from her rig. What'd you do, knock like a gentleman, then slap her around once she was kind enough to let you inside?"

"Something like that," Bates grumbled.

"Punched, Hes. This asshole punched me, damned near knocked my teeth out." She spat to the side, then licked a circle around her pink, wet lips. "He took my pistol!"

Heston wanted to lick those lips. Along with her other just-as-luscious body parts.

"Then take it back. Why'd you let him in?" he asked, again keeping his tone neutral. Supportive. Not judgmental. Not to the woman who deserved every bit of his respect.

London pointed her knife at Bates' crotch as she reclaimed her weapon from his jacket and stowed it in her rear waistband. Next, she pulled his pistol from the holster on his hip and tossed it aside. "My mistake, Hes. He lied, said he was proud of me. That I deserved a medal for locating Alex and Kelsey. Guess he's not so proud now." She giggled like the minx she could be.

"I'm bleeding, you bitch! Can't you show a little mercy?" Bates whined, his fingers red with blood.

"So? You're bleeding. Big deal," London replied. "Where were you taking me, Devon? What were you going to do with me, huh? Give me a party?"

"I was keeping you safe!" he shot back at her. "You don't know who you're messing with. These guys are dangerous."

"Says the man who slaps a woman half his size," Heston murmured as he unchambered the round from Bates' pistol, ejected its magazine, and secured the weapon inside his own inner jacket pocket.

Another piercing scream shivered over the trees. For the first time, Bates glanced in the direction of the sniper hide. Looked like he was having a hard time swallowing.

Heston ran his fingers over his chin, then dropped his hands between his knees again. "Where were you taking London?"

"Umm—"

"Show us," London commanded.

"I can't walk," Bates hissed. "You cut me, you lousy c—"

"You won't finish that word if you want to live," Heston snarled. "Enough with the name-calling. Grow a pair. Be a man for once in your worthless life."

"Tracks, Hes." London nodded toward the size-eleven boot prints in the fresh snow, leading to her camper from the river trail. "Let's see where he was before he paid me a visit."

"Then let's go," Heston agreed easily. He pushed to his feet, strode over to where Bates lay panting, took hold of the back of the guy's jacket collar, looked over his shoulder, and told London, "Get your butt in gear, babe. Times a-wasting."

Then, as if they were just taking a walk with a large, unruly child, Heston dragged Bates backward on his butt, flailing his hands and complaining all the way through the trees. Past Shaw Creek drainage and Tamanos Creek Camp, which Heston already knew was closed for the season, all the way to the wide-open meadows surrounding Owyhigh Lakes. The distance they walked was a good three to four miles, but hey. With London skipping along beside him like the happy woman she used to be, Heston was content. It was a singularly beautiful day for a hike.

He paused at the end of the trail. Bates had stopped thrashing by then. Heston let go of his collar. Bates leaned back on his hands, breathing hard, but was still whining plenty. Like anyone cared?

"Will you look at that," Heston breathed. The view was outstanding. Snow-covered Governors Ridge provided an impressive backdrop to the two shallow, glacier-fed lakes. If it'd been earlier in the year, the meadow would've been rich with bluebells, asters, and columbine. Maybe a few deer, mountain jays, chipmunks, and pesky marmots. But the two shallow lakes were both frozen solid. Snow covered everything except the trail of boot prints carved through the five, six inches of white stuff. They led to a hole in the ice some *fisherman* had drilled in the center of the nearest lake. Judging by the size eleven prints that matched Bates' boots and the single three-legged, collapsible camp stool parked beside the hole, he hadn't been worried about London's safety. Hadn't intended to teach her to ice fish, either.

Heston pursed his lips. It was one thing to see bodily damage inflicted on your woman when she could fight back. And London had, quite efficiently. But it was another to see the preparations taken to murder her in cold blood.

"That your handiwork, Bates?" he growled, ready to strangle the jerk with his bare hands. The mere thought of what this guy had intended for London, sent every last one of Heston's good intentions to respect her decision spiraling dangerously close to the red zone.

"I don't know what you're talking about," the bastard whined, panting now, probably exhausted from being dragged. "I can't see nothing from here. Never been here before."

Heston bit his tongue. Until now, he'd been okay with London tormenting Bates. It was her show. Her kill. Not. Any. More.

"What were you going to do to me, Devon?" London asked as she sank to one knee beside Bates, that pointy blade still in her hand. "Huh? Teach me to fish? Give me a nature lesson? Or put me in that hole? Drown me? Sit there and watch me die?"

Bates said nothing, just lay there huffing, puffing, and bleeding.

Heston crouched at Bates' other side, then trailed the back of his index finger down the man's bristly jaw, to his neck and on down to his collarbone, digging his fingertip into the loose flesh there like a hook. Hmmm. That was an idea. "Ever been tortured?"

Bates shook his already bobbing head. "Never been military, you asshat. Told you that. Can't you soldiers remember a gawddamned thing?" He was scared now. Finally. Damned well should be after what he'd intended for London.

"No? Then you're in for a treat." Heston's face cracked with a sinister smile he didn't let reach his eyes. His index fingertip dug deep into the hollow of the guy's sweaty neck. With one vicious stab, he could end Bates. Punch his fingertip through the man's trachea. Watch him choke. Let him suffocate until his gasps produced bloody drool, and no matter how hard he flailed and groaned and cried, nothing would save him.

But that wasn't what this little exercise in physical prowess was about. The threat of torture was enough to get most men and women answering questions. Didn't matter if the questions concerned national security, classified intelligence, or personal info, most people broke long before blood, tears, or violence entered the picture. Fear was the key, not propane torches, pliers, or the scalpels Hollywood portrayed. Those psycho props were about making a buck off audience ear and horror, not Humint. Human Intelligence. This come-to-Jesus meeting was about giving Bates what he deserved, true, but more, it was the purest form of information gathering. Let Bates figure that out by himself. It was time to up the game. If he cried like a baby after a little rough play, too damned bad.

Heston shoved to his feet and dragged Bates to the fishing hole.

Chapter Sixteen

London could barely believe what she was doing. Threatening to kill Bates? Torture him? Was Heston serious? Could she go through with any of it if he were?

Yeah, she'd like to see Bates pee himself, but the knife in her hand was only for show. Yes, she'd used it on him, but that was when he meant to kill her. She'd acted in self-defense. He was unarmed now, and even though it sure looked like he'd meant to kill her, that he'd planned it, she knew from her FBI training that intent was not the same as the actual crime. People could plan to terrorize or torment others all they wanted. Ex-husbands did it all the time. But unless their intended victim was the President of the United States, nothing would ever happen until the ex actually carried out his plan. Any police officer would tell you that. Which was why abused women often didn't stand a chance. Restraining orders were merely official recordings that a woman feared for her life from a specific individual. They didn't come with police protection, bodyguards, or safe houses. No, a woman afraid for her life had to pay for protection herself. Or end up dead.

London wasn't a killer. Was she? She'd been trained by Quantico's best, sure. She knew how to shoot, could hit body mass nearly a mile away, could handle herself in most hand-to-hand fights, unless someone smacked her head, that is. And yes, she'd passed the torture lessons exacted on her and her fellow class members in the hidden forests of Marine Corps Base Camp Lejeune a couple years back.

She'd been proud of how long she'd lasted under extreme duress. But damn, those were was the hardest drills she'd ever been subjected to. She'd come out of the exercise bloody, sweaty, her face tear-stained, and with every bit of her reserves spent. Hell, demolished. Despite the fact that they were the ones who'd broken her, the Marines who'd worked her over, all gave her shitty grins and knuckle-bruising fist bumps for being the only female who'd endured. Now she knew what waterboarding, electrical shock, and psychological mind games were about. Bad. Really, really bad.

Swallowing hard, she kept up with Heston's stern march to the center of the lake. He'd changed in the course of this hike. At first, he'd been easy going. Now he'd turned scary. His jaw was rigid and sharp and his dark brows were clashed into a stern V over his nose. Even his nose had turned knife thin. He wasn't hiking, as much as speed-walking, and his eyes were so dark, she couldn't see any brown in his irises. He was angrier than she'd ever seen him. Angry enough to kill.

She wanted to stop and ask him what he meant to do to Bates once they got to that hole, but she was afraid he'd turn her question back on her, for her to decide, who, if anyone, should kill Bates. She didn't want to show weakness or disrespect, didn't even want to chat in front of Bates. So she approached the hole and—

One look at that twenty-pound boat anchor sitting on its side next to the hole…

One glance at the metal handcuffs…

At the leg irons…

At the slick black hood sticking out of a forest green USFS canvas bag. A hood like those sickos used on sicker sickos in those stupid BDSM games ,where people paid to get whipped and suffocated and...

"You bastard!" exploded out of her.

She'd been worried about frightening Bates? The man she'd once enjoyed working with. Had spent time talking to. Hours even! Sharing ambitions and dreams and—and stuff!

In seconds, Heston had Bates' wrists fastened behind his back with those cuffs, had his knees bent, and his butt at the edge of the hole, which was frozen over. With one savage kick, Heston broke the ice, then dragged the heel of his boot around the edge and widened the hole back to its original foot-and-a-half width. He sized Bates up and went back to kicking the edges until he made the hole as wide as Bates' shoulders.

London couldn't believe what she was seeing. Stupid her, she dropped to her knees to take a better look at the icy hole that would've been her grave. The water was frothy and black as death. Full of broken shards of ice. Fresh ice had already reformed at the edges.

"I was just gonna play with you," Bates murmured, his voice trembling, and his whole body spasming with fear. "A little. Not too much and not for long."

"You bastard! Stop lying! You were going to put me down that hole and under the ice!" she shrieked, pointing at the damned thing as if he didn't know it was there. "In freezing ice water! In handcuffs! With a hood over my face so I couldn't breathe!"

She grabbed the hood. Damned thing was elastic or spandex or something stretchy, with Velcro straps in the back that had very little give. There were no holes in the front of it for a person's mouth or eyes, just two tiny slits for a nose. The stupid thing had a shiny silver buckle under its chin and a loop, like for a dog collar. *Shit!*

"How about we try this crap over your big head, Devon! Let's see if you like it?" London's gut pitched acid up the back of her throat at the thought of anyone volunteering to be suffocated like that, of anyone putting it over someone else's head and face for—for fun! Stifling black spots swarmed her vision. She had to lean back on her haunches to keep from face-planting. It was hard to breathe imagining that hood over her head. It was a struggle to suck in enough air. Everything in her screamed bloody murder. But she refused to embarrass herself in front of this jackhole. What the hell?!!

"And then what, *Captain* Bates?" Heston asked darkly, twisting this jerk's rank, making it sound like an insult instead of the honor it should've been. London leaned closer to better hear him. It would sure be nice if he'd lean her way and wrap one of his strong, protective arms around her. She had never been so close to falling apart. And okay, he was right. She did want him to protect her and keep her safe. Now. Here. How could anyone hate her so much they wanted her dead? To die so horribly? In a dark, frozen lake, kicking and crying and fighting for air. Fighting to live!

"Nothing," Bates murmured. "Honest. I wasn't gonna drown her, just—"

Heston's fist shot out of nowhere and plowed into the side of Bates' head, knocking him to his side away from the hole. "Honest? You don't get to even think that word. You're a disgrace to the Forest Service. To your fellow rangers. To America! Just what did you intend to do to LT Wilde?" He was on his knees now, his chest heaving, both fists clenched, his knuckles white, and spitting mad. "*Almost* drown her! *Almost* suffocate her! *Almost* let her slip under the surface of this frozen lake and *almost* freeze to death? *Almost* scare the fuck out of her? *Almost* let her body not be found until next spring! Just what were you going to do to her, you son of a gawddamned bitch!"

"Nothing! I wasn't supposed to kill her. Just shut her up. She knows too damned much!"

London fell back on her ass, speechless. *I know too damned much? Like what? What do I know?*

Heston didn't ask. He was long past playing games. Like a pro—because he was one—he twisted Bates' ass around until the guy had both boots stuck in freezing water. The chicken shit hissed as his boots filled. Good. Because that was just the beginning. The rule was to make sure black op assassinations looked like accidents, and therein lay a problem. Not *the* problem, just *a* problem. Truth was that ice fishermen died all the time if they were unprepared. If they were idiots. If they didn't heed the signs of hypothermia. If they were overweight and broke through thin ice. If they drilled their fishing holes along crack lines. The reasons were endless. But ending this asshole while London watched? That was the real dilemma.

Heston looked across the hole at the woman he adored. London's eyes were no longer their usual pretty turquoise green. They'd turned dark blue. Even her hair seemed darker. Colder. Nothing like the cozy warm tropical hues when she was happy. He pursed his lips and let loose a plume of overheated angst. Make that outright rage. If anyone deserved to die beneath this ice, it was Devon Bates, bastard extraordinaire. And London should decide his fate.

"What do you want to do with him?" Heston asked, dialing his rage back enough to offer her the calm respect she deserved, to let her know this particular decision was hers. She was the intended murder victim here. Bates hadn't brought that anchor just to 'play.' Heston jerked the canvas bag that had held that extreme bondage mask, pissed at the sickening fad sweeping the nation. If he lived to be a hundred, he'd never understand the thrill a man got out of beating a woman. Not after what he'd seen done to women and girls in Afghanistan, Iraq, and Iran. India. China. Thailand. Fuckin' Hollywood USA. The bag needed to sink with Bates.

Shit! There was something beneath the mask. A Nikon camera.

London gasped like she'd been shot. Her hands went to her throat, and everything went from bad to worse. Without warning, she shoved Bates into the hole. The man sank. Bubbles sputtered over where he'd disappeared.

Panicked that she'd over-reacted, that she'd eventually regret killing Bates, Heston stuck his arm into the cold water, up to his armpit, until his cheek was flat against the ice. He spread his fingers and made contact with Bates' short as shit haircut. Like it or not, Heston extended his arm down deep, grabbed Bates by his ear, and pulled him to the surface. Up came the bastard. Once he surfaced, Heston got a better hold on his neck and jerked him out of the hole.

Bates sat at the edge, crying like the chicken-shit he was. "I had no choice! He made me do it! You gotta understand!" Sputter. Choke. Whine. Bitch. Whine some more.

This time Heston growled at London instead of Bates, needing her to understand the consequences of what she did there today. "I appreciate you want to kill this creep, but be sure you understand that if you drown him, some hiker or fisherman, maybe a little kid, will find him next spring, and it won't be pretty. But if that's how you roll, say the word and I'll push him back in. Hell, I'll load his boots with rocks to make sure he sinks. Doesn't matter to me. They're already as heavy as the anchor he would've used on you. He'll go straight to the bottom. He's weak from blood loss. Won't last long. Is that what you want?"

Tiny crystal tears clung to the tips of her lashes. "I never did anything but support and encourage him," she replied. Her voice was so damned small and lost, it was all Heston could do to keep his hands to himself and not pull her into his arms. "I thought he was my friend, Hes. We shared shitty canned meals together and worked twelve-hour shifts and" —she swiped a hand over her eyes— "stuff. Like… like friends."

"I do know," Heston agreed. But he also knew this was the precise moment she'd reached the pinnacle of all that independence she'd been chasing. And here she was, immersed in a man's dirty world, faced with the ugliness soldiers abroad carried out in hopes their loved ones back home wouldn't have to. "Kelsey didn't deserve getting shot, either," Heston reminded her as kindly as he could.

"I didn't do that!" Bates bellowed. "Uh-uh, that's not on me!"

"Then talk," Heston ordered. "Who shot Kelsey and Alex Stewart?"

"You'll let me live?"

"You think you can bargain? With what? The hairy balls Asher has no doubt already cut off your sniper friend?" Heston gave Bates a rough shake that had him leaning face first over his watery grave again. "No deals. I want names and I want them now."

"Drop him," London said, her voice oddly flat. "He's lying. Everything he's ever said was a lie. Just do it, Hes. Push him back in, now. Before anyone sees us."

Heston stared her down, caught her sly wink at the same moment Asher walked up behind her. "You sure?" Heston asked, playing along with whatever was going to happen next.

London's head bobbed, making her turquoise hair shiver and ripple like waves in a tropical lagoon. Heston put a hard hand in the middle of Bates' broad back and—

"Former Sergeant Ryan Malloy of Defense Forces Ireland!" Bates screamed like he'd been electrocuted. "He paid me to shut her up. Said she's too damned nosey, doesn't listen to her superiors like the bitch should. That she needed to learn a lesson, once and for all. He's the best of the best! You can't kill him!"

"Already did," Asher said matter-of-factly from behind London. As if to prove it, he tossed a bloody bag over her shoulder. The way the bag bounced before it rolled alongside Bates sure looked like it held two balls instead of a head.

Bates tipped onto his hip away from the trophy. "No, no, no! Fuck! He'll kill me for sure now!"

Ah, so Ryan Malloy wasn't the mastermind behind the scheme to end Alex and Kelsey.

"Malloy can't kill you. He's already dead, right, Agent Downey?" Heston asked.

Asher smirked. "Yup. Caught him sighting-in on my good buddy, London, with that fancy computerized rifle of his. Never saw me coming. Sliced a big smile under his chin, neat as a whistle. Chucked his fat ass out of the tree he was hiding in. Sure ain't smiling now."

Bates' groan was almost comical.

"Who'll kill you now that Malloy's dead?" Heston snapped. "Tell me and I'll keep you safe."

"He can do that, you know, Devon." London was back in control. But Heston couldn't help wondering where her knife was. Sure wasn't in her hand.

"I can't, I just c-c-can't," Bates whined. "You guys don't understand how these things work."

"Then don't tell us," London replied easily, almost kindly. "It's okay. We understand. You've had a really hard day, Devon. I bet you're tired. Why don't you lean back and—" She whipped an arm around Bates' neck and, in a heartbeat, her blade was under his chin and against his bouncing Adam's apple.

"No need to worry, good buddy. I'll take good care of you," she soothed wickedly. "Either you tell Heston what he wants to know, or I end you right here and now. You won't have to worry about Malloy's boss killing you. Think about it. Won't be much left of you next spring once the trout in this lake feed on you all winter long. I'll bet they're real hungry this time of year. Ravenous. They're carnivorous, you know, and they like bacon. Uncooked. With a lot of fat left on it. Fat, Bates. Just. Like. You."

Made cutthroat trout sound—well, cutthroat. London also had Bates eating out of her hand. She'd tucked the blade's dull side against his throat. Her knife wasn't hurting him as much as it was helping Kelsey and Alex. Heston pursed his lips and blew her a kiss and a wink. She winked back. The lady was damned good at PsyOps mind games.

"Tristan O-O-Obermeyer," Bates muttered.

"Secretary of State Tristan Obermeyer?" Heston asked in disbelief. "That Obermeyer?"

"Yeah, yeah, him. He's tight with the guy running to be the next US ambassador to Ireland. Michael Keane. Guess Wilde saw Malloy with them in DC last month. Obermeyer was pissed. Said Wilde recognized him. Even said hi to him and Keane. Said she had to go before she blows his cover and ruins everything. Told Malloy to finish the Stewarts, then asked me to, you know…" Bates blinked down into the frigid hole where his water-filled boots still dangled. "Malloy sub-contracted me to take her out because… Shit. Because I owe him for… for…"

"Spill," London whispered. "I remember that trip to Washington DC, and yes, I saw Secretary of State Obermeyer with Keane. They were talking outside Estadio's on Fourteenth Street, Northwest. Didn't know Malloy was there with them, though. Why do you owe him?"

Bates' chest puffed before he wheezed, "I gamble, all right? Got in a little over my head the last time I was in New Jersey. Malloy put in a good word for me and—"

"And now you owe some shark who works for Keane. How much?" Heston asked.

"Fifty thousand. Doubles in forty-eight hours if I don't pay up. You gotta understand, I didn't have a choice!" Interestingly, Bates didn't correct Heston saying *'now you owe some shark who works for Keane.'* Was Michael Keane the new Irish Mafia boss? Or had he always been the top dog in charge of drug and gun running, prostitution, extortion, and a dozen other illegal enterprises in Boston? Which begged another question: Did Alex know?

London chuckled. "What body part you gonna lose?"

"I'll lose my wife!" Bates made it sound like his betting on the wrong banker was London's fault. "He's got my wife!"

"Don't blame London for the choices you made," Heston corrected. "You're a lousy gambler and a shittier husband. You've got no choice. You're stuck between a rock and a hard place. Where's Malloy holding your wife? What's her name? We might be able to save *her*."

"Kitten. Kitten Bates," Bates replied, his gaze gone flat but still on that hole.

Well, wasn't that just precious? Heston huffed in disgust. Wanna bet Kitten was the alias a clever call girl used to lure idiots like Bates into crooked card games run by sharks? Who in turn maintained an unbelievable profit margin—for the Irish mafia?

"Kitten?" Asher asked, surprised. "As in 'here kitty, kitty?' Or as in the slam, bam, thank you, ma'am, kind of kitty?"

"She's a cocktail waitress, you son of a bitch! A good one."

Heston grunted. *I'll bet.* Things kept going from bad to worse for Bates. Yes, Heston would ask Mark to check out the dubious Mrs. Bates, but he suspected Kitty worked for Keane, and Keane wouldn't hurt the girl who brought in suckers like Bates.

"I say let's take him back to Alex, Hes and Ash," London said, her voice firm, her decision made, and Heston's way forward as clear as the light dancing in her tropical blue eyes again. "Alex will know what to do with him. He might even let him live."

Finally, she was at peace with herself. And she should be. London had done damned good today. And if she was happy, Heston was going to make sure she stayed that way.

Chapter Seventeen

It took two hours to get Bates back to London's camper, where, lo and behold, an armed Tom Landry stood guard over Ryan Malloy. London laughed at herself. That balls-in-the-bag trick must've been Asher's way of either impressing her or, as it turned out, frightening the shit out of Bates. Legendary sniper Malloy looked pathetic, hogtied on his belly like he was, squirming with his ruddy face in the wet chipped-cedar bark at the rear of her camper.

"You asshole!" Bates screamed when Malloy came into view. Lurching forward, he stuck one water-logged boot out in a vain effort to kick Malloy. "This is all your fault!"

Heston jerked Bates away. "Shut it, or I'll hog-tie you next to Malloy and let you two roll around in the mud awhile. Then we'll see who kills who."

The threat silenced Bates. Heston leaned him against the nearest tree and ordered him to, "Sit. Make a move and I'll shoot your head off." To prove it, he unholstered a pistol, but kept it pointed down.

London crouched to one knee for a closer look at the alleged world's greatest sniper. Malloy wasn't bad looking. He was blond, had a manly, square jaw with reddish-blond scruff that almost made him handsome. She guesstimated him at around a hundred seventy pounds, six foot two inches tall, maybe three. Which made him underweight for his frame.

But there was something wrong with him, something she didn't expect in a sniper, least of all in the world's best. Malloy's skin had a yellowish tint, his eyelids were puffy, and the whites of his eyeballs were scarlet, the irises nearly non-existent. His pupils were blown, dilated so wide only black showed. Flat-black. No sparkle. No nothing. It was like looking into emptiness. He didn't look up at her, much less give any indication he recognized the trouble he was in. There was no sense talking to him. The lights weren't on and nobody was home.

"What's he on?" she asked her camping neighbor.

"My guess is meth," Tom answered, crouched protectively beside her with the tip of his boot under Malloy's chin. Which she was beginning to understand was what good men did for their female counterparts—protect them. Not because they disrespected women, but because they really were bigger-boned, heavier set, and didn't think twice about using their larger bodies to shield those they'd been trained from childhood to protect and serve. Made her girly parts tingle remembering how hard it had been for Heston to stand down when she'd talked with Tom. She was beginning to understand honorable men, and how much she'd hurt Hes when she'd walked away. How much he'd truly cared for her. How much he still cared.

"And before you ask," Asher cut in. "You're right, London. There's no way Malloy would've been able to shoot accurately in the condition he's in. I suspect he's been a long-time user and he very well could be the man who pulled the trigger the day Kelsey went down. But the second I came face to face with him, I knew he wasn't capable of killing anything except maybe a beer. Ever hear of precision-guided munitions?"

Asher glanced over his shoulder at what looked like an assault rifle on steroids lying on its side on her site's picnic table. "That's most likely the same weapon he used the day he shot Kelsey and Alex. Looks like a stand-alone rifle, but it isn't. It's part of a highly technical system."

She nodded, still trying to figure out what made a good-looking man destroy himself with drugs. PTSD maybe? The competition that came with being 'the best of the best,' as Bates said? Which made Malloy sound more like one of those silly military guys in the sci-fi movie, *"Men in Black." 'Best of the best of the best,'* nothing. Malloy was the worst of the worst.

"The system works like this, London," Heston said. "A shooter laser-paints the exact location he intends to hit, in this case, Alex's shoulder or Kelsey's head. Just the tip of her left ear would've been enough, especially since that's closest to where she was grazed. The next time, Malloy only had to point the rifle in her direction and squeeze the trigger. The system would've done everything else. The smart bullet followed its programming, homed in on the laser designation, clipped Kelsey's skull, and made Alex believe he'd seen red mist, when all he'd seen was skin, tissue, and the small amount of blood splatter caused when the round grazed her skull."

"And yes, Agent Contreras" —Tom looked up at Heston— "that same rifle is one of the hundred *'fire and forget'* proto-types stolen from McCormack Industries out of Rosslyn, Virginia, last year. I expect you know the place I mean."

Heston blew out a huff. "I do. Jed McCormack's a good friend to Alex, helped him start his business. I agree with your conclusion. A killer with this technology only has to get close to hit his mark."

"And anyone else could have laser painted Kelsey's head or her ear. Someone with a steadier hand," Tom said.

"Works like horseshoes and hand grenades," Asher added. "Close is good enough. No wonder Alex couldn't determine direction or source."

"Oh, my," London breathed. "Smart bullets can adapt their flight path? They can change trajectories?" Sounded like science fiction. "What if Obermeyer's plan is to kill the president? What if someone already laser-painted President Adams?"

"Jed already thought of that." Heston tapped his temple. "As soon as McCormack realized what he'd created, he built a failsafe into the program that distorts any signal aimed toward the President, making one of his smart bullets just another dumb round that'll fall to earth once it's spent."

"Deck's on his way," Asher informed Heston. "Not sure we should send Bates with him, though. You know how loyal Deck is to Alex and Kelsey."

"Not worried," Heston clipped, his gaze hard on Bates. "Accidents happen."

"He's gonna throw me out of that chopper, ain't he? Once he gets high enough." Bates kicked one water-logged boot out like a kid throwing a temper tantrum. "I ain't going! You can't make me. You can't do that! I have rights!"

"Said the man who planned to torture and drown my woman," Heston growled.

My woman? "Shut up, Devon," London snapped, secretly pleased Heston had publicly claimed her. "Decker isn't anything like you. He's a Vietnam vet, not a chicken-shit, gambling addict. Shit! Here I'm trying to make you feel better, when I should be the one throwing you out of that helo." This guy was getting on her last nerve.

"N-Not… k-kill… Prez… Not… Adams," the meth-head on the ground sputtered in a sing-songy voice. "Wrong, bitches. Wrong. Wrong. Wrong."

London turned toward Malloy as Heston took a knee beside their suddenly talkative prisoner. The girlish giggle coming out of Malloy's throat was creepy.

"Can I get you to loosen his ropes?" Heston asked her.

"You bet." She scrambled to obey, but before she could, Tom reached one long arm past her and snapped the tie between Malloy's hands and feet loose that kept him on his belly. All tension went out of his restraints.

"Thanks," she told Tom. "Guess those knots weren't very tight, huh?"

"Just your basic slip knot, ma'am."

Well, damn. These guys knew a few things she didn't. *Mental note to self: Learn how to tie all kinds of knots.*

Malloy wiggled over onto his butt, stretched his arms, legs, and fingers. Then crossed his legs, stared at Heston, and started singing a disjointed version of the theme from some cop show in that same weird girly voice.

"Alex got a call from your boss earlier today," Heston interrupted the nonsensical crap. "He wants Alex to accept President Adams' offer to take the VP position. Said that's the only way Alex will be able to keep Kelsey safe, by doing what he's told from now on. Sound familiar? Will your boss be good for his word if Alex signs on with President Adams as your boss's snitch?"

London knelt there transfixed and silent, recalling Heston's conversation with Mark in the camper. *'Alex will never do that. Not after what they did to Kelsey. Hell to the no.'* This had to be what they'd been talking about. But what on Earth did Obermeyer want Alex to do if he agreed to become VP? Or was Hes talking about the as-yet unnamed Irishman who'd threatened to kill Kelsey? Who exactly was the boss?

Malloy blinked as if he'd finally noticed Heston. "Yup." He popped that damned P like killing Kelsey was a joke. "Boss wants Stewart to be the next VP so he can bust the Senate's hold on the arms race. A couple other things, too. Heh, heh, heh."

"What arms race?" Heston asked patiently, his tone mostly neutral, just a titch inquisitive.

"You know. The. Arms. Rac-c-c-c-ce." Malloy dragged the last word into a hiss.

"What the fuck?" Asher roared.

"*'The Vice President of the United States shall be President of the Senate, but shall have no Vote, unless they be equally divided,'*" Heston replied evenly. "United States Constitution Article 1, Section 3, clause 4. Look it up."

"Your boss wants Alex to throw a congressional vote? On what, Malloy? Which House Resolution?" Tom asked, his voice as calmly calculating as Heston's. Him using Malloy's name was a smart move.

Malloy shrugged. "All I know is arms race and some bill that needs signing and some committee to... hmm..." He cupped his chin in one palm and rested that elbow on his knee as if he needed help holding his bobbing head still. "Something about the Taliban... Yada, yada... err... something about the Shah of Iran and... all the shit they wanna do over there... No. That's not right. Geez. I get mixed up." He shook his head then shrugged. "My head's killing me. Thinking is hard, man. I don't know, all right?"

Asher turned his back on the group and cursed, "You've got to be kidding me. This guy's the world's best sniper?"

London knew exactly how he felt.

"House Resolution thirty-seven," Heston said quietly, "concerns Michael Keane's nomination to become the next ambassador to Ireland. The vote's divided. The Senate won't approve him until the FBI completes their investigation. The House claims the GOP's spreading propaganda and lies about an innocent man. Fact: Keane is accused of complicity with the current terrorist insurgency in northern Burkina Faso, West Africa. FBI believes he's behind the uptick in gunrunners channeling stolen US Army weaponry through Ghana to Ansar ul Islam, the terrorist group behind the worst violence. If Alex accepts Adams' offer, he'll be the one casting the deciding vote on that resolution. Which makes Keane ambassador, but gets Kelsey killed if Alex doesn't vote how Keane wants."

"Where do you keep all this information?" Asher asked. "Sounds like you're quoting straight out of an encyclopedia. You got a brain chip or something in your head I don't know about?"

Heston tapped his temple again. "OCD, remember?"

"Not OCD, Agent Contreras," Tom stated. "You have an eidetic memory. You can recall verbatim, images or written pages you've only seen once, right?"

Heston nodded.

"Impressive."

"You guys are so screwed," Malloy interrupted, sing-songing again, his hands clasped around his ankles, rocking back and forth like a kid on a sugar high. "Bitches, all of you. Americans are bitches. Ah ha, ha, ha!" He tipped his head back and grinned at the branches overhead. "Told ya so. Told ya so!"

"This is getting us nowhere," Asher grouched.

Heston pushed to his feet. "On the contrary. We need to get this intel to Alex so he's prepared for whatever the Irishman demands of him next time he calls. H.R. 37 won't become public law until the stalemate in Congress is resolved. If Alex has to vote—"

"He'll never side with that stinkin' Irishman," Asher declared.

"Mr. Stewart's no Benedict Arnold," Tom agreed staunchly. "He might be the orneriest son of a bitch I've ever worked with, but he'll die before he betrays his country."

"He is that," Heston agreed.

"What'd you say your boss's name is, Ryan?" London snuck that question in as innocently as she could.

Malloy grunted. "Nope. Sorry, sugar pie, but nope, nope, nope. Not gonna tell you. Not gonna tell anyone. Ober… Ober-What's-His-Name'll kill me. Nope. Not telling you nuthin' so stop winking at me. You ain't that cute."

London sat back on her butt and crossed her legs Indian-style. "Just like Bates said. Michael Obermeyer. The Secretary of State is the man who ordered Kelsey's murder."

"I never said that!" Malloy bellowed. "You're lying! I never told nobody it was him. You're gonna get me in trouble."

"Is he Irish?" Heston asked.

London stilled at that question. The name Obermeyer didn't sound Irish, and if Heston was thinking Obermeyer was the Irishman, she doubted Obermeyer would've traveled across country from the East Coast just to give Alex a burner phone. For now, the Irishman was still an unknown quantity, but he needed to go down as much as Bates, Keane, Malloy, and now Obermeyer did. Talk about a conspiracy.

Malloy huffed. "Are you daft? Not everyone's lucky enough to be Irish, you eedjit."

Asher turned and growled, "Let's shut the fuckers down. All of them. Now. Today. Come on, guys. The sooner we get this done, the better."

He wasn't wrong. "Not necessarily," London said, mostly to herself.

Heston cocked his head and grinned at her. Tom was already staring at her.

She shrugged both shoulders. "I've read about Secretary of State Obermeyer. He's a powerful man, Ash, and there's rumors about mysterious deaths and missing bodies on his way to becoming Secretary of State. Can Alex Stewart take down this big of a politician? Is he powerful enough to overcome Obermeyer and his paid assassins? Look around us, guys." She waved a hand at Bates and Malloy. "He's got a network, not just a couple friends in high places. Look what he did to me. Alex doesn't need to be *as* powerful. He needs to be *more* powerful. Is he?"

Asher winced.

Tom crossed his arms over his chest and spread his boots. "Understand what you're saying, London. And you're right. Alex needs to get ahead of Obermeyer—somehow. I have no idea how he'll do it, but he's dealt with crooked politicians before. All you guys need to do is get these two jerks back to Alex before they end up dead, too."

London watched Heston tug his cell phone up from one of his many pockets and thumb-dial a number. "Mark, Heston here," he said, then paused. "Yeah. Soon as Deck shows, we're on our way. Bringing a couple guests." He nodded at her and paused again. "Yup, we'll bring them in the back door as usual. Understood. Look for us at eight, but expect us at midnight. Also…" He went on to tell Mark about H.R. 37, the stalemate in Congress, Obermeyer's backing Keane, and the death threat to London.

How she wished she could hear the other side of that conversation. She'd met Mark and his wife briefly at the hospital. They were an adorable couple. And to think he was as lethal a sniper as Heston, and his wife was a physician. Mind boggling.

Heston ended the call with, "Copy that." He winked at London and announced, "We're Oscar Mike, people. Get these two jokers ready to fly."

Bates, who'd been quiet during the discussion, whined, "Uh-uh. I ain't going nowhere."

London couldn't believe he'd take Bates and Malloy into the same hospital that housed Kelsey. It didn't make sense, but instead of questioning him and making him explain, she threw her support behind him. "What Heston said goes, Devon. Tied to a helo skid or belted inside, your choice. But you're going wherever Heston says."

"You always were a bitch," he sneered.

She stepped into his space, stuck a finger in his chest, and declared, "Yeah, well, I'm a live bitch. So move your ass!"

Chapter Eighteen

Look at that woman go. If they'd been alone, Heston would've kissed London after watching how she'd intimidated her former supervisor, then manhandled Bates onto the helo as quickly as Deck touched down. Then, while Asher secured Malloy, she'd harnessed Bates into the rear seat, which was extra thoughtful since his hands and ankles were cuffed. She'd run back and locked her camper, and asked Tom to watch over it until she returned. By then, Heston was already in the helo and the sun had set. There was just enough ambient light to watch London and Tom say a quick goodbye. No hug. No sign of emotional attachment between the two. Confirmed Heston's opinion of Landry.

The mystified expression on London's face when she climbed back up into the helo was priceless. She had no idea that *'Look for us at eight, but expect us at midnight'* was simple TEAM code for four hours, the difference between eight and twelve pm, the amount of time it'd take Deck to get them to the *backdoor*—aka TEAM HQ.

Alex didn't need a face-to-face meeting with the men who'd tried to murder his wife. Not only did he not have time to fly across country, Alex would've killed both Malloy and Bates on sight if he did. Effective solution, yes. Justifiable murder, probably not. But killing suspects was no way to conduct interrogations, and Heston needed answers more than

Alex needed revenge. The puppet master had to go down, not just his puppets. Heston wasn't sure who that mastermind was. He suspected Obermeyer ran the show, as Malloy declared. But he hadn't ruled Keane out, and the mysterious Irishman needed a name. There'd be no coming back from what Heston did next, so he needed to get it right the first time, for both Alex's and Kelsey's sakes.

Assisted by a steady jet stream, Pilot Decker Edison made it to Virginia, within the prerequisite four hours. Heston checked in with Mark, gave him names and the rest of the intel. Told him Malloy and Bates were in custody. That Obermeyer and Keane had contracted Malloy to murder Kelsey. That Malloy had, in turn, contracted Bates to kill London.

The helo's skids had barely touched down on the tarmac at TEAM HQ when Renner Graves jerked the side door open and declared, "Welcome home, boys." He flashed London a big smile that Heston wanted to knock off his ugly face. "You must be London Wilde. Glad to finally meet you, ma'am. Been hearing nothing but good things about you. Name's Renner Graves. Need a hand down from there?"

"Sure don't, but thanks, Agent Graves," she replied, already free of her harness and on her feet. "I assume you have a secure facility for our visitors?"

She made Bates and Malloy sound like honest citizens.

"Yes, ma'am. But these men aren't visitors, they're prisoners. FBI Director Tucker Chase is on his way. He'll be taking them to the FBI's facility in the District for questioning." Renner looked at Heston. "Sorry, but this case falls under the Bureau's jurisdiction. Alex called Chase direct. Probably not what you want to hear, Heston, but—"

"That's bullshit!" Asher roared. "We nailed Bates and Malloy. They're ours!"

Heston put a hand on Asher's hefty biceps to keep him from exploding out the door and taking Renner down. "Let Chase have this case, Ash. The FBI should handle Malloy and Bates. It falls within their jurisdiction, and Alex trusts Director Chase."

Alex and Tucker were tight. Tucker might've been an annoying Navy SEAL like Tom Landry back in the day, but Tucker Chase commandeered the only psychic unit in the Bureau. Heston had heard that Chase had some talent in that area. Bates and Malloy might live longer this way. Might yield more factual, hard evidence instead of the promised bloodletting if Alex ever got his hands on them.

"How's Isaiah?" Heston asked as he dropped off the helo with a solid grip on the chain between Bates' cuffs, while Ash assisted the zoned-out, world's greatest sniper to the tarmac.

Renner grinned. "Now how'd you know Isaiah was here?"

"Because he's standing behind you." Heston reached around Renner to shake Isaiah's hand. "Hey, Isaiah."

Renner peered over his shoulder. "Damn, you're sneaky, Zaroyin."

"Me?" Isaiah teased. His dark blue eyes sparkled as if this were an easy hand-off, but Heston caught sight of the hefty nine-millimeter, fifth-generation Glock pistol loose in the holster cup on Isaiah's hip. The son of Abraham Zaroyin, the mad scientist behind the catastrophic plan to implant mind-control chips in active duty military members, Isaiah was one of very few Level Ten psychics in the world.

He and Eden Winchester, another Level Ten, were the first agents to serve the federal government in that capacity. Their record for intercepting murderers, spies, and other miscreants was phenomenal, bar none. There were a few other Level Tens scattered across the world, from Russia and China to England, Algeria, Iraq, and Israel. Even on a peak overlooking the winter capital of the Dali Lama in Himachal Pradesh, India. But to date, only a handful worked for the Bureau.

"Tuck wants to meet your girlfriend, Heston. Hope you don't mind waiting," Isaiah said.

My girlfriend? Heston knew Isaiah never said anything in jest. If he said girlfriend, he was seeing something Heston hadn't yet admitted. Was it possible? Did he stand a chance of getting back into London's good graces? Was he worth her? Hell, Isaiah was probably inside Heston's mind right now, listening while he argued with himself. He shot Zaroyin a grin and told him, "Stop it, smartass."

Isaiah grinned. "Not for me to stop anything." While he reached out and took a firm hold of Malloy's cuffs, he stuck his chin at London. "She's the one in control. Surprised you aren't."

He had Heston there. "Working on it," was all the intel Isaiah was getting on that subject.

Renner grunted when a bright red Dodge Challenger careened over the tarmac, its wheels squealing. "Tuck's here. I gotta go."

"Good seeing you again, Renner," Heston replied evenly.

Tucker Chase, forever a badass former SEAL and the only FBI Director without a filter, would never change. Proof positive was him slamming on the brakes and sliding that monster car sideways on the tarmac and into a perfect stop alongside the helo. Six feet of tough-guy muscle poured out of the driver's side, while an elegant blonde with mile-long legs stepped daintily from the passenger seat.

"Heston," she called out. Smoothing one hand over the front of her skirt, she extended the other to him as she joined the group.

He pulled her in for a quick hug instead of just a handshake. "Hey, Eden. Didn't expect you. Where's Ky?"

She fluttered her fingers as if she was dusting the air. "Oh, you know. Off saving the world with Tate and Keller. Texas, again."

London was suddenly at Heston's side, nudging his elbow out of her way as she burrowed in close. She stuck a hand at Eden. "Hi there, ma'am, I'm—"

"London Wilde!" Eden exclaimed, releasing Heston and reaching for London. "Former FBI Agent in training, former Forest Service law enforcement officer." She grabbed both of London's wrists. "Also currently investigating—without federal oversight, I might add—the attempted murders of two of my very best friends, Alex and Kelsey Stewart. I am so glad to make your acquaintance. Did I miss anything? Oh, yes, you graduated with honors from Texas A&M University. Weren't you valedictorian that year? My God, you're too pretty to work for the Bureau. Isn't she, Heston?"

"Well, umm, yeah," London admitted sheepishly as Eden released her wrists and gave her a quick girly hug. "I mean, about the other stuff. Not about being pretty or anything like—"

"She's too pretty for government work," Heston agreed, still wondering if Isaiah was right about her being in control.

"London's my best friend. Probably the smartest agent the FBI ever let slip away, too."

He smiled down at the timid woman inside the circle of his arms, that London had turned into. Her fingers were splayed possessively on his chest and her cheeks were pleasantly pink. But she'd turned shy and quiet. His breath hitched at this new perspective of the woman he still loved. So this was what she looked like embarrassed. So damned beautiful, it was hard to breathe. Her jealousy was a joy to behold, and her being possessive of him was downright thrilling. But her being bashful in front of another strong woman was just plain adorable.

Guess Heston wasn't the only one staking out territory tonight. Isaiah was right. She was Heston's woman.

Tucker stalked up to where everyone but Decker had gathered. Deck was still inside his helo, probably checking off an end-of-flight safety list.

"Get these two out of here," Tucker ordered.

"I've got Malloy. Can you handle that one, Eden?" Isaiah asked as he pulled Malloy toward the sleek, black, FBI sedan parked nearby.

She shot him a dazzling smile. "You know better than to ask. I can make former United States Forest Ranger Bates bark like a dog if I choose. Come on, Bates. You're riding with me."

True to her word, she strong-armed Bates and led him away. The guy was bigger than Eden, but he looked damned meek with her hand on the cuffs behind his back, the other now filled with a pistol identical to Isaiah's. Which neither of them needed to take these two men into custody. Not with the psychic talent Heston knew Eden and Isaiah possessed. What he wouldn't give to watch them interview Malloy and Bates.

"Ma'am," Tucker huffed as he took hold of London's free hand and tugged her away from Heston. "My unit could use—"

"No," Heston declared, his hand already clamped on London's shoulder, needing to protect her from this oversized, arrogant gorilla who right then thought he was charming and irresistible. "She's with me."

"…an investigator with your talent—"

"Save the job offer, Chase. I'm telling you."

"…and your natural aptitude for—"

Damn, this was not going well. "London!" Heston snapped.

She looked straight at him and blew her jewel-toned bangs off her face. Those pretty turquoise eyes turned cold and calculating. Instead of answering, she gave him her chin.

Shit. He was doing it again. Bossing her. Walking all over her. Thinking he knew better, that he knew everything. Which he didn't. She hadn't needed his advice or his interference before. She didn't need it now. Hell, she didn't need anybody's advice.

What London needed wasn't him telling her what to do any more than she needed Tucker Chase pressuring her to work for him. She needed time and space to decide her future for herself. It might not include working for The TEAM. Might not include being bullied by the idiot who'd only ever wanted to love her and protect her for the rest of her life, either.

Yeah. That. Heston finally recognized how his internal caveman's need to control her was pushing her away. He stopped ranting. Just let go, gave up, and trusted London like he'd trust any other TEAM agent. Like he trusted Asher and Renner and Mark and Alex.

London *was* intelligent and experienced. She *had* proven her worth—over and over. While he'd proven he was mostly stuck in the Middle Paleolithic period—again and again.

Heston swallowed hard. It was hard admitting he'd been a dumbass. Harder yet to let her go.

He'd looked up that name she'd thrown at him. He now knew precisely who *Donna Reed* was, and what she represented to today's women. Also knew how brainless that sitcom had made women look back then. How her smiling, willing subservience might've been the norm for the nineteen fifties, but it had set the bar so low, no man nor woman should ever consider it again. Especially not London.

Heston admitted defeat, nodded at her, *message received. I love you. Goodbye.*

She sent back the barest nod, then tossed her head like a winner should, and Heston accepted that, too. He had to. She *was* a winner. Always had been. Bottom line, London didn't need him like he'd once thought she did. She was independent. She'd go far. She might not be a good fit for the Forest Service, but she'd find her way. That was what strong women did. They shrugged off the yoke of other people's expectations and they flew.

With a gut full of regret for not being smarter sooner, he turned his back on the high-pressure employment negotiations taking place on the tarmac at TEAM HQ. It might be best if Tucker got his way. Working with psychics the caliber of Isaiah and Eden was a tantalizing offer. London would bring a lot to their team. Heston had no doubt she'd fly higher if she wasn't working with him. He'd hold her back. That wasn't what he wanted for her.

It was a bitter pill to swallow, but London's happiness was more important than her listening to his 'manly wisdom.' He didn't know everything. The encyclopedias in his head were worthless stores of facts. He had an after-action report to write. He kept walking.

Isaiah was wrong. London wasn't Heston's girlfriend, wasn't even his woman. In order for her to fly, to truly succeed and excel like he knew she would, she had to be on her own. Heston had to set her free, and he would. So he did. *Damn it.*

Chapter Nineteen

Alex stood over his wife's bed. He'd overstayed his welcome. Now that Dr. Kang, the neurosurgeon Alex had flown in from the East Coast, had performed the second surgery and replaced the portion of Kelsey's skull he'd previously removed, she needed more than this understaffed joint had to offer. Like absolute safety and privacy. Protection. Anonymity.

"I'm taking you home, sweetheart," he told her, as if she might suddenly wake up and argue with him. *That'd be nice.*

Her stats were good. Too good. Libby, Judy, and Doc Fitz all agreed how extraordinarily well Kelsey had breezed through both brain surgeries. Some doctor on staff here, Alex hadn't cared enough to ask the man's name, disagreed. Like a phenomenal prick, he'd stormed out of her room in a huff because Alex had deferred to Dr. Kang's opinion instead of his.

"You do that, you fly her across country and you'll kill her!" Dr. Nameless had spat on his way out.

Alex disagreed. Between Dr. Kang's, Dr. Libby Houston's, Dr. McKenna Villanueva's, and Lead Trauma Nurse Judy Mortimer's professional care, Kelsey would be in the best of hands.

Alex had given this place a generous donation when Kelsey had first arrived. Nobody'd argued with him then. But somewhere between then and what would surely be her quicker departure now, the administrator and his staff had turned on Alex. Which made him think. *Think,* his motto. His number one rule.

He damned well knew it. He should've figured it out sooner. The damned Irishman had infiltrated this hospital and paid someone off. Possibly the administrator. It explained how the bastard knew which room Kelsey was in and the phone number to that room. Which also meant some asshole had her in his crosshairs right damned then.

Alex jerked his new TEAM satellite phone up from his jeans pocket and thumb-dialed the secure line to TEAM HQ, which, right then, Mark Houston was carrying on his hip. Mark was somewhere on the hospital grounds, or inside, hunting Kelsey's killers. Many TEAM agents were. Most had come to Kelsey's aid. But things still happened and Alex was done taking chances.

"Houston here," Mark replied.

"Activate TEAM protocol Spirit One."

"About time. Consider it done. You take care of our lady. We'll do the heavy lifting."

Alex pursed his lips at the outright loyalty he'd come to expect from his TEAM. There were none better. None more loyal. None more dedicated.

Spirit One was the covert transfer of precious intelligence, high-level resources, or cargo. In this case, Kelsey. The heavy lifting would be his TEAM getting her safely out of this hospital and securely into the TEAM jet waiting for her on the same private landing strip she'd been flown in on.

Alex should feel better than he did, but the lump in his throat made it difficult to tell Mark thanks. "You—ahh—"

"Stow it, Boss. We've all been through crap before. Know what it's doing to you now. Take a breath and chill. Order a beer. Relax. Put your feet up on the back porch. Kelsey's tough. She'll breeze through this next surgery like a champ. You'll see."

Mark's words were what any good friend would say to a worried husband. In this case, *back porch* was code for TEAM HQ, where Kelsey would soon be safely ensconced below ground in the TEAM's high-tech on-site hospital. *Next surgery* was code for the covert operation to get Kelsey out of the hospital, sight unseen, as efficiently and quickly as possible. She was Spirit One, and Alex meant to spirit her out from under the noses of hospital staff and that damned Irishman. Whoever the son of a bitch was.

The decompressive craniectomy Dr. Drake Kang had performed on Kelsey was no simple operation. Which was why Alex had called the acclaimed neurosurgeon and his team of experts from the East Coast to handle it. Kang's team included reconstructive surgeons, anesthesiologists, critical care experts, radiologists, and rehab experts, to name a few. Once the initial surgery was completed, the swelling in Kelsey's brain had reduced significantly. Alex would forever be thankful for that early sign she'd survive.

Until Dr. Kang had expressed his concern the day after the first surgery that Kelsey was doing too well, that she didn't seem to be experiencing any pain or distress, both expected aftereffects of a decompressive craniectomy. Especially after the pounding her poor skull had endured in the river. Her blood pressure should have spiked. She shouldn't have been as quiet as she'd been. She certainly shouldn't have been a model patient. She should've been in pain. Should've tossed and turned in some sort of agony. He'd expected she'd at least be nauseous. Maybe have thrown up. Instead her BP remained low, signifying a total lack of stress after the hours-long surgery.

"Either your little wife's stronger than she looks, or I'm missing something, Alex," Dr. Kang had told Alex privately the morning after the second surgery. "I've run more diagnostics. There's no indication of stroke, seizures, or intracranial bleeding, and that's good news. But she's too— too placid. Too calm. I've seen miracles before, Alex, but my gut's telling me the sooner you get her back East where I can monitor her progress without someone looking over my shoulder, the better."

"You don't trust this hospital?"

Dr. Kang had shaken his head. "I didn't say that, but I'm OCD like you. The helo you've got waiting on her is already equipped to transport critical care patients. I'll be with her every step of the way. I suggest you get her out of here, and do it fast."

"See you soon, Mark," was all Alex could come up with.

"Copy that."

Only when Kelsey was safely at TEAM HQ would he be able to chill. It'd be better if she woke up and smiled. But Alex had a feeling that wasn't happening anytime soon.

Chapter Twenty

"Yes, sir, I'll be sure and let you know." *When pigs fly. No way am I working for this obnoxious guy. Who does he think he is?*

"I'll take that as a definite yes. See you Monday morning, bright and early." Director Chase grinned. Then, as if that wasn't enough of a lame come-on, he shot London a cocky wink. He still hadn't let go of her hand. Was he flirting with her? Seriously? A man his age? He had to be in his late thirties, maybe early forties. Yeah, he was okay looking, but too damned old to think he was, in any way, impressing her. There was at least ten years difference in their ages. *Eww.*

'Take it any way you want,' she thought, but said, "Monday, yeah. I'll let you know by then." *Like I said.*

"Great! You've got my card."

"I sure do," London answered as she pulled her fingers out of his big, warm grip. *And I've got your number.* The man acted like he already owned her. *Gross.*

"I'll get your workspace ready," he called out even as she turned and walked away from him. "Ever had an office to yourself?" *No, and I don't want one now.* "Well, I'm the guy who can make it happen."

"I'll call you," she repeated, more firmly this time, then kicked up her gait and speed-walked to the one-story brick building Heston, Asher, and Renner had disappeared into.

"Bye now!" Director Chase yelled.

Oh, for the love of God, give it up! London didn't look over her shoulder this time. Didn't wave. Didn't answer. Uh-uh. No sense in saying anything to this obnoxious guy. Man, was he pushy.

She'd learned a few things working for the government. Most government agencies were inefficient, bogged down by redundant regulations, ROEs, and a shit ton of lessons they hadn't yet learned from their prior errors. Add to that the fact that all federal data systems were outdated, some as old as World War Two. The very socialist nature of government employment, which had to have been the harbinger for today's woke generation's rule that everyone gets a participation prize, prevented hardworking civilians from excelling. Which stood to reason. Corrupt politicians created those agencies, and the only thing politicians ever excelled at was covering their asses.

Case in point: the Federal Bureau of Investigation had enough rules to choke a twenty-mule team, like the ones that had once hauled tons of borax out on the Mojave Desert! And the Bureau's egregious errors were legendary. Yet they kept making the same ones. Over and over again they'd proved how partisan and corrupt they were. Why she'd ever wanted to work for the FBI boggled her brain now. And that Tucker Chase guy?

No. Just no!

Finally, at the brick building, she jerked the entry door's steel handle and—*Ouch!* Darn near pulled her arm out of its socket. Locked? Heston locked her out? Damn him. Furious at being treated like a nobody, she raised her fist to give the door a good pounding when—

It opened inward and there he stood. "You finish your job interview?" he asked politely. Too politely, damn him. He thought she'd told Director Chase she'd work for him. Well, guess again.

"I'm not working for that pompous jerk. Come to think of it, how can your friends, that Isaiah dude and Mrs. Winchester, stand him? He's an ass."

"Most alpha males are asses, London. They're driven to succeed and exceed. Can't tolerate slackers. Won't tolerate cheaters. You'd be smart to accept his offer, and you'd get used to him. He's one of the few decent bosses around."

"I don't care how decent *you think* he is."

"No, of course you don't," Heston replied with something that sounded a lot like indifference in his tone. "Sorry, that just popped out. I won't make assumptions again."

London slapped both palms onto his chest and shoved him backward, tired of the uneasy truce between them. "For your information, I told him I'd think about it, that I'd call Monday and let him know my decision. But I lied. I'm not dumb enough to call him—ever. He thinks he's hot shit. But he's not and he's certainly not the man I want to work with."

Heston's deep brown eyes blinked. Sadness glittered there. Didn't he know she meant him? Did he really think she'd kiss him like she did in her camper if she'd planned to walk away again? Hadn't they cleared the air between them? Didn't he know she'd give anything to take back the rash decision she'd made that night? Didn't he know anything?

She stabbed her index finger into the thick wall of his muscular chest. "I don't want to work for the FBI. I've already got that t-shirt. It didn't fit!" She stabbed him again.

Instead of fighting back, he calmly spread his palms to the wall behind him.

His complacency made her mad. "Who's walking away now, Hes? It's sure not me."

"I'm giving you time and space," he whispered. "I'm giving you enough room to make your own decision without my interference."

"I don't need time and space!" By this time, they were nearly flush against each other, yet he hadn't taken hold of her like he used to. Hadn't tipped his head to kiss her. Wasn't acting friendly. He looked sad. *Not acceptable.*

London flung herself at him, just wrapped her arms around his stubborn neck and her long legs around his waist. He was too good for her. Too smart and so much better trained, the whole enchilada. Damn it, she wanted him to want her as much as she wanted him.

He didn't make a sound, didn't even say, *'Oomph,'* when her body hit his. But his hands automatically caught two big handfuls of her ass. That was encouraging.

She took a frantic, deep, wet taste of his mouth, bound and determined to light this man's fire again. "We've both made mistakes, Hes," she mumbled against his lips. "I hurt you, I know. I've hurt you a hundred times worse than you've ever hurt me. I get that. I'm sorry." She peppered his face and neck with more kisses. More determination.

At last, "I'm trying," murmured out of him.

Sill not good enough.

Returning to his mouth, she licked his lips, then bit the bottom one. Licked it again in case she'd bitten too hard. Wormed her tongue into his mouth and combed her fingers up his neck and into his hair. They were both panting hot, short breaths into each other's mouths. His body had changed from cool, calm, and collected, into a coiled, deadly snake who might bite her.

Bring it on.

Switching tactics, London attacked his shirt, pulling it out of his pants, needing to be skin-on-skin with this man. Her man. "I haven't been with anyone since I left Killeen," she told him without preamble.

"I've never loved anyone but you," he replied huskily. But there was still a heavy hint of sadness in his tone.

London tipped back at his confession. "You haven't slept with anyone else? Really? But…"

Heston was a god among men. He was so good-looking. Bronzed by his lineage. Muscled by the physical demands of his vocation. Short, shiny black hair, always trimmed and neat. Even the five o'clock shadowing his chin was sexy. His body was honed into a chiseled, lean, mean fighting machine. He was smart and honest and— "What's wrong with women in Virginia?"

"None of them are you," he whispered.

London blinked then. His pain at her leaving him was still fresh. She'd been off thinking she was saving the world when all this time, she should've been saving him. Seeking his forgiveness. Healing the pain her impulsive decision had caused. Keeping him safe and protected. The world had never really needed her, but he did. And she needed him.

"I never stopped loving you," she choked, her fingers once again running over his head, into his hair, petting him like she should've been doing all those missed years. "But if you can't forgive me—"

"Can you forgive me? I'm the one who started this mess."

"No, you're not. There's nothing to forgive."

"Let's agree to disagree. Can we talk more about this later because…?" Heston released one hand from her backside to palm the door behind them open. It bounced against the inner wall. He didn't seem to care, just took firm hold of her ass again with both hands, kicked the door shut behind them with his boot, and plunged them into darkness.

By the quick glimpse London caught before everything went dark, he'd chosen well. Big, empty conference room. Nice long table. A bank of computers and monitors on the far wall. Lots of chairs were scattered around a conference table. Heston kicked a couple of those chairs out of his way and sat her on the edge of the table. Her greedy hands went to his belt and zipper. He pulled her shirt over her head and tossed it away. His shirt went next. She had no idea where her bra went, because all of a sudden, her breasts were in Heston's warm palms. Both of them. She couldn't breathe. His hands were big and callused and rough, and his thumbs were working magic on her aching nipples.

She tipped her head back, remembering the days and nights they'd spent worshipping each other's bodies. Soaking each other in. Adoring the way they'd fit together. Playing. Damn it, she hadn't played once in all the years they'd been separated. She needed this. Wanted this man with a passion that was tearing her apart. "Marry me," she commanded.

Heston shook his head, as he inhaled her nipple into his mouth and suckled. A shock of awareness slammed straight to her core. Instead of arguing, London gave into her body's response. Her eyes rolled back at the suction of his wet mouth on her. At the thrill of his teeth scraping over her begging nipple.

A fierce flood let loose between her legs.

Releasing her nipple with a sloppy 'pop,' Heston took a step back and tore her jeans down her legs. He needed to take his clothes off, too. And be quick about it! But he didn't. Her naked, him still dressed. So damned naughty. Downright dirty. Shivers raced up her spine at the game she was caught in. She was the bad girl. He was the man in charge of bad girls. Tingles raced up her spine at what that might mean for her.

Discipline.

Bring it on.

He attacked her breast again. Oh, that mouth. That hot, slick mouth of his felt so, so good. She could've sat there all day letting him suckle and nibble her boobs, squeeze and lavish those girls. Until his tongue migrated up between her breasts to her neck. To her mouth. The moment his teeth grazed her bottom lip she opened for him. His hands went firmly to her neck. Her hands went to the sides of his head. He tilted her head sideways. Their teeth clashed. Their tongues tangled and tangoed. His breath became the only air she needed.

A steady, primal beat began low in her gut, in her womb. Her blood was on fire, drumming a rhythm through her veins as old as time. A beat her body remembered. The sensual magic it had needed for so long. Like a fine line of det cord, magic flashed bright and hot, sizzling between her core and his mouth and…

"Oh, Heston. Oh, man, Hes… Hes…" She writhed into his touch. Into his mouth. Against the manly palm pressed firmly over her mound. Against the strong, thick fingers curled inside her trembling body. Plucking at the erogenous flesh deep within. First one finger, then two, then… "Heston. There, yes. There. Right there!"

Her words rolled off her tongue as if she were being tortured. By love. By the glorious consummation of two stubborn, hard-headed souls finally mashed back together. By the conflagration caused by his busy fingers inside her body. By finally understanding how much love hurt, but only because she'd finally given her heart away. All of it. Completely. Like she should've done years ago. To Heston. Without regret or ego.

In the blessed heat of this reunion, this once-in-a-lifetime second chance, she mentally tore it out of her chest and handed it to him. Living without Heston Contreras in her life was the greater loss. She knew now that he'd always owned her heart. He was right. She had run from him, from this. But no matter how far she'd run, she'd still loved him, and from this day forward, he owned her. Like she would soon own him.

But he needed to lose those clothes. She was hot and sweaty and nearly naked. He was still completely dressed. She'd only gotten his belt loosened. His zipper wasn't even down the tiniest bit.

As if he'd read her mind, Heston's slick lips moved up to her neck and he distracted her once more. He sucked a mouthful of her skin into the warm, wet depths of his mouth, then pressed his jaw together and bit. No bloodletting, just a possessive, claiming bite on her neck that she hoped left a mark to last forever.

"Do it again," London commanded, her arms circling his neck again, and her voice husky. Her entire body quivered with aftershocks from the magnificent orgasm he'd given her.

"Oh, baby, I've missed this. I've missed us," he breathed, his mouth barely open, still hot and slick on her neck. "I can feel every one of those after-orgasm quivers. I'm here, baby. I've got you. Let yourself go. Lean back and feel."

"But you're still d-d-dressed," she managed to stutter before tremors lifted up her back at the heat pouring out of Heston's mouth. He'd always been the one for her. She needed him to understand that. She'd only left him to protect her independence. Which now seemed a woefully pathetic reason.

"Marry me," she ordered again, her pupils flaring to catch the faint, blinking light from the far wall of monitors and big screens and—stuff.

Heston pressed his sweaty forehead to hers. Man, they were both shaking. London inhaled the spicy, musky aroma pouring off the warm, slick body holding her. Then inhaled again. Heston. Old Spice aftershave. Maybe Old Spice deodorant. Manly sweat. Combined, they were her favorite scent and the most delicious flavors in the world. She licked a sloppy line up his neck to his jaw, right under his ear, and savored the taste. Didn't matter what he'd splashed on. She knew the scent of this man's skin and his breath. With just one sniff, one lick, she could pick him out of a line-up of a million guys and never be wrong.

He growled into her hair, "I'm not telling you no, baby, but first, we need to talk."

"Now?" she asked like a simpleton, her fingers still threaded into his hair. "Here? But you haven't even undressed yet, and you didn't—"

"I'm fine. Honest, babe." His hands still cupped her bare backside, but she was the only one who was naked. Well, nearly naked. Her boots were the only reason she hadn't completely lost her pants and panties, but Heston hadn't undressed at all. Only his belt was loose on his hips, and she'd done that. Something was wrong.

"This was about you, not me," he continued. "My place, babe. Let's get dressed. We can grab breakfast on the way." Tugging her right hand away from his head, Heston folded her bra and shirt inside her curled fingers. "Let's get you ready to go."

Was he dismissing her? Sure felt like it.

London's heart still pounded in her head from the first orgasm she'd had in years. Her blood was boiling and bubbling in her veins. Her brain was slow, foggy with afterglow. Breathing hard to get her emotions back on track, she fumbled her arms and shoulders into the shirt Heston held for her. Her bra went into her pocket. He helped her off the table. The instant London's feet were back on the floor, she stooped and hurriedly pulled up her panties and pants. Suddenly, everything they'd just done felt awkward and wrong, like she'd wanted all of him, but he'd only wanted a piece of her. What now? She had no idea.

Chapter Twenty-One

This wild, impulsive, audacious, headstrong woman was *it* for Heston. London had been *it* since they'd met in college, and yet he'd just mugged her in an empty conference room like a horny inexperienced teenager. Once again, she'd shaken his world. Uprooted the damned thing. Shook it like a dog shaking a rug, then threw it down between them. A challenge: *Where do we go from here?*

To bed. His bed. Not at the walnut conference table that would be damned hard to sit at during upcoming meetings. Not that there weren't other conference rooms at TEAM HQ. But how could he sit here and pay attention while remembering how she'd tasted on that table? How she'd panted into his mouth when she'd come? How much he loved her?

The ride to his place was short and sweet. Unfortunately, it was too quiet and he understood. London thought she was getting her way, and she had, up to a point. But there was so much more going on between them than just what happened after that foolish fight in Killeen. She didn't need to apologize. Not anymore. Their problem now was that he wanted forever, but, at the same time, he refused to stand in her way. She had so much potential and he didn't want to be the past mistake holding her back. She was made to fly. She could and should leave him behind. A woman with her uncanny investigative talent should never settle for less. For him.

Heston stopped at a local bakery on the way. The tiny shop was owned by Charlee O'Donnell, the blonde, amber-eyed woman Asher'd had his eye on for months. Up to now, Asher turned into a tongue-tied moron whenever she brought cinnamon rolls and fudge brownies to TEAM HQ. Which was at least twice a week. The idiot had better make a move on her before someone else did.

Whatever. Heston didn't have enough brain bytes to solve Asher's relationship problems tonight. He purchased a dozen donuts, then hustled London to his place. While she grabbed the treats from the backseat, Heston climbed out of his black Challenger, ran around it in time to open her door, then headed up the walk and inside. The irony that he drove the same type of car as Tucker Chase didn't escape him. At least his wasn't a flashy red neon sign.

"Nice place, Agent Contreras," London said quietly after he'd unlocked the deadbolt on his front door and gestured her inside.

At that Agent Contreras comment, Heston had a feeling he'd missed something. He re-engaged the deadbolt, took the box of donuts from London, dropped them on his kitchen counter for later, and started a pot of coffee brewing.

His place had been a garage back in the 1950s. Its inside walls sported raw, unpainted brick on both levels, a concrete floor at ground level and a massive loft that overlooked most of the lower floor. The common area, kitchen, full bathroom, and his office were tucked under a wide staircase that led to the loft. Besides his bedroom, upstairs housed a furnished guestroom and a smaller room full of storage.

He'd bought the garage during his one-and-only house-hunting trip to Virginia, and he'd been remodeling it ever since. There was still plenty to be done, inside and out. Funny how he'd always pictured London there, had even included certain items in his renovation plans—just for her—just in case. And now, there she was.

"I should've asked earlier," he said, peering around the kitchen door jamb. "I'm making coffee, but I've also got beer, wine, or whiskey, if you'd rather something stronger."

"Coffee's fine," she replied from where she stood gazing up at the framed portrait on the mantle. "Is this picture recent?"

"Yes, taken last year. That's Mama and Dad in the middle, as you know. Good photo, huh?"

"Roberto's still not married?"

Heston shrugged. "He's too busy touring the world. Last I heard, he was in Manchuria, headed for India."

"What's he do?"

That was a tough question. "Mama says he hasn't found himself yet. Guess he's still looking."

"Hmm…" There was something odd in London's tone, as if she were being extra-polite. Extra nice. "You look like your dad."

Heston let that observation slide. Carter Contreras might look like a nice guy in the photo, but he was and always would be a badassed Marine. Gruff. Rude. Sharp-tongued when dressing down a kid who spilled milk at the dinner table. Growing up, he'd been unreasonably tough on his boys, but never Belinda. He'd spoiled her, which had always been a sore spot between Carter and Bellisa, Heston's mother. His Mama.

"Where were you when it was taken?"

"Afghanistan. Alex sent Mark, Harley, and me to track down a friend of his, to bring him and his family to America."

"And did you?" Again, her tone sounded remote, like she was holding back. Was she having second thoughts about her marriage proposal?

"Mostly," Heston answered, remembering locating the wizened, little man, Arzad and his worried wife, Gulnar, in their tiny mud-brick home. How small they'd looked inside the giant C-130 that had flown them to Eglin Air Force Base in Florida. Worse, how Gulnar had cried for their only granddaughter when the plane lifted off, and left the dust and stink of Afghanistan behind. Najela was still living somewhere near the abandoned American Air Base with her aid-worker husband, Benny. With their three small daughters. In abject poverty, like most of the country, now that the Taliban was on the move again.

'I need to get them out,' he thought to himself. *'Their country's turning back into the shithole it was before. That's my next mission. God, I hope they're still alive.'*

"Hey, where'd you go?" London asked, her brows narrowed in that adorably inquisitive frown he adored.

Heston shook off the worry for the young woman a world away and looked into the turquoise eyes blinking at him now. "Just thinking. Coffee should be ready."

"Stay here. I'll get it." London was back in seconds with two mugs of steaming brew. "You still drink yours black, right?" she asked, one cup extended toward him.

Heston took the mug and set it on the side table. "I do, thanks. But first, conversation."

She wiggled her backside into the corner of the couch opposite from him, put one knee between them, and balanced her mug on that knee. Like a barrier. "So talk."

He pursed his lips, not sure where to start. The knee between them looked like a castle wall with a steamy cup of ammunition between them. Whether she knew it or not, she'd created a boundary he knew he should respect, not breach.

But it was now or never. "I can't survive another break-up," he said quietly. "If you need to leave me behind so you can fly, London, go. Please, just go. I won't hold you back. I'm proud of you, and I'll support you every way I can, even if it means letting you go. I understand the drive that propels you to serve your country, I do, and I don't blame you. I feel the same call. It's a powerful force that doesn't allow for much compromise, does it? When called to action, we're the ones who jump first, ask questions later. While others run from it, we run into trouble. We never give up on our dreams, which is precisely what you did the night you left me. You followed your dream. You jumped at your chance to serve. I just—"

"For your information, I left because you attacked me and my dreams," she said firmly. "Not because I no longer loved you."

He nodded. "Copy that. I did attack your dreams. I minimized you as an individual and as a woman, and I'm damned sorry." Heston swallowed hard. "I'm not the modern thinker you are. I'm still the guy from the stone age who wants to be the only man in your life. The one who runs to protect you."

"You *are* the only man in my life."

Heston noticed she didn't admit she might never need his protection. Looking down at his boots, he shook his head. He couldn't change who he was. The drive to protect London was fiercely strong, maybe too strong for a modern-day relationship to work. He refused to be less than who he was. And yes, his inner caveman didn't have a submissive bone in its body. Or in its pants. "I'm not the only strong one in your life, London. You don't need me for that. You're strong enough all by yourself. I see that now. And because I do, I love you enough to finally let you go. If that's what you want." Man, he hoped it wasn't, but she needed to know she had choices. That he wouldn't stand in her way.

"Not good enough, Contreras," she bit out, moving her mug from her knee to the coffee table with a sloshy thump. "Is that why you didn't go all the way with me back there? Is that why you stayed dressed while it was okay to get me naked and finger me? Why you wouldn't let me love you back?"

"No," he exclaimed, shocked she'd even think that. "Hell, no. But it's been a long time, and I couldn't resist, and I—"

"And once again, you thought you knew better than me, right?" London said that with a cocky shoulder swagger that sent out a loud and clear, *'Danger, Will Robinson!'*

He dragged a hand over his head. "I can't win, can I? I didn't have a condom, and I didn't allow myself to fuck you because I wanted to make love with you, London. Make love, understand? I wanted to make love to the only woman I've ever loved, not screw you on a hard table like a one-and-done. Would it have been fun? Maybe. But the first time I sink into your beautiful body again, I want you to be comfortable and somewhere safe and—"

London jumped to her feet, huffing through her nostrils like a bull in a china shop. "That's not love, Hes. That's chicken shit and you know it."

He'd screwed this up and now she was pissed.

"What's so wrong about both of us being strong, huh? Can't you handle me being a smart, capable woman and making my own decisions? Is that it? Does one of us have to be weak before this thing between us works?"

Lifting off the couch, he took a strong step into her. "Is that what you want, London? Is that what'll work for you, us being an even match?"

Her brows slammed together. "There's nothing even about us, Hes. Look at you." She waved her hand, flipping all five fingers at him. "You're sexy and handsome as sin, and you're stronger than me. Hell, you're stronger than most guys I know. You're Superman to my Lois Lane, only my Lois Lane is more like—"

"Wonder Woman," he breathed, finally understanding the difference between them through her eyes. London wanted strong because she was strong. Not naïve. Not inexperienced. She'd learned her lessons the hard way, by failing and getting up again, by fighting for the right to be what and who she already was. Strong and perfect.

"No, I was going to say like wimpy What's-Her-Name in that *"Avengers"* movie," she snapped.

"You mean Scarlett Johansson? But you're precisely like her."

London dismissed his comment with another dismissive wave of her hand. "Not her. The other one, Tony Stark's wife. That blonde. Wait a minute." Her head jutted back a notch on her spine. "You think I'm like Scarlett?"

Finally, she was getting it. "I sure do. Look at you. You're beautiful and you're stronger than most men I know. You know what you want, and you go after your dreams. Only…" He took another step toward London. "You're hotter and smarter than Scarlett."

She shook her head, sending those long turquoise bangs tumbling into her eyes. "Really? Me? I guess I am kind of strong. I do work out, and I like a good run every morning. But I'm no good at hand-to-hand fighting." She tapped the side of her head. "Two strikes, remember? I'm not even up for even matches. I'll always lose."

Heston took another step into her. This conversation was all over the place, and he wasn't sure she was hearing what he'd meant at all. His voice sounded weak and whiney, and he wasn't portraying himself as the strong personality he truly was. How could he turn this around? He needed to understand her better. Might as well jump into the fire.

"Are you planning on leaving the first time we disagree, argue, or fight?"

She cocked her head, her eyes bright and as belligerent as ever. "No, Hes. I'd really like to stay if you'll let me. We've got things to figure out, I get that. And yeah, I realize we'll still argue. That's what people who love each other do. We've both changed these past few years. I've made plenty of mistakes, starting with the night I took off and left you." She swiped a hand over her head, tossing those jewel-toned locks away and making sure they'd fall back over her eyes as she did. "But I'm here now, and you're here, and I don't like it when you decide who gets to keep their clothes on and… and I never stopped loving you, damn it."

Her bottom lip trembled.

Heston took that final step, took a firm hold of her hips and, hopefully, the situation. "There hasn't been anyone since you. Promise. We were always good together."

London draped her hands over his shoulders and ran her fingers up the back of his neck into his hair with a sultry, "Aww."

He closed his eyes, time-warping back to the days when one touch of her hand was all it took to get him hard.

"And we can be better, Hes. Both of us, individually *and* as a team. A team of two. Our team."

He liked the way that sounded. "Stay?" he asked, so damned smitten with this amazing woman that he felt like a fool. A fool in love with a woman with wings. Wings he meant to protect and guard the rest of his life. If she wanted to fly, by hell, he'd make sure she could soar as high and go as far as she wanted.

Her lips slammed together in a pout. "Of course, I'll stay. Think you can get me an interview with that Mark Houston fellow?"

Heston shook his head, charmed to his socks. "Baby, I'll get you anything your heart desires. Mark will be thrilled to talk with you."

With that, negotiations were over. He grabbed her waist and hoisted her over his shoulder. "This is me being a caveman," he told her, in case she had other plans. "Want me to stop?"

"No! Don't ever!" she squealed even as she ran her hands over his ass and down his thighs. "Is this where you give me a tour of the house?"

He landed a playful smack on her rump. "No, baby, this is me dragging you off to my cave and thumping my chest all night long while I fuck your brains out."

"Aww. You're such a romantic. But I wanted to—"

He landed another sharper smack on the gorgeous ass that would soon be bare, blushing red, overheated, and—his. "You'll want what I give you, brat, and I'm going to give you exactly what you need. What you've been asking for." *What I was once too dumb to see that you needed.*

"A spanking?" she teased, wiggling that warm ass under his palm.

"I was thinking a nice, hot bath." This time he smoothed a gentler hand over her backside while he climbed the open staircase to the loft.

She froze. "Seriously? A bath? What? Do I stink?"

He was on the top step by then, outside the master bath off his bedroom. "No, never. We'll skip it if you don't want to." She'd want to. He knew that for sure. He tipped her off his shoulder onto her feet and told her, "Close your eyes."

Once she did, he opened the bathroom door, turned her around to face the delicately fashioned surprise, and whispered, "Welcome home, London."

When she opened her eyes, her mouth fell open, as she took in the red brick walls across from the door, their reflections in the mirror over the sink, and the bright white ceiling overhead. He flipped the switch beside the door to heat the dark gray slate under her feet. For once, Heston kept his mouth shut and let her process his gift.

London entered the room, her bare feet on the slate a mere whisper, her eyes wide. He'd bought the antique, hammered-copper tub on a whim after he'd remodeled the loft. Two giant Boston ferns sitting in hard-as-hell-to-find wrought-iron plant stands, graced one end of the free-standing tub. London used to love ferns. Another hung from the ceiling like a leafy piñata. He flicked the switch on the wall behind him, and the fairy lights he'd strung around the floor-to-ceiling window became flickering fireflies in the dark room.

Shelves of all the scented candles, soaps, bath bombs, and lotions she used to love lined the wall at opposite end. Fluffy white towels waited on warming racks. London might think she was badasssed, that she had to be, to compete like a man in this dog-eat-dog world. But she was also a girly-girl who loved to relax in a steaming tub of bubbles, with a glass of wine at the end of a hard day. In here, she'd be safe to be herself. The ugly world wasn't welcome.

"It's a really big tub," she said quietly.

He held his breath, afraid he'd done it again. Overwhelmed her with his idea of what she liked, instead of first understanding what she thought was important. Maybe this wasn't such a grand surprise after all.

London was studying her reflection in the beveled mirror over the double sink. One hand went to her cheek, the fingers on her other hand went to her lips. She looked shocked standing there, as if she were seeing herself for the first time. Maybe she was.

Heston backed out of the door and let her have whatever time she needed to decompress. Damn. He'd done exactly what she'd told him not to do. Thought he knew better. Had to be the hero. Never earnestly listened to understand what she tried so hard to tell him.

He was still as dumb as a box of rocks.

"Hes," she said, stopping him before he moved too far away. "Join me?"

His heart skipped a beat. "Me? Yeah, sure. If that's what you want."

"I've only ever wanted you." She turned her back to the sink, and in one fell swoop, ripped her t-shirt over her head. "I want you. In that tub. With me. Now. Crank up the water. I like those twinkly lights, but leave the others off. Let's party like we used to. Remember?"

"Yes, ma'am." Heston couldn't help the grin that cracked his face. Party like they used to? That, he could do.

Chapter Twenty-Two

London couldn't wait for Heston to undress, so she did it for him. Just unzipped his pants and stripped him out of his jeans while he tried to toe out of his boots without falling. His shirt went flying, then, jumping from one foot to the other, she fumbled out of her pants. He did the honors of peeling her panties off. At last, they were who they'd been before this whole mess started. Just Heston. Just London. Nothing in between.

Her heart pounded when his hooded gaze flashed over her nakedness with lust. Everywhere he looked, each time he licked his lips, flames ignited in her belly. This was what she'd wanted from him in that dark conference room. Them. Finally together in heat and passion. An answer to her marriage proposal would've been good, too.

His brow lifted, giving him a devil-may-care vibe. "Birth control?"

"Oh, yeah. Almost forgot," she breathed, wishing she'd been as responsible as him. "Implant. Nexplanon."

"How long ago?"

"Umm, four, no four and a half, maybe…" She had to think when she'd gotten the tiny implant. The tiny get-it-and-forget-it choice of birth control was only good for five years. "Damn. Nearly five years ago, Hes."

"Should still be good. I get tested every year, and you already know I haven't been with anyone else since… then."

"But what if—?"

"We get pregnant?"

Oh, she loved the way he said '*We.*' Not just '*you.*'

"Then we'll have a blonde baby girl who'll look just like you running around this place."

"Or a gorgeous baby boy with big brown eyes and shiny black hair."

That was all it took, him talking about making babies. Quivering with anticipation, London pounced, her slight weight pushing him against the wall, her fingers dancing over his body like a blind person's fingertips fluttered over Braille. This was her way of remembering the rigid cords in his neck, the hard tension of his pecs when he flexed, the furrowed musculature of her man on her way down his stomach to—

Ah. There. That's what I want.

He groaned. But once her nimble fingers curled around his cock, once she had a good firm hold, he was hers and she knew it. The big, beautiful length of him thickened in her hand while she feasted on his mouth. Kissing. Tasting. Licking his lips and biting his tongue—until he took charge, picked her up and stepped into the tub with her. By then every part of him was steel. London kept working him. Pumping. Sliding her curled fingers up. Gliding them back down. Licking her lips and wondering if—

"Woman, you keep doing that, and I'll be done before we get started." Leaning to one side, he flicked the faucet on, then adjusted the showerheads that ran the length of the tub, converting their bath into a misty rainforest pool.

"Would it be so bad?" she asked breathlessly, water running down her face and into her eyes. She'd done that to him. Made him weak. Made him needy. She'd never thought herself powerful before, but now she realized she was. The femininity within her body and soul had bent this man to her will. Made him tremble. Made him bossy. Made him want her enough to give her what she needed.

"As long as I've waited for you, yes, damn it. I'm barely holding on as it is. Now bend over and show me that gorgeous ass. Hands on the edge of the tub, babe. Look outside while I take care of business. Hang on."

"Ooo, businessman, huh?" London wiggled her backside, teasing even as she spun around and her palms hit the window beside the tub. Not looking out. Not caring who might be looking in. Finally sure of what she'd wanted during her years of missing Heston.

He dropped to his knees behind her, his hands smoothing down the sides of her ribs to her hips. "Spread 'em, babe," he ordered huskily, his fingertips dancing over her bare ass while his tongue slipped down her spine. Then lower. Lower…

Quick as a wink, she complied. He'd always loved looking at her, touching her secret places. Testing her limits, even play spanking her sometimes. The fever in her blood spiked at the possibility this might be one of those times.

"Farther," he ordered, landing a gentle slap to her butt. "Wider."

Like a hungry hooker in a back alley, she shifted her feet apart until she was nearly doing the splits. Her heart pounded a staccato salsa in her chest, knowing the view she was giving him. Her right foot pressed over the drain while the other argued with the slippery back of hammered copper over where the best footing was. The slippery slope won. Her foot ended up braced at the edge of the tub, giving Heston more to see and better access.

As if he agreed, he pressed both thumbs deep between her cheeks and spread her apart. London's breath caught when his hot breath fell on that tender stretch of feverish skin. Her toes curled. Her body clenched in eager anticipation. The tantalizing scrub of his scruff over her tenderest flesh was enough to send her flying all by itself. She'd never had whisker burns *there* before. Part pain. Part pleasure. *Ahhh.*

Warm wet rain trickled into her hair and eyes. Into her panting mouth. Down her back. Over her bare backside and—there—where his tongue teased and demanded. Fire scorched everywhere his tongue touched. London's libido sprang to life. She closed her eyes, lost in the paradise she'd nearly given away. Why? To prove what? That she was every bit as strong and as smart as a man? She no longer cared what the world of men wanted from her or thought of her. The only one she cared about was Heston. He mattered. No one else.

"Hang on," he ordered, his fingernails digging into her flesh, reminding her who was boss. That he owned her. He'd better be careful. Between the heat of his breath and the scintillating drag of his whiskers against her slick skin, as well as the feral, needy mewls coming out of her throat, he might own her sooner than she expected. London was a hot, jumbled mess of hormones, fire, lust, and desire. Her blood was hot, so hot. She was already dancing on her toes, ready to come. Needing the building orgasm to explode and blow her world apart.

Without asking, his tongue speared into her core and… and…

Those lovely fairy lights twinkled brighter and faster. Or maybe it was her. Maybe she was the one twinkling. But when he lit that greedy string of det cord between his mouth and her core, she was a jittery breath away from coming all over him.

Thrusting her backside against his face, London growled. "Heston… Hes… Hes-s-s-s… M-more."

He pinched her butt cheek and feasted where no man had feasted before. Adding his fingers to the mix, his voice turned growly deep. "Not yet," he ordered. Him stroking the erogenous tripwire just inside her body vibrated her heartstrings. He knew how to pluck those intimate chords until she was wound tight. Tighter. Until…

"Ahh," she ground out, her body pulsating under his skillful touch, tensed for the pleasure winding up from her toes.

"Hands flat against the window, babe."

She hadn't realized her fingers were in her hair or that she'd jutted her breasts forward as far as she had. "Please, Hes. Harder. I need this. So do you."

"You ready?" he rasped, his voice moist and hot in her ear as he joined her in the tub and braced one foot against the drain.

Her foot slid out from under his, then against his, using him for support. "Yes. Yes, yes, yes. Hes, hurry, I'm… I'm…"

"Don't you dare come. Get those hands back on the glass. Look at yourself in the window. You think someone's outside watching? If they are, they can see every inch of your naked ass and how sexy you look. How beautiful your tits are. They'll get to watch you come undone, babe. Trust me, you never looked hotter. Great tits. Best ass in the world. Look at you. Look at me!"

She couldn't comply fast enough. Just spread her fingers wide apart on the steamy windowpane, as far as they could reach, until her wet skin squeaked against smooth, cool glass. One quick right-handed action wiped a circle of condensation from the glass. And—there she was. Her turquoise green eyes wanton and wide. Her lips swollen, wet, and red. Her breasts were heavy, her nipples diamond hard and taut. She'd become every bit a sultry, shameless siren from the depths of the wildest seas.

And there stood Heston, tall and broad behind her. His eyes were bright and eager. His hair had flopped into his eyes, and those pits of steamy black were so damned hot. Every bit of him screamed warrior. Protector. *Mine!*

"I s-s-see you," she stuttered, her pulse pounding.

"I see you too, babe," he growled, his fingertips dug into her hips, his thumbs pressed into the small of her back. "Every last piece of you. You're so damned beautiful, and you're mine. All mine." He delivered that last declaration with a stinging smack to her ass.

Felt so, so good. Like a lovesick sex-kitten, she mewed, "It's raining, Hes."

A handsome smile covered his face. "You noticed? Good. Now count to ten like you used to."

She nodded, keeping eye contact. With every tortured breath, her breasts heaved as if they wanted him looking at them. Just them. Naughty, naked girls.

"The rain's running down your back and between your butt cheeks," he told her, his gaze zeroed on her ass.

"I'm so wet. For you, Hes. Only ever for you." He needed to know that.

"Fuck, yes, you're dripping." With that heady innuendo, Heston jacked forward and pushed that magnificent spike of his into her slippery folds. Not teasing. Not hinting. Just a wicked thrust that came with throbbing veins and power.

The impact forced a purr from her throat. Maybe even from her vagina.

"One," she whispered as he withdrew with aching slowness. Missing the heat of him, she arched farther back to keep him in place. Wanting more of him. Daring him to shove that thick, hard weapon back into her greedy sheath where it belonged.

"You like this," his deep baritone rumbled.

"I do."

"Eyes on me, babe," he ordered as he—oomph!— slammed in deep again.

A breathy, "Two," sighed out of her. London blinked through the raindrops running over her face, then swiped the window clean again, needing to watch the fierce expressions on his face as she counted. His eyes had turned dark and hungry. He took sex seriously, like he was on a mission. His muscular, hair-roughened thighs bunched against her hamstrings. His thumbnails dug deeper. The muscles in his back coiled and—

"Three," she wheezed, trying to hold back. Needing to come, but not without Heston.

"Don't you dare," he growled, the stiff, crisp hairs on the sides of his knees abrading the insides of her thighs.

"Then hurry."

He hurried. *Oomph.* "God, that feels so good."

Another hearty slap stung her ass. "I mean… f-f-four!"

He pounded into her again.

"Five!"

Then a slippery quick, "Six!"

A smoking hot, "Seven!"

Her feverish body matched the brutal pace he set. She fell in love with the sounds of his muscles smacking against her flesh.

"You'd like a good spanking, wouldn't you? You like it when I'm in charge." He shoved in deeper, grinding into her.

She stared him down in the window. London was on her toes by then, braced for that quintessential more. "Yes, Heston. I love you like this. And a good spanking… Hmmm." The naughty idea made her wiggle. "Yeah. I'd like that. With you."

No sooner whispered, when a solid slap landed on her buttocks and, "Eight!" screamed out of her.

Without pulling all the way out, he slammed deeper and ordered, "Tell me again."

"I'd love it. I love you. Anything you do is okay with me. Nine!"

Heston buried his forehead between her shoulder blades and rasped, "What comes next, baby girl? Tell me. Say what comes next or I'll blister your ass."

"M-m-me," she squealed, pushing backward into his pelvis, needing him inside so badly that tears filled her eyes. She'd never been anyone else's baby girl before. Hell, she'd never been anyone else's anything. Had never been disciplined or spanked. No one in her life had ever loved her enough to draw a hard line.

But the thought of Heston bending her over his knee and delivering a no-kidding spanking sounded incredibly naughty. Her nipples were so hard, they ached. Her ass begged for another gentle smack—just because Heston would be the one delivering it.

"What number?" he snapped. Grunting like the powerful beast he was, Heston bucked one last, bone-grinding time and—

"Ten!" she snapped back at him. Just as he—*Oh, God, oh, God*—slammed home. Deeper in. Further. All the way. In so deep it burned. His pubic bone hit her pelvic cradle. The stimulation of those rough, coarse hairs nesting his cock was too much. She was almost there. Almost…

Until she slowed her breathing, wanting to last longer than Heston. The sight of his reflection in the window was too precious to miss, this memory a once-in-a-lifetime keeper. Through love-struck eyes, London watched their joined reflection. Heston lifted his handsome face to the rain, his eyes closed with the intensity of his release. His darker, masculine hands clenched her pale, white hips. She watched him bite his bottom lip, how he smiled as he ground his body against her.

London drew in a breath. There he was, her ardent, ferocious lover. Her man. Her dearest companion. Her best friend and the only man in the world she would ever love. The big, brave man who adored her in return. He was gloriously beautiful. Carved out of caramel granite. Perfection in every way. Drenched and dangerous. Vehemently in love with her. A beast undone. Her beast. Her utterly gorgeous, handsome beast.

London's heart stuttered at the beauty framed in the window. Him behind her, his magnificent male body planted deep into her much smaller body. Protective—always. Strong and devoted—forever. She'd hurt him, yet here he was, worshipping her. Loving her. Forgiving her and giving his everything to her, his heart, his body, and his soul.

The sight of Heston finishing first, pushed London over the edge. He hadn't done that in all their times together. Had to be the feminine power she held over him tonight. Greedy flames of pleasure burst through her body, scalding her at the same time with his seed and promise and—Heston.

London let go. She planted her soles on the bottom of the tub, arched backward, and let her head fall on his shoulder. His hands tightened into manacles on her hips. His thumbnails were tiny, biting cuffs, cutting crescents into the pillowy tops of her backside. She knew the truth now. He had always loved her. Always believed in her. He'd never let her fall.

The grandest orgasm ripped through her. Brilliantly hot, like a comet, its tail whipped sizzling aftershocks through her core, lighting up every nerve and tiny receptor, clenching every strand of muscle along its path. Laser bright starlight shot from her fingertips. All because he'd reached the pinnacle before her. There was no struggle or contest between them. He'd made her whole again, as he'd poured himself into her emptiness.

London let the truth pour into her. She was enough by herself, but she was a thousand times better with Heston.

Powerful aftershocks rippled through her body, then dissolved into wicked, steamy fragments. Sobs caught in her throat. It was hard to breathe. Hard to do anything but absorb the brilliant liquid golds, bright shiny silvers, red throbbing hearts, and sparkling white ribbons pouring down on her. This wasn't rain. This was heaven. How did one human vessel hold so much heaven?

A fragment of scripture flashed in the dark like an answer to her question. *No greater gift…*

It caught her unprepared. Unaware. But it was true, wasn't it? No man fought harder than a man for his woman, than a husband for his wife and child. Even when they'd been apart, Heston Contreras had never stopped fighting to keep her and her country safe. He would die for her, simply because that was who he was. He loved her. No greater gift, indeed. The greatest gift a man and woman could give the other. Living and dying for each other. For better or for worse…

"I think we're already married, Hes," she whimpered, out of breath and her legs weak, but her vision finally clear. "I think I just did it to us, married us. We did it together, I mean. Together." She was babbling, and had no idea if what was in her heart could even be translated into words. Only knew that her place had always been at Heston's side, and today, she'd been given another chance to love him.

He stood at her back, panting like a beast who'd just run—and won—the race of his life. His large body curled protectively over her smaller one. One muscled forearm rested against the sparkling windowpane, the other around her belly. Holding her steady, keeping her shaky legs from collapsing. "Why do you say that?"

"Because," breathed out of her. "This has to be what heaven feels like. You and me. Where we are right now. Here. Just us and… and I… I love you so much. Never stopped, not even when I was angry with you. There hasn't been anyone else. There never will be."

Like the knight in shining armor Heston was and always would be, he lifted her still quivering body into his arms and climbed out of the tub. Tucking her wet head under his chin, he whispered, "I've always loved you, London. You've been it for me since that first day in Econ 101."

She closed her eyes, not remembering Econ 101, only the handsome man who'd taken the seat next to her. "It stopped raining,"

"Because I turned the faucet off," Heston explained as he tossed her a warm fluffy towel. Once they were dry enough, he carried her into his bedroom, tossed the blankets on his bed aside with one hand, and then laid her down.

London looked up at him, her body weak and limp, her bones fluid, and her heart full. There were no words.

He dropped to the floor at her side. "Now about that marriage proposal."

She knew what he needed to hear. "I'm sorry. I should've let you do it, I know it now. You're the man. Your culture's big on tradition, and it's traditional for the man to—"

His index finger landed on her lips. "Shush, babe. Listen a second. Why do you think I'm kneeling?"

"Umm, because that's the traditional pose for a guy who's about to… propose? Which you should. I mean, if you want to. I mean—"

He tugged her hand to his mouth and pressed a warm, wet kiss in the center of her palm. "It's also a damned good position for a man to tell the woman he adores that, yes, babe, I accept *your* proposal. I'll marry you." His eyebrows lifted as if he was waiting on her reaction.

She rocketed up onto her elbows. "Really, Hes? You don't mind that I proposed?"

"You. Me. What's the difference? As long as we're together, I don't think anything else matters. So where's my ring?" There went those brows again.

Her jaw dropped. "I don't have a ring. I didn't think. Oh, no! I should've planned better, but—"

Leaning to one side, he pulled the nightstand drawer open and drawled, "This little thing's been lying around a few years, but I think it'll fit." Turning back, Heston took her left hand and slid a brilliant, blue-topaz stone onto her ring finger. Enhanced by a string of white diamonds on the rose-gold band, the oval stone sparkled with fire.

"Ohmygod, ohmygod, ohmygod!" she squealed. It was the most beautiful thing she'd ever seen. "How long have you had this? When did you get it? For me?" Her squeals turned into heartfelt sobs. "You've had this a long time, haven't you? Even when we... Before I..." The word got stuck in her throat. She couldn't say *'left.'* Just. Could. Not.

Pushing her gently to her back, Heston climbed on top of her. With his elbows on the mattress alongside her head and his knees between her legs, he threaded his fingers into her short hair and held onto her. He had her full attention.

All she could do was lick her lips and blink up at him like the fool she'd been. Her heart was breaking. She hadn't gotten him a ring. Hadn't gotten him anything. Had only caused him pain. He should hate her. But he didn't. The evidence was on her finger. He'd had this ring the night she'd left, she knew it. She didn't deserve it. She'd hurt him too much.

The dim lighting from downstairs illuminated his loft, making his already dark eyes seem black. Extra serious. He trailed a fingertip over her forehead, between her eyes, and down her nose. Cupping her jaw, he lowered her head and pressed his lips to the middle of her forehead. "I bought it the day I joined the Army. Remember the errand I ran after we visited your folks? That's where I went. The jewelry store texted me while we were at your parents' place, but I couldn't give it to you then. The mood was all wrong. You were upset that night, so I waited for another time. Just didn't think it'd take this long."

Oh, no. She squeezed her eyes shut. "The night they said those awful things?"

"The night you defended me, London. I was proud of you. You have so much on the ball. You're smart and beautiful, the perfect woman in so many ways, and the only one for me. You stood firm that night. Didn't let your dad bully you. Didn't take crap from your mom. I know they were just looking out for their only daughter. I'm sure they didn't mean what they said, but right away, you set them straight. You defended me. Then you walked away from the toxic home you grew up in, and you chose to stay with me."

"I was so angry with them. So disappointed." London bit her bottom lip.

Her father had called Heston a *'useless Hispanic'* that night. But Heston had no idea what hateful pejoratives her father used the next day when he'd called, trying to convince London to come home. To use her brain, for God's sake. To leave that lazy Latino behind, that she could do better. To pull her head out of her spoiled ass and grow up. That Heston was just another lazy *'beaner'* who'd never amount to anything. He'd even called Heston a *'muchacho'*, another derogatory slur that inferred Heston was just a *'boy'*. That he didn't deserve the respect a man extends to another. Yeah, *those words*.

London's neck muscles worked hard as she swallowed the pain her parents' words caused Heston. But what had she done then? In a fit of ego and stupid, stupid, stupidity, she'd done precisely what her parents had wanted her to do. She'd run off and left him. London wanted to bang her hard head into a harder wall. Instead, she told him, "I am so, so sorry for leaving you. I'll never hurt you again, Hes. I was so dumb. I thought I needed to prove something. All I did was prove I'm as bad as my parents."

"No, babe, you're not. You aren't anything like them. Trust me. I know." That warm finger pressed over her lips again, ending her rant. "How about we let the past stay in the past? We're here now, London. We're together and we're in a good place. You were brave and took a chance. I understand. You did what you had to do, and now you know. Let's focus on the positives we've learned from our time apart; the smart things we've done instead of the mistakes we've made. Hey, congratulations. We're engaged." His brows lifted like he was surprised.

"Even if we weren't, we'd still be in love," she whispered, trailing her fingers up the back of his head and into his soft, lush hair. "I promise, Heston Contreras, I will spend the rest of my life loving you. Now snuggle with me."

The warm smile on his face was exactly what London needed. He did as she asked. Stretched his long legs over her, then settled his handsome body close behind her. With his front to her back, he wrapped her inside his arms and whispered, "You've just made my mom very happy."

She wiggled her butt into his lap. "Because we're engaged?"

"Yes, babe. She thought I'd never settle down."

"It's been so long since I've talked to her. I'll call her tomorrow so we can start making plans."

His chest expanded with a deep sigh. "She missed you. I think she likes you better than me."

"No mom loves anyone better than her own son."

"Mama does. You were always special to her. She's proud of your accomplishments. I think because you've accomplished what she always wanted to do. It's your college graduation picture on her wall by the fireplace, not mine."

London squirmed around until she faced Heston. "Are you lying?"

"Promise. Mama likes you best. You'll see."

"But I hurt her when I left you. I know I did. I need to apologize, but what can I say?"

"Just show up, babe. I promise, all you have to do is show up and she'll take it from there. Oh, yeah, bring Kleenex because Mama's a crier."

London swiped a finger under her leakiest eye. "So am I."

The tenderest smile bracketed Heston's mouth. He leaned into her and kissed the tear away. "My dad's another story. But Mama? Yeah, bring Kleenex. Maybe a box of it, because she's going to cry all over you the second she sees you. If she scolds anyone, it'll be me for not telling her you're back."

"I don't understand why your mom's always been so nice to me."

Heston took her jaw in both hands and pressed a kiss to the end of her nose. "Because she loves you. Now go to sleep. Tomorrow's another day, and we'll be busy. You can call her then."

London did him one better. Got up in his grill and French-kissed the hell out of her man. "I love you, Hes," she declared, licking her lips when the steamy kiss ended.

He pulled her back under his arm. "I know, babe. Go to sleep."

"I am tired," she admitted.

Before long, Heston's breathing evened out. But try as she might, sleep wouldn't come for London. She lay there listening to his heartbeat, wishing she could go back in time and make better decisions that night. She'd hurt him more than she'd ever realized, and she'd hurt his beautiful mother, too. Regret was a sucker punch she hadn't seen coming. How could she ever make those wrongs right? What do you say to the woman whose son you nearly destroyed just because you were a selfish brat and acted out? London had no idea. She eased from under Heston's arm, so her tossing and turning wouldn't disturb him. He grumbled in his sleep but after the day they'd had, she knew he wasn't waking up.

The night dragged on, but no brilliant plan for forgiveness came to mind. Sleep eluded London at every turn. Insomnia and guilt nagged until—

"Enough," she told herself, somewhere between two and three in the morning. Quietly, she gathered her scattered clothes, washed up at his bathroom sink, and dressed for the day. She brushed her hair with his brush and used Heston's toothbrush because morning breath—*Ewwww*.

Maybe a good run would settle her brain. She tiptoed past him, pausing a moment to gaze down on him as he slept. Heston was the most beautiful man in the world. His olive-skinned face was boyishly slack with sleep, and his dark lashes laid like crescents on his cheeks. There was a fierce hardness about him that hadn't been there before. Which stood to reason. She'd changed during their time apart, too. In some ways, she was stronger and tougher. She knew how to draw a hard line when push came to shove. She knew how flawed the federal government was. But while she'd drifted from one federal job to another, Heston had gone to war. He'd seen horrible things, might've done a few horrible things, too. But he'd served his country instead of himself.

London leaned over and softly pressed her lips to his cheek. "You're all mine," she whispered, "and I'm going to molest the hell out of you when I get back. Sleep, Heston. I won't be gone long."

Wouldn't he be surprised when he woke up to coffee and breakfast?

Stealthily, she crept downstairs and quietly unlocked his front door. Once outside, she sucked in a bellyful of crisp, night air and took off running down the street. She hadn't kept track of how they'd gotten to his place. Just knew she needed the chilly wind in her face to clear her mind. She wasn't worried about Heston's dad, but for sure, she owed Bellisa an apology.

She didn't intend to go far. Had gone around the block he lived on when an idea struck. Why not stop at that cute little bread store and take Bellisa a box of sugary sweetness? What was the owner's name? Charlee O'Donnell? Sounded right. The store sat in the middle of the block. Maybe the next one over? Why not surprise Bellisa *and* Heston?

Intent on setting things right, London grinned as she ran. She couldn't wait to wake Heston. Maybe she'd jump his handsome bones before he even knew who was assaulting him. Maybe she'd wake him up with her tongue and her mouth. She grinned wider. He *was* the best ice cream cone she'd ever licked.

London was two doors north of the elongated, pink-and-white striped dome awning of that quaint little bakery when she spotted it. Great! The day was looking up.

Until two gnarly guys dressed in black suits stepped out of the alley.

She cut to her left, giving them the inside track, just to be courteous. Also to keep her distance. Women running solo had to keep their guard up.

Instead of stepping aside, the guys spread their feet and blocked her way forward.

"Hey, guys," she offered breathily. "Coming through. Either get out of my way or—"

Some moron grabbed her from behind and yelled, "I got her! Open the trunk!"

She squirmed to loosen his hold, the ass. Reared her head back to bash his nose. But he was bigger and the arm around her neck was tight. With a grunt, he lifted her off her feet.

She kicked and thrashed, fighting his stranglehold. Not giving up, damn it!

By then, his two buddies were at the car parked by the curb. The trunk was open.

"No!" she hissed, putting all the vehemence she could muster into escaping. She scratched. She kicked. She yelled. "I'm not going into that trunk! Help! Someone help me!"

The other creep ran to assist.

"No! No! You can't do this!" London screamed louder. But the streets were empty. This was her fault. She should've stayed in bed where she belonged. With Heston.

The guy behind her clapped a gloved hand over her mouth and jerked her head to the side.

She cocked her knee, intending a backward kick to his nuts.

A tiny sting hit the crook of her neck. With one shuddering breath, her world melted into murky darkness. They were bigger than her. She was too late to the fight. Too weak. There was no way she would win. She could barely keep her eyes open. Wasn't sure what was happening to her until her limp body crashed inside the trunk of that truck, car, whatever. Her cheek burned when it met the harsh, cheap interior carpet.

Everything went black. She couldn't see, couldn't tell which way was up. Didn't matter. She jerked her arm out from under her, then rolled to her side. Her poor head buzzed. She tried to focus, to make her eyes work. To remember. Not happening. Every self-defense move she'd learned vanished into the ether.

When a tiny yellow light flashed overhead, she came face to face with two blank eyes staring at her. *Oh, shit. The Irish sniper. Ryan Malloy.*

Chapter Twenty-Three

Heston woke up slowly, happily. At last, he knew what his life would be like today, tomorrow, and every morning after. The talk with London last night had been long overdue. He now understood why she'd left him. She'd turned her back on her parents when they'd denigrated him. In doing that, they'd questioned her moral compass, her sanity, and her beautiful brain. They'd treated her like a foolish, inexperienced child instead of the very savvy adult she'd been. To save herself, she'd walked away from them and everything they stood for. Their plan for her to take over their business. Their plan for her to marry a nice white boy who worked for them.

That was the night she'd chosen Heston over them. But what had he done? Precisely what her parents did. Exerted too much dominance. Disrespected her. Demeaned her accomplishments and her dreams. Treated her like an idiot. Which was why she'd left him. She'd only left him to save herself. And she should have. London was not only independent, smart, funny, daring, sexy, and perfectly whole by herself, she didn't need anyone to complete her. Never had.

She didn't need to be babied, led around by her nose, or directed, either. She was that butterfly on the breeze, so damned beautiful. Fragile, but strong. A creature of light whose greatest need was not to be protected, but to be set free to live her life the way she wanted. The way she needed.

She was all his now, and he intended to slather her in love and kindness the rest of her days. But the sun was high. He'd slept too late. Heston opened his eyes and turned to London, his beautiful queen.

Her side of the bed was empty.

"Hey, babe, where are you?" he called out as his palm swept the bed. Not even warm. She'd been gone for a while. The shower wasn't running. No aroma of coffee in the air. Where could she be? Heston bolted upright and called again, "London?"

No answer.

His place wasn't that big. She couldn't have gone far. Maybe she was in the garage? Though why, he didn't know. He'd been in too big of a hurry to get her inside last night, and his car was still in the driveway. Hurriedly, he threw on a pair of athletic pants and a clean white t-shirt, then the ragged pair of running shoes beside his bed. Her clothes and shoes were gone. Damn.

Hammering down the steps from his loft, he cleared the common area with one sweeping glance, then hit the kitchen to verify what he already knew. London wasn't there.

He jerked the door to the garage open and flipped ton he overhead lights. Not there, either.

Panic started tapping his shoulder. Doubt crept in. She wouldn't have walked out again. She wouldn't do that to him, would she? Back at his front door, he jerked it open—too easily. It wasn't locked, yet he distinctly recalled engaging the deadbolt last night.

The tapping at his shoulder morphed into full-blown panic.

"London," he bellowed as he ran to the end of his walk and looked both ways down the street. God, he wished it had snowed. Then there'd be tracks. But it didn't snow in Virginia in September and London was nowhere in sight.

"Shit," he hissed. A quick glance over his shoulder zeroed in on his car. If she'd run again…

"No," he said, if only to convince himself. "Not this time. She didn't leave me. She wouldn't. She loves me. We're getting married. Either she's just gone for a morning run or she went somewhere to grab breakfast for us. That's all. I'm panicking for nothing. I trust her. She'll be back. I know she will. She wouldn't just leave like—"

Last time.

But she was gone and she'd left no note. She used to at least tell him where she was going. Back then, he'd loved finding her decorated scraps of notes. She ended each one with Xs and Os or hearts. Lots of hearts. But this morning? Nothing.

Heston took off running, quartering each well-kept yard he flew past, scanning ahead, hoping he'd see her pretty ass ahead of him. She'd preferred to run before the sun came up and traffic got in her way. Back in Killeen, she'd pound out as many as five miles on a good morning. She'd come home sweaty but exhilarated. Sometimes he'd run with her. But she preferred to run alone. It was her time to get her head right. To think clearly. To plan her day and focus on her coursework.

Damn. Where could she be?

Heston circled the few blocks of his subdivision. Once upon a time, it had been part of an industrial area. Now it was mostly gentrified, but with an emphasis on low-income and middle-income housing. The few warehouses left from the fifties hadn't been repurposed into swanky bars or elite hangouts, where only the rich could afford to dance and eat. Instead, the upper floors were opened to middle-class malls, Mom and Pop diners, eclectic boutiques, bookstores, shoe stores, you name it. Gas stations, doctor and dental offices, necessary stuff like that. What had once been the rundown, neglected part of town had been turned into a no-kidding neighborhood where people knew each other.

A good neighborhood, but a neighborhood where Heston still couldn't locate London. He widened his search. The sun was high overhead when he barreled into Le Petite Sunrise Sweets Confectionary. The noon crowd was there, most of them sitting at the pink and gold bistro tables across from the bakery display case.

Charlee O'Donnell called out a cheery, "Good afternoon, Heston!" from behind the counter. "Are you back for more donuts? Already?"

"Good, they were good, yeah," he answered automatically. He stepped to the counter and instantly recanted. "Actually, we haven't eaten them yet, but—" he let his gaze sweep the bakery's interior one more time— "have you seen a pretty woman with short turquoise-colored hair today? She's about your height and she's always smiling. Same color eyes as hair, well almost. She might've run this way. I don't know." His fingertips drummed the countertop.

Charlee's expression turned serious. "No, I haven't, but it's Saturday, and I've been extra busy. Weekends are my money-making days. Who is she?"

"London Wilde." He swallowed hard, not ready to divulge too much information. He went to tug his wallet out of his rear pocket to show her the picture of London he always carried, only—

His pockets were empty. No wallet. No cell phone. *Shit.* He'd left home with nothing but panic. Rapping his knuckles on the counter, he told Charlee, "Never mind. Just thought she might've come this way. You, umm, wouldn't have a security camera, would you?"

"I'm sorry, no. It's a pretty safe neighborhood so I haven't invested in one yet. I know I should for insurance purposes, but right now every cent I make goes back into my business." She wiped her fingers on the towel in her hand. "I've got your number so if I see her, I'll let you know. Go home and grab your phone. Hey, maybe she's already gone back to your place."

"Good thinking. I'll check. See you later."

"Bye, Heston. Good luck finding your lady friend."

God, he hoped he did. He took off running when he hit the sidewalk. If she wasn't at his place, she hadn't left voluntarily. He'd barely hit his front walk after he'd retrieved his cell phone and wallet, when a bright, arrest-me-red Jeep screeched to a stop at his curb. Could only be Harley Mortimer.

Sure enough. The TEAM's senior agent reached over the console and shoved the passenger door open with a curt, "Get in!"

Didn't have to ask Heston twice. He jumped in to ride shotgun. "London's missing," he blurted. "I've been all over the neighborhood. I can't find her."

"Yeah, well..." Harley stomped on the gas, turning his Jeep into a rocket.

The sudden acceleration jerked Heston back into his seat. "You know where she is, don't you?"

"Not precisely, but we will soon. Been calling you for a gawddamned hour." Harley jerked the steering wheel, and an illegal Indy 500 race was on. Harley wasn't his usual teasing self this morning. At the intersection, he ran the red light and swerved into oncoming traffic. He didn't slow down on the road to TEAM HQ, either.

"We got home late last night," Heston explained. "We were tired. When I woke up, she was gone. I was worried and ran out without my phone, so sue me. What's going on?"

By then Harley had slammed on the brakes, parked the Jeep, and was taking the steps into TEAM HQ three at a time, waving for Heston to hurry up.

Heston stayed dead on his heels. He'd no more than cleared the entry when Mark Houston slapped a tactical headset at him and told him, "Put this on. You're tip of the spear today."

"Me? Why? Where's London?" Heston asked as he inserted the tiny device deep into his ear.

"Here," someone bit out from behind The TEAM's customer service desk.

"Where?" Heston bellowed. London wasn't anywhere in sight as far as he could see until—

Oh, God. There. On the big screen. Behind the desk on the wall. A vicious growl percolated up his throat when his eyes zeroed in on the still image of a bloodied and battered London Wilde. She was hanging by her cuffed arms, the chain of the cuffs draped over three pipes in the ceiling wherever she was. Dressed in her clothes from the day before, she was unconscious. The side of her face that he could see was shiny with blood, her hair was wet with it. Dark bruises marked her face and neck. She was gagged.

"Who did this?" Heston bellowed, unable to control the raw panic clawing up his spine. "Where is she? Do we know?"

"Not yet. Mother's tracking—"

"Not good enough! I will kill the bastards who did this!"

"Heston," a calm voice of authority spoke.

"What?" he snarled, needing to run and rescue London. Needing to hit something.

Just. Not. Alex. Who, with that one spoken word, had gotten through to Heston. He still couldn't control his mouth. "What are you doing here, Boss? Where's Kelsey? Why aren't you still back in Washington with her? What'd you do, leave her?"

A quiet hush fell over the crowded lobby at that vehemently tossed insult.

Until Alex quietly enunciated, "Kelsey is here. At TEAM HQ."

Heston's panic was so far out of control, he didn't comprehend what 'here' meant. "She's" —he looked around— "where? I don't see her."

"She's here, downstairs in The TEAM clinic, you dumbass," Murphy snarled, "Judy and Libby are with her. So's Doc Fitz. Maybe you oughta think before you smart-off again."

Heston looked around the lobby. Okay, yeah. He was pissed, but he shouldn't've taken it out on Alex. Looked like everyone was there. Every agent. Some of their wives. Each of them fierce enough to start a war all by themselves. Or finish one.

"Taylor Armstrong, Gabe Cartwright, and Maverick Carson are also with Kelsey," Mark added gently. "They'll protect her and the ladies if anyone breaches this facility."

"Which ain't gonna happen," Beau Villanueva cut in. "Not while I'm breathing, gawddamnit. I'll blow the sons of bitches back to Hell!"

"As will every TEAM agent here," Mark continued calmly. "We all know what you're feeling, Hes. Kelsey's in good hands, and soon London'll be in good hands, too, because she'll be with you. Take a breath, brother. Let us explain."

"Hurry," was all he managed to spit out. His chest was hollow and his ribs were caving in. He couldn't breathe.

He was nearly out of his mind when Harley spoke up. "The hospital in Washington was no longer safe. We couldn't control all exits or entrances, and the hospital administrator didn't appreciate Alex taking over. So we brought Kels home last night. If you'd call in a sit rep once in a while, you'd know that." He waved his hand dismissively. "Not like it matters, but after that last threat—"

"Christ! Another one?"

Heston got a stern head shake from Harley. "No, the same threat the caller made when he told Alex he could get to Kelsey anytime, that the next time he'd kill her."

"We knew we had to move her," David Tao said quietly. "Just needed to make sure we could do it quickly and safely. She's just undergone her second craniectomy, and she's a critical care patient. Moving her had to be done correctly."

"My wife's making sure Kelsey gets the care she needs," Beau declared.

"As are Judy and Libby," David added.

Heston inhaled a shallow breath. "Good. Okay. So Deck—"

"Not Decker. His helo's too small for the task," Mark interrupted. "Adam Torrey flew her home. He was already on standby, and we knew we'd need more equipment than Deck's helo could handle. We snuck Kelsey and her equipment out through the hospital maintenance elevator—"

"And now she's where she belongs," Harley cut in. "With us."

Heston all but bellowed, "But where's London?"

Chapter Twenty-Four

London kept her head down, feigning unconsciousness for as long as she could get away with it. Her poor arms were stretched high over her head. She was hanging by her cuffed wrists, and the cuffs were metal. They'd long ago cut into her skin. Blood tracked down her arms, into her armpits and over her stretched-to-breaking, battered ribs. Whoever'd taken her had tossed the chain between her cuffs over three metal pipes traversing the ceiling. There wasn't one part of her that didn't hurt. Her backside, ribs, chest, and gut. Her face, head, neck, and shoulders. Her poor ears. At least two of her front teeth were loose, and her arms were numb.

Some chickenshit had woken her by tying a bag over her head, then by drowning her. He'd aimed a hose at her face, and the cloth bag had absorbed water so quickly that, for a few frightening, disoriented moments, she'd panicked. Couldn't get a solid footing, not as slippery as her bare feet were on the wet floor. She'd been helpless and scared and sure she was going to die. Still was.

After waterboarding, some asshat delivered a stinging slap to her still-covered face. A punch to her gut followed, then another to her ribs. When one of the bastards called, "Timeout!" she'd foolishly believed Heston or maybe his TEAM were storming the place, wherever she was, and they were going to save her. Not hardly. Not when she'd heard the sound of a cell phone taking a photo. Crap. It'd kill Heston to see her like this. She was such a failure!

"Why are you doing this to me?" she'd asked between the next breath-stealing blows.

"Where is he?" The brute who'd hit her had an Irish accent or brogue or whatever it was called.

"W-who?" she'd asked, turning her face away so he couldn't make direct contact with her bleeding lips again.

Jerking her back around, he bellowed in her face, "That cocky bastard, Alexander Stewart, you shite! You know where he took her! Where is he?"

Another round of backhanded cuffs made one thing painfully clear: Alex and his wife were no longer in that hospital in Washington, and this guy, who had to be the Irishman that Alex hated, didn't know where they'd gone. Interesting. The Stewarts were safe. Good for them. London planned to make sure they stayed that way.

"Stop," she'd begged. "I don't know where h-h-he is." Because she didn't, and she'd never tell this jerk if she did. Alex was living through the most desperate time of his life. The last time London had seen Kelsey, she was lingering at death's door, and this bastard wanted her to rat out Alex? Never.

The harder the hits, the more determined London became. She was stubborn. She could beat this Neanderthal at his own game. And she did, just locked her brain down and refused to save herself at the Stewarts' expense. Alex loved his wife. They needed to live happily ever after, damn it. And London would make sure they did, even if it killed her.

After the Irishman gave up, another jerk came in. He didn't ask London anything, just slapped her until she spun with every hit. The cuff's chain didn't allow a complete rotation. It jerked her wrists each time she reached the end of it. The force of each blow sent her back for another slap. Neither man touched her breasts, though, which she'd thought unusual—then.

The second guy took the hood off of her when he left. Not like it mattered. By then, her eyes were swollen shut, and she couldn't see. The overwhelming sting of fertilizer in the air made it hard to breathe. Stifling. Broken ribs and swollen, bloodied lips sucked.

She had no idea who'd kidnapped her, but suspected the Irishman who'd just beaten her was behind everything. Or Obermeyer. Or Keane. Maybe Devon Bates. Couldn't be Malloy. She was pretty sure he was the dead guy in that trunk. It made sense it'd be one of the others. Or all of them. They'd already gone to great lengths to silence her for something she'd supposedly seen or heard in DC. Sure'd be nice if she'd known what their big secret was back then. Because she was pretty sure she knew now. Which also explained why her breasts hadn't been beaten along with the rest of her.

Despite her pounding head, she'd heard muffled voices coming from the room behind her. Frightened women's voices. Young girls' cries and sobs. An occasional bang, something slamming hard against metal. Like steel doors closing. Bars ramming. Locks clanking. Big, heavy, industrial locks that secured massive doors. Like the ones on semi-trailers and containers. The kind loaded onto ships and stacked five high and twenty deep.

Obermeyer and Keane were involved in human trafficking. The sex trade. That was why there were women and children in the next room. If this were a container, which the hollowness of every sound convinced her it was, the chance of it being offloaded with her and those women and children onto a ship headed somewhere overseas was downright frightening.

She rolled her tired neck at the very real possibility that she, those women, and the poor children had already been sold into prostitution. Or worse. The pain and confusion in her poor head made London consider her place—her station—in life. Was it only to serve men, like so much of the world thought, in order to stay alive? Was it to bow and scrape like uneducated people used to do? Like Black slaves before they'd learned to read? Like women who, in many parts of the world, were still considered chattel, owned by a man at birth, then bartered away for a couple goats as wife to another man she hadn't chosen?

Hell to the fuckin' no. London would die before she'd let any pervert defile her. No way would she ever—ever!—submit willingly.

The problem was how to get both feet on the floor and out of there. She had no cell phone or strength. Her poor head hurt. Everything was muddled and her focus was spotty at best. Thinking was difficult, and logical planning was damned near nil. Which meant concussion. *No shit.*

But wait until she felt better to escape? Wait for someone to come rescue her? Might as well curl up and die. That stupid solution earned itself another, "Hell, no!" Which didn't come out of her mouth with as much venom as London intended.

Man, she was in the worst situation ever.

One thing she knew about sex traffickers, they were all ugly, sweaty pigs who got off on slapping women and children around. They were sadists, into slavery, bondage, whips, and chains. Into rape. Some were so morally bankrupt, they killed the women and children when they were done fucking them. Then there was the porn industry. Slasher and snuff films. Femicide. Some princes, kings, and presidents participated in the perversion. Some might look handsome, suave, and debonair on TV. They might smell good and dress to the nines—if any man dressed to the nines. She had no idea if guys did that or not. But guys who dabbled in the industry, lied to make their country and constituents think they were good and decent. When they weren't.

Damn. London dug a thumbnail into the back of her little finger to get her mind back on track. Hysteria served no purpose. She had to stay calm. Her wrists were bleeding, and she had no idea how much blood she'd already lost or could stand to lose. She'd give anything to be sitting on the metal chair in the corner over there. The one with the big rusted wheel chained to its front legs. She couldn't remember when or how it happened, but the toes on her left foot were mashed and bleeding. She might've been made to sit in that chair, she had no way to know. The jerk who'd beaten her probably dropped the wheel on her bare foot and laughed. *Asshat.*

And who cared how pedophiles smelled or dressed? She didn't. They were all worthless lowlifes. All selfish bastards who deserved to have their balls cut off with a dull knife and shoved down their throats. While they were still alive. And screaming. That'd be a nice touch. Though screaming might be hard to do once they started choking on their nuts and—

Damn. It was hard to stay on track, much less focused on the essential task of getting out of those cuffs, then out of this place, wherever it was. Trembling at her helplessness and shaking from the cold, London forced her thoughts to Heston.

He'd be awake by now, probably wondering where she'd gone. Was he looking for her? Was he worried? Or worse, did he think she'd run off and left him again?

She lanced her little finger again, harder this time. *No. Just no.* Heston had proven his love a thousand times over. He'd be pissed at her for leaving so early, sure, but by now, he'd know something was wrong. He'd be looking for her. He wouldn't just forget her. She wasn't worried about that. Only about what would happen to her before he found her. The bad guys were sure to come back. What would they do to her then?

Sucking in a deep breath of chemical-laced air, she strained against the unyielding cuffs. But damn. She was too weak to lift her weight, and her wrists were torn and raw. Okay then. What else?

Think, London. You can do this. Wouldn't these jackasses be surprised if they came back and she was gone? God, that'd be something. Or maybe she'd hang around and be the one who castrated them. With a rusty knife. Only…

Swallowing hard, she scuffed her bare toes against the cold, wet floor in a silent fit of nerves. Her vision was compromised and her range of motion sucked. To castrate anyone, she needed a knife, and a way out. Not in that order. Shit, she might need a white knight after all.

Dropping her chin to her heaving chest, she squeezed her poor puffy eyes tighter and prayed for her life and the lives of the poor women and girls trapped with her. "Heston," she whispered, salty tears coursing over her cheeks and down her neck. "I didn't leave you this time, honest. I'm here, and I… God, I need you, Hes. Hurry. Save me. Please, hurry."

Chapter Twenty-Five

Heston turned to the man he'd insulted. He'd been so worried about London, he hadn't asked Alex about his wife. "Holy shit, I'm… I'm sorry, Boss. How… how is she?"

Alex looked haggard and weary, but still lethal. The man's blue eyes were pits as dark, black ice and bleak as the unforgiving depths of the deepest ocean. His expression was carved from the same black ice. Sharp. Jagged. Damned deadly. Take one wrong step, and just like that ocean, he'd end your dumb ass and never look back.

Twin SIG pistols graced both cups of the worn leather holster strapped over the plates of his tactical vest. A damned evil knife lay at his hand on the counter. Odd. No sniper rifle, Alex's strong suit, in sight. Which stood to reason. He was kitted out for close combat fighting. The killers who had London wouldn't die by a shot they didn't see coming. No. This was personal. Alex wanted the Irishman, whoever he was, Obermeyer or Keane, to know precisely who was killing them. What happened today would be lethal, up close, and gawddamned personal.

"No need to apologize. I've been in your shoes. Kelsey's holding her own," Alex replied evenly. "She's not out of the woods yet, but—" he paused— "soon. You'll see. She'll come back to… to us."

Christ, the man was wound as tightly as Heston. "What's your plan?" he asked with as much patience as he could muster.

"For now, we're waiting on more intel from Mother. She's on her way up. Just—"

"Here! I'm here, Alex. I'm running as fast as I can. Don't start without me," Mother ordered, her heels clicking menacingly from the rear hall elevator to the portable tables Heston had just noticed along the wall behind the counter. "Where are the maps I asked for, people?"

He swallowed his OPSEC mistake down. He hadn't heard the elevator. Hadn't even heard its doors open or close. It'd been a damned long time since he'd lost track of situational awareness. It wouldn't happen again.

Everyone in the lobby shifted to the tables. Heston took quick stock of the crowd. Mark and Harley stood at Alex's left. David Tao, Connor and Izza Maher, Rory and Ember Dennison, Cassidy Dancer and her husband, Jude were there, too. Lee Hart and his wife Tess. Hunter Christian. Eric Reynolds. Beau Villanueva, of course, since his wife was attending to Kelsey.

Renner Graves stood alongside Beckam Garner, both with their arms folded across their chests. Jameson Tenney stood smartly at Alex's right side, his hair combed as usual, dark glasses covering his eyes, white cane tucked firmly alongside his left leg. Tripp McClane and Jake Weylin looked ready to brawl, both grim and stiff across from Alex. Shane Hayes and Everlee Yeager, all but stood at attention with them. Even the agents who normally operated OCONUS, outside the continental United States, were present and accounted for:

Walker and Persia Judge. Zack Lennox. Seth McCray. Cord Shepherd.

Heston didn't recognize the older Black gentleman with Murphy, but they seemed to know each other so he let that lack of detail slide. Murphy's secretary, Page Royal, stood at his elbow. Geeky Axel Cho, Mother's technical assistant, and the guys and gals from TEAM Two were there, as well. Grissom McCoy, Phoenix Bond, Avery Branson, Jenna Bates, Cole Hemmingway, Leisha Warner, and Byron Shields. Asher Downey jerked his chin at Heston. Christ, everyone was there to support Alex and Kelsey. And now London.

Mother assumed a stern position alongside Jameson, then turned on him with a curt, "I know you pulled your own map. You know where she is." Not questions. Outright declarations.

"Yes, Mom, I did and I do. Is everyone here so we can start?" Jameson asked, his head rotating as if he were surveying his audience. Which he absolutely wasn't and would never do again.

Former Navy SEAL Jameson Tenney had lost his sight during a classified overseas combat mission gone wrong. But whereas many injured vets came home to drug addiction, homelessness, and suicide, Jameson threw himself into learning to live without seeing. First came Braille and learning how to maneuver in public with just a cane and his other senses. After accomplishing that, he'd tackled—and conquered—two extreme sports: parkour, the obstacle course that involved precision jumping, wall running, climbing vertical walls, and other seemingly impossible feats of daring; and Krav Maga, the extreme fighting system from Israeli Defense Forces that combined aikido, boxing, karate, and wrestling techniques. Somewhere amidst the incredible physical skills he'd acquired, Jameson had also become uncannily adept at profiling. A couple of TEAM agents swore he could read minds. Maybe he could. The son of a bitch could still nail the high-caliber, thousand-yard gong at the gun range. Maybe because his other senses were sharper now? Maybe because he simply listened better? Who the hell knew?

"Go ahead, Jameson," Alex ordered.

Jameson nodded and began. "As we all know, Alex suspects that either Secretary of State Obermeyer or the proposed next ambassador to Ireland, Michael Keane, are behind the attempts on Alex's and Kelsey's lives. And now they've kidnapped" —his head rotated until his dark glasses aimed at Heston— "your friend, Hes. Former USFS Lieutenant London Wilde. Mother and Cho located security footage that show her abduction outside Le Petite Sunrise Sweets Confectionary, at zero three-hundred hours this morning. Three men were involved. Two slowed her run, the other came up behind and tranq'd her. She went down like a lamb. They stuffed her into the trunk of a black Lincoln town car. License plate came back as stolen, so that's a dead end. But…"

He turned to Mother, who pointed the remote at her fingertips to the big screen and brought up another image. "A traffic camera across the street caught this image when the trunk was open." The picture was shadowy and grainy, but there was enough morning light to reveal the stark white face and blank eyes, as well as the bullet hole in the forehead, of the deceased male stuffed into the right rear wheel well.

"That's Ryan Malloy," Heston declared.

His inner caveman roared to life. *Protect London! Run! Now! Save woman!*

"Who the fuck's Ryan Malloy?" Beau Villanueva growled.

"Former Irish Ranger. Extraordinary sniper. Jack Malloy's son," Heston replied, his heart pounding at the obvious threat to London.

"Shit, he's famous," Beau hissed. "How'd anyone take out Ryan?"

"Who cares?" Izza Maher spoke up. "But I'm betting they took her over the bridge to Anacostia. Plenty of deserted derelict buildings over there to stash bodies." Her dark eyes cut to Heston. "Sorry, but you know I'm right. Two dead drug addicts were found there just last week. It's a valid dumping—"

"She's not dead," he bit out, pissed that Connor's wife would go there so quickly. London couldn't be dead. He'd know if they'd already killed her. He'd feel her sweet spirit leave the Earth. He would!

"The river's not frozen, but it's still damned cold this time of year," Jake Weylin said quietly. He ought to know. He'd been pulled from the Potomac in the middle of a fierce winter storm a few years back. Almost died.

"Shut the fuck up," Asher cut in before Heston could knock Jake on his ass. "London's not dead and she's not in the fuckin' Potomac River! We'll find her, gawddamn it. Where'd they stash her?" he barked at Jameson. "You oughta know."

"At the tip of my finger, Ash, Hes," Jameson replied evenly.

Swallowing hard, Heston glared down at the spot in the map where Jameson's fingertip still rested. He leaned closer. Really looked this time. It wasn't in the middle of the District. It was nearer the east end of the Tidal Basin, the man-made reservoir between the Potomac River and the Washington Channel in Washington DC. "They've taken her to the Jefferson Monument?"

Jameson's dark glasses aimed at Heston as if he were truly seeing him. "East of the monument."

"Why?" Heston asked, striving to—somehow—remain as calm as Jameson. Something about the blind guy inspired confidence. For the first time since he'd seen London's battered image, hope lifted its weary head. Jameson believed London was still alive. Heston could feel it.

"We're dealing with two alpha predators, Hes, not deadbeat addicts or brainless lowlifes who kill on the spur of the moment, then dump bodies wherever it's convenient. Think about it. Obermeyer and Keane are both connected with powerful people in Congress, and they're arrogant. They want Alex to suffer. They're making a statement. They want him to understand, at least to think, they're powerful enough to make him do what they want, whenever and anywhere they say. It's early Saturday, and today, like every week until the middle of October, there'll be a farmers' market in the parking lot east of the monument. Right now, there are a hundred or so vendors setting up tents, E-Z Ups, and stands to sell produce and crafts. Before noon, the place will be crowded. Directly east of those vendor booths, between the parking lot and East Basin Drive Southwest, lies the District's Inner-City Gardens, a green zone set aside to encourage inner-city families to raise their own produce. There you'll find individual family plots, gardening sheds, and" —Jameson's finger tapped the location he'd uncannily pointed out before— "three shipping containers repurposed as organic greenhouses. Keane owns them, and he's made sure everyone knows the produce for his chain of pubs along the East Coast is grown there."

Sounded plausible. Hes had seen Keane's ads and billboards. He'd made quite the name for himself. And those were his much-touted, much-advertised containers lined up side-by-side with the fenced-in community gardens. What better place to stash London than in plain sight?

Jameson's slender finger tapped again. "That's where you'll find her, in one of those containers."

Heston agreed. "I think you're right."

"Keane and Obermeyer stashed her there because, sorry, Hes, Jake's right, too. It's close to the river. More importantly, Keane thinks he's untouchable. With Obermeyer flying cover for him and campaigning for his ambassadorship, Keane believes he can get away with anything. Even murder."

"Look at the photo again," Alex said. He'd been uncharacteristically quiet for a man with a vendetta. "What do you see?"

The TEAM's focus rotated back to the big screen, where Mother had once again displayed the shot of London, bound and gagged and—hanging by her poor arms. Heston's eyes filled. It was damned near noon. She'd been missing for hours. Keane and Obermeyer'd had more than enough time to torture her. And worse. She wouldn't last much longer.

"I see a flooded linoleum floor with a drain in the center," Harley replied. "Plain metal walls. London barely standing on her toes and—! Look at her pant leg, Hes."

Heston's eyes jerked to the bloody symbols scrawled on the side of London's thigh. Scribbles, really. But the Xs and Os were clear enough to make him panic all over again. She'd sent that message to him before she'd been strung up. Was that her way of telling him goodbye? Had she given up?

"Why'd they take her?!" *Why not me?*

Jameson breathed a drawn-out sigh. "When London outed Bates, she made it personal. Obermeyer's carefully orchestrated plan to make Keane ambassador fell apart, as did their other plans."

"Other plans?" Heston asked.

"Obermeyer and Keane own a warehouse full of containers just like these three, on a dock in Delaware," Jameson replied soberly. "That's where they stash the women and girls they've kidnapped before moving them to South America."

"I'm still tracking the ship that left Delaware last night," Axel piped up. "I'll find those poor women. Don't worry."

"South America? This shitshow's about human trafficking? That's what Obermeyer and Keane are into?" Heston turned on Mark, ready to knock the guy's head off at that despicable insight. "I knew there was a mole inside Stewart's house. I abso-fuckin'-lutely told you! Who is it? Do you know? Have you even looked for the person who knew where the Stewarts were going? Didn't you take me seriously?"

Mark was a big, broad bull of a man. Standing at six feet three inches tall and weighing around three hundred pounds, he could easily snap Heston's neck if push ever came to shove. Instead, he crossed his arms over his chest and quietly replied, "I always take you seriously, Hes. You know that. You're one of our best, and yes, we found the mole. Arlette Kramer is the Stewarts' neighbor and one of Lexie's friends. But she's only six years old, and she had no idea that the nice man with the funny accent who fell off his bike in front of her house was pumping her for information. Of course she told him everything she knew. Ask any kid. Kids love talking to anyone who'll listen. I've already chatted with her parents. They also knew where Lexie's parents were going on their secret getaway."

"Because my daughter can't keep her mouth shut," Alex added wearily.

Well, shit. Heston knew Lexie. She was her mother's Mini-Me, but also so much like her father. He scrubbed his face, not sure how to ask, but going to ask anyway. "She has a photographic memory? Like you?"

"Not photographic," Alex whispered. "Eidetic. Like you. Kelsey and I outlined our route on a Trails Illustrated map of Mount Rainier National Park. We put it away. Made sure we didn't talk in front of Lexie. But obviously, she found it and shared it. Us. We're the breach in TEAM OPSEC."

"It's not your fault," Mark said. "Kids—"

"Yes, it is." Alex cut him off. "I should've known better. When Lexie gets her little posse together, the whole damned house sounds like a son of a bitchin' chicken coop."

"But we don't know for certain it was Lexie, Boss. Bates might've turned on Malloy," Mark persisted.

"Not possible," Heston said. "We turned him and Malloy over to Tucker Chase, and I doubt Tucker'd let him make any outgoing calls. How'd Obermeyer get Malloy?"

"Tuck had no choice but release Malloy when Obermeyer sent the Secret Service to Tucker's boss with orders to collect him," Murphy spoke up. "Gawddamned diplomatic immunity applies to that jackass."

"How'd Obermeyer know Tuck had Malloy and Bates in custody?"

Murphy shrugged. "Might be the same way the Irishman knew where Kelsey's been all this time."

"Which tells me they had eyes on us every step of the way. We played into their hands. Where's Obermeyer now?" Heston demanded to know. "Where's Bates?"

"Obermeyer's whereabouts are unknown," Alex answered, "and Tuck has one of his best psychics working over Bates. We should get better intel soon. Listen up, people." All eyes were already on Alex. "Deck and Adam will fly us into Reagan. From there, I've got a fleet of unmarked vehicles on standby that'll move us to this location."

His index stabbed a long, rectangular position just east of East Basin Drive Southwest. "This is Keane's container one. Mark, hit it and hit it hard. Take whoever you need to make it happen with you." He stabbed the next container. "Murphy and Roy, take container two. Take whoever you need. And Hes…" Roy had to be the older Black guy with Murphy.

Heston looked up into the deadly eyes of one weary, but pissed-off killer. "Bring your blowout bag, get an IFAK kit if you don't already have one, and enough painkiller to keep London comfortable until medics arrive. You and Eric are with me."

"Copy that," Eric answered.

"You know which container she's in," Heston breathed.

"Of course he does. I've had drones in the air over those containers for weeks," Mother cut in. "Just wish I'd known there were women in there, I'd have called the FBI. Speaking of which, the FBI will be on hand. Don't ask me how they know—"

"Psychics," Heston spat. "Tucker met us when we landed last night. Shit! He's got intel he's not sharing."

"The Bureau has no need to share anything with us," Murphy pointed out.

"Like hell they don't!" Heston yelled. "If Tucker knew London was there—"

"He would've called me," Alex said tiredly. "Damn it, Hes, they're not omniscient and Tucker's on our side. Trust me. His wife was kidnapped years ago. Nothing brings out the beast in him more than men who abuse women."

Mother cut in with, "Things might get messy. FBI's after Keane, too, so—"

"We're going covert, Mother, not rogue," Alex bit out. "We do this by the book, people. If the Bureau takes Obermeyer and Keane into custody, let them. But if anyone— any-gawddamned one—dares come after my wife or any of you again—in my house—on my land!—kill the sons of bitches!"

Heads nodded and The TEAM moved out. Heston, Eric, and Alex were at HQ's entrance when Alex's phone buzzed.

"Libby? What's—?"

"You need to come down to Kelsey's room. Now."

Heston cocked his head at the loud, stern command coming from Mark Houston's petite wife over the phone.

"Is she—?"

"She needs you, Alex. She's trying to wake up, and the first person she needs to see is you. Hurry."

"On my way." Alex stuffed the phone in his pants pocket and turned to Heston. There was a spark in his tired blue eyes for the first time in days.

"Go, Boss. Your place is with Kelsey."

"Kill them, Hes," Alex bit out. "Kill them all. Make them bleed. Make those sons of bitches pay."

"Yes, sir, I will. Now go. We've got this," Heston answered with equal venom.

Alex turned for the elevator that would take him down three levels to The TEAM's high-tech sickbay. Heston and Eric turned to the East, toward Washington DC and the Jefferson Monument. To London. Obermeyer, Keane, and that damned Irishman might think they were running this show, but they were dead-assed wrong. They'd made a fatal mistake. The biggest, baddest apex predator on the East Coast wasn't Alex Stewart. It was Heston, a caveman at heart maybe, but a caveman who would damned well defend London to the death. Their bloody, painful-as-fuck deaths. Today—there would be blood.

"Stay strong, babe," he projected across the distance between them. "I'm coming."

And I'm bringing Hell with me.

Chapter Twenty-Six

Alex arrived at Kelsey's door out of breath and, for the first time in forever, unsure of himself. He'd prayed for this moment, but now that it was here, he was afraid to hope. Kelsey had taken one helluva beating in the White River, enough that she might never recover completely. She very well could have permanent brain damage. TBI, for hell's sake. There was no way to know for certain until she woke up.

Hesitating, he ran a hand over the knotty scar on his scalp. He'd been beaten years ago, bad enough his brain had also swollen. He'd had the same surgery as Kelsey. Had nearly the same section of his skull removed. The same scars. She and he were a matched set.

"Alex," Libby said behind him. No hope resonated in her voice. No emotion. Just the calm professionalism of a strong woman who'd transitioned from nurse to physician. The same woman who'd survived her own near-death experience before she'd married Mark. Libby Houston, now a mother of five, a doctor, and Kelsey's best friend.

Alex lifted his eyes to Libby's sweet face. He might never tell them, but he loved Libby and Mark. There were no better friends. Well, except for Murphy and Roy, both senior agents who'd retired years ago, but had come back. Harley and Zack. Their wives and… *Shit*. He was rambling.

"Let's look in on Kelsey and see how she's doing, shall we?" Libby suggested, her slender hand already palming the door open. And there she was. His goddess. His everything. Alex's breath caught, just like it did every time he looked at Kelsey. Quickly, he stepped past Libby and went straight to Kelsey's side.

"Judy, McKenna, and I decided you should be the only one with Kelsey when she wakes."

He nodded like the dolt he'd turned into the second Kelsey'd been shot.

"She was drugged, Alex. Understand? Someone at that hospital in Washington was giving Kelsey too much painkiller. We think that's the main reason she didn't regain consciousness once the swelling subsided. Not because of any severe brain damage. In fact—"

His head swiveled back to Libby. "Drugged? By who?"

McKenna peeked around Libby and joined him at Kelsey's bedside. "Axel hacked into the hospital's security, but couldn't find anything conclusive. Mark and Beau, on the other hand, installed Tattle Tails in the hallway outside Kelsey's room after you got that first threat."

Tattle Tails were Mother's invention. The tiny things were expertly camouflaged to be nearly invisible, at least, unnoticeable, and crafted to record audio and video. Once inconspicuously placed, they remained active until their batteries died or until Mother killed them. She'd patented the miniscule batteries that powered them, had yet to reveal how she'd packed so much clever technology into such small devices.

Alex blinked. He hadn't once thought of Tattle Tails. He'd been too worried about Kelsey. But he should have considered the damned Irishman would have someone inside the hospital. Thank God for friends who'd flown cover while Alex had been running around like a chicken with his head cut off. "And?"

McKenna pulled a four-by-four photo out of her scrubs' pants pocket and handed it over. "Axel did a background check and found this. The woman played her part well. I never doubted she was part of the staff there."

"Sorry to say, but neither did I," Libby added.

"Her name's Jolie Montgomery, and she is a nurse, just not an American nurse."

"She's from Ireland," Alex growled. He should've seen that coming, too. "Son of a bitch!"

"The photo shows her injecting something into Kelsey's IV. I believe it was fentanyl. Every time she entered Kelsey's room, she injected just enough to keep Kelsey sedated," McKenna continued. "Libby, Judy, and I suspected something was up when Kelsey's stats returned to normal so quickly after her first surgery. Relieving the pressure on her brain did what it was supposed to. Yet she didn't regain consciousness like she should've and—"

"And we know our girl, Alex," Judy, Harley's wife, bit out. "Kelsey's a fighter. The minute Axel told us that woman is a fraud, we started tracking every shot that went into Kelsey's IV. We asked questions. We stuck our noses in everyone's business, and we pissed a lot of people in that hospital off."

"Not like we care," Libby added haughtily.

"Her?" Alex asked. The kind nurse who'd told him to keep doing what he was doing, that his presence had stabilized Kelsey's blood pressure?

Damn. He'd been so consumed with all the what-ifs of losing his wife, he'd thoroughly neglected OPSEC countermeasure. He'd failed to recognize critical intel. He'd mis-identified threats. Mark and Beau were the ones who'd assessed his and Kelsey's vulnerabilities. He'd analyzed some risks, but had zeroed in so intently onto that damned Irishman—whom he still didn't have a name for—that he'd been blind to others. These three women were the ones who'd encouraged him to bring Kelsey home to Virginia. They were the ones who'd developed and applied no-kidding countermeasures. Them. Kelsey's girlfriends. While he'd been running scared and—

Alex wasn't afraid to admit it. "Kelsey's my everything," he told the three women he trusted with her life. "I was a mean, hateful son of a bitch before I found her. When I…" He paused, his heart so damned full of love for his wife it might break all over again. "I'm nothing without her. Absolutely nothing." He would've used Heston's *abso-fuckin'-lutely,* but Libby, Judy, and McKenna were ladies, and Kelsey might overhear, and he'd already cussed enough, and—

And now, he was rambling.

Libby's cobalt blue eyes glistened. "Then stay with her, Alex. Be the first one she sees when she opens her eyes. She's been more active since we brought her home. It won't be long now. It still might take days, but you'll see. She is going to be okay, honey."

God, that endearment killed. "Thanks," he choked out, his voice so damned tight.

Libby gave him a very feminine chin nod. "You need anything, you hit the call button. We've got your back, Boss."

That did it, her calling him Boss. His eyes teared up. He had to blink to keep them from falling, as the ladies he loved almost as much as he loved his wife, filed out of the room and left him alone with his one and only. If they thought Kelsey was going to be okay, then he believed.

Carefully lifting her covers, Alex laid down beside Kelsey and made sure to cover her again, except for her already exposed foot. There were no lines, tubes, or wires to deal with this time. She was warm and soft but sleeping. Breathing evenly. Her poor head was still in that protective helmet, would be until Dr. Kang confirmed ed she was stable without it. Still so close and yet so damned far away.

Gently sliding his right arm under her shoulders, he tucked Kelsey's back to his front. She didn't stir, didn't moan. But Alex did. Like the weakling he'd become, he dipped his face into the space between her helmet and her neck and let his tears fall. What was loving a woman if a man wasn't scared to death to lose her? What did he have to live for if she died? Yes, Alex adored his children, but Kelsey leaving them would change everything. He'd be hollow, not just bereft, but empty. Gutted. The precious light and laughter he depended on would be gone, and with it, his soul.

God had blessed him with Kelsey and Alex knew it. He didn't deserve her, never had, never would. Which was why God might still take her back. Because she *was* pure, and Alex was one of the filthiest sinners on Earth. He might be one of God's children, but he wasn't a favored son, and Alex wouldn't change that if he could. He wasn't one of God's avenging angels. If anything, he was more like the Destroyer, Satan. A killer. A wolf. One of those necessary evils in this wicked world, but evil, nonetheless.

"I have faith in you, sweetheart," he whispered. "Take your time. Just breathe. Just rest. If you have things to do before you can come back to me, that's okay. I understand, because I have things to do here. Please know that whatever happens, I love you. And if it takes forever—"

"Quiet," she mumbled, her voice thick and drowsy. "I'm tired. Leave me alone." Damned if she didn't yawn and stretch. Her warm backside flexed against his cock. Which had no interest at all in performing, not since the lady of his heart had come so damned close to Death's door.

"Kelsey?" he asked, needing more than just those few words.

She sighed a tiny grunt. Turned her face into her pillow.

"Am I boring you?" he teased, so damned hopeful that he was. That she'd heard him. That she'd come back with her memories intact.

"Hmmpf…Uh-huh…"

She'd heard! She'd answered! She knew him!

Alex could've roared, he felt that lighthearted. That lucky. Instead, he bowed his head and inhaled the essence that was pure Kelsey. Her unique, sweet scent. Her indomitable spirit. Her faithful soul. If anyone believed in God, she did. Alex's doubts fled like ice in the morning sun. She'd survived other nightmares. She would survive this one. She *was* coming back to him. They *would* go home together. They'd cry and hug their children and—

"So tired," she whispered.

"Then rest," he whispered back.

Looking at the ceiling, he silently told The Man Upstairs, *'Thank you for saving my wife, Lord. Thank you so damned much. But there's still work to be done down here, and You know it. So forgive me, Father, because I'm definitely going to sin.'*

And Alex hit the call button.

Chapter Twenty-Seven

"I've got eyes on container one," Lee Hart reported from high in a sturdy Douglas Fir between the Jefferson Memorial and Keane's containers. "Windows cover the entire west wall, Mark. All clear. You're good to go."

"Copy that," Mark replied.

For now, Heston was concealed with Murphy behind a hedge on East Basin Drive Southwest, across from the site of Keane's containers.

Another all-clear came from Renner Graves, the sniper watching container two from somewhere just as inconspicuous as Lee's fir tree. "Murphy and Roy, only bogey in sight is Keane. Keep your heads on swivels. He's armed. Two pistols, both holstered under his sports jacket."

"Copy that," Murphy answered.

From Tripp McClane came a raspy, "Stay put, Heston. Eric. The two Chevy Suburbans parked at the rear of container three are moving. Four big guys in one, a skinny guy driving the other. Two men just exited container three. Crap, they're carrying a body bag. One's Obermeyer and—sorry, can't make out the other guy's face. His ballcap's pulled down real low and his collar's turned up. He's the only one in a suit jacket, dress slacks, and fancy shoes, if that helps."

"He's wearing a suit?" Heston hissed.

"Whoever he is, he knows we're here," Murphy added.

"Get a picture, Tripp. Shoot it to Mother," Mark ordered.

"Done," Tripp answered. "Sorry, Hes, know you don't want to hear this, but Obermeyer and his buddy tossed the bag into the lone guy's SUV. They're getting in with him."

Within an hour after meeting with Alex, The TEAM had converged on the green space east of the Jefferson Monument, with permission from Tucker Chase and President Adams. Before they'd arrived, the Metro Police Department had swept in and evacuated the farmer's market, as well as cordoned off all streets nearest Keane's containers. To avoid panic and the usual gaggle of looky-loos wanting selfies, Metro PD claimed someone had reported a gas leak. That the area wasn't safe. They'd further substantiated the lie by bringing a dozen or so utility vans with them, vans that concealed SWAT teams. FBI Director Tucker Chase and his team were somewhere in the area as well. Heston hadn't spotted them yet.

The TEAM had worked closely with MPD for some time. While DC's officers were known for their professionalism, as well as for tackling impossible missions, it was TEAM agents who voluntarily policed the poorer hangouts of the District, where homeless vets, vagrants, and other down-and-outers congregated. It was Alex's men and women who sought out the sick and handicapped, stood overwatch throughout the District for people in trouble. They'd infiltrated the rougher neighborhoods of Anacostia, formed friendships that weakened gang influence and affiliations, protected at-risk teens, assisted single-parent families, and passed out food to the homeless on a daily basis. The TEAM had become the arms and legs of the District's police department and that synergy worked. Alex had put

Tripp McClane in charge of the TEAM/MPD effort. Looked like he had some diplomatic talent after all.

"Both SUVs are pulling out, people," Tripp reported. "Turning left onto East Basin Drive Southwest."

"Fuck!" Heston bellowed. "I need a gawddamned car!"

As if it'd been waiting for him to lose his cool, a sleek black Porsche rolled alongside. Damned if the passenger window didn't roll down as Zack Lennox yelled, "Get your ass in here, Contreras! Move it!"

Eric slapped his back, "Good luck, Hes."

Heston didn't answer, just jogged to the Porsche, threw himself into the passenger seat, and ordered, "Go, go, go!"

The moment Obermeyer's Suburbans passed the Porsche on East Basin Drive Southwest, Zack shot into the far-left lane and followed, leaving four civilian vehicles between them.

"Shit," Heston fumed. "We're too late. We should've been here sooner."

Chatter between the teams breaching containers one and two disintegrated into the unmistakable pops of flashbangs and a hurried, "Go, go, go!" order from Mark to his team.

"No one in container three so far," Cassidy Dancer reported evenly. "But we've only cleared one room and it's not very big. Eric, you find anything?"

"Not yet. Advancing to rear exit—Gun! Shooter!"

Gunfire erupted over the tiny earpieces. Zack cocked his head, a finger to his ear as he listened.

Heston lost his edge completely. "Shit, shit, shit! What am I doing? I've let everyone down. I left my post. I should be there, only—!"

"Will you shut it?" Zack growled. He was as hefty as Mark. Not like Heston cared whose was bigger. He'd failed

The TEAM and he'd failed London. This time, she'd be gone for good. Because of him! He'd gotten his second chance and he'd blown it. Knew the odds of Karma granting three chances to an idiot like him were damned near nonexistent. What if—?

"You good, Cass? Eric?" Murphy asked.

"Copy that, Murph. We're good, yeah," Cassidy replied steadily.

"Wyatt took both assholes down," Eric added. "Two wannabe gangster-types in camis and sporting AKs. You oughta see the middle room of this container, guys. Someone was definitely hung from three overhead pipes. Blood spatter's everywhere, even on the ceiling. Water's an inch deep on the floor. Proceeding to yet another damned door in this zoo."

"Hope it's the exit," Wyatt Browning added. "This kill box keeps going. Crap!"

Another flurry of gunfire erupted from what Heston guessed was still inside container three. It was hard keeping up with the action with only one audio and no visual feed. It should've been him taking those shots. It should've been—

"Two more assholes down," Wyatt reported breathlessly. "Both armed with AKs. Both dumber than shit. Cassidy and me are good, Murph. We found a dozen or more kids and battered women in cages. Eric's got his gear out. He's triaging now."

"Same in container two," Harley replied. "No guys with guns, just little girls locked in dog crates. Wire dog crates. Place reeks of piss and decay, and some of these darlin's are sick."

Heston's fingers went through his hair as children's cries and moans came through his earpiece. He couldn't help feeling like a heartless pig when he asked, "Any sign of London?"

"No, Hes," Cassidy replied, "but…"

"But what?" Heston snarled. More chatter from Mark's and Murph's teams kept him from digging a bigger hole full of angry words he would regret later. Turned out greenhouses only filled half of containers one and two, none of three. Which was the container Eric, Cassidy, and Wyatt had stepped up and handled after he'd left them hanging.

A sudden battery of shots rang out, silencing all chatter. At last, Mark came back with a breathless, "Keane down. Thanks, Maverick. Totally self-defense. Proud of you, brother."

"You think?" Maverick snarled. "Shithead had a .44 magnum on you! Everyone else okay?" It was good knowing Maverick Carson had Mark's back, but damn, he sounded pissed.

Quiet confirmations came from the snipers on overwatch. Eric, Cassidy, and Wyatt replied with affirmatives, followed quickly by Jake, Beckam, the Mahers, then Rory, Walker, and—of all people—Jameson. How did that guy get around?

"We thought something like this might go down," Zack told Heston. "When in doubt, overcompensate. Obermeyer wanted a fight, now he's got one."

"But no London," Heston reminded everyone with venom. He bit his tongue before he lost his temper.

"Wherever she is, Hes, she'll need you when you find her, so shut up and stop bitching!" Cassidy yelled. "Wherever they're taking her, she's hurt, and if the blood in here is all hers, she's hurt bad. Take care of your woman when you catch up with her, and put those bastards down while we take care of these jerks. Christ, don't you trust us?"

"I do, but—"

"You already knew Obermeyer and Keane were involved in human smuggling," Zack reminded him.

"Yeah, but—" Heston was ashamed to admit he only cared about London. Where the hell was she? In that bag in the rear of Obermeyer's Suburban? Already in the Potomac? Eric said someone had been hung, that there'd been blood spatter. Was that someone London? How bad had they hurt her? How—how hurt? Tortured? Raped? Christ, he couldn't handle the ugly thoughts racing through his mind.

"Same here," Lee Hart announced grimly, from which container Heston had no idea. "No little girls, but around twenty young women. They're scared of us, they're skinny, and they're dehydrated. Eric? Can you give us a hand when you're done in three?"

"You bet, but I'm going to need help."

"Stand by, people. Metro PD just called and an army of EMTs are on their way to you," Mother announced solemnly.

Selfishly, all Heston wanted was for Zack to slam the accelerator to the floor and catch up with those SUVs. Listening to this complex take-down and not participating in it was killing him. His TEAM had all put their lives on the line to rescue London. But they hadn't found her!

Out of the blue, Zack cuffed the back of his head.

"What the hell, Lennox!"

"Knock it off, Hes. If Obermeyer's got her, and you know damned well he does, then she's still alive. Trust me. She's in the back of the Suburban the old guy's driving. Want to bet he's the Irishman?"

"I don't give a shit who he is. He beat her. I'll kill them all."

"And I'll let you, brother, but we can't take them out on the George Washington Parkway, can we? Collateral damage is unacceptable. You still got us covered, Mother?"

"You bet. We're tracking your GPS, and we've got two drones in the sky overhead. Both on the SUVs you're following, in case one splits from the other. The Parkway will take them all the way to Maryland, but I doubt they'll cross state lines."

Heston choked. "Why not? Because Obermeyer's politically connected? One of the elite? A fuckin' upstanding citizen?"

"No, smartass, because we've identified two of the men with him, the Branson twins, Bernie and Buzz. They're on parole for the same armed robbery. They set one foot out of state and they'll be headed back to prison."

Like that mattered to armed assailants, felons who shouldn't be carrying the hardware these guys probably had, to begin with. "And again I ask—"

"Shut the hell up, Contreras!" Mother yelled. "I'm not stupid. You follow your gut, don't you? Well, I follow mine, and when I tell you what's going on, you'd better listen up and believe me, understood?"

Zack snickered.

Well, damn. Heston wasn't going to win, and honestly, there was no sense arguing with Mother. He zipped his lips and watched the scenery fly by, as the GW snaked along the southern shore of the Potomac River. The farther northwest they went, the deeper the forests the GW ran through and the darker the shadows over the highway. Virginia's hardwood trees were ancient giants. Thick, gnarly branches arched over miles of some sections of the road, creating shadowy tunnels broken only by rare bursts of sunshine. Even that dimmed as the predicted easterly weather front moved in. Heston's mood dimmed along with it. He needed to get to London. The advancing rain and the casual chit-chat between Mother and Zack didn't help.

"Just passed Snake Island," Zack advised her. "Next exit will put them near US Park Police District, Station Two, if they take it." He turned to Heston. "You think Captain Bates had input on Keane's and Obermeyer's plans for London?"

Heston couldn't answer. It made sense that Bates might know someone at Station Two, though. Both the US Forest Service and Station Two ahead, along with the Bureau of Trust Funds Administration, the Office of Surface Mining Reclamation and Enforcement, US Fish and Wildlife, as well as US Geological Survey, fell under National Park Service oversight. NPS, in turn, fell under the Department of Interior. A USFS ranger from Washington State might've worked with someone from Virginia's Station Two in the past. Hell, Bates worked for Malloy, who'd worked for Obermeyer and Keane. There could be a link between any one of them and Station Two. Probable? Not likely, but still possible.

Because he couldn't do anything to help London, Heston's brain kept spewing good-to-know but useless information. Such as Sterling Johnson, successful businessman and trusted friend of President Adams. Also nominated to his current position as NPS director by Adams and just as quickly confirmed by the United States Senate.

After Senate confirmation, it was the newly promoted NPS director's responsibility to hire six senior executives to manage NPS national programs, policies, and budget. Each of those senior executives was given the power to hire regional directors who, in turn, managed the various branches of the National Park Service, including, but not limited to: Forest Service Rangers, Law Enforcement Officers (LEOs), Park Management, Fire Management, Resource Management, Marketing, Publicity, Administration, et cetera. The scope of NPS was as far-reaching as DoD's scope. It was likely that Bates knew at least one person in the police station ahead. In fact—

A veritable lightning strike hit Heston's frontal lobe and lit up his neural receptors like fireworks on the Fourth of July. A person's frontal lobe was where logical thinking, planning, organizing, and deductive reasoning, and—

No. More. Shitting minutia!

"I know who the Irishman is," he hissed, as his agile, intelligent mind continued to identify logical links at the speed of that same lightning strike. "Miles Wirth is the Senior Executive over NPS Administration. His father's from Ireland, still lives there. Lancaster Wirth from County Armagh—"

"Isn't that in Northern Ireland?" Zack asked.

"Yes," Mother replied. "So?"

"Figures," Zack snorted.

"Okay, so Northern Ireland, yes, but not Belfast. Not involved, that anyone knows of, in any car bombings or assassinations or—"

"That anyone knows of," Mother interjected.

"Guys. Listen. Lancaster was up on racketeering charges in the States seven years and eight months ago, but the only eye-witness who could have identified him died in an unexplained explosion. Problem was Wirth had diplomatic immunity. The FBI couldn't make charges stick without their witness, and—" *Shit!* Heston couldn't get his brain to stop spewing details from the news articles he'd read years ago.

"Be advised both vehicles are exiting," Mother interrupted calmly, which allowed Heston to draw in a breath after rambling like the eidetic idiot he was. "The right turn will take them into Station Two's parking lot. The left puts them back on the GW with ramps that'll head in either direction."

"There's also a dirt trail on the far west loop of that left turn that'll take them down the banks of Turkey Run," Zack replied.

"Yes, and that river empties into the Potomac. I hear it's good fishing," Mother said.

"Good hunting, too," Zack added darkly.

"And Lancaster's the asshole who put that hit on Kelsey!" Heston bellowed to get Mother's and Zack's attention. "Listen to me! He's not the Irishman. He didn't give Alex that burner phone. His son did. Miles is the Irishman. He was never as strong nor as respected as his old man. I know that because I've read the trial transcripts. All of them!"

Because I am just that anal.

"Lancaster's pulling the strings. Miles is just another one of his puppets. Trust me on this, guys. I'm right. Miles' oldest daughter is Katherine, aka Kitten. Kitten Wirth Bates. She married Devon Bates. She's the cocktail waitress who set Bates up with one of Keane's loan sharks. Now he thinks he owes them or they'll kill her. But they won't because the Wirth family runs the Irish Mafia in America now. Only the real boss lives in Ireland. Lancaster is that boss!"

"In Ireland where he's untouchable," Zack surmised.

"Your gut telling you this, Hes?" Mother asked with enough snark to choke a horse.

"That and listening to you guys yack. The second Zack mentioned US Park Police District, Station Two, my thoughts splintered off to a news article I read a few years back on the Wirth family. At the time it meant nothing. But with Miles now Senior Executive over the NPS Administration, it makes sense. He's connected to the Irish Mafia. Hell, he is the Irish Mafia, and I'll bet each of you a hundred bucks nobody knows that, not even our President."

"You do realize Miles would've gone through extensive screening before he was hired for any government position, don't you?" Mother asked.

"And you realize how easy it is for the Irish Mafia to grease the right palms, pay somebody to look the other way in our messed-up federal government, right?" Heston had her there and he knew it.

"That's true, but… damn it. You might be right. Hold, please. I'm getting Mark on the line and… Mark? Heston knows who the Irishman is, and Alex isn't going to like it."

At last! Not *'thinks he knows'*, but *'knows'*.

"Who?" Mark barked.

"Tell him, Hes," Mother ordered. So Heston repeated what he knew to be true, then explained his line of reasoning and how he got there.

"Alex'll go ape-shit crazy," Mark muttered. "Where are you guys?"

"West on the GW, on Obermeyer's tail," Zack answered. "Pretty sure Miles is driving the SUV with Obermeyer and Lancaster, also London, if that's her in the body bag. Mother, have you run him through your facial rec program yet? Can you verify the driver ahead of us? Is he the Irishman?"

"If he's Miles, where's his old man, Lancaster?" Mark asked before Mother could reply.

"Unknown," Heston answered. "But if Miles and Obermeyer are here—"

"Let me worry about Lancaster. There's got to be photos of Miles online… Traffic cams…" Mother must've muted her headset, because suddenly her voice belted out, "Found him! Miles Wirth is driving the first SUV. The older guy with Obermeyer is—Shit! It's Lancaster Wirth. You're following the men responsible for trying to kill Kelsey and kidnapping London."

"End them," Mark ordered vehemently. "You heard Alex. Kill the sons of bitches."

"Copy that," Heston barked back. "After London's safe."

Mark disconnected and Zack glanced at Heston. "How the hell do you know all this?"

Heston didn't have time to explain how his brain worked. It was nothing to be proud of, not as long as it had taken him to connect the dots between Bates, Keane, Obermeyer, Miles, and Lancaster. "It stands to reason. Lancaster worked closely with Pops Delaney," Heston postulated, "which is how he knew about Alex."

"Because Mel Stewart ran with Delaney, yeah. I get that."

"And because Mel's a braggart and a do-nothing. Back then, he probably wanted to get in good with the boss. It would've made him a big man to hang with someone as powerful as Lancaster. So he sucked up like any spineless, wannabe gangster does with a drug lord." Which essentially, Lancaster Wirth was.

"Okay, yeah. Mel blabbed about how successful Alex and his business were, about Alex's wife, kids, and—"

"And when President Adams publicly invited Alex to stand with him as his next VP," Heston cut in, "Wirth saw a way to get inside the White House. He figured all he had to do was put the fear of losing his family into Alex, and Alex would fold like his own weak-kneed son did."

"Giving Lancaster undue influence in American politics," Mother breathed. "Son of a bitch!" And now she sounded like Alex.

"Hold on, London," Hes whispered. "I'm coming, baby. I'm—"

"We're coming," Zack snapped. "You tell her *we're* coming. You and me and Mom, and *we're* taking every last one of these motherfuckers down!"

The Porsche leaped forward at Zack's command. The quick response of the horses under its sleek black hood pushed Heston into his seat. He turned to really look at Zack then. The big man was a bald chunk of bronzed, carved granite and just as hard. A Marine like Alex, mean and mad as hell. His knuckles were big and white on the steering wheel. His dark brows were slammed together over the angry scowl of a fire-breathing gargoyle. It helped knowing a man like Zack had his back. Heston took a breath and let himself hope. Obermeyer and Lancaster thought they'd backed Alex into a corner by sending Malloy and his smart gun after Kelsey?

Guess again, assholes. You pissed off the wrong Devil Dogs. You're already dead. You just don't know it.

Chapter Twenty-Eight

London fell to her knees, then scrambled as quickly as she could into the prickly cover of the thickest briar patch she'd ever seen. Thorns dug at her already-bruised skin, tearing long scratches down her battered arms, chest, and belly. The wiry brambles were as sharp as barbed-wire. The deeper into the brush she went, the harder those thorns gouged every bit of her naked body. Regardless, she plowed through, needing to be out of sight and hidden within the depths of this naturally made hellhole, instead of trapped in the one waiting for her if Obermeyer and his hunting buddies found her. She was damned if she'd go down easy. Not here. No way. She absolutely planned to save those other women. They deserved a chance, too. She would rescue them. She would!

But to do that, she needed to live, and to live, she had to hide for as long as it took to catch her breath and form a workable plan. When Obermeyer and his creepy friends stuffed her into that body bag and smuggled her out of that stinking container, at first, she'd thought they'd dumped her on a couple dead bodies. Until one of them moved and another whimpered. That tiny sound led to quiet questions and muffled answers. She now knew there had been three other women with her: Maria, Tandy, and Felicia. Then. Now—only two remained. London was the only one who could save them.

So she would—somehow. The game they were caught up in was as barbaric as the jerks hunting them.

The moment Obermeyer unzipped the body bag, he ordered her and the other women to, "Take your clothes off! All of you! Hurry! Drop 'em! Everything goes. Faster, gawddamnit!"

Hurriedly, she'd undressed, but tried to maintain some level of situational awareness while she did. She didn't have a clue where she was, and she didn't recognize the bikers in leather vests with Obermeyer. Had never seen them before. Neither did she recognize the two gentlemen in suits—make that assholes—with him. Both watched her and the other women undress like a couple perverts.

Once she and the other women were naked and shivering, Obermeyer lifted his rifle, which she was pretty sure was a Ruger Bolt Action, aimed it at her head, and bragged, "This rifle's same as the ones Alaskan guides use to hunt grizzlies and Kodiak bears, little girl."

"Get it, sweet cheeks?" the red-haired, whiskered man at his elbow aimed that insult at her.

Obermeyer wore a pea-green cloth hat and what she thought were hunting clothes. Everything looked new, crisp, and clean. The creepy guys with him were another story. All wore flannel shirts under vests, ragged jeans, and dirty work boots. The other two men—the perverts—were in suits. Nice suits. They were armed with pistols that—hopefully—wouldn't hit the moving target she'd intended to turn into.

London covered her breasts as much as she could. Why were they all staring at her? Besides the obvious fact that her face was swollen, she probably looked like a Halloween mask, and the rest of her was black and blue.

"I don't think she gets it." The older guy in immaculate, *pleated dress slacks, a pressed white shirt, and a dark red tie, stuck his chin at her. "Why don't you explain it for Miss Wilde, Biff?"*

Biff, the red-haired moron, snickered. "Bare, not bear, get it, toots? As in bare-assed bitches who are right now gonna run for their fuckin' lives!"

"'Fore we shoot 'em in their pasty-white asses!"

"Yeah!" The guy with the green mohawk crowed like a freak out of a science fiction horror show. "Prey don't need underwear, so git going, chickies! Run, run, run!"

While the men laughed and yelled ugly obscenities after the other women ran, London held her ground, thinking the least she would do before she died was tell these bastards to go to hell. Until Biff raised his rifle, took aim, and shot Tandy in the back.

"You killed her!" London shrieked, her tiny shred of confidence now as dead as her new friend.

"Sure did. Bagged me the fat one," he bragged. "Weren't even hard, as slow and wide as she was."

Tandy. The blonde. The mother with a tiny baby at home.

"Keep standing there and I'm gonna bag me another," Biff declared.

"No!" Obermeyer yelled. He lifted his rifle stock to his cheek, shut his non-dominant eye, and aimed at London. "The blue-haired fairy's been a thorn in my side long enough. She doesn't need to run. Get over here, Wilde. Don't make me come get you."

"Let me get her for you," the mohawk-sporting jerk crowed. "I want a piece of that."

London understood then why discretion was the better part of valor. Living to fight another day wasn't cowardly, it was smart. She turned her bare backside on those asshats and she ran as fast as her poor battered, bloodied feet allowed. Zigzagged through the brush. Kept away from clearings and trails. By then, the men behind her were laughing and howling, peppering the forest with gunshot. Birdshot. Buckshot. Blanks or whatever. They didn't hit her, but they'd kill her the first chance they got. At least wound her, and who knew what they'd do once she couldn't run anymore.

Like the pompous prick he was, Obermeyer bellowed, "Listen up, ladies! There's only three of you left, so I'm going to be gracious and give you three chances. First three times we catch one of you, we'll let you go, promise. Might not let you go easy, but them's the rules. You get caught, you'll have to offer up a little something extra" —his buddies grunted and laughed— "before you get to run again."

London shivered at what that something extra would be.

"But the fourth time we find your sorry asses…" Another shot rang out. "Fourth time's the charm, sweet cheeks. That's when you end up dead and your ass gets hung by your ankles in one of these trees for your girlfriends to see. So run, little girls. Run fast. Run far. If you're lucky and survive this little contest, you get to live and we'll never bother you again. Promise."

Again with the snickers and obscene comments. The lies.

Something rustled in the trees over the briar patch where London was hiding. She looked up and—shit—straight into the bright red dot of a laser beam pointing down at her. Not fair.

Obermeyer pursed his lips and blew her a kiss. "Got you. Now get your ass out of there, Wilde, so I can get a better look at them long legs. Nice and easy. Don't want more scratches on that sweet ass of yours. If you're real good, I won't alert the others. They don't have to know I found you. That means you get four chances instead of three. Sound good?"

Like hell.

He licked his lips. "Never expected I'd be the first to fuck a blue-haired pixie."

The first? Bet me he isn't going to tell the others. Liar.

Turning around as quickly as her bloody toes and feet allowed, with her heart pounding in her chest, London scurried back the way she'd come. On her hands and knees, sure. There was no other way out of those wicked brambles. But faster this time. Knowing he might be getting an eyeful, but daring to hope—

No. Not daring. Knowing. Believing with all her heart that Heston was in these same woods looking for her. Right now. He loved her. He always would. He was coming for her.

Once she cleared what would've been a thorny barricade between her and these red-necked assholes, she dug the tips of her mangled toes into the hard dirt under her feet and took off at a sprint. Toes were now expendable. These bastards wanted her to run, so she ran. For her life. For the lives of her two remaining friends in these woods. The ground turned to mush and mud the farther she ran, not like that lessened the pain in her feet. But if nothing else, she'd die trying.

No sooner wished for than—something hit between her shoulder blades and down she went, hard. Her poor, bare backside roller-coasted over a slippery slide of wet greenery that sent her through more barbed-wire-laced underbrush, until it finally dumped her feet first in the shade of towering oak.

Obermeyer thundered down that same slope, on his feet, not his ass.

London scrambled to her feet. God, they hurt.

Too late. Too slow. Obermeyer attacked before she caught her balance. He had her by her throat and shook her so hard that tiny red stars glittered at her peripheral.

"Gotcha," he growled, his fingertips dug into her windpipe.

She couldn't breathe. Striking back, she raked her nails across his face.

Lifting his other hand, he slapped her.

For one brief instant, she wondered where his fancy rifle went. But her head pounded with that slap, and her vision went bonkers. More than intel, she needed air. All her battered, bloodied nostrils dragged in was the reek of sweat and men's cologne. She remembered that smell from where she'd been beaten. He'd punched and slapped her.

"You stink like shit," she breathed, wishing she were strong and brave like Scarlett Johansson.

"You think you're so damned smart," Obermeyer hissed. Lifting his free hand over her head, he slapped her again. He shook her and she turned into a loose-limbed doll. "But I've got you now, and you're gonna pay for fucking with me. On your knees!" He threw her to the ground. "It's my turn to fuck you!"

London managed to roll to her back before he could deliver on his threat. She had no doubt he'd rape her. He was a big guy, not big like Heston, but heavy. Overweight with a fat roll around his middle, Obermeyer probably raped all the women and girls he kidnapped before he sold them. She already knew he was a greedy bastard.

Isn't that what pedophiles and perverts did? Think of themselves first?

"I said, on your knees!" he ordered, whipping the leather belt out of his pant loops, making it crack like the whip it was.

"No!" she yelled back, as loud as she could. Too bad her defiance came out like a whimper.

Obermeyer took a menacing step forward.

London crab-walked backward, keeping her swollen, blurry eyes on him. She wouldn't get far. There were bushes and trees behind her.

In seconds Obermeyer had her by the neck again. She kicked. She flailed. Without enough air, all her efforts went into fighting the grip he had on her.

'Hurry Hes. I know you're coming. I know you love me. So hurry.' She could feel him in the air. He was nearby, almost there. She believed it with every noisy beat of her panic-stricken heart. He would save her. He would! All she had to do was stay alive long enough until—

Darkness closed in.

Chapter Twenty-Nine

Heston heard that belt snap. One look at London turned him into a red-zone killer. There she was, on the other side of that bush, caught like a tiny, fluttering bird in Obermeyer's fist. She was naked! The jackass was on his damned cell phone, bragging, "I caught the blue-haired pixie. This little bitch cost me plenty, and trust me, I'm taking what she owes out of her backside. You wanna watch, get here quick because I'm not waiting."

The fuck you say! Heston silenced his comm link, tuned out the rest of the world, and zeroed down on Obermeyer. Lowering his shoulder, Heston turned into a freight train and charged straight through the bush. Obermeyer didn't see or hear him, probably thought Heston was one of his *good old boys* come to watch him rape a defenseless woman. Who weighed next to gawddamned nothing!

Before Obermeyer could cry out, Heston tackled the pompous prick to the dirt and pressed his forearm to the guy's windpipe. London collapsed on her side in the dirt. Heston shot her a quick, appraising look to make sure she was breathing. She was the important one there. She'd always come first, even if saving her meant letting Obermeyer get away.

Once it was clear that London was coming around, Heston leaned his weight on Obermeyer's throat. "Let's see how you like it!" he hissed, so damned angry he was spitting.

Cocking his free arm, Heston delivered a wicked right hook that wiped the smug off the bastard's face. Again! Again and again!

Obermeyer was dressed like the stolen honor bastard he was, in high-priced cammies that had never sweated out a forced five-mile march. The spiffy Boonie hat strapped under his double chin hadn't seen one second of combat, much less war. Probably hadn't been worn for anything other than hunting defenseless women. No tactical vest and no gawddamned sense. Fool was completely unarmed. His fancy rifle lay on the ground. Probably tossed it when he couldn't manage it and London at the same time.

But Heston was armed to the teeth, outfitted for close combat, and trained in all the ways there were to kill a man. And he would kill this pig. That was all Obermeyer was.

Heston let his inner caveman loose. That feral beast, along with Heston's tactical knuckle gloves, made short work of Obermeyer's plump lips, his perfect, straight teeth, his elegant nose, and his wide-open eyes. Heston had no fucks left to give. In short order the arrogant ass on the ground was reduced to a blubbering pile of snot, shit, and blood. Obermeyer couldn't see anymore. His face was hamburger. His orbital bones were mush inside the ragged skin of his swollen face. Big red gaps replaced his front teeth, and Heston hoped he'd swallowed every last bit of that perfect dental work.

Obermeyer batted Heston's gloved hands away. Not happening. He begged for his life. He cried like a weak little girl. The murderer and rapist swore he was sorry, that he hadn't meant to get carried away or hurt anyone.

Like Heston cared? Obermeyer had the nerve to mumble apologies, to swear on his mother's grave he'd never, ever hurt another woman again.

Too fuckin' late.

"Man up, you gawddamned motherfucker!" Heston roared into Obermeyer's battered face. "You're tough enough to terrorize women and little girls, yet you can't take an ass-whipping when you deserve it? Fucking coward!"

Tipping back on his haunches, Heston pulled out his knife, snapped it open with a quick flick of his wrist, and stabbed Obermeyer's windpipe. The breath wheezed and bubbled out of him. He was a mighty big guy when he was hiding behind a high-powered rifle and threatening women. But he was out of shape, overweight, and he hadn't come prepared to fight like a man.

Like the bloodthirsty devil it was, Heston's inner caveman roared for more blood. He was out of control and it felt gawddamned good. This was why he'd been born, to rid the world of despicable bastards like Obermeyer and his cronies. With a wicked swipe of that razor-sharp blade, Heston severed Obermeyer's carotid arteries, then jumped away from the asswipe who'd dared harm London, to avoid the blood spurting from the guy's throat.

Obermeyer gurgled, but didn't do a damned thing to save himself. Didn't try once to compress the spigots Heston opened in his neck. In seconds, his heaving chest stilled.

It was over. Justice was done and revenge was sweet.

Stooping over, Heston wiped his blade on Obermeyer's trendy camouflage pants, and finally looked for London. She hadn't gone far. Sheathing his knife, he located her easily. She'd curled into a ball behind a bush. Typical of victims, making herself as small as possible. Her arms were around her bare legs, and her battered face was buried between her bloody, scraped knees.

Heston's heart melted. Ripping off his blood-stained gloves, he stuffed them in his rear pocket and walked to her, uncertain of what she'd think of him now. She'd just seen him murder a man. Righteous? Abso-fuckin'-lutely. Legal? That remained to be seen. Heston wouldn't contest a murder charge if it came down to that. He did it. He killed Obermeyer. He broke the law, and he knew the consequences. But he'd do it again to save London's life.

Dropping to one knee at her side, he turned his comm link back on and asked, "Mother? You still with me?"

"Yes, Heston. I'm here for you, honey. How's London?"

Honey? That was new. Heston had no idea how Mother knew he'd found London. He cared less when she told him, "Everyone not guarding TEAM HQ is on their way to assist you. Should I send EMTs or will Eric be enough? He's closest to your location. Is she hurt bad?"

"Just Eric. Thanks."

"Talk to me, Hes. How is she? Really?" Was Mother crying? Sure sounded like it.

"She's alive and she's scared. Not sure how badly she's hurt yet. But Obermeyer's dead."

"Good," Mother replied without hesitation. "Err, umm, I had drones overhead, remember?"

Oh, yeah. Drones. Damn. Mother'd seen everything.

"I'd do it again," he growled defensively, daring her to reprimand him and ready to fight the world for London if he had to.

"I know. Honey, trust me, I know. I'm so glad you got to her in time. That rat bastard needed to die, and London needs you now. Take care of her. Eric is five minutes out." Mother could be a nosy gal, but she really was all heart.

"Thanks, Mom." London sniffed and Heston disconnected. "Babe," he whispered, swiping his forearm over his forehead in case it wasn't sweat dripping into his eyes.

London lifted her chin. Blinked. Then lurched forward and crashed into him. "Th-thank you," she cried, pressing her bare body against his chest. "He… he was going to rape me, Hes. Him and… and those other guys. There's seven of them, h-h-him and four bikers and two creeps in s-s-suits."

Hiccups punctuated every sentence. Her shoulders shuddered and her chest heaved with short, hard gasps. She was sweaty and hyperventilating and still providing intel. Seeing her broken like this tore Heston apart. Gently, so as not to hurt her anymore, he gathered her onto his lap. It didn't take long to jerk the roll of extra clothes out of his go-bag and get London dressed. She was all thumbs, tears, and stutters, trying to help, and he'd never been more sure of his love for this beautiful woman.

"I thought I'd lost you," he said, as he tugged the extra pair of pants up her long, dirty legs. Those poor bloodied toes. She'd truly been in the fight of her life. "Sorry. No underwear. You'll have to go commando. But you can't walk, sweetheart. I'm carrying you out of here."

"I-I knew you'd c-c-come. Only had to l-l-live long enough and… and f-f-fight… and… and…" Breaking down, she buried her face in her hands. Poor sweet thing hadn't stopped fighting, not even after Obermeyer'd had her by the throat. The bastard!

"Lift your arms, babe." Fighting to control his rage, Heston pulled his extra TEAM shirt over her arms, head, and shoulders. It was long enough it covered her bouncing knees. She was still in fight-or-flight mode, her nerves strung tight and adrenaline kicking her butt. But she was safe.

Tenderly, Heston tucked her under his chin again, one palm flat to her back, his other unholstering one of his pistols. There was no way he wouldn't shoot the next fucker who came after London. He laid the loaded weapon within reach beside his hip, then wrapped both arms as tight as he could around London without hurting her.

She settled into him with an anxious whine. They were both shaking. Both suffering the after-effects of too much adrenaline. Her ear was flat against his heart. Her nails dug into his ribs, as if she didn't dare let him go. He was her lifeline, and he'd never been more content than right then. Even with Obermeyer dead nearby.

"Am I hurting you?"

"I'm sorry, but, yeah. M-my ribs, Hes. It's hard to… to catch a breath. I think one's broken."

Heston bit his tongue. She'd been beaten and nearly raped—gang-raped, for Christ's sake! She'd been humiliated, made to strip for Obermeyer's fucked-up idea of entertainment. In front of his asshole friends. The mere thought of what she'd lived through enraged Heston all over again.

His soul screamed to wreak the bloodiest vengeance on Obermeyer's buddies. To rip every last one of them apart. To make them pay and cry and beg for mercy. The first chance he got, once London was safely out of there, he'd hunt those asswipes down, gut every one of them, and hang them by their intestines, high in the trees. They'd never, ever hurt anyone else—

"Th-thanks for rescuing me." London's soft whisper interrupted Heston's feverish need to wreak mayhem.

He squeezed his eyes closed, fighting to be the gentle man she needed, not the brutal barbarian with blood-stained hands and the stink of Death clinging to him. She *was* safe. She *was* his. And best of all, Obermeyer *was* dead. Sometimes a man had to focus on what—or who, in this case—was in his hands, instead of wishing the moment away and going after worthless scum.

A quiet, "Pssst" broke the moment. In a flash, Heston's pistol was in his hand and whoever that fucker who'd whispered was, he'd better be prepared to die.

Zack. Thank God. It was Zack in the shadows with an index finger to his lips and his rifle across his chest, stock up, barrel down. Striding straight for Heston, he dropped to his knees. Digging out a black canteen from under his tactical vest, Zack unscrewed the cap and handed it to London. "Here, darlin'. Have a drink. Easy now. Not too much. Not too fast, either. There you go. My car's just a hop, skip, and a jump away, Miss London. Feel like letting me take over this hunt of yours while Heston gets you to a hospital?"

"Ah-huh, yeah," she mumbled, water dribbling over her chin and running down her neck.

"You're scaring her, Zack. Step back!" Heston growled. *Before I have to beat your ass, too. Cuz I sure as fuck will.*

But London surprised him. With a deep, shuddering breath, she faced Zack, handed the canteen back, and replied through swollen, torn lips, "Yeah, I think I've had enough f-f-fun for one d-d-day."

Zack put a big, gloved hand on her shoulder. "I'll bet you have, kiddo. You can be certain of one thing. These guys aren't ever going to hurt you again. Our friendly FBI's in these woods, too. Guess we interfered with their ongoing investigation into Obermeyer and his friends. No need to worry about anything, London. Heston'll take good care of you."

"Tucker Chase and his team? They're here?" Heston hoped.

Zack nodded but added nothing more.

"Anyone know where Obermeyer's boss went?" Heston asked.

Zack's gaze dropped to London, before he shook his head and looked over Heston's shoulder. "No, but I understand there's an old cougar scavenging near the river today. Don't worry about anyone but London, Hes. Get her inside my car. Eric'll be there soon."

Heston hoped that scavenging old cougar had ice-blue eyes and a razor-sharp hunting knife. If that cat was who he suspected, the Wirths wouldn't last the day.

"Will do. Thanks for the intel." It was time to relocate London. The farther from Obermeyer's stink, the better.

Zack pushed to his feet. His dark eyes flickered into the trees beyond. "No problem, Hes. Stay frosty."

"Wait! Don't go! Zack!" London panicked. "You have to save them. He killed Tandy. Shot her in the back, but Maria and Felicia are still out there, hiding. P-please. You have to find—"

"Shush, darlin'," Zack whispered, running the back of his gloved fingers down London's cheek. "They're already safe. Promise. A couple of Heston's friends found Maria, an FBI agent located Felicia. Your friends are on their way to the nearest hospital. Tandy's been recovered and cared for, too. You done real good."

London went limp in Heston's arms. "I didn't. I should've saved Tandy, b-b-but—thank you. Thank you so much."

Zack's brown eyes glistened. "You can't save everyone, Miss London. Sorry, but that's just a fact of combat. You save who you can, then you live to fight another day. You're an extraordinary woman. Bet you thought you had to rescue Maria, Tandy, and Felicia all by yourself, didn't you?"

She nodded. "They needed someone on their side."

Zack looked to Heston. "Take this warrior home, Hes. She's done enough. We'll take it from here."

"Appreciate it," Heston replied, his throat so full of respect for London's bravery that he could hardly speak.

"It's been really nice meeting you, Zack," London murmured against Heston's chest.

"London Wilde" —Zack touched two fingers to his forehead in a salute of respect— "the pleasure's all mine. Now go. My car'll take you anywhere you want." With a curt nod, he disappeared into the dark.

"Wow, he's a really, really big guy," London whispered.

"And one of the best." Heston cradled her tenderly, as he lifted to his feet and set a course for Zack's Porsche. It wasn't far, and Hes made good time. He'd barely settled London onto the passenger seat when he clocked Tucker Chase stalking around one of Obermeyer's SUVs. Tate Higgins rounded the other SUV, the one with two pairs of muddy boots extending from the rear gate. Tucker said something to Tate. Tate stuck his chin in Heston's direction.

Heston covered London with the blanket Zack kept behind the driver's seat. She was quiet when Heston straightened and stared at Tucker and Tate across the roof of the Porsche. Both men were kitted-out in black FBI SWAT gear and carrying enough armament for a small army.

"Your boss with you?" Tucker asked without preamble.

Heston shrugged. "Far as I know, he's back at TEAM HQ with his wife. Why?" He wasn't about to admit anything, much less indict Alex or any member of his TEAM for what had happened or might happen today. Chase was still FBI and, technically, the Bureau was supposed to follow some ridiculously redundant ROEs to cover their federal asses.

Thank heavens, Tucker didn't press for more information on Alex. Good thing. Because Heston wasn't up for fighting two guys. Both Tucker and Tate were big as bears, and Heston had other places to be.

"Kelsey snapped out of it?"

"Not as far as I know. But Libby said Alex needed to be there when she did, so her waking up sounded imminent." Heston nodded toward the boots. "You taking out the trash?"

Tucker scrubbed a hand over his face. "Yup. Been investigating Obermeyer and what he calls his hunting club for over a year now. Your woman okay?"

"She will be," Eric Reynolds declared, as he stepped out from the bushes at the edge of the trees. "Where's London?"

"Here," Heston told him. "Thanks for meeting us."

"It's what I do." Eric came swiftly to Heston's side.

Eric was USMC down to his boots, but he should've been a practicing physician. That was his true talent.

Heston tipped his head inside the Porsche and told London, "Babe, Eric Reynolds is The TEAM medic. He's going to take a quick look before we evac you to Georgetown. You can trust him. Are you okay with him checking you over?"

She swallowed hard and nodded, but didn't say anything. Heston had a feeling something had changed since he'd sat with her under that bush. She wasn't looking at him anymore. Her head was down. Was she embarrassed or hurting? He wasn't sure. It was his turn to swallow hard. Was this the beginning of the end?

Chapter Thirty

Alex cocked his head at the sound of dead air in his earpiece. Zack wasn't answering. Not unusual for a man when he went dark.

"That's the problem with this younger generation," Alex told the man straining against the expertly knotted red silk tie binding his too-soft-to-have-ever-worked-a-day-in-his-life hands, over the thick branch of this ancient oak. "They don't think they need to keep in touch with their elders."

Straining and kicking wouldn't help Lancaster Wirth. He wasn't going anywhere, not with his bare feet barely touching planet Earth and a gag in his mouth. Which was exactly how he'd treated London inside container three.

The best payback involved giving pricks like Lancaster a taste of what they'd brazenly dished out to others. He got off on beating, demeaning, and raping women? Now it was his turn in the barrel, so to speak. Alex had to admit, the idea had merit, stuffing this bloated ego into a steel drum, soldering the lid shut, leaving the screaming gunrunner, drug lord, murderer, and flesh peddler in the dark for the rest of time and eternity. But...

Alex shook off all the morbidly creative ways this day could end. He hadn't brought a barrel with him, damn it. Maybe next time. Because there would always be a next time in this messed-up world.

At the moment, Tucker Chase had three agents from his psychic team combing through the forensic evidence in Keane's containers. They'd collected plenty of DNA evidence. It was everywhere, more proof that those slick bastards thoroughly believed they were untouchable. But, since DNA took months to process, Tucker also sent his star investigator, Eden Stark Winchester, into container three to work her psychic magic.

All she'd had to do was simply touch the floor that London had bled on, that her poor toes had slipped and slid over while she'd been beaten. With her sensitive fingertips, Eden had *seen* the ghastly minute-by-minute replay of what London endured. Eden had already proven that Lancaster had restrained London in container three and how. She knew Obermeyer, Keane, and Lancaster were joint owners in their illicit business. But with her psychic skills, Eden had *seen* Lancaster deliberately hang an unconscious London by her wrists to those overhead pipes. She'd *watched* him joke and chat with Obermeyer and Keane while he'd tied a thick, dense hood over London's head. She'd *watched* him turn on the hose that Keane had so obediently provided. Lancaster was the bastard who'd waterboarded London, and he'd damned near drowned her.

Eden *heard* Obermeyer and Keane ask London multiple times where Alex was.

What Alex hadn't known, until Tucker relayed Eden's findings, was that, somehow, Lancaster, Obermeyer, and Keane had known Kelsey was no longer in Washington, that they couldn't use her to get to him. Alex stiffened as he recalled how many times London had begged them to stop hurting her. How over and over, she'd told Lancaster, "I don't know where h-h-he is."

Which was true. But instead of inventing a plausible lie to forestall more pain, she'd simply taken the hits and endured to the end. Foolish? Yes, but also damned brave.

Cocking his neck, Alex lifted one shoulder to squelch the tension radiating up his neck. London, God bless her, shouldn't have protected him, shouldn't have bled a single drop of blood for him. She should've given him up. That would've been smart. But he had to respect a fellow warrior who'd given all, who'd stared into the face of Death and spat in its eye, if only to prove that she could. Which made her USMC material in his book.

All Wirth and Obermeyer'd had to do was ask. Alex would've told them precisely where to find him. Of course, he would've killed them when they'd arrived, that was a given. Overall, it would've saved everyone this troublesome day, and London wouldn't be suffering like she was. But they hadn't asked. Instead, they'd tortured the courageous young woman Alex owed his wife's life to. Big fuckin' mistake.

Eventually, the coroner and the DNA would corroborate Eden's intel. Too bad that wouldn't happen fast enough to save Lancaster or his son, the infamous, chicken-shit that Alex had erroneously dubbed 'the Irishman.'

Irish, nothing. The Wirths might've come from Irish stock, but they were lowlifes. Certainly nothing like Patrick Bradley Stewart, Alex's paternal grandfather, a true Irishman who'd fought bravely at Iwo Jima in World War Two, who'd come home injured, then taken in Alex and his mom. That after Mel, Gramp's son, also Alex's deadbeat father, had deserted his wife and only child to run off and play bigshot with Pops Delaney, the kingpin of the Irish Mafia in Boston. Delaney, who Alex now knew had been his gawddamned uncle. The ungrateful son who'd changed his name from Stewart to Delaney. The child Gramps had never talked about, not even once.

Talk about a rude awakening, to find yourself in line to inherit a 'family business' you never knew existed. Which was why those thousands of dollars of alleged 'insurance' money from the Irish mob had rained down on Alex, since Jameson had righteously ended Delaney's daughter in Boston. Lancaster must've been the one sending it. He'd honestly thought Alex could be bought?

Hell, no. That money was blood money and Alex made sure the local police charity received every last tainted penny. Alex didn't want it. Would've sent it back if he'd known Lancaster Wirth was behind it.

After container three, Eden investigated the other containers and revealed the names of the women and children Keane had kidnapped and kept in those containers until he could transport them overseas. Like cargo, the bastard. Like get-rich-easy merchandise. With Keane now on a slab at the county morgue, Alex would make damned sure London was the last woman Lancaster ever touched again. Alex couldn't destroy every pedophile and flesh peddler in the world, but he could end this one. And he would.

Karma was a sneaky bitch. She'd provided the perfect branch of the perfect tree at the perfect height for this perfect meeting. Alex had used it before, that time to hang a six-point buck he'd shot during a long-ago deer season. Coincidentally, this branch was every bit as sturdy as those metal pipes in container three, the ones where Obermeyer, Keane, and

Lancaster Wirth had hung London Wilde. Where they'd taken turns battering her. Asking her stupid questions.

All by itself, this branch was just a nice piece as oak. Fairly round. Bare of bark. Strong as steel. Hard. It hadn't bowed when it accepted Lancaster's full, dead weight. Well, not exactly, dead. Not then, and not yet. Alex had only knocked Lancaster out once he'd caught up with him in this dark, primeval, Virginia forest. But he was wide awake now.

The saliva in Alex's mouth dried at the nightmare Heston's poor woman had lived through. Especially now that, thanks to Mother, he knew everything there was to know about Obermeyer's elite 'hunting club' for the rich and famous perverts he'd called friends. Alex knew about the missing women up and down the Eastern Seaboard who'd been kidnapped, hunted like wild animals, raped for sport, then murdered in these same woods. He knew about the families who would never find the closure they needed to heal, who'd never know what happened here. Which made Obermeyer's and his lackeys' crimes all the more reprehensible. There'd be no funerals. No last rites. No comfort. Those poor families would live in hell wondering and worrying about what happened to their sisters, daughters, girlfriends—their wives—for the rest of their lives.

Alex had a list of other names to go along with the crimes against those murdered women now. Two US senators, one from New York, the other from California. Several successful tech giants, one in Texas, the other in California. A Canadian billionaire. A prime minister. Three princes, none of them from Europe and none in line for any throne. A son of a bitchin' priest. A recently wedded movie star. Numerous others who wouldn't live long enough to so much as wish they'd never partied with the powerful, generous Secretary of State Tristan Obermeyer.

Alex tipped his aching head damned near to his shoulder to control the grip of tension on those stubborn neck muscles. He used to enjoy hunting. Man against beast was an honorable contest, when the kill was necessary to live and high-powered scopes weren't used. But today? He was nothing but a garbage man.

As silent as a wraith, Zack stepped out of the thickening gloom brought on by the early sunset in any forest. Shadows had grown longer and darker as the day drew to a close. Without a lick of regard to his unwilling passenger, Zack jerked the dangling body off his shoulder and tossed Lancaster's son Miles to the ground at his father's feet. "Found your fuckwit son."

The senior Wirth thrashed, grunted, and whined, no doubt begging for his son's life.

Yeah, that wasn't going to happen.

A wicked, animalistic growl from Zack silenced him. The bastard thought he had a dog in this fight? Hardly.

The son certainly hadn't been cut out to follow in his father's footsteps. *Tsk, tsk.* But Miles had aided and abetted the attempt on Kelsey's life, the cold-blooded murder of Tandy Lockwood, and most likely, what happened to every last one of the missing women. He had delivered the burner phone to Alex on Mount Rainier. He'd known damned well then what his old man had planned for Kelsey. Miles had, in fact, contracted the hitman, Malloy, to shoot-to-miss her. The Wirths hadn't wanted her dead. They'd only wanted Alex in their pocket, frightened enough to willingly do anything to save his wife, enough to sway congressional votes their way.

So here Alex was. Frightened? Of these bastards? Never. Not even breathing hard. Certainly not *in* either of their pockets. They thought they could scare him? That he'd ever betray his country? That he wouldn't hunt down any man or woman who ever—EVER—threatened his wife? *Fools.* All they'd done was piss him off. If they'd done their research, they'd have known not to challenge a United States Marine. Ever.

The fact that Miles had been in these woods playing hide-and-seek with his father, proved the younger Wirth's complicity in all London had endured. True, she hadn't officially signed onto The TEAM, but inadvertently, she had protected Alex and Kelsey, and she was Heston's woman. And no one—NO ONE—fucked with Alex's family.

Rolling his head back, he let his lungs fill with the pleasant scents of the approaching cool weather. Maybe snow. Autumn for sure. Crisp evergreens, cedars, and fallen leaves, absolutely. The rich loamy scent of decay that spoke eloquently of September's demise and winter's approach. At last. It was time. The stage was set. Alex was done playing.

He stepped into where Lancaster was hanging and looked up at the man. The bastard glared down at him from between his stretched arms as if he could hurt Alex. Not hardly. Lancaster had worked up a good sweat, though. The pits of his fancy shirt were stained, as was the front, where spit from the soaking wet gag in his mouth trickled over his chin and down his neck.

"So..." Alex breathed, braced for what was to come. "You think you can order a hit on *my wife*, hunt *my TEAM*, invade the privacy of *my family*, threaten and rape defenseless women? You think you can beat London Wilde? And what?

I'd just roll over and cower in fear—of you? What are you, Lancaster? The dumbest fuck on the planet?"

The senior Wirth whined and kicked at the ground his feet couldn't quite reach.

Poetic justice, that. Alex couldn't help the evil smile twitching the corners of his lips. Turn-about was fair play after all.

Lancaster was now feeling the same fear London felt. Like her, he wasn't up against an equal. Not by a long shot... No pun intended.

Ironically, Wirth writhed against the strength of his own pretty, red tie. Silk. Spun by worms a world away. Just like the oak branch, strong and durable. Bet he never guessed he was sealing his fate with that early morning decision of his to look—dapper.

"I'll make you a deal," Alex said conversationally. "I'll let you live long enough to watch Zack skin Junior alive. He'll start slow with your kid's face, then his neck and chest. You know, the way you guys beat London Wilde. You worked her face over pretty good. She's got a concussion for sure. Her neck's bruised as fuck. Why? Because you thought choking her would make her climax? That you could get her off before you killed her? Who broke her ribs? You?"

Wirth shook his head for all it was—*worth.*

Not much.

Alex kept going. "She's probably bleeding internally. Must've been hard, punching a small woman's belly, a little thing who couldn't fight back. Three against one, you like those odds? Maybe that's what I'll do. I'll give you three-to-one odds Junior here won't live long enough to wake up and cry for his daddy. You like the odds you gave London Wilde now?"

Wirth moaned and squirmed like a whore at a biker convention.

"No?" Alex asked as if he were surprised. Which he wasn't. Men like the Wirths were cowards first, dishonest, dirty businessmen second. "Guess we'll see. But by the time we're done with your baby boy, we'll have carved every square inch of hide off his body. If he's stronger than he looks, if he isn't dead by then, I'll personally cut off his limp dick, stuff it down your throat, and let you choke on it. How do you like the odds you gave London Wilde now?"

Wirth screamed, moaned, and bellowed into his gag. Already dark and frayed, it was only getting darker. He lifted his knees and kicked both feet out, aiming to strike Alex. But missing. He pitched his head back. The veins on his forehead and in his neck looked like they were ready to pop. He huffed and puffed and he cried. He might've been pleading. Alex couldn't tell. Didn't care. He'd never learned to translate chicken shit.

By now, Wirth also knew he'd lost everything he should've valued more than the blood money he'd spent his life squandering.

With a chin nod, Alex signaled Zack to get to work.

Zack bent over the younger Wirth, bullied him over his shoulder, walked over to the nearby Loblolly pine, and dropped Miles into the hole beneath the tree. Alex had dug the grave after he'd stepped off The TEAM helo's skids earlier. Digging graves was easy when a guy used small charges.

The tree itself had to be at least sixty feet tall. Most of its remaining branches were higher up its trunk, leaving the lower trunk bare. Loblollies grew like that in forests packed with other pines. They dropped their lowest branches while reaching for the sun. That left a lot of room for graves at their feet. A country boy from Virginia knew things like that.

Lancaster should've done his homework.

What no one else in America and the world knew, except President Adams, was that Alex and Zack were two of the ten deadliest assassins to come out of the Iraq and Afghanistan wars. Back in the day, before Alex lost Sara and Abby, they'd been part of a top-secret black ops team, and President Adams had been their commanding officer. They'd taken out higher value targets than those named on the infamous Most Wanted deck of playing cards. Also unknown to Americans, not all those HVTs had been in Iraq. Some were taken down deep inside Turkey, Egypt, Russia, China, and Ukraine. Bosnia. Segovia. Canada. France. Even in America. Another thing most Americans didn't care to know or understand: America's enemies were everywhere.

"Finish him," Alex ordered without venom. Another form of torture was to make the victim believe that their suffering had no effect on you.

Zack dropped into the hole, straddled Miles' prone body, flicked his hunting knife high over his head, and commenced slicing. Which was all for show. Also in that hole was a plastic bag full of cloth strips soaked in red dye that, in low light, resembled flayed strips of human skin.

When the first 'bloody' ribbon flew over Zack's shoulder, Lancaster screamed into his gag. He kicked harder. He cried. Sobbed. Sweated. Writhed as if he were the one being sliced. Which was precisely the result Alex wanted: the father to believe the son suffered for the sins the father had inflicted on

Kelsey and London. On every single woman and child whose lives he'd destroyed. On their families.

Alex and Zack hadn't gotten this far in the covert surveillance business by being stupid. They both knew the worst torture took place in the mind. Miles wasn't being skinned, wasn't being touched by that shiny blade. But Lancaster thought he was. Fear was the abso-fuckin'-lutely perfect torture for a bastard who sold human flesh, raped, and beat women. Mental torture. Imagination at its best and its worst. That was what produced the loveliest, most gruesome horror—the mind.

Lancaster was right then choking. If he kept that up, he'd stroke out and suffocate before the first round bell rang. All while Miles lay napping inside that nice cool hole. Completely unaware of how close he was to his father. To death.

Tsk, tsk. Can't have that.

Zack grunted and sawed his arm, as if he'd gotten to a particularly tough piece of meat. If Lancaster had a lick of sense, he'd realize this was a set-up. Miles wasn't screaming or fighting back. That should've been Lancaster's first clue. A smart person would've come to at the first slice of Zack's blade. But fear, not logic, ruled Lancaster now. Precisely what Alex wanted.

Making it look believable, Zack slapped both bloody, gloved hands to the sides of the grave and pulled himself out of the hole. With a show of bravado, he tossed a handful of bloody 'skin' at Lancaster's squirming feet and bragged to Alex, "Cut the bastard's dick off so you don't have to get your hands dirty. He's all yours."

Those bloody, loosely knotted strings looked nothing like skin or a guy's dick, but Wirth was deep into believing. More grunting. More whining. Wordless begging. More thrashing hysterics that wouldn't make a lick of difference in the end.

Enough was enough. How many women had Lancaster made bleed and cry? What'd he do then? Laugh in their face, while they curled up and died? Walk away like they were nothing? Alex honestly didn't want to know.

"Shut the fuck up!" he bellowed. "You started this shitshow, Lancaster Wirth. I'm ending it." Alex pulled the SIG from the holster cup under his left arm and shot Lancaster Wirth in his high and mighty forehead. Twice. Playtime was over.

The man's body went slack. At the same time, Zack ended Miles Wirth with a double tap. Alex retrieved his blade and cut Lancaster down, then dragged his body to the grave where his son lay.

"We didn't used to bury them," Zack commented drily.

"This time's different." Lifting one knee, Alex booted Lancaster over the edge. Kelsey's would-be murderer landed face-down on his dead son's body.

"Shoulda buried them alive, both in the same grave," Zack muttered. "Made them stare at each other until Hell swallowed them."

"Yeah, I thought of that. But this bastard needed the same kind of Hell he condemned his victims' families to. His last thought was that his son was being butchered. That you were torturing the baby boy he might've loved at least once in his life. Let him rot in Hell believing that."

"You're getting soft."

"Nope. Just better. Let's bury this shit." Alex handed Zack one of the two folding shovels he'd brought with him, while he used the other. "Heston took care of Obermeyer?"

"Sure did. You might want to talk to him about what he did in the Army, though. Got a feeling he's more like us than we thought."

"Already talked with Adams, and you're right. Contreras was black ops, too. Who's left?"

"No one. Tucker Chase took out the ones I didn't. It's over. Let's finish burying these two and get you back to the pretty saint you married."

Alex nodded in the dark. He had married a pretty saint, and he'd done a lot of hard thinking these past few troublesome days about all Kelsey meant to him. About who mattered most. About the kind of man he was and the person he wanted to be. About The TEAM and the men and women he served with. About President Adams' upcoming nomination for Alex to be his vice president.

A dozen years ago, Alex never thought he'd be the successful businessman he was today. He'd been a has-been back then, a morally bankrupt assassin, starting a business of like-minded mercenaries, all in the name of service to their country. Call it what you will, The TEAM was just that, a team of assassins. Yes, he'd hired only honorable, decent people who cared about this fucked-up land called America. He'd made a few blunders, but he'd more than made up for those missteps. His reputation for getting the impossible jobs done made him who he was today. He had more business than he needed. More money than he could ever spend.

It was time to call a spade a spade. Kelsey and the kids were more important than any amount of money and he didn't give a flying rat's ass about his reputation or being VP. It was over. Finally. He'd done all he could. He'd given enough to his country. Kelsey had too.

"Let's go home," he told the steadfast man at his side. Alex got the answer he expected. "Copy that, Boss."

Chapter Thirty-One

Instead of going home in Zack's Porsche, Eric and Heston were taking London to Georgetown hospital in one of the many TEAM SUVs that had converged on Turkey Run today. The place looked like an SUV parking lot, with a helicopter on standby, its rotors whirling dust in the clearing by the road. Ironically, it was sitting in the same place where Obermeyer had made her, Maria, Tandy, and Felicia strip. And now Tandy was dead. Thankfully, the other women were on their way to a hospital. London didn't know which one. Heston had asked Mother to locate their whereabouts so London could speak with them, if they wanted to hear form her. They'd all survived a horrific day together. They needed each other, right? At least London needed to see them, to be sure they were okay after… after…

She turned to the window, afraid to let Heston see her. After Eric had examined her and found nothing bleeding or badly broken, he'd very carefully wrapped a warm blanket around her and set her with Heston in the back seat of the SUV Eric had arrived in. Heston had wanted her on his lap, but Eric insisted she wear a seatbelt.

It was better this way, them sitting side by side while Eric drove. Heston had still tried to pull her across the seat and under his arm, but she'd whimpered. He said he understood, that he was sorry he'd hurt her. But her ribs were only partially why she'd whimpered. Her world had been flipped inside out. She needed distance from Heston, from everyone, to sort herself out. Everything had changed since she'd slipped out to grab breakfast. Before she'd been grabbed off the street.

What a fraud she was. A delusional liar, who'd convinced herself she was better and stronger than she was. Quicker. Smarter. But she wasn't any of those things. She was a loser. A very foolish, weak, helpless loser. A dreamer—just like Heston had said.

London bit her poor, swollen lip, making it bleed again as the first drops of rain hit the windshield. The view outside turned blurry. A storm was blowing in from the East and the weak September sun had already set in the West, making everything grayer and darker. Bleaker. As if life wasn't already bleak enough.

Growing up in her parents' home hadn't been easy. All her life, London had bolstered her own self-image and convinced herself she had confidence. That she could ace physics, calculus, and track in high school. That she was smart enough, that she knew enough to pass the ACT test with nearly perfect scores. And she had. That she could be accepted by Texas A&M University. She'd done that, too. Out of years of emotional neglect, she'd learned how to be her own cheerleader. She'd become a self-taught expert in positive reinforcement. At ignoring her parents' jabs. Her cell phone's photo app was full of encouraging memes. Feel-good banners and posters had decorated her bedroom. She'd even painted an aquamarine rainbow once, then painted over it in bold, black brush strokes that declared, "God loves you, so smile!" Just watercolors, nothing as spectacular as oils. Nothing that would ever end up in an art museum. But it had meant something to her, and it had helped her smile through some terribly long stretches of loneliness. Of being the odd man out. A loner inside her own home.

London had no idea how she'd done it, but at an early age, she'd realized she was different from her parents. They were naturally unhappy. She was the opposite. Somehow, their bitterness didn't affect her. It didn't stick or sink in. As joyless and depressing as they were to be around, she was the opposite. Where they avoided social lives, she'd always enjoyed people. She'd never had tons of girlfriends, but she'd found a way to be happy, even when she was alone.

Simply by focusing on being all she could be. On excelling. Their social circle consisted of the few individuals they employed, who, unfortunately, were like them. Unimaginative. Boring. Which stood to reason. Their business was selling boots. Work boots. All ordered by mail. Never in person. No one came to their store to try boots on, because they'd never considered expanding their business to accommodate walk-in customers. Just boots. The same styles year after year. Only available in black and brown. Take it or leave it.

So London left them and put herself through college. Why not? She'd excelled in academics and athletics despite their criticism, lack of support, and name-calling. She'd accepted their low opinion of her because she knew, deep inside, she'd never seen the world the way they did. She was a glass half-full person. Always had been.

Not anymore. Her parents were right. She had no business thinking she'd ever make a difference in the world. She wasn't strong or smart or clever enough. Some guys had glass jaws, she had a glass skull. She couldn't fight, didn't match most guys in weight, strength, or skill. Couldn't take a punch. She hadn't survived FBI training, sucked at being a forest service LEO. She was a fraud.

"You okay?" Heston asked, his arm around her, despite her edging closer to the window.

"I'm fine," she lied. Then, because he knew her too well, she added, "Just sore and tired. I want a long hot shower and aspirin. And sleep."

"No sleep for a while, London," Eric said from the driver's seat. "You're definitely concussed. We're taking you to the hospital, and we won't leave your side until we're sure you're okay. If you do fall asleep, we'll be there to wake you every half hour."

Well, damn. "I don't want to go to a hospital. I just want to go home. I'll be okay, promise."

Like it or not, Heston released his seatbelt and gathered her back under his arm. "Sorry, but you need a thorough examination, X-rays, maybe an MRI or two. You already threw up twice. That's a definite indicator."

"I know, but..." London let her next argument hang. There was no choice. To get Heston off her back, she needed to be seen by a doctor. Her head *was* killing her. He might be right.

She used to be happy there under his arm. She used to be safe. But safety was just another illusion. There was no such thing. It was as big a lie as she was.

What weighed heaviest on her mind now, was how she'd treated Heston years ago. After just one fight, one simple misspeak on his part, on the day he'd seen two of his men die, she'd run off like a spoiled brat. Why? Because her itty-bitty feelings got hurt. She'd bailed on the man she'd loved. Like a cold-hearted bitch, she'd hopped a jetliner to the East coast and left him. She hadn't even said goodbye. Or written a letter to explain. Or called to tell him where she went, that she was okay, or why she'd left. No, she'd treated him like he was trash.

Just like her parents treated her. A painful sob caught in her throat at that cold truth. Her chest hurt, but this pain came from her heart, not her ribs. She was no different than her mother. As far back as London could recall, her mother had never hugged her or kissed her boo-boos when she was little. She'd never had a no-kidding talk about girl things. Womanly things. Not about her changing body when she'd started her period. Not about her breasts when they'd grown from an embarrassing C to a double D—at twelve. Girls were mean at that age. Boys were meaner. Luckily London's gym teacher encouraged her to sign up for track. She'd also taught London about sports bras and deodorant, about tampons and the differences between men and boys. More than anything, Mrs. Summers had cared for London.

But London had only cared about herself. And now Heston had proven—with his life—how much he loved her, while all she'd proven was she was a fraud. A thoughtless, headstrong, foolish fraud.

Chapter Thirty-Two

Awareness came to her like a slow-moving tide in the middle of a dark moonless night. Cautiously. Stealthily. For every inch it advanced, it reeled backward a thousand footsteps before it began the tediously slow process forward again. Teasing with a sunrise of promise, then drowning that promise in darkness and fog. So much fog. Over and over, the tide rolled in and then retreated. So many futile attempts to rejoin the land of the living.

She wanted to run, to escape the endless surge and retreat. At least to wake up. To remember. No sooner thought, than the tide ebbed away from the promise of clarity again, extinguishing her power of reasoning and dashing her spirit. Dousing hope with wave after wave of endless nothingness.

Until…

"Sweetheart?"

That voice. That one word was powerful. It stopped the tide in its tracks. It meant something. It was more than an endearment. It was a promise. A vow. A pledge of forever. Of family and safety and security. Of warmth and strength. Of sizzling warmth and absolute strength. Of… someone.

With a deep breath, the fire in her lungs at last dissipated. She could breathe.

The throbbing noise in her head stilled. She could hear herself think.

Her brain hadn't failed her after all. Better, a delicious scent teased her nose, daring her to inhale more. It spoke to her of tall cedar trees, smoky campfires, and children's laughter—of all the absolutes that used to be her universe. Of a man. A single man. Her man. Of his willingness to fight for her, to die for her. He'd taught her how to fight. He'd saved her, showed her how to save herself. And she had. Could do it again.

Just not right now.

Fighting lethargy and a dizzying loss of equilibrium, she dared open her eyes. She wasn't blind after all. The cold, damp world around her wasn't the shore, but a hospital room. Its walls and edges blurred and shimmered, came in and went out of focus. The lighting overhead dimmed, offering instant relief. Her pupils widened ever so slightly, as they eased her brain into her new normal.

There he was. The most magnificent male in the world, standing beside her bed. Alex towered like a stalwart redwood above her. Not over her. His eyes were closed. He was obviously in prayer. His head was bowed. His forehead was creased with worry. His lips were thin, as if he didn't like the answer he'd received.

There was no dominance in her man. Not over her, at least. But she did see lines across his forehead, and a skosh of fear crinkling the corners of his eyes. Her hand was gently held between both of his, as if she were fragile. Which she was, since the hand he held was bandaged down past her wrist and—*ouch*—a twinge of pain stabbed at her shoulder. That arm just might be fragile, too.

Not like she'd pull her hand back. No way. The pain in her shoulder was nothing compared to the loss she'd feel once he let go. Come to think of it, her chest felt as if it were tightly wrapped. Had she broken a rib? My goodness, what else?

Her man was the fiercest warrior, but also, the gentlest lover and father. He commanded legions with great courage, yet he gave his heart tenderly and absolutely. He served to please. The steadying scent of him reassured her. He was her Alex, and she was his Kelsey. They had five children together, three angels, Abby, Jackie, and Tommy. Two noisy, very much alive, mischievous scamps who filled their home with spilled milk, empty candy wrappers, life, and laughter. Lexie and Bradley.

Kelsey smiled. They needed to stop calling him Baby Bradley. One of these days, he'd be a man like his father, and he wouldn't appreciate that handle.

Her chest heaved with gratitude. When the tiny movement caught Alex's attention, she found herself bathed in the purest, deepest, bluest sunshine.

"Kelsey?"

Funny how a woman instantly recognized trepidation in her husband's tone.

"Alex," she answered, giving him reassurance and all of her love.

"You're back." His voice broke.

She gave his much larger hand a squeeze, signifying a hearty yes! Not that he'd understand, given how limp her bandaged fingers were.

He squeezed back just hard enough for her to know he understood.

Her gorgeous hero leaned his handsome body over hers, slid one arm beneath her, and scooped her out of bed. "Am I hurting you?" he asked as he dropped into the recliner at her bedside and carefully arranged her on his lap. "You've been out of it for days, and you've got several broken bones. You're healing and you've had surgery, sweetheart. You have to keep that helmet on, and I don't want to—"

"I have a helmet? Who cares? Kiss me," she whispered as she looked up at him.

"Yes, ma'am." He pressed the tiniest kiss into her hair.

"No, here." She pursued her lips.

The stubborn man blessed her forehead with a softer kiss.

And that would have to do. For now.

"How are the kids?" she asked groggily.

"Missing their mom. Please tell me if I'm hurting you."

She lifted her bandaged hand. "What'd I do, break a finger?"

"You don't remember, do you?"

The way he asked was telling. Kelsey gulped. "Umm, I guess... no? We were looking at the sunrise up on Mount Rainier and then—" She drew a blank and shrugged. "Nothing. What'd I do? Slip and fall down the mountain? And, oh yeah, umm... where are we? We're not still in Washington?"

"No, sweetheart, you're in our critical care unit at TEAM HQ. Libby, Judy, and McKenna have been hovering over you ever since..." His belly expanded against her left side, but it radiated around her back to her other side.

She winced. "Ouch. My side—do I have a broken rib?"

He held up three fingers. "Three broken ribs, one broken hip, clavicle, wrist, and three broken fingers, all on your right side. I don't want to frighten you, but someone shot you the morning we were up on Emmons Glacier."

She had to look up at him then, to make sure he wasn't joking. "We were talking about Mount Saint Helens and… and then… I got shot?"

Alex traced a fingertip over the curl of her right ear. "Give me your left hand. It's okay. I'll be gentle."

She did, and he directed it to her scalp behind that ear. "Stitches? Did someone shoot me in my head?"

"Bastard tried," Alex growled.

"Did he shoot you?" she nearly screeched.

"Kelsey, yes, but nothing serious. Sit back. Lean into me. Please."

"You always say it's nothing serious, Alex. Let me see. Let me take care of you. That's my job." By then she sounded hysterical, and Kelsey didn't know why she'd gone from zero-to-sixty so quickly.

With one big, warm hand, Alex pressed her cheek to his chest. "That's one of the reasons I love you. Here you are, battered and lucky to be alive, but worried about me. Give me this, sweetheart. I need to hold you more than I need anything else right now. You. Just you, safe in my arms and alive and breathing on your own. Please, give me this. You're all I need. Just you, back from the dead. I thought I'd lost you."

She relaxed into his big, warm, muscular body, content to breathe the scent of him back into her soul. Epithelial by epithelial. Cedar and campfire smoke, forever her favorite fragrances. "I have no memory past us talking about Mount Saint Helens."

"Good. The asshat who shot you didn't intend to kill you, just nick you. After he succeeded, you slipped and fell into the White River. The bastard also got a shot off at me, but it's only a flesh wound."

"Alex," she said as threateningly as she could manage. "I need to see it."

"Honest. It's already healed. I'll show you once we get home."

She nodded, willing to compromise for now, because Alex didn't lie. "Okay then. Go on."

His belly expanded with another deep inhalation. "There are lots of moving parts to this mission, sweetheart, but it all comes back to Mel and his ties to the Irish mob. Pops Delaney was Lancaster Wirth's lieutenant, his go-to man for his dirty business in Boston. Delaney wasn't the true Irish Mafia boss. Neither was his daughter. Lancaster Wirth was, and his son was in it up to his neck, too. It's a long, complicated story, but the bottom line is you're safe now, and every last bastard behind your getting shot is either in FBI custody or in the ground."

Kelsey lifted her bandaged hand to his chest. She wanted to flutter her fingertips over those hard-as-rocks pectorals, but settled for patting him instead. "I'm always safe with you."

He made an odd choking sound deep down in his chest and Kelsey knew precisely what he was thinking. "Stop it. I'm alive, Alex. Hold me. Never let me go."

A gruff "Never," reverberated under her ear.

"Good," she snapped. "I know damned well I wouldn't be here today if not for you and your TEAM. Let go of all the what-ifs. I made it. We made it. That's all that matters."

"I'll never let you go," he breathed into her hair. "Thank God for ice-cold water."

"Oh!" She bolted upright. "I remember that, but... but..." The memory was lost as quickly as it had come to her.

Kelsey sank back against Alex. "Remember what you told me that time you recovered from almost dying?"

"You mean when Harley finished the job I should've and sniped your ex before I could?" he replied bitterly.

"Yes. What'd you tell me after I pretended to be your nurse and unwrapped the packing on your eyes? Remember?"

He should. Her ex had tried to kill her, and Alex had survived one hell of a beating the same night. He'd temporarily lost his sight as a result of severe head trauma. The doctors hadn't expected he'd survive. But he had. Once he'd come to, he'd been an ornery beast and had ordered Kelsey to get away from him. To leave. And she did. But after she'd had time to think, she'd returned on a mission to save him from himself. She'd worked a deal with his doctor and surprised Alex by standing in as his nurse the day the bandages came off those poor, sad blue eyes. She'd been the one who cleaned the medicinal residue from his eyelids and lashes. It was still a very intimate memory. Him so helpless and still so angry. Her so timid, afraid of hurting him. So tentative that she'd known he'd lost patience with her. That was when she'd fallen in love with this grumpy man all over again.

"Yeah, I remember."

"Well? What'd you say?"

"Just that I wanted to go home."

"Me, too," Kelsey whispered. "I just want to go home, Alex. Can you make it happen?"

Her crazy, bossy man huffed like a spoiled brat who wasn't getting his way. There was no way he'd be able to refuse her. He couldn't. Because he'd already made it happen.

Kelsey was home the moment she opened her eyes and saw him.

Home to her was simply—Alex.

Chapter Thirty-Three

London was broken. Not just broken, but withdrawn and growing farther away from Heston each day. Worse, hopeless. There was no spark in her. The light in her eyes was gone, and she'd replaced that sassy turquoise with the mousey blonde Heston hadn't seen in years. The zest that had once fired her soul, fervently enough that she'd stood up to her parents for what she believed in, then left for the same reason, had retreated to someplace deep within her psyche. If it was still there at all. Heston didn't know.

He'd cajoled, pampered, and gone out of his way not to mention what happened the day she'd been rescued. All with no reaction. It was as if her insides had been hollowed out by what she'd lived through and what she'd seen. Heston worried she'd had enough, that she was on the verge of leaving him. That she didn't want to live with the killer she now knew he was.

He took time off, then he took more time off, needing to be there for her. Whatever it took for as long as it took. Still… nothing. Physically, she'd recovered. The bruising had faded. Her ribs were still tender, but she was back to breathing without cringing with every breath. The signs of stress remained. For nightwear she'd traded her tiny tees and boxers for long flannel bottoms and long-sleeved tops. She said she needed to keep warm, but Heston knew better. She wanted distance from him and to keep him at bay. She didn't want to look sexy, so she wore layers. She flinched when he touched her. She never stepped into his side anymore. Never bumped hips, and she retreated whenever he came too close. She hadn't teased him once in the week they'd been home. Didn't smile. Refused to leave the house.

Despite how much she'd needed Heston after he'd found her with Obermeyer, she didn't seem to need him now. Wouldn't talk about it. Refused to share. He was afraid he knew why. She must've been raped, but she wouldn't admit it. She hadn't allowed him to join her in the examination room at the ER, so he had no way to know for sure. Maybe just because he was a man? Maybe because of what she'd witnessed him do to Obermeyer?

Worse, London didn't seem to want to live anymore. She'd lost the effervescent joy that was her trademark, her way of facing life head-on. She'd become indifferent. Numb.

Heston now knew Obermeyer, Keane, and the senior Wirth had personally beaten London in that damned container. They'd laid their hands on her. They'd hurt her. The knowledge turned him nuclear if he thought on it too long. If he could, he'd dig Obermeyer's dead body up and kill him again. He'd gotten off easy.

Miles hadn't touched London, though. He wasn't behind Malloy's murder or London's abduction. Not like that made him any better than his old man. He'd still acted on his father's orders. He'd been an active accomplice.

It was an interesting side note, given that his father seemed to have favored Alex over his only son. Lancaster had certainly used Miles as nothing more than an errand boy to get at Alex, then as chauffeur. While Lancaster had focused his very persuasive power on the man who could get him and his schemes inside the White House, he'd treated his only kid like a lackey. Which seemed logical. Miles had never served in the military. Had no weight training. Hadn't worked out. Hadn't known how to shoot or defend himself. His federal career was lackluster at best. His only value was that he was his father's son.

The difference between Alex's and Miles' ambition, dedication, and drive could be measured in light years. Hell, they weren't even in the same universe. Not to mention Alex's love for his wife and family, his loyalty to his TEAM, and his love of country. America surely had her flaws, but with men the caliber of Alex Stewart standing guard at her moral frontiers, jackals, wolves, and snakes the likes of the Wirths, Obermeyer, and Keane, didn't stand a chance.

The TEAM meeting Alex called this morning was an unwelcome interruption to the uneasy truce between Heston and London. She'd flat-out refused to go into TEAM HQ, like Alex requested. Said she wasn't a TEAM employee, that she'd reconsidered and might work for Tucker Chase after all. That she needed time and distance. She'd staked out Heston's spare bedroom as her own. They hadn't slept together since he'd brought her home. If he gave her any more distance, she'd be out the door and gone. That worried him the most. That she'd leave again, only this time he'd never get her back.

Heston dragged a hand over his head and down the back of his aching neck. Didn't help. There had to be a way to get through to her, but damned if he knew what it was. He'd never thought of her as fragile before, but she was now. Beyond fragile. Obermeyer had broken London's spirit, and Heston didn't know how to help her pick up those fragmented pieces and put herself back together again.

His phone buzzed in his pocket. Caller ID showed Mother on the line. *What now?* He'd already called in and taken the day off, opting to spend it with London.

"Heston," he answered.

"Alex is on his way," she said.

"He's coming here? Why?"

"To talk to you, why else?"

"I'm not coming in, Mother, and neither is London. I don't care what Alex wants. I'm not going on call-outs, either. Already spoke to Murphy and told him no out-of-town missions or overnight ops for a while. I'm… I'm…" What? On hold? Afraid if he left, London would leave and he'd never find her again?

"Will you shut up and listen? Get dressed. Alex should be there by now."

"But I—"

Sure enough, someone with a damned big opinion of himself pounded on the door with a sharp, bold knock that sounded more like, "Let me the hell in," rather than, "Please answer your door."

"There he is. I hear him knocking. Open the door, Hes. Alex brought someone who'd like to speak with London."

"She doesn't want counseling, Mother. I've tried. If she thinks I've set her up, she'll leave me for sure. I can't do that to her. It wouldn't be fair. You don't understand."

"That's the thing, honey. I do understand." Suddenly, Mother's voice was softer and sweeter than Heston had ever heard. "I know exactly where London's head is right now. I've been in her shoes, and so has the woman with Alex. Trust him.

Trust her. Give London a chance to talk with someone who understands. She needs this particular woman on her side. You'll see."

"But I—" Heston shut his mouth at the sound of London's bare feet on the stairs behind him.

"You gonna get that, or should I?" she asked, still in her too-warm layers of winter wear.

"No, babe. Don't open—!"

Too late. She'd answered the door in the clothes she'd slept in. And there she faltered, staring open-mouthed at Alex.

"About damned time," he chuffed.

"Bye, Mother. I gotta go." Heston pocketed his phone and went straight to London. Damn it, Alex had no right to do this, this—whatever he thought he was doing.

London had turned white, as if she'd seen a ghost. Heston had half a mind to slam the door in his boss's face—until he saw who else was on his doorstep.

"Kelsey?" That changed everything. "Come, come in. Please…" He gestured his smug boss and Kelsey inside, then closed the door behind them. Speechless, Heston had no idea what to say to smooth over this fiasco before London lost it. Poor thing had taken a definite step back, and damn it. Alex had just blown the progress Heston thought he'd made. If this didn't look like betrayal—

"Hi, London. I'm Kelsey," Alex's wife said, her big dark brown eyes shining. But her voice was too weak and her face too damned pale for her to be out and about like she was. "I hope you don't mind me stopping by. I'd lie and say we were in the neighborhood, but I felt I needed to see you. So here we are."

Heston now knew one of the Wirths had planted a nurse in the Washington hospital and used her to slip Kelsey fentanyl. Again, not enough to kill her, just enough to keep her asleep and keep Alex on edge.

"She knows who you are, sweetheart. London Wilde is the woman who found us the night the trailer blew up, right, Hes?" Alex asked.

"Yeah, right. Sure. London ducked her boss that night and took me and Asher to this trailer she'd been scoping out and…" Heston shook his head, needing to shut up before he said something London didn't like.

Her sad eyes were still fixed on the fragile-looking woman in the wheelchair. Kelsey would be in that chair until her ankle and hip healed. The helmet on her head was a sure giveaway as to her condition. She couldn't go to London and Heston wouldn't dare suggest anything, except… "Coffee?" he blurted. "Anyone want coffee?" *Because I sure do.*

Shit! This was turning out so, so bad. Alex had his nerve. He never should've—

"Hi," London said quietly, shyly. Just to Kelsey. Not to Alex. Heston wasn't sure London even knew Alex was there.

"Could we go somewhere private, maybe to another room, just to talk?" Kelsey asked, her attention focused entirely on London.

Heston opened his mouth to answer, but London beat him to it. "Umm, sure. But my bedroom's upstairs, and you don't look like you can walk. Is, umm, the laundry room okay? It's just down the hall." She gestured toward the garage. The mud slash laundry room was just inside the side entry.

Alex stood ready, his hands on Kelsey's wheelchair grips. "Long as it's warm, that'll be fine. Kelsey's body temperature is still stuck in the Arctic. Point me in the right direction and—"

"This way," London interrupted. "It's right here and… Here, let me move the clothes basket."

"No problem," Alex assured her, in his gruff, kindly way. Once he'd maneuvered the wheelchair down the short hallway and around the corner into Heston's laundry room, he backed out, closed the door behind him, and said, "Don't mind if I do. Make mine black."

So Heston made coffee. By then, Alex had made himself comfortable on Heston's front porch, which was nothing more than a four-by-four concrete pad with three steps to the walk. Heston handed over the mug of hot caffeine and took a seat beside his boss.

"She's not going to leave you."

Heston wasn't going to argue. What did Alex know? Nothing, that was what. Not a damned thing about how messed-up their relationship had been and still was.

"She'll come around. She needs a woman to talk with, that's all."

"You think you've got it all figured out, huh?"

Alex stretched one long, lean leg down the steps. "No, but Kelsey does. Once she knew what happened to London, there was no stopping her. She had to come see London."

"This was her idea? To come here today? Not yours?"

Alex took a hit off the scalding brew in his hand. "I'd rather Kelsey was still in The TEAM's hospital, where she should be, but, yeah. She wouldn't have it. This is the first time she's been outside since that day on Emmons Glacier, and she wanted to come here first. Let me rephrase, she needed to speak with London. It's a coping thing."

Heston stared at the fingers of vapor curling off his mug. He refused to divulge anything personal between him and London. All he said was, "Thanks."

"The wives want to meet London. All of them."

That was interesting. "Why? They don't know her."

"True, but they're a nosy bunch of females, and a few of them have been through worse. If you ask me—"

"Worse?" Heston spat. "What worse than being beaten by grown men, then nearly gang-raped?"

Alex set his mug on the step between him and Heston. "Having your little girl stolen right out of your arms. Being buried alive and damned near freezing to death. Losing a race with a train and getting twelve inches of skin ripped off your hip and thigh. Being beaten by a Mexican drug cartel when you're eight months pregnant. Watching the man you love get shot and nearly bleed out in your arms. Losing custody of your newborn son to your asshole father. Need I go on?"

"Some wives have gone through that? Seriously?"

"Starting with Kelsey." Alex crooked his neck like he often did when he was tired, pissed, or stressed. "You know how I met her?"

Heston shook his head. "Sure don't."

"During the worst time in my life. I'd recently lost my first wife and daughter. Sara and Abby were killed in an accident with a… a delivery truck. Back then, I hated everyone. Then I got this hairbrained idea to start a business, like I knew anything about that. First damned thing, one of the guys I'd hired went rogue and I had to pay the Air Force millions for breach of contract. Decided I'd had enough shit and split. Abandoned my TEAM. Headed for a cabin I used to own east of Spanaway, Washington. Found Kelsey on the porch when I got there. She'd been beaten by her ex-husband. Worse, he'd killed her two sons. Drowned them. Only she didn't remember any of that, and honestly…" Alex brushed a hand over his face. "I wasn't any better than her ex back then."

Heston set his mug aside and waited for the rest of the story.

"But things changed. The more I helped her, the more I treated her wounded fingers and knees, and God, her poor battered face... The bastard punched her before she got away from him. After he'd had the nerve to tell her he'd murdered her boys. She jumped out of his truck. Damned near got caught, and Nick would've killed her if he'd found her. But he didn't, least not right away. Thing is, being with her every day, watching her cringe when I just wanted to help, and listening to her scream when nightmares got the best of her, damned near broke me. I'd dig Nick's worthless carcass back up just so I could kill him again."

Heston knew *that* feeling.

"I'm just sorry it wasn't me who ended the bastard. But Harley sniped Nick after the bastard got hold of Kelsey and damned near killed her. Long story short, yeah, most of the wives have been through hell just as deep and ugly as what London survived. They know precisely what she needs, and Heston, she needs Kelsey. Kelsey knows what to say and what to do. Good women are like that. They get a little bossy, but they reach out to their sisters and hold them tight when they need it most."

Heston shook his head. That might work for The TEAM's wives, but London was independent. "She's leaving, Boss. I screwed up. I killed Obermeyer in front of her."

"Like hell she's leaving. I know what a woman looks like when she'd had enough, but that woman inside looks at you like you hung the stars, damned if I know why. Right now, she's hurting, Hes. Give her time. Talk to her. You might be surprised to know, but most women want someone to kill their would-be rapists. London might not be as upset about what you did as you think."

"I've tried. I can't get her to open up. She's left me before and..." Shit. The story poured out. By the time Heston finished, Alex's hand was a lump of hot iron setting on his shoulder.

"Women don't think like men, Hes. Took me a while to understand all that encompasses. They process information differently, probably better than us guys. They look at the whole picture. They're not task-driven. Sometimes they're not even logical. They're emotional and touchy-feely. We're not. Which is why we fall in love with them. They... well, Kelsey anyway, sees right through me. Always has."

Heston took a hit off his coffee. Mother had seemed okay when he'd ended Obermeyer. Heston had an idea there was more to her story, but he'd been too worried about London to dig into it. Not like he would. Mother was no pushover. She might take offense if he asked about the day she'd called him honey. The day he was positive she'd been crying while she worried about London.

"How about another cup of coffee?"

Alex squeezed his shoulder before he let go. "You were black ops," he said.

Heston cranked his head around and really looked at Alex. "If I were, you know I won't talk about it."

That seemed to be all the confirmation Alex needed. He scraped a thumb under his chin like a prizefighter challenging an opponent.

Heston said nothing because there was nothing to tell. Yes, he'd been one of damned few Rangers selected to go undercover in the Ukraine a while back, how far back didn't matter. He'd done his duty more times than he cared to remember. He'd taken out more HVTs than anyone would ever know. Not even Alex. And that was the end of it. Loose lips still sunk ships, damn it.

"You'll work with Zack Lennox when you report back to duty. You okay with that?"

Heston nodded. "Zack's a good man. I'd be honored to work with him, but nothing OCONUS until I say."

Alex grinned a cocky grin and held out his empty mug. "Another cup would be fine."

"But first…" Heston let that hang. There were things he needed to know, other things he needed his boss to know. "I killed Obermeyer and I'd do it again."

"We already went over that."

"So who ended Lancaster Wirth and his worthless son?" Heston suspected Alex had, but he needed to know for sure.

"I thought you knew," Alex breathed.

"No, I don't, but if they're still out there, if they dare come after London—"

"They won't," Alex declared. "Rest easy, Marine. When I say no one's coming after London, it's because they can't, got it?"

"Oh? Oh." Heston swallowed hard. And here he'd been expecting his home to be breached any minute by the Irish Mafia. That Lancaster had put a hit on him, and that his men would storm over him and London with guns blazing. That he'd fall and, in the process, fail London. That they'd kill her. Or worse. "Umm, thanks, Boss. But I was Army, not USMC."

Alex shrugged. "Too bad. You would've made a better Marine. Sorry, should've told you sooner. Please tell London they're both dead. It'll help her rest easy, too."

Heston realized he and his boss weren't much different. They'd both killed the bastards who'd dared hurt their women. There was profound comfort in that knowledge, knowing he and Alex were cut from the same hard piece of leather.

"So, umm, Mother. I mean Mom, umm, err—"

"Spit it out."

Heston took a deep breath. "She called me honey that day at Turkey Run. I'm pretty sure she was crying when she said it, and… God, she had drones in the air over us, over me. She saw everything, and I wonder if maybe… if Mother…"

Alex hmphed. "I'm surprised she wasn't cheering you on when you ended Obermeyer."

"Well…" Heston had no idea what to ask. He'd just refused to share sensitive intel about his past. Alex should refuse, too, especially since this intel concerned someone who wasn't present. "Never mind. I'll ask Mother myself." *Someday. Not today, but some other day. Maybe.*

"Mother had a little girl named Dempsey," Alex said quietly. "She picked that name for her daughter because Dempsey was born with birth defects they both fought the rest of her life. Sadly, Dempsey died sooner than Mother expected."

Heston stared at his empty coffee mug. "I'm sorry I asked."

"Don't be. Suffice it to say that Mother understands grief and loss the same as the rest of us. A person doesn't need to go to war to have their heart crushed."

Heston sucked in a full breath. There was more to Mother's story, but that small insight was helpful, and one day, she might share it with him. Heston could wait.

"Another thing you might not know, Lancaster beat London because she refused to tell him where Kelsey and I were." Lifting his free hand, Alex waved Heston's next question off. "I know, I know. London didn't know I'd already moved Kelsey, but the point it, she wouldn't betray us, Hes. She refused to tell the guys who beat her anything. Just took those slaps and punches like a man. I'm damned sorry about that, but I'm also damned proud of your woman."

Heston's hand clenched into fists. "Gawddamn it! She's not a man! She's… Shit! She wasn't trained for that crap. Why didn't you let me kill him? I would've torn him—"

"Because your number one job was, and will always be, protecting London. She needed you that evening, not anyone else, certainly not another man. And Lancaster needed to meet the man whose wife he almost killed."

Heston was still breathing fire. But yes, London had surely needed him then. Certainly, no other man should've held her while she'd cried. His heart rate slowed as, little by little, logic wrested control from his inner caveman—again.

"Lancaster and I had a very insightful discussion," Alex continued conversationally, "of course, I did all of the talking. But him asking London over and over for my location told me that he had more than one person inside that Washington hospital working for him. I've tasked Mark and Murphy to track down everyone who had access to me or Kelsey. Also, you might as well know, I'm hiring London. Told Mark to do the paperwork. She's got an uncanny sense for investigations, and she was willing to die for two people she'd barely met. Think she'll accept my offer?"

Heston ran a hand over his head. "I'm not even sure she'll stay with me."

"She will, Hes. London's smart. She isn't going anywhere without you," Alex said with more confidence than Heston felt. But Alex believing that she'd stay—helped.

Heston lifted to his feet and walked inside for another round of caffeine.

Chapter Thirty-Four

"I don't know," London breathed. Kelsey wanted to know why she hadn't confided in Heston since her abduction or told him how she felt. London had no good reason. Only knew it would take time for her to put the mess with Obermeyer, Keane, Malloy, Bates, and Lancaster and Miles Wirth behind her. She'd have to work through that. She just didn't know how. She'd faced miserable pain at those men's hands. For the love of God, recovery was going to take time.

"I hate to ask but… were you raped, sweetheart?" Kelsey asked gently. "I was. I've been in your shoes. I know what you're feeling."

She was a tiny but beautifully elegant woman. There was a section of shaved scalp above one ear, but London only noticed because she knew where to look. Kelsey was still a little banged up from her near-death experience. The fingers on her right hand were bandaged together, making it look like she was wearing a white mitten. She must've hit that cattle guard with her right side since that was where most of her injuries were. Her right wrist was wrapped and her right arm was in a sling. She was still fighting pneumonia, maybe more, which explained her raspy, smoker's voice.

The woman's pretty brown eyes were the problem. Kelsey seemed to see through London. No one had done that before. It was unnerving but, in a weird way, it was also—

kinda good. London shook her head at that inane, random thought. She didn't need anyone inside her head, not until she figured her head out herself.

So she told Kelsey, "No. He, he didn't get that far, but the look on his face when he told his guys to come watch while he… while he…" London choked. Shivers raced up her spine as the evil gleam in Obermeyer's eyes that day speared her all over again. She wanted to throw up. Fighting the instant chill in the room and the nausea in her gut, she scrubbed her palms up and down her biceps. If only it worked.

But nothing warmed her these days. Not Heston. Not all the layers of clothes she wore. Didn't matter how many blankets she cowered under on the twin bed upstairs in Heston's extra room, or how far she turned up the thermostat. She'd ruined everything with Heston the moment she'd decided to go for that damned morning run. How she wished she'd stayed in bed. She'd be plenty warm now.

London crossed her arms and leaned her butt against Heston's washer, setting a firm boundary, not wanting to hear whatever Alex's wife thought she had to say. Words were no help. Why bother saying anything at all? London was stuck in a hell of her own making, and she knew it. She used to be stronger. So much braver. She used to know precisely what she wanted from life. But now? All those silly dreams felt like one big lie.

There was a wall between her and Heston she didn't know how to breach. A wall she'd built and reinforced daily. He hadn't known before that hiding, running, and pushing people away were what she did best. Being lonely was a well-learned survival skill from her childhood. It worked within the four walls of her parents' home. Avoiding her mother was probably the first thing London learned as a toddler. It worked then and it would work now.

She'd let Kelsey give her polite, little spiel. She'd be courteous and act like she was listening. What would it hurt? Once Kelsey realized how useless her buck-up-and-get-over-it solutions were, she'd get good and gone. London planned to tell her goodbye, run upstairs, lock herself in her bedroom, and lick her wounds then. Maybe she'd have a good cry. Maybe she wouldn't. Who knew what she'd do when she was alone again. London didn't.

She had no idea what to tell Alex's wife anyway. They had nothing in common. Kelsey was one of those supremely confident types. She was a CEO's wife and belonged in the spotlight with her OCD husband. She probably met with prime ministers', celebrities', and other important men's wives all the time. Probably knew how to work a crowd. Probably—

"Come here, sweet girl." Damned if Kelsey didn't jump to her feet so fast that it startled London. She spread her arms wide open and continued with, "I know you love Heston, but he's a man and you need a mother right now. Get over here and let me hug some loving back into you."

Oh, my gosh! The nerve! Kelsey was exactly like her husband! Brash and bold and bossy and—!

Those damned high walls crumbled. Frightened and not feeling brave in the slightest, London took a tiny step toward Kelsey.

Kelsey matched her with another fragile step forward. There she was, walking with a broken hip when she should be sitting down and—

Oh, what the hell. London caved, and for the first time in her life, found herself wrapped inside a real mother's arms. Kelsey wasn't a large woman. Petite, maybe five foot tall. Maybe not. Thin, probably too thin and still pale and weak. But her arms felt so, so good, and she was here. She'd come straight from her hospital bed just to hug London. Just to be here with her, and for her, just for her, and… and…

The notion that a stranger wanted her when her mother hadn't, was just too much. London squeezed her eyes tight. Hot, salty tears slipped between her eyelids anyway. In mere seconds, this kind woman's thoughtfulness reduced her to tears, snot, and stupid, noisy hiccups she couldn't stop. The harder she tried, the harder she cried, and the harder she cried, the more those hiccups hurt.

Kelsey didn't seem to mind the mess London was making on her blouse. She pulled a handkerchief out of nowhere—a cloth handkerchief. *Who even carries one of those anymore? Who even knows where to buy one?* They got used and abused with disgusting human waste and had to be laundered and… and… Kelsey just kept holding on, smoothing one warm hand over London's shivering back, and murmuring while she wiped London's eyes with the other. "You poor, poor thing, I've got you now. Everything's going to be okay. There, there, let it all out. I promise, you'll feel better. You'll see."

"No, I won't," London bawled. She wanted so hard to believe. But really? "How's anything ever going to be okay? N-n-no, I'm…I'm not… I'll never be okay a-a-again," she stuttered like a silly teenager after her first breakup.

"Oh, yes, you will, because you're smart and you're stronger than you know. You're a winner. Anyone with a brain in their head can see that," Kelsey whispered against London's teary cheek. "It takes a while, sweetheart, but eventually, time softens the sting of cruelty. It really does. The pain and grief never go completely away, but you learn to live around them. They become a big old rock in our hearts. We can't make it go away, and we wouldn't if we could, but we can learn to live around it. To be happy again. Alex told me a secret, back when all I wanted to do was curl up on my babies' grave and die. Want to know what it was?"

London pulled away from Kelsey to really look at her. "You lost a baby?" *Oh, my God!* She couldn't imagine the pain and sorrow. And here she was feeling sorry for herself, crying sloppy tears all over a woman who'd lost so much more than she had.

"Two," Kelsey replied somberly.

Oh. Babies' grave. Not baby's grave. Two babies were in the same grave. Now London understood. Kelsey had lost two babies, not just one.

The light in Kelsey's brown eyes dimmed. She was so pale and had no business being out of her hospital bed. Yet here she was. The sparkle faded, and London put an arm around her for a change, to comfort her so she'd know she wasn't alone, either. "My two perfect little boys were murdered by their father," Kelsey whispered. "He was abused as a child. His mother was a foul, disgusting old toad who poisoned his mind until he... until he did what he did."

"I'm so, so sorry," London anguished.

Kelsey nodded. "Thanks, London. I was pretty dumb back then. I didn't recognize the man Nick really was. Or should I say, wasn't? When Alex found me at the cemetery that day, I'd given up. I was done. Life wasn't worth living. I didn't have a speck of the will to live left. With all my heart, I wanted to die. I just wanted to be with my boys again." Her hand lifted to her chest. Her fingers splayed over her heart as if she were reliving the worst time in her life.

Which London knew she was. How sad!

"But that big, gruff bear of a man sitting out there with Heston," Kelsey continued, "just picked me up and brought me to Virginia to live with him, as if he did crazy stuff like that every day. Which he does, doesn't he?" She wiped a slender finger under her leakiest eye.

"Heston gets pretty crazy sometimes, too. So… so what's the secret?"

Kelsey eased out of London's embrace and leaned her left hip into the dryer, mirroring the stance London resumed. "That it's not the load that breaks you down, sweet girl. It's how you learn to carry it. The one sure thing about life is that it will be one long string of endurance tests. Abuse. Murder. Divorce. Even rape. Pain, disappointment, and death will come to everyone, eventually to us again. But it's how we deal with those tragedies when they return that will make or break us."

Wow. That actually sounded—wise. And it came from Alex? The man who'd been half-insane with rage and pain the night he'd found Kelsey in that burning trailer? The man who'd snarled at everyone who'd tried to help him?

"W-what were their names? Your boys. I mean, if you don't mind telling me." London strived to change the subject, to get Kelsey's focus off her.

"Jackie and Tommy. And no, I don't mind talking about any of my children. Those little boys are very much a part of our life, as much as Abby, the sweet daughter Alex lost, and the two little rascals who decorate our lives today."

"How on Earth did you deal? What'd you do? My God, how'd you ever get through that?"

"First…" Kelsey took a deep breath, then pursed her lips and let it hiss out. "I just… I let Alex in. I was a battered spouse back then, and I was pretty much worthless as an intelligent human being. Despite my college education and my teaching certificate, I had no opinion on anything. I was afraid to think for myself. I thought I was weak. I'd been told I was useless so many times, I believed it. That's how my ex controlled me. By verbal abuse first, then physical. I was so messed up when I met Alex that I firmly believed it was my fault my deranged ex-husband killed my boys—"

"I never should've asked!" Guilt for causing more pain for this brave woman stole London's breath. She was an idiot to think she'd suffered more. Being beaten and 'almost' raped was nothing compared to what Kelsey had lived through.

"I'm not sorry, London. I'm very glad you asked because I can honestly tell you I'm a stronger woman today because of what happened back then. What's past, is past. Bad things happen. Look at Alex. He lost his first wife and daughter to an automobile accident while he was deployed overseas. He was so hateful and angry when we met. But he was suffering as much as I was. Somehow, we realized we needed each other in order to heal. I reached out to him, and he" —she shrugged both shoulders— "he did what Alex does best. He stepped up and took it from there. And we fell in love."

"I… I don't know how to… reach out to Heston…"

"Oh, yes, you do. It's hard, sure, but that man sitting out there with Alex is dying inside. Heston's here for you, baby girl, he just doesn't know how to reach out to you. He's trying so hard to respect your boundaries, but he's just a man, not a mind-reader."

London snorted. "Him, help me? I can't even help myself."

"Honey, trust me. The men women like us fall in love with are overbearing, confident to the point of being arrogant, know-it-alls. They live hard and will probably die younger than we'd like. But while they live, they'll give their all for what they believe. As much as that confident strength annoys us sometimes, it's precisely what we need and want in our men. Because we're also who we are. We *are* strong, and they know that. We *are* brave, and they know that, too. And we've fought just as many ugly battles as they have. Look at you, girl. You're a survivor. I'm so proud of you."

London could've basked in Kelsey's praise all day.

"Ask yourself this: Could you be happy with a man who isn't brave enough to stand up to you? To stand for you? Like Heston did and still does?"

That very real fact slapped London upside her head. She *had* survived a brutal beating by multiple assholes, hadn't she? She *had* been humiliated, made to strip and run for her life. And yes, the whole day had been utterly demeaning. But she *was* still alive. She *had* fought against being gang-raped with every fiber of her being. She hadn't been raped, and best of all, Heston *had* come for her, and his righteous rage *had* been glorious to behold. He'd gone nuclear on the asshat who'd hurt her, who'd thought he could rape her while his asswipe buddies watched. Who'd thought she'd go easy. Well, she'd showed him, hadn't she? She'd hung on until Heston showed and because Heston loved her more than he cared about himself, Obermeyer was the dead one. *Not. Me!*

"I never wanted to be like my mom," she admitted for the first time ever. "And my dad…" London shook her very hard head. "My dad's afraid of my mom. He's never stood up to her. Never will."

"I take it he never stood up for you, either."

"Well, yeah. I mean, no. He never minded bad-mouthing Heston, but not Mom, when she'd go off on one of her bitch sessions. She wasn't physically violent as much as she was loud, and she'd say the most hateful things. She called me names and she knew how to destroy any confidence I talked myself into. Dad would just sit there and watch and kinda shrink, like he didn't want her to see him and lash out at him next. And she would've, if he'd… if he'd… just once…" Oh, what the hell? Why bother?

"If he'd ever come to your rescue. If he had ever defended you, just once, like a real man will always defend his child," Kelsey said pointedly.

"Well, yeah. That…" London replied in a tiny voice. She wiped a quick hand over her still bruised, aching ribs. Man, it was hard talking about home sweet home. Ha! What a joke. The home she'd grown up in had never been sweet.

"London, I am so sorry your mom didn't know how great a gift you are. She missed out. That's her loss. And your father's a pitiful excuse of a man. No real man tolerates any child being verbally or physically abused, especially not his. Ever," Kelsey said with vehemence.

"Doesn't matter. Honest, Kelsey. I figured out pretty early I didn't want to be like her. And yet, I am, aren't I? I'm still my mother's daughter and… and…" London couldn't say it, that she'd treated Heston the same way her mother had treated her. All her efforts and choices to prove she was better than him, that she could serve her country better than he could, had only brought her full circle, back to her thoughtless cruel mother. "I suck. I'm just like my mom. All this time I've been competing with Heston. I thought I always had to be better than him. I had to prove I was just as strong and capable and patriotic. But I'm not."

Kelsey reached across the space between them and took hold of London's wrist. "First of all, it doesn't matter that your mother chose not to love you. That's on her, not you. I see you, London. I see a beautiful woman who thought she had to fight the world alone, but you don't. Not anymore. Because now, you're part of *my* family. You're part of Alex's family. He doesn't just hire, he adopts. He'll deny it, because the family he calls The TEAM has grown larger than he ever anticipated. But that's what it is. The TEAM and every single agent and their wives and husbands—and their children—are your family from now on. Just like Heston, they will always have your back. They'll stand with you and for you, and, if needed, they will die for you."

Wow. London swallowed hard. She had no idea what to say.

"And I hate to break it to you, honey, but you're not a man, and you weren't created to do what men do. You're better than any man on Earth, simply because you're a woman. You might need a man's help getting there, but you're the only one who has the power to conceive, carry, and give birth. And trust me, babies usually come pre-assembled but without any operating instructions, and the labor it takes to get them here hurts like a bitch. No man on Earth could survive what we women can. Neither can men ever hope to perform miracles like conception and childbirth without a shit ton of medical technology and, these days, publicity. Bearing a child is a unique and precious gift, London. Even if you never choose to use it, it's still very much a part of who you are."

London's shoulders lifted with a deep, cleansing sigh. "But Heston saw me break down, Kelsey. After Ober… Ober…" *Shit!* She couldn't bear the slimy feel of that bastard's name on her tongue. "After he did what he-he d-d-did…" London hated with all of her heart that the creep still had a hold on her. He might not have raped her, but in a way, he did. The hateful intent she'd seen in his eyes was just as bad.

Again, Kelsey was there, squeezing London's wrists, pulling her back from the ugliness lingering in her soul. "Breathe, London. That son of a bitch is dead. Heston killed him and he did it for you. And…"

London couldn't help it. "You cussed! You said s-s-son of a bitch. You sounded just like your hus-husband." She stuttered between the girly giggles she was trying hard to suppress. Then, oh, what the hell. Why not? She laughed. Out loud.

Kelsey laughed with her, and the sound was heavenly. It was joy, the simple joy of a mother and another woman's daughter connecting honestly and lovingly. Just as quickly as it started, the laughter turned to tears. Kelsey seemed to understand London's mood swings. She grabbed hold of her again, pulled her into her shoulder, and cried with her.

At last, London took a deeper, better breath and regained her composure. She stepped back from Kelsey. "If Heston heard us, he's going to think we're insane," she said as she wiped her tears and blew her nose. Thank heavens for that handkerchief. She might throw it away instead of washing it, but it was a lot gentler on her sore nose than the toilet paper she'd been using. Because, duh, she'd been afraid to cry in front of Heston, so she'd hid in the bathroom when crap got the best of her. Not anymore.

"Feels good to get some of the poison out of your heart, doesn't it?" Kelsey asked.

London nodded. "Yeah. It does. It really does."

"But you know what feels even better?"

London couldn't imagine.

Until mischief lit up like sparklers in Kelsey's eyes and she whispered, "Make-up sex."

London burst into another fit of giggles. "Never—ever—did I think you'd say that."

Kelsey grinned. "Why not? Men aren't the only ones with sex on their minds all day. I've been confined to a hospital bed or a wheelchair for days, London. Days! I'm tired of getting patted and kissed on my forehead. I want some action, girlfriend!"

Girlfriend. London loved the sound of that. She couldn't help but fall in love with this feisty woman. Kelsey wasn't as meek as London had thought. But she'd certainly worked a motherly, womanly kind of magic on London's heart. She felt strong again and ready to take on the world. Her spine stiffened. Breathing came easier. So did letting go. It no longer mattered what her mother and dad had ever said. They weren't a part of her life, never truly had been. And Obermeyer and his buddies? They were no better than dog shit, and who gave dog shit a second thought? *Not me!*

Kelsey had convinced London that she could and would make a difference. Maybe she already had. She *did* matter, and from now on, she wouldn't hold anything back from Heston. What he said mattered most. With a deep breath, London let the fabric-softener scent of the laundry room fill her lungs and her spirit. The real London Wilde was back, baby.

She turned to Kelsey. "Do you know what I'm going to do?"

Kelsey's eyes widened. "No, what?"

"I'm going to the nearest drugstore and I'm buying a couple boxes of turquoise hair color and tons of extra-large condoms!"

They both burst into fits of laughter… and joy. Silly, magical joy.

Chapter Thirty-Five

Heston glanced over his shoulder at the hallway. Was that laughter coming from the laundry room? *London's laughing?*

"Sounds like they're done talking," Alex said.

Heston lifted to his feet in case… You know, just in case. He heard the laundry room door open. Heard Kelsey callout, "Alex. We're done in here, sweetheart. I'm tired. Come get me."

Alex was already on his feet. It didn't take him long to retrieve his wife and wheel her chair backward out of the hall and into the living room. London followed.

The moment she'd stepped into sight, Heston froze. Couldn't move. Didn't dare. As much as he wanted to run to her and scoop her into his arms, he wouldn't. She'd rebuffed every advance he'd made and every sweet word he'd uttered since he'd brought her home from the hospital. If her mind was made up and she needed to leave in order to save herself, it would kill him, but he'd let her go. For her, he'd do anything, even that. Only she mattered, only her happiness. Her mental health. Just. London.

"We're heading out," Alex said grumpily.

"Thanks for letting London visit with me," Kelsey added. She looked even more drained than when they'd arrived.

"You okay?" Heston asked.

"I am now. Take good care of my girlfriend, Heston." Kelsey stuck her chin at London. "She's a keeper."

"That she is. Goodbye," Heston replied hastily, then thought better. "Umm, sorry. Not what I meant. Thanks, Kelsey. Boss." *Now, please leave.*

"Anytime," Kelsey chuckled.

Alex had her at the door by then, so Heston pulled it open wider to facilitate getting that wheelchair onto the front step. "You need a hand, Boss?"

"Nope. Just need to get my nosey wife back home where she belongs," Alex growled.

As the wheelchair thumped gently down the steps, Kelsey tossed a glance over her shoulder, and winked at London. "Call when you're ready to meet the rest of the girls, London. They're going to love you. Just wait and see."

"I will. Thanks, Kelsey. Now go home and rest, okay?"

"I will. Love you, London. See you soon." Lifting her left arm, Kelsey fluttered her fingers. "Bye!"

With that, the wheelchair settled onto the front walk and Alex aimed his sweet wife toward their car.

Heston closed the door behind them. Finally, he was alone with London and the elephant in the room. "What girls?"

London shrugged both shoulders. "Kelsey's friends, the TEAM wives. Did you know Mark's wife is a general practitioner, and they have five kids?"

"I did, yeah. Most of the wives work. Libby's no exception. I mean, err, outside the home. Most TEAM wives are professionals and work outside their homes, but not all of them, but... I mean…" Heston clapped his mouth shut to keep from making more mistakes. When had relationships between men and women become minefields of political correctness?

"Hes." Just one word. One quietly spoken word. But when London said it, it came with so much feeling. So much promise.

Not believing it could be this easy, Heston breathed, "London."

That was all it took., and she was in his arms, peppering his face with kisses.

Slowing the tender assault, he cupped her jaw between his hands. Tears fell, his and hers. "I love you, babe, so much more than I can ever tell you. So damned—"

She slammed into his lips and cried into his mouth, "Shhhhh. It was me, not you. It's my fault. I'm sorry, I'm so sorry. I—"

"You have nothing to be sorry for."

She tipped back on her heels and looked up at him. "I do. I was scared of what you'd think of me. I felt dirty and used, and I couldn't understand why, because I was still alive, and you came for me, and—"

"Did he… rape you?" Heston asked as gently as he could. He needed to know how to proceed and who else to kill.

She shook her head. "N-no, but…" Her shoulders lifted. "He made us undress in front of him and his creepy friends, and then we were supposed to run for our lives, and if one of them caught us… but he caught me and… and he said… he was going to…" London scrubbed a hand up Heston's chest, not petting him. Just seeming to need reassurance he was still there. That whatever she said next or whatever happened before wouldn't make him leave.

He took hold of that nervous hand and plastered it flat to his chest to get her full attention. "I'm not going anywhere, babe. I'm here for you, and no matter what, I will never leave. We're in this together. We're getting married, remember? You and me."

Her free hand skimmed into her drab, mousy-brown hair. "Oh, yeah, I… I forgot… I… ah, I lost that beautiful ring you gave me, and he said… he said…" London looked up at him, her bottom lip caught between her teeth.

"I know what that piece of shit said to you, babe, and I heard what he'd planned. Don't worry about that ring."

"But you bought it for me and it means so much and—"

"Hear this now and know deep in your wild, crazy heart, London," he interrupted, "that none of what he did is your fault. You didn't kidnap, beat, or kill anyone. You don't sell children or girls or women. You meant to rescue Maria and Felicia, for Christ's sake."

"Well, yeah. B-but I really need to see them again," rushed out in a frenzy. London's nerves were strung tight. Her body was literally vibrating with fear and anxiety.

Heston dropped a kiss on her forehead and told her, "Agreed. Anytime you're ready. I'll drive you wherever you decide to go, but be prepared. They may not want to see you again. Keane had them longer than he did you."

"Were they—?"

"Raped? I have no idea, but I've been around trauma victims enough to know they don't always deal well with triggers, things or people that remind them of what they've been through."

"Oh," London breathed. "I guess I'm a trigger, huh? I never thought of that. I mean… I should've, but…" Her voice trailed away.

Heston tipped her chin up with his thumb to get her to look at him again. "They're probably as nervous to see you as you are to see them. Give them time. If they reach out, you'll know what to do. In the meantime, you need to decompress. You don't have to rescue the whole world, you know."

"Yeah, but…" Her heart rate was still too high and her pulse fluttered in the hollow of her neck, that tiny divot above her breastbone.

Heston opted for distraction. "What was funny? What were you and Kelsey laughing about?"

"Umm, make-up sex."

"Make-up sex?" Not what he'd expected. London's face relaxed at the change of subject, though. That tiny signal helped Heston relax, too. "Wish I'd heard the start of that conversation."

For the first time since he'd brought her home, a twitch teased the corners of London's lips.

"She's tired of Alex hovering over her and treating her like she's broken. She should be. She's been through hell, but she's not. Kelsey has bones that still need to mend, and I know this visit wore her out, but she made me laugh when she said she wanted some action."

"Kelsey said that?" Now Heston had heard everything.

"I can't believe it, but yes. She said she's ready to get on with her life and put all this crap behind her. She has this amazing outlook on bad things that happen, you know, death and p-pain a-and… c-c-crap. Did you know she was married before and that her ex murdered her two baby boys?"

"Alex just told me, yes. How about we pick up where we left off, London? Can I interest you in taking a bath with me?"

"I want to, but…" She swallowed hard enough that Heston heard it.

"Lights off. No play-spanking. No worry about anyone looking in, either. Just us doing what we want to do." Those things only worked when or if London wanted them anyway. Time to fess up. "The glass in the upstairs bathroom is tinted polycarbonate, babe. No one can see in, not even if they put their nose against the window." He slapped a clenched fist to his chest. "Me, caveman, remember? I'd never let anyone see you naked."

"Oh," she breathed. "Good. But why—?"

"Because you're a closet exhibitionist. At least, you liked the idea of being caught. Of being seen."

The loveliest blush pinkened her throat. "Umm, I guess. Long as I'm caught with you."

"And I only swatted your bottom because you seemed to like it. Spanking isn't my thing. I'm not into that BDSM bullshit. But you got so turned on when I turned you over my knee that one time, and I thought—"

"Yeah. Let's not d-do that anymore, okay? Maybe l-l-later. A lot later."

Her anxiety was back, and it was time to change subjects. Heston stooped low and swung her into his arms. "No worries, babe. Not with me. Not ever. You want vanilla, you get vanilla. You want whipped cream and chocolate sauce over that vanilla, say the word. Whatever you say, goes, got it? I'm yours to command, so command me."

At last a tiny giggle. "Like my very own genie in a bottle?"

Heston climbed the stairs to the loft. *Their loft.* "You bet. Though it better be a big bottle, because I'm a big genie."

Another giggle. "Yes, you are, on all the best ways."

"You know it." The tight hold on his neck loosened. London pressed her head and one hand against his chest. They were at the bathroom door. "Bed or bath?" he asked.

"Bath. Then bed with you. I'll… umm, move back into your room later today, and then—"

"Our room. Our house. Our bathroom and our tub, London. Move when you're ready. No need to rush. You might still need time to yourself, and I under—"

"No, Heston." London tipped back in his arms enough to stare up at him. "If Kelsey can be strong, so can I. She's been through worse shit than me. I'm sorry I've made you feel like you have to walk on eggshells around me."

Before he could argue, she continued. "I know how I've been. But now, I… I know I'm strong enough, that I'm good enough, all by myself." There went another tough swallow. "I'm not my mother, and I don't care what she or my dad say or think. I only care about you and me, about us. We're the ones who matter, and I'm so, so thankful you came for me." Her pretty eyes overflowed. "I don't want to be a man. I'm not built like you, and I can't compete with you. I just don't want to."

That insight explained a lot. Why she'd left him. Why she'd bombed out of the FBI. Possibly why she hadn't lasted in the Forest Service. All her life, she'd been busting her ass, thinking she had to think, work, and be better than men.

He sat with her on his lap on the edge of the tub. "Babe, I've never expected you to compete with me."

"I know, but ever since I was little, I got it in my head that—"

He knew where this was going. "That you weren't good enough?"

"No. That I'm not good enough for anyone or anything." She snorted. Laughed. Then broke into tears. "I can't take a hit, Hes. Not even a little one. Look at me. I have a couple broken ribs, and my nose is still sore, and I don't want to work for the FBI. I'm not even sure I should work with you." She dashed a quick hand across her eyes.

Heston pressed her under his chin where she belonged. She melted easily against him. *Thank God.* "You were completely helpless, babe. They cuffed and beat you, London. No man could've protected himself in that situation, either. And I'm still going to say things wrong sometimes, but know this: You are so much better than most men I've worked with. It was you who defied Bates and kept searching for Alex and Kelsey when he quit on them. You led me and Asher to that trailer fire. You knew all along something was hinky with that piece of junk. You're the reason Bates is in FBI custody. Another thing, I will never, ever stop protecting you, babe. Call me an ape, hell, call me a chauvinist pig. I'm okay with whatever you decide to call me. But you will always— always—come first in my life, and I'm not going to apologize if that hurts your feelings. I'm selfish, babe, but I simply cannot live without you in my life. Hell, I could hardly breathe the morning I couldn't find you. And once I found you..."

His body stiffened as the memory of Obermeyer holding London by her neck, her bare feet completely off the ground, killed him all over again. "Sorry, but I will destroy every rat bastard that ever touches you. I can't NOT take care of you. I'm not made that way."

"Okay," she breathed, her fingertips dancing over his chest. "Settle down. I get it, Hes. I understand now, and I love you, too. I don't have to be as good as you because I'm already better. Sorry, but yeah. I'm better than you. Kelsey reminded me us women are the only ones who can have babies. It's not just how we're made, it's because we're made completely different than guys."

Heston nodded, his blood running hot with rage thinking how close he'd come to losing her. But getting worked up now was not how to help London relax. He controlled his breathing and let her talk.

"And I need to go to the drug store." Her fingers raked over her short hair. "I want to be me again."

"Turquoise?" He hoped.

She nodded a timid little nod. "Yeah, if you like it."

"Uh-uh, it's not what I like. Only thing that matters is what you like. It's your hair. But honestly…" He gave her his most lopsided grin. "I loved it. It was so—you."

That seemed to be what she needed to hear. "Yeah. Turquoise, then. I like turquoise."

She'd gone from supremely overconfident to downright timid. This was going to take time, but Heston had two weeks off, and if London needed more time, all he had to do was ask.

"After or before our bath?"

Her arms circled his neck, and for the first time since she'd come home, she ran her fingers up his neck and into his hair.

Heston closed his eyes and enjoyed the sensation of her touching him again. He'd been so worried she was too traumatized to ever want to be with a man again, but now, he could breathe again.

"You like when I do that," she purred.

"I do. It's…" He drew in a deep breath, searching for the right word.

"Intimate?" she whispered just before she kissed the corner of his mouth.

"Umm…" It was difficult to concentrate.

"Hot?" she breathed into his ear.

Shivers raced up his spine.

"Affectionate?"

"*'Killing me softly'*," he said, quoting the old Roberta Flack song London loved.

His eyes were still closed when she tipped onto one foot, lifted her other leg over his thighs, and straddled him. "I changed my mind."

"Women's prerogative," he whispered, his voice gone gruff and so damned hopeful.

"Bed first. Bath later."

Opening his eyes, Heston met the fiery jewel-toned, sparkling eyes of the woman he adored. London was finding her way back to him. She was taking the first steps. She'd opened up with Kelsey, and now, she was talking with him.

"Abso-fuckin'-lutely," he breathed into her face.

London smiled, and that was all Heston wanted, his woman to be happy.

Lifting to his feet, he cradled her ass in his hands and took her straight to bed.

Their bed.

Chapter Thirty-Six

London was on her back. She stretched both arms over her head and grabbed the slats in Heston's headboard because he told her to. She enjoyed him being bossy in bed. There was a definite submissive streak she hadn't admitted to before, although he'd probably guessed, given how often he'd spanked her. Playfully, she reminded herself. Not hard. Never just for the sake of pain. Mostly for stimulation. Heston was always careful with her, always tender, even when they got rowdy. Still...

Knowing that didn't squelch the panic simmering at the back of her mind.

His chest was on her belly, and his long, hairy legs were nestled between her bent knees. He'd sucked one nipple into his mouth, the other was caught between his thumb and finger, getting pinched and rolled. This man was taking his time. His talented fingers had already lit the invisible line of det cord between her nipples and core. If he kept doing what he was doing with his oh, so warm mouth on her breast, she might—

"Hes-s-s-s..." she hissed as lift-off commenced.

With both hands in his hair, she pulled his head closer and shoved her wet nipple farther into his mouth. Lust and desire. Fingers and mouth. That was all he'd touched her with so far. She'd never climaxed without him coming with her. Probably because he was her one and only. She didn't want to now. But he was in charge, and he was playing her body like a musical instrument with legs.

Both breasts heaved as her second orgasm rocketed through her, leaving effervescent trails of aftershocks up her spine, throughout her bloodstream, hell, everywhere. There wasn't one molecule in her body not bubbling when he pulled back and blew a warm breath over her wet nipples. Both ached so much that they, in turn, recharged that invisible det cord. That single puff from his mouth turned her nipples cold, and along with the cold, they reverted into wanton, naughty school girls. And…

Again? Not physically possible. Not this soon. Three would be an all-time record.

Heston nuzzled his warm face between her breasts while those greedy diamond tips cooled. Before what… what had happened in the forest… she didn't yet know how to safely reference—*that*—without getting rattled. She'd never speak the names associated with *that* terror again. Not ever. There was a time she might've been brave enough to face anything life threw at her, just not—*that.*

"Hey," Heston murmured, his elbows planted in the mattress above her shoulders, his arms alongside her head, and his fingers in her hair. "Where'd you go?"

London blinked up into his ruggedly handsome face, at the tenderness glistening in his dark brown eyes. She'd lost track of him and where they were for a moment. Damned panic was a stubborn bitch, and that bitch was right then pounding a noisy drum in her head, as if it had complete control. Irrational fear gripped her throat just like… h-he had. H-him. The bastard who tried to kill her. R-rape her.

Heston might've gotten too close, too soon. A headache loomed. Flashbacks blinded her view of the man at the end of her nose. All she could see was… then. That ugly man. Him. What almost happened then. How utterly helpless she'd been. How frightened and horrified.

There would be no third orgasm.

Heston bowed his forehead to her breasts and whispered, "Nice and slow, babe. I've got you now. It's just you and me until the end of time. I'm here and I'm not leaving. Breathe for me."

Unable to answer, she did as he asked, just dropped her nose into his hair and inhaled the comforting scent of his scalp, his shampoo, and the raw masculinity that was her man into her soul. Her man, damn it. It was Heston who was there with her. No one else. He'd never left her, and she'd never, ever leave him again. He wasn't ever too rough. If anything, he was being too gentle with her. And that was good, but it also made everything worse. She knew why. He didn't want to set off any triggers, and man, did she have triggers. This wasn't them being them. They weren't okay yet. Not by a longshot. And yet…

The scent of him in her nostrils quelled the raging thunderclouds building in her head. She inhaled deeper, drawing in every last sensation of comfort. The slightest hint of his sweat. The masculine scent of his shampoo. The scrub of his scruff abrading her tender nipples. Heston had always been good enough to eat, and this time, now, suddenly, inhaling him was the same as inhaling life. Their life. London desperately wanted back the life they'd had before. She wanted to be carefree and confident again. If only she could get over the mountain of doubt in her way.

"You have goosebumps," Heston whispered. "You're shivering." He rolled to her side and had her bundled inside the blanket and facing him in no time.

"I'm... I'm..." *Speechless? Scared I'll never recover? That I'll always remember? That Kelsey's wrong and there will never, ever be anything easy between me and Heston again?*

Fighting for control, London reached a nervous hand down past Heston's belly, through those crisp, curly hairs to—there. Right there. "Now I... I have you." If only her voice hadn't quavered. *Sheesh!* She wanted so badly to get back to who she used to be, not the weakling who'd taken her place.

He flexed his abdomen to give her hand more room. "Are you sure you want more? I'm good with—"

"Yes, Hes. Not just more. I want us to do everything we used to do. Don't hold back. Please, I need us to be us again."

"Okay, but let's take it slow. How about we go for three?"

"Three times?" London would've laughed if he hadn't pushed to his knees, thrust his hips forward and—slid deliciously into her. She growled at the stretch of his friendly invasion. Of the girth. The depth.

Heston could've been one of those high-priced male escorts, at the least, a male model in those high-priced men's magazine. He had the sexy, dark looks women swooned over, and his toned, bronze body was made to be adored. But he was all hers and he had a nice long reach. Right then, he was hitting all the best ridges inside of her. Her body clenched at the possibility he'd created. Three orgasms? Unbelievable. But worth trying.

London squirmed beneath him, focused on the mantra that if she believed it, she could be it. Confident. Sassy. Not scared. Not hesitant. "Yes. There. Hes… Yes. There. Ahhh…"

Let those stupid swooning women suffer. Heston Contreras was all hers.

"Legs around me, babe," he ordered. "You know what I like."

Oh, yeah. As quickly as London wrapped her legs around his hips, Heston slid both manly hands under her butt and tilted the lower part of her body upward. His hair flopped over his forehead and the tenderest smile graced his rugged face as he looked down at her. Even after all this time, after what she'd done to him, he still loved her. He'd been faithful when she hadn't. He'd searched for her when she'd deserted him. How could she ever make up for that?

"You're thinking too hard. You're too much in your head. Stop it, babe. Look at me. It's just you and me in this bed. Just feel. That's all you need to do right now. Feel," he said as he thrust that magnificent cock into her, then ground himself in deeper. "Just know I'll always love you."

London kept her eyes on him, and sure enough, the rest of the world fell away. It *was* just Heston and her in this time and this place. She hadn't noticed how or when it happened. He'd distracted her.

"Know how much I love you," he said, softly pulling out, then sliding back in just as softly. "With every beat of my heart, babe." Those manly hips moved forward again and again. "With all of me. My heart. My soul." In and out. "Never doubt us." And again. "We belong together. Just you and me, London. Just us."

"I do know that," she breathed.

"I don't think you do," he grunted, setting a sensual rhythm as old as time. Rocking gently into her. Pulling out just far enough to tease and make her body miss his. With every stroke of his rock-solid cock against her inner walls, with every backward glide and forward thrust, Heston was unlocking the door to them—only them.

"Forgive and forget," he ordered. "Our bed. Our home. Our life."

She didn't get the chance to answer before he slid home again, so, so deep. She closed her eyes. Heston and she were *here*. They were *now*. Only them. Sweating and earnestly striving to stay together—as one. Locked in each other's arms forever.

London was afraid to blink. If she did, her nearly overflowing tears would stream down her temples, and Heston would stop, and—

His forehead dropped to hers, which meant he'd seen and now he'd back off. But he didn't. Instead, Heston took her mouth by storm, kissed her long, hard, and thoroughly. They breathed the same air. He feasted on her lips and tongue and… gradually, the fear that had interfered with their pleasure subsided. Heston was right. All she had to do was focus on the feel of his muscular thighs flush against her backside and his cock, hot and thick, inside.

A voracious hunger flared for this man. For his heart. Her body knew his, and right then, his body was keeping her soul alive.

Fireworks crackled with heat. The rub. The friction! London squeezed her eyes shut as pure, hedonistic pleasure rolled up her spine. The fierce masculinity Heston offered was her undoing. She crashed, just fell into the moment and came in a blinding white light. A new life. A new beginning. Together. There was nothing else worth chasing or remembering. Nothing but… this. Just them.

They were going to make it.

"Three!" Heston huffed triumphantly.

Dazed, London opened her eyes. Her breath caught at the sight of the man crouched between her legs. Dark, shiny hair hung into his eyes. Tiny beads of sweat dotted his brow as he chased his release. He hadn't found his release yet, but he was hilt deep and pushing deeper, the veins on his lower abdomen dark and pronounced, his callused fingertips digging into her butt cheeks. Heston owned her and that was everything she'd ever wanted.

At last, London understood what Heston Contreras owning her meant. Not servitude. Not domination or that he thought he was better and smarter than her. Not this man. All London saw was Heston's unadulterated adoration of her. This was him worshipping her body and loving her as a woman. His woman.

Heston withdrew gently, then slammed home, making her very feminine boobs bounce and her too-big womanly ass jiggle. He spread his much larger, harder body over hers, leaned forward and, still cupping her butt, he took her mouth sweetly. Earnestly.

Heat speared her body. Her toes curled. The erotic sounds of steaming hot male flesh slapping wanton female flesh was the music her heart needed. She loved giving herself to Heston. Always had. Wanted so badly for him to come with her. This would make four—for her. The first for him. The knowledge that he'd held back to satisfy her was too much.

"We're going to make it, Hes," London whispered, listening to the music of her man's body loving hers.

Heston Contreras was magnificent. He was darkness, but he was also light. Her light. The epitome of strength, but also gentle. Best of all—he was here and he was hers. His pace quickened. He knew what he was doing. With his fingertips digging into her hips, he slammed forward. Tilting his chin upward, he stilled, then roared his release to the ceiling.

He was planted so deep, London wasn't sure where his body ended and hers began. They were both humming the same melody of sex. Of love.

The pad of his thumb traced the sweaty crease where their bodies were joined. "What a view," he panted. His warm hands smoothed beneath her, gently mapping the curves of her butt. "This pretty ass is mine, London. All mine. So you need to get over yourself. Because, where this ass goes, I will always follow." He landed a soft smack to her hip.

That love tap was precisely what she wanted. His hands on her again. In love and in play. That was all those play spankings had ever been about. Not pain. Just them playing. Like naughty kids.

With a grumbly grunt, Heston rolled to his side and took her with him. They settled with their legs tangled, her back to his front, both of them warm and satisfied. Sated.

London pressed her backside against his pelvis, needing to stay as close as she could to the man who'd brought her back to the land of the living. Heston reached down and pulled the sheet over them. She snuggled deeper into the protective curve of his body, loving the smell of his sheets and the scent of sex in the room.

"I've always loved you, London," he rumbled in her ear, easing one arm beneath her neck and the other over her chest and between her breasts.

Her first inclination was to tell him again how sorry she was, but London resisted. Instead, she gave Heston the same thing she needed to heal. "I'll always love you. Thanks for having my back."

She could feel his lips curl into a smile in the crook of her neck. "I have your front, too, babe." He tweaked her nipple to prove it.

That did it. London felt it coming. Knew it was probably inappropriate but did it anyway. She tipped her head onto his broad shoulder and—she laughed. Giggled like she used to after she came, back when they were still new and everything was perfect. Because everything was perfect again.

"That's my girl!" Heston exclaimed happily, nuzzling his nose into her hair. "I knew you had it in you."

Crazy man. What he said. How he said it. Of course she'd had *it* in her. And *it* was a good eight inches of pure Heston. London laughed harder. He laughed with her. They laughed like kids. Because they were kids again, kids who played exceptionally well together.

Chapter Thirty-Seven

Heston lay on his back with London gathered under his arm long after she fell asleep. He was wide awake, on guard for no other reason than she might need comforting. Although she hadn't been sleeping with him, he knew nightmares hounded her every night since she'd come home. He meant to intercept the next one before it got out of hand. That was his job, to protect her from everything, even herself.

Except for the scented plug-in glowing in their bathroom, the house was dark. He'd bought this place as a fixer-upper when he'd first moved to Virginia. Back then, it provided distraction, manual labor, and almost... helped him forget about London. At least, it helped him try to forget. He knew now there was no way he could ever move beyond the love they'd had for each other then. Theirs was a love story for the ages. It would be again. He'd make sure of it.

The way his fact-gathering, very logical, extremely anal mind worked frightened him sometimes. Like now. It kept telling Heston that London would run again, that she'd survived too much neglect as an infant and child at the uncaring hands of her parents. That those years of abuse had a cumulative effect on her, a bow wave of potential dysfunction, so to speak. That everything would catch up with her one day, that she'd fall back on the survival skills she'd been forced to learn as a child, and that everything Heston did wouldn't be enough to save her. Or them. Obermeyer and his asshole buddies had hurt London more than she realized. Heston worried she'd need more than he could offer. Once bitten, twice shy, and all that.

She moaned in her sleep and splayed her slender fingers over his chest, then up his neck and under his chin. Her hand was damp and sweaty. He needed to tell her Lancaster and his son were dead. That Alex planned to hire her. Maybe then she'd be able to put the incident at Turkey Run River behind her.

Anxious for all the unknowns facing him, Heston eased out from under London and stepped into the bathroom. Closing the door, he settled on the edge of the tub and thumb-dialed the one person in the world he knew would understand.

"Heston?" Mama mumbled when she answered. "Do you know what time it is? Madre de Dios! It's two in the morning. What's wrong?"

"Nothing, Mama. Really, I just… I just…" He ran his fingers through his hair.

Rustling ensued over the connection, which meant his mother was getting out of bed to go somewhere else to talk without his father's know-it-all comments in the background. "Okay, Heston," she ordered once she settled, probably at her kitchen table. "Now tell me why you needed to call me so early in the morning. Are you okay? Are you injured?"

"No, Mama, I'm sorry I worried you. I shouldn't have called so late. I'm still working in Virginia and—"

"And you're happy there, I know, I know. So you tell me over and over again. That is good. But is that handsome boss of yours still good to you? That's the question I want answered." Bellisa Contreras had a crush on Alex since

Heston introduced them. She was always hinting he should bring Alex over for dinner sometime, but that was never going to happen.

"Mr. Stewart is good to all his employees."

"Heston, you called me. Why? What's wrong?"

"I found London," he answered. "We were both on the same operation, only we didn't know it."

"Great! Then bring her over for dinner the next time you're in town. Promise me, Heston."

He nodded to himself. "Of course. Sure. I promise."

A moment of silence stretched between Arizona and Virginia, until his mother asked, "What's troubling my boy? Is London hurt?"

"She did get hurt, but she's going to be okay, and… and that's why I needed to talk with you."

"I'm listening."

Of course she was listening. That was what Mama did best. She kept quiet and she listened and she cared.

"She's had a tougher life than I ever realized, Mama. I knew her parents were indifferent, but they never hugged her or held her when she was little. Never told her how awesome she was, never gave her a shred of confidence, or attended any of her school activities. They didn't even see her graduate from college, and she was valedictorian that year. Her mother's a witch—"

"Shhhhh, Heston, you mustn't say that. We never know what others have gone through."

"Exactly. I never knew how hard it was for London to live in her own home, Mama. Can you imagine not wanting to go home after school? Being afraid to show your face because your mother would rip it off? Her childhood was nothing like mine. You made our home a sanctuary, Mama. You made Christmas cookies in July, remember? Just because Roberto broke his arm climbing out his bedroom window when he was running away."

"Eh, it was nothing. He needed to smile, so I made him smile. What is it you tough guys say, mission accomplished? Well, that is my mission in life, to always make my kids smile. Do I need to make Christmas cookies for you?"

Heston could feel the warmth and encouragement of his mother's love across the miles between them. Instead of launching into all the ways his love for London wouldn't be enough to hold her, he told his Mama, "Yes, please. Teach me and London how to make Christmas cookies. We both need to smile."

"Then bring her home to Arizona, my perfect boy, and I will teach you both how to love each other, and…" He could feel her shrug in that noncommittal way she did when she was reading his mind. Which he was sure she was. Couldn't all mothers? "…and we'll make enough cookies to last until Christmas."

This was what Heston hadn't known he needed, simply to reach out to his one sure touchstone in life, the woman who loved him unconditionally. "I love you, Mama."

"And I love London, my perfect son." Bellisa Contreras had the nerve to chuckle under her breath. Like he couldn't hear that? "And you, of course. When can you be here?"

"You always did like her better than me," he teased, going along with his mother's way of pulling him out of his gloom.

"Well, she's better looking, what can I say? And she's so much smarter."

"She is that. I'll talk with her first thing in the morning, and we'll plan a good day to visit."

"Any day you come home will be a good day to visit. Hurry, talk to London. Tell her I need to see her beautiful face again. I miss her!"

"But not me?" He feigned being offended.

"Ah, but you grew under my heart, my perfect boy. I've missed you since the day you were born and decided to leave my body. But it sounds like poor London was born under a cold, hard rock. Let's spoil her until she forgets how thoughtless her mother and father were. Let's make sure London knows how very much she's loved."

"Yes, Mama." By the time he disconnected, Heston was grinning. There was no one in the world like his mother. No. One.

He crept quietly back to his bed and into London's arms. "Mama said to tell you she still loves you best," he whispered. "And, oh, by the way, we're going to Arizona first chance we can. Maybe tomorrow. That good with you?"

"Ah huh," London answered drowsily. "I miss her, too."

Heston couldn't resist. She was still mostly asleep. "But you missed me more, right?"

"Oh, yeah… Sure…" London yawned. "But I really miss your mom."

Heston had to smile. He'd been worried about all the what-ifs that might destroy what he had with London. He'd been focused on the wrong things, on the negatives. Because life didn't come with guarantees. Hell, the world might end. London might not really be in love with him. They might not make it. It could happen. Couples fell apart after ten, twenty years of living together. Things might still go wrong.

But what if they didn't?

Chapter Thirty-Eight

The day after Kelsey visited London, Alex pulled up to the young Marine guarding the White House point-of-entry off Pennsylvania Avenue. As usual, he handed over his driver's license, contractor ID, and his personal pass from the Oval Office. Beneath those was a plastic container storing the oversized cinnamon roll Kelsey had sent along.

The sharply trimmed, immaculately groomed, young man in USMC blues scrutinized the documents and handed them back. Then carefully, he accepted Kelsey's gift and tucked it, face up, under his arm. "Thank you, Mr. Stewart. Sure hope you sign on with President Adams. It'd be an honor to protect you."

"Do I look like I need your protection?" Alex snapped.

The Marine stiffened to attention, his eyes forward. "No, sir!"

Alex nodded his approval at the loud and proud Devil Dog answer. "At ease," he said more gently. "Don't forget, you and the guys are coming over Christmas Eve. Bring your families if you got them. Remind everyone for me, Tony?"

Corporal Antonio Esposito relaxed as much as any Marine could. "We're all planning to be there. You may not need my protection, Mr. Stewart, but it'd still be an honor to serve with you."

Alex grunted. Kids in uniform. How was an old dog like him supposed to deal with a young pup's blind loyalty? 'We'll see,' was what he relied on with Lexie. But Esposito had served in combat. He deserved more. "How about you look me up when you're done wearing that uniform? You know where to find me."

A no-kidding grin cracked Esposito's proud face. "Yes, sir!"

"But knock off the sir shit," Alex growled. "I'm not military, understand? And I don't tolerate ass-kissers."

Grinning like a fool, Tony kept his lips zipped and waved Alex onto the White House grounds. Minutes later, Alex was admitted into the Oval Office, where he took the seat at the left of President Adams' desk and waited for him to finish the phone call he was on.

Several years earlier, President Thomas Beauregard Adams had been the dark horse in a fiery presidential race between two mud-slinging, lying politicians. Adams had run as an independent, and he'd won by a landslide. Seemed the silent majority had been as sick of the ever-escalating political drama, backstabbing, and lies as Alex had been. Americans wanted a straight shooter and, in Adams, they'd gotten one.

The President was a dead-ringer for Mark Houston. Could have passed for him any day of the week. Had the same dark looks. Same work ethic. Same heft and country boy charm. But Adams was more polished, as a President of the United States of America should be. His brown hair was always fastidiously trimmed. His nails were short, his cuticles clean and neat. He could've passed himself off as a metro male, as good-looking as he was. The ladies of America certainly loved him. But Alex knew different.

Adams might look like he belonged in Hollywood, but there wasn't a narcissistic bone in his body. He'd gotten elected because of his willingness to listen to the American public, to respond to them personally when needed, to meet them on their level in order to understand what most presidents never would—how to truly serve the people. Adams looked out for the little guy, for families struggling to make ends meet, for the homeless, and small business owners. He met one-on-one with illegal immigrants, not just popes, prime ministers, and others who thought they were God. He showed up with his shirtsleeves rolled up and ready to work when hurricanes devastated the shrimp industry along Louisiana's shoreline. He probably drove the Secret Service crazy, but he'd worked twelve-hour days, then had the audacity to show up early the next morning, ready to start all over again.

He was known for his uncanny skill of compromise, as well as his commitment to the military. The man was a tactical genius, profoundly adept at talking obstinate senators and congress men and women into seeing things his way.

Unbeknownst to the American public, Adams was also behind the mysterious helicopter crash that had killed his first vice president, VP Winston, along with several renegade Secret Service agents, a few years back. But only after he'd discovered, via his man undercover, aka Alex Stewart, that Winston had orchestrated President Adams' assassination. Winston had never wanted compromise, only revolution. To that end, he'd funded several radical malcontents who'd agreed that Adams had to go, including the subversive *Chaos Now*. Through President Adams' devious, but well-planned counterattack—which included making it look as if Alex were murdered—Adams saved the nation's capital, as well as thousands of lives.

In short, there was a genuine, diehard warrior in office for the first time since Teddy Roosevelt. A warrior Alex had come to disappoint.

President Adams ended his call and turned to Alex. "How's Kelsey?"

"Getting stronger every day, Mr. President."

"Tom. Call me Tom, damn it. You hired Special Operator Heston Contreras."

Alex cocked his head, remembering Zack's opinion of Heston. "He's a fine operator."

Tom was no dummy. He had a reason for bringing Heston up. "He broke up with Tuesday Smart?"

"He never hooked up with her, sir. Why do you ask?"

Tom pursed his lips. "Tom. Not sir and not Mr. President. Damn it, Alex. We've been over this before."

Alex coughed and amended his reply with, "Tom then." Problem was that respect was in Alex's nature, and calling the President of the United States anything but Mr. President, seemed damned pretentious.

"I know damned well why you're here today. You're not accepting my offer of VP."

"Correct," Alex replied, not sure what his being VP had to do with Heston or Tuesday Smart. "It's time I step back and let the young men handle The TEAM. They're as much a part of it as I am, and these days, they're a helluva lot smarter."

"I doubt that. But if you step back from your TEAM, you'll have more time on your hands. We can make this work. You'll be my team."

Alex chose to wait his president out instead of arguing with him. Tom might rely on that country boy charm of his in public, but in private and in combat, he was a tough son of a bitch who usually got what he wanted.

Not. This. Time.

President Adams huffed. "The reason I asked about Heston is Ms. Smart needs a bodyguard. Senator Hyde from Texas asked who I'd hire. I recommended you. Thought Heston would be good for the job, but if he's busy—"

"I have other agents who are every bit as good as Hes."

"Understood. Just thought it'd be a good match if they were already tight."

"They're not, and Heston is unavailable for at least the next month. I only hire good men and women. Send me the specifics and we'll take care of Ms. Smart."

"You sure you're not VP material? Winnie would sure appreciate having a close friend like Kelsey in this damned mausoleum."

Alex dipped his head in the affirmative. "I know Kelsey would love spending time with Winnie, but right now she needs me at home, sir, and I'd—"

"Tom."

"Tom. I appreciate the trust you have in me, but my mind's made up. I will always serve you, but this time, I cannot serve with you."

"That shit with the Irish Mafia?"

"I'm lucky she's alive."

"Yes, you are."

"That and I've promised Kelsey for years I'd retire. It's time I honor her by living up to my end of our deal. I'm not getting any younger."

"And neither am I." Tom shoved his chair back and stood, ramrod straight with his right arm extended. "I understand, Alex. We would've made a great pair."

"Yes, we would've." Alex lifted to his feet and accepted the handshake. "Thank you again for your continued friendship."

"You don't have to be my vice president to have that," Tom replied, releasing Alex's hand. "Tell Kelsey that Winnie and I would love to drop by when she's up for a visit."

"Will do."

"We sure married up, didn't we?"

"Yes, we did. Good seeing you again, Mr. President."

"Tom, damn it."

"Yes, sir. Tom."

"Give that wife of yours our best."

"Will do."

On the drive back to TEAM HQ, Alex stopped by a florist and selected a simple bouquet of red roses for the love of his life. For now, he and his family were staying in a private suite inside TEAM HQ, near the Intensive Care unit. Libby, Judy, and McKenna were adamant she needed more care than they'd be able to give her if she were home. So Alex asked Mark to collect his kids and bring them to TEAM HQ. Lexie and Bradley needed their mom, and it would do Kelsey good to see them. Alex couldn't wait to have his family together again.

Once inside TEAM HQ, he crossed the lobby to the elevators and ran into Mother. "You shouldn't have," she said, eyeing the bouquet.

"I didn't. Any news yet on who in that hospital worked for Lancaster? Besides Jolie Montgomery?"

"She's the only one I've found so far. If I were her, I would've put some kind of Tattle Tail inside Kelsey's room to keep track of you both, just like Mark and Beau did to track her out in the hall. Maybe she did. Maybe that was how Lancaster knew you'd taken Kelsey out of there. Maybe he was watching you the whole time."

Which made perfect sense. That would explain how Lancaster had seemed to be one step ahead of him. "So just Jolie Montgomery then?"

"I believe so, yes. What do you want me to do with her?"

"Nothing. Where's Mark?"

"He just took your kids down to see Kelsey. They've gotten so big, Alex."

Alex heard the ache in Mother's comment. He'd forgotten how much she loved his children and still grieved for Dempsey. The last time she'd seen Lexie and Bradley was last Christmas Eve. And here it was, nearly Christmas again. Alex knew how bleak this time of year had been without Sara and Abby to share it with. It had to be just as bleak for Mother.

"Come with me," he ordered, punching the down button with the side of his fist.

"Well, I… I can't… I mean… I just…" Mother sputtered as the door closed her in beside him. "I've got work to do, and—"

"Work can wait. This can't." The elevator took them three levels below ground level to The TEAM's high-tech sickbay. The Stewart suite, as Libby named it, was across the hall.

When the elevator opened, Mother crossed her arms over her chest. Like Alex cared if he annoyed her? Not today. Usually not ever. But he also knew he needed to set things straight, starting with Sasha Kennedy. He wasn't sure how yet, but it would come to him.

Mother took a deliberate step back when he stepped out. Cocking his head at her, daring her to tell another lie, he reached in, took hold of her elbow, and steered her into the hall with him.

"I really have work to do," she grumbled, pulling out of his grip.

He palmed the door to the Stewart suite open. "So you don't have time for these rascals?"

"Daddy!" Lexie squealed, already running full steam toward him, her dark brown curls bouncing on her shoulders.

Alex caught her under her arms and swung her high over his head. "There's my best girl," he crooned while she giggled. "Look who I brought to see you. It's—"

"My other Mother!" Lexie squealed again, deserting Alex's arms for Mother's. "I missed you so much! Did you miss me?"

"I…. I sure did, sweetheart." Mother had no choice but to cuddle the snuggle bug who was right then pushing her face into Mother's neck and patting her back like little kids were prone to do. They loved everyone. Even their grouchy father, who'd just been tackled by his year-and-a-half-old son.

"Hey, Bradley Boo," Alex said, lifting his son against him and getting a sloppy wet kiss on his cheek in return. "What've you and Sister been up to today?"

"Mommy!" Bradley growled, bouncing on Alex's forearm. "My Mommy!"

Alex cast his gaze across the room at the woman he adored. Without the protective helmet, Kelsey looked like hell. Her fingers were in her braid, loosening the long plaited strands of silky chocolate, but her face was too pale. Dark circles underlined her eyes, and she wasn't smiling. Not even a little. "You okay?" he asked, alarmed.

"I'm fine. It's just been a long day," she replied, licking her lips as if she'd just run a mile and was dehydrated.

"I'll bet." Maybe bringing the kids to stay with her wasn't the good idea he'd thought it was.

"She's just tired. Seeing the kids again wore her out," Libby announced breezily as she strode out of Alex and Kelsey's bedroom and into what passed for their open space. "We don't have any vases, so put those flowers in a pitcher. Leftovers are on the counter. Warm what you want and put the rest in the fridge. Kelsey's on her way to bed, so give her a hug and tell her goodnight. The kids are yours for the rest of the day. I'll be back if you need me, but make sure Kelsey sleeps."

Mark exited the kids' shared bedroom. "Hey, Boss. Finished installing childproof locks on all bathroom cabinet doors in this place and put safety plugs in all the electrical outlets I could access. I lowered your bed so Kelsey can get in and out of it easier, and I installed a baby monitor in the kids' room in case Lexie or Bradley want you during the night. I'll be across the hall at the clinic if you need anything."

"Anyone there I should know about?"

"Just the most beautiful woman in the world. My wife."

"You are so getting a hug for that later," Libby said.

Mark lifted an eyebrow. "And a kiss?"

"Maybe something else, too." Libby shot him a suggestive wink and—

"Get out," Alex ordered. "Play on your own time."

"I intend to," Mark replied as he ducked out the door with Libby in tow.

Alex handed Bradley to Mother. "Here. Hold him while I put Kelsey to bed."

"B-b-but…" Mother stuttered as a little boy joined the wiggling little girl already in her arms.

"Like riding a bike, it'll all come back to you," Alex told her as he strode over to Kelsey, leaned forward, and lifted her carefully out of the easy chair she was sunk into. "You. Bed. Now."

She circled one arm around his neck and leaned into him. "Thank you. I am tired."

"I can see that." He hip-checked their bedroom door open and took Kelsey to her side of what would be their bed until she was strong enough to go home. Which might take weeks. He pulled back the blankets and carefully laid her down. "Need help changing?"

"Yes, please."

Alex closed the door, then proceeded to help his wife undress. By the time he had her in sleep pants and a tank top, she was drained, and he'd gotten an eyeful of the purple thong she was wearing. He winked salaciously. "You want to ask me something?"

Strenuous activity like sex wasn't in Kelsey's immediate future, not until her ribs, hip, wrist, clavicle, and fingers healed. She'd insisted on visiting London, but in no way was she ready for intimacy. How on earth had she gotten that thong on anyway?

Her mouth opened wide with a yawn. "I had plans, Alex. Good plans. I wanted you all to myself tonight. But then Mark showed up with the kids, and I needed time with Lexie and

Bradley, and before you know it…" With a huff, she sent the dark brown tendrils that had escaped her braid flying.

Settling on the edge of the bed, Alex curled his index finger over her ear and tucked that silken lock back where it belonged. "When did you eat last, sweetheart?"

Kelsey ran an index finger under her eye, catching the tear before it fell.

"Just before you came from Tom's place. Libby grilled hamburgers, and Mark made enough German potato salad to feed the entire TEAM. It was good. You should try some."

Alex loved that she called the White House Tom's place, like visiting the most powerful man in the world was no big deal. He lifted her hand to his mouth and kissed her knuckles. "But did you eat enough?"

"Yes. Half a burger and a spoonful of salad. You should've seen Bradley chow down on that salad. You would've thought he was starving the way he gobbled it up and wanted more. Mark laughed his head off."

"You know how us guys love bacon." Alex tucked the blanket under his wife's chin. "If the kids are too much for you to handle, I can hire someone to—"

Screech! Stop the damned train. If the kids are too much for her *to handle? His* rowdy kids? *After she'd survived what should've been her death? Oh, hell no.* "Never mind," he said, mentally chastising himself for being as dumb as ever. "I'm not going anywhere. I'll take care of you and the kids." *Me. Just me for a change.* "And the day you're ready to play, I'm your guy."

The tiniest smile brightened her pretty face. "Well, of course you're my guy. Who else would I play with? Could we at least kiss like we used to?"

That he could do. Alex leaned over his wife, took her jaw gently between his hands, and started out slow. Which lasted for all of two seconds. Kelsey bit his bottom lip, licked it, then pushed her tongue into his mouth, and that started a fire. His hands slid down her shoulders to her hips, then onto her backside. Her hands slid up his chest to his neck and around it. She held onto him just as tightly as he was holding onto her. They were both breathing hard when he came to his senses and slowed the roll. He stopped squeezing her ass. With one last provocative lick across his lips, she eased off, too.

Alex tucked her back under his chin, against his pounding heart. "What you do to me. How am I supposed to walk into the other room with a spike in my pants?"

He felt her lips curl into a smile against his neck. "Thanks for letting me have my way with you, even for a few minutes."

"This downtime won't last long, sweetheart, you'll see. You're getting better every day."

Kelsey's shoulders lifted with an unconvinced sigh. "I want it all behind me, Alex. I want my life back. I want to go home to our house. I want our kids playing in their back yard. I never minded running your dad to the clinic or running Raymond's Place."

"Hey, save room for me on that to-do list, because from now on—"

She pulled back far enough to stare up at him. "You turned Tom down?"

"I did. VP isn't anything I ever wanted. I don't like people enough. In fact, most days I don't like people at all."

"I am so, so glad. I never wanted to be a VP's wife, either. Although, if that VP was you—"

"Not me. Nope. Never." He couldn't help it. Alex grinned like a lunatic. It'd been years since he'd felt this free. "I'm retired."

Her brows lifted to her hairline. "Sorry, but you'll have to convince me of that, buddy. I've heard it before."

"No, really," he said sincerely. "Mark's managed TEAM One for years now, and Murphy's done great with TEAM Two. They're both better than I ever was at pulling in men and women from all services."

"You did lean pretty heavily on the Marine Corps."

He shrugged, never going to admit anyone was better than a Devil Dog. At least, not out loud. But she was right. He had only hired Marines when he'd first hung out The TEAM shingle. But now, both TEAMs included sailors, soldiers, and airmen. He had yet to hire a Coastie, but that day wasn't far off. Alex ran a thumb over his chin, wondering which of his senior agents would hire the first Coastie, Mark or Murphy?

"Sorry. You're tired." He could see it in her eyes.

"I am," Kelsey agreed. But first…"

Alex leaned back to give her room. He was pretty sure he knew what was coming. A man in love didn't miss the hidden clues and tiny nuances of the woman he loved. Not if he was smart, he didn't.

"My nightmares are back." There was a tremor behind those four words.

"Tell me about them?" he asked. The biggest thing he'd learned with this, his fourth marriage, was to use his ears more than his mouth. Talking was about him. Listening was about her.

"I'm drowning, Alex," she whispered. "I'm somewhere dark and cold, and I can't breathe, but I can't stop myself from diving deeper, because I'm… I'm…" Her body shivered with the same fear that had driven her when she'd first lost Jackie and Tommy. For months Alex had listened to her scream as nightmares tore her heart apart. She'd been living with him, but locked behind his guest bedroom door back then. Only after he'd taken her to his bed after their first crazy night of lovemaking did those nightmares back off. Kelsey was the one who'd taken the step that turned their platonic relationship into heaven. Maybe it was time to lift his no-intimacy ban and join her in this oversized hospital bed like she wanted.

"I'm searching for my boys. For Jackie and Tommy. I hear them giggle. I'm so close my fingertips brush through their hair" —Kelsey's body stiffened as she fought the upcoming meltdown "—but I can't grab hold of them! My fingers never connect! I can't reach them, but I can't give up, and I keep going deeper and deeper and… Alex!"

If the unspoken *'save me!'* in her tone wasn't the last straw, nothing was. Alex jerked his tie off first, then his dress shirt and pants. Hurrying, he folded everything neatly over the free-standing valet chair by their shared walk-in closet—like a good Marine. Then, he climbed into bed behind Kelsey and pulled the blanket up to her chin—like a good husband. The kids were with Sasha and the most important job in his life began now.

"Sweetheart, I need you to know what happened to me on Mount Rainier."

"Oh, no. What?"

And now he'd frightened her. Not his intention. Alex eased one arm under her neck and resting his other hand between her breasts, needing to feel her heartbeat. Poor thing was fluttering like a tiny bongo. His throat and mouth went dry. Alex coughed. Swallowed again. At least, tried to swallow. This was about her, not him. Kelsey's tiny hand landed on top of his, and her touch was all he needed to continue.

"I dived into the White River after you fell, which was probably a dumb thing to do, but..." He shrugged both shoulders. "I am who I am, and I wasn't letting you go without a fight."

"Oh, sweetheart," Kelsey breathed, her fingers now circling two of his between her breasts.

"Scared the hell out of me when you fell in and disappeared so fast. That river was wicked. Tried to drown me, and you're so much smaller. I knew what you were going through, and I fought the son of a bitch the best I could, b-but I...." Damn it. He never stuttered. Not with anyone. He commanded, and he ordered, and he led!

But he'd also failed. Alex loved Kelsey enough to tell her that. "I failed, sweetheart," he choked. "No matter how hard I stroked and kicked to get to you, the river beat me back. It was killing me. But for me to find you, I had to s-save myself first. I had to get to shore. I had to live. I am so gawddamned sorry." The tears he'd denied for weeks, broke free. Alex buried his face in her hair and held onto his one true lifeline.

"You did save me," she reminded him, her nightmare seemingly forgotten, which was not what he wanted. This was about her, not him. *Get to the point, Stewart!*

"A man saw me struggling. He came into the river far enough to grab hold and pull me out. He got me to shore. He gave me warm, dry clothes, a jacket and water and food, so I could keep looking for you—" This was harder than Alex expected. "He and his kid were already searching for you. He knew who I was."

Kelsey's slender fingers intertwined with his much thicker, callused fingers. "It's okay, Alex. You can tell me anything."

"I know, but—"Alex dragged a rough hand through his hair. This was not supposed to be about him. "His name's Tom, and you're not going to believe this, because I sure didn't, but his little boy looks just like Lexie, and his name's Jackie, and…" Alex had no idea why he'd started down this road, or why he'd thought Kelsey needed to know he totally believed the Lord had a hand in her rescue. A mighty big hand. Alex lifted his upper body enough to look over her shoulder and down at her. He needed eye contact.

Tears glistened in the corner of her pretty brown eyes. "Are you telling me that... Jackie and Tommy…?" She pulled her bottom lip between her teeth, a sure sign she knew what he was going to say next.

A chill raced up the back of Alex's neck. "Yes, sweetheart. God sent your boys to help me find you. I prayed—never prayed so hard in my life—and He sent…" Alex bowed his face into the side of Kelsey's head. "He sent Jackie and Tommy. I'm sure of it. Only Tommy's a grown man and Jackie's his son." Alex now realized why Tom's password, *JackieNTommy,* had had such a profound effect on him that night. He'd been in shock, sure, but the Lord had obviously known he had a hard head and needed to hear those names more than once before they sank in.

"Wow," Kelsey breathed, her fingers tight around his. She was trembling. Her poor heart was now a damned kettle drum.

"I'm sorry. I thought telling you would—"

Her fingers squeezed tighter, cutting off his apology. She was shaking so hard her teeth chattered. Alex pulled her against the entire length of his body. His leg lifted automatically over hers to protect her from the pain he'd caused.

"Wow," she breathed again. "Thank you. I… I needed to know that. So, so much." She was crying. Instead of being the domineering asshole he knew he was, Alex waited until she decided to roll over and face him. He tucked her under his chin when she did and he held on. "I believe you. Who else would God send in our time of greatest need? *Ghostbusters*?"

He pursed his lips and forced a breath. If she could poke fun at him, they were going to be okay. And just maybe, her knowing that her first two sons were still very much part of her life, was the weapon she needed to fight the nightmares. Nothing destroyed nightmares faster than truth. A little faith didn't hurt, either.

"They both look like you. I want you to meet them. It might be hard, but—"

"But it's the proof you wanted, isn't it?"

Alex wasn't sure what she meant. "Not so much proof, sweetheart, but—faith. Tom Landry and his son Jackie were the only bright lights in my world right then. They gave me precisely what I needed to get back on my feet and find you. To take that step into the dark and know that…" Alex gulped. "He'd catch me." He, as in God, not Tom Landry.

"And to remember who you are," she added, her breath warm against his skin. Both Kelsey's shoulders lifted. "Maybe it's God's way of telling us you still have work to do."

Licking his dry lips, Alex chose to believe his wife would always know more than he did. "Maybe."

"Sara's visited me before," she whispered. "She's happy, Alex, and she's watching over you. Over us. You're never as alone as you think, and I guess, neither am I. The ones who've gone before us are only a step ahead, which means we're just a step behind. Sometimes we forget they're just out of sight, not lost forever. Thanks for helping me remember."

Threading his fingers into her lush chocolate tangles, Alex tipped her face up, needing one more taste. "I love you so damned much, woman," he whispered before he covered her mouth and branded her as his once more. He kept the kiss short, but wet, hot, and thorough. There wasn't one part of his body not aching for her when he eased back and wrapped her tight in his arms. "Tell me if I'm hurting you."

Sighing, she planted a kiss to the underside of his chin. "Just the opposite. You did it again, sweetheart. You saved me. I feel better."

"Then sleep." Alex pulled the blanket over her exposed shoulder and up to her ear. "If you need anything, I'll be here."

"Thanks." It didn't take long before she went limp and fell asleep.

He lay there watching her. Loving her. Reaching out, he traced a fingertip over her plump bottom lip. Her lips weren't blue or thin like they'd been when he'd first found her in that godforsaken trailer, and her cheeks were pinker and fuller, not drawn like when he'd arrived earlier. The network of worry lines at the corners of her eyes were once again perked upwaed, and he could only hope they'd turn back into laugh lines once Kelsey processed everything he'd just told her. Because it was true. Tommy and Jackie had saved him, and in doing that, Alex had been able to save Kelsey, who, for time and all eternity, would always love her first two baby boys.

Taking a deep cleansing breath, Alex thanked God again for allowing him more time with the miracle that was his wife. He held Kelsey close for as long as she needed, but when she groaned in her sleep, Alex recognized the difference between an upcoming nightmare and annoyance that he might've been holding her too tightly. Because, hey. He wasn't holding her for her sake as much as his. Relaxing his arms, she rolled away from him. Ordinarily he'd spend hours spooning with her, but he needed to save Mother from his kids.

Lifting carefully out of bed, he dressed. It'd been a long time since he'd been as scared as he'd been these past weeks. Losing Kelsey would've destroyed him, and he wasn't ashamed to admit it. Kelsey was every last breath in his body and the reason he was able to keep on keeping on. Might sound cliched, but without her, he really was nothing.

Closing the bedroom door behind him, he drew in a sigh of contentment and assessed the new life unfurling before of him. Handling his kids was a given. Yes, Lexie and Bradley would keep him busy, but time spent with them was pure pleasure, not work. Caring for his dad was another done deal. Mel wasn't going anywhere but back home with Alex, once Kelsey was strong enough to make the move. The light in his life might be a fragile glow at the moment, but Kelsey had proven her courage and determination before. She'd soon be back on her feet.

As if on cue, the persistent tension that had plagued his shoulders and neck for most of his adult life gave up their hold. A startling wave of warm oxygenated blood rushed up his scalp into his brain. The goosebumps caused by the loss of that grip chilled him.

So this was retirement, huh? Felt like a brand new life, like a hearty dose of exhilaration and freedom. Okay, then. Upward and onward. The TEAM was in excellent hands. With Obermeyer and the Wirths in the ground, Kelsey and London had nothing to worry about. Let the future begin.

He stopped in his tracks when he caught sight of Mother sitting with Lexie and Bradley. Leaning against the wall outside his bedroom door, Alex crossed his arms over his chest to enjoy what he was seeing: Mother on the couch across the room, reading one of Lexie's storybooks to his children. Bradley was sitting quietly on her lap, listening, but nosey Lexie jabbered away beside her as only she could do. That girl was too smart for her age. She needed more mental stimulation and—

"But why don't rats have fuzzy tails like squirrels?" she asked.

"Because rats and squirrels grew up in different neighborhoods," Mother answered. "Squirrels live in tall trees, so they had to grow furry tails to help navigate through the air when they jump from branch to branch. But rats don't want to live in trees. They like keeping their grubby, little rat feet on the ground."

"But why?" Lexie asked earnestly, her brows knitted together, which made her look so damned cute.

Alex rolled his eyes. *Lookout, Mother. Here comes the never ending, 'Why, why, why?'*

Mother looked her in the eye. "Think about it this way, honey. Were all of your daddy's Marines just like him?"

Lexie's lips puckered into an adorable pout. "That's a really silly question. Of course not. Not just anyone can be like my Daddy," she replied with attitude and the cutest, "Hmmpf. Everyone knows that."

Alex nearly laughed out loud. Yup, Lexie was his daughter all right.

The loveliest smile broke through Mother's usually stern countenance. "Well, it's the same with squirrels and rats. Not every animal in the world wants to fly through trees. So squirrels grew furry tails to help them fly better. They use those furry tails like rudders, while rats use their furless tails to keep cool, and sometimes, to run through tunnels and grip sewer pipes beneath the ground."

Lexie stared up into Mother's face. "What's rudders? And if rats can grip pipes, why can't they grip branches? Why don't they want to live in trees with squirrels? Then they could be friends and maybe they could teach each other fun stuff. Besides, climbing trees is awesome. My Daddy built me a treehouse, and it's my favorite place in the whole wide world because I can see forever when I'm up there. Sounds to me like squirrels and rats use their tails for the same reasons, Sasha. Are rudders like steering wheels? My daddy's got a steering wheel in his car. He lets me sit on his lap and drive sometimes. I even get to honk the horn."

Alex didn't need to hear more. He knew who needed to spend more time with his kids. Someone who could challenge Lexie. Someone who was a helluva lot smarter than him. Mother. And to get her to agree, she needed to be happy again, like she'd been when she had Justice Sandler in her life.

Alex intended to get to the bottom of what happened with their alleged marriage. Sasha hadn't ever given him a straight answer. Had she divorced Justice or had she run out on him? For that matter, had they ever legally married? Was he pining away the same as she was? Had he cut himself off from his family and friends, too? Alex needed to know. Because the woman reading patiently to his children had motherhood stamped all over her. The false mystique Sasha Kennedy had created to keep everyone away, was about to end. Alex might not be her boss anymore, not that she knew it yet, but she deserved to be as happy as he was.

And he was just the man to make it happen.

Epilogue

"I'm so excited!" London squealed when Heston stopped his Challenger at the entry to his parents' circular drive. The white stucco, red-clay tiled hacienda ahead radiated the same glow coming off London, and the driveway would take them right to his parents' front door. Just. Not. yet.

The lazy trip from Virginia to Arizona had been time well-spent. Maybe it was just the steady vibration of wheels on the road. Maybe simply being together long enough to really communicate did the trick. Heston didn't want this unique time of their lives to end. As soon as they stepped into Mama's house, everything would change. Not in a bad way, but he'd have to deal with his dad, Mama would take up all of London's time, and Heston didn't want to share.

Until this cross-country trek, their life together had always been packed too full of studying and tests, planning or working, and both of them striving to reach that unreachable 'all they could be.' Whatever that meant. It no longer mattered. The only thing Heston cared about now was bouncing in the passenger seat like a kid at Christmas. He'd had no idea how badly London had missed his mother. But then, he hadn't understood how bleak of a childhood she'd lived through, either. That was about to change.

Heston just wasn't sure he wanted their lives to change. The last three days had been filled with nothing but long, private conversations, impromptu stops along the way to see some out-of-the-way attraction, too much junk food, and intimate nights spent making love and getting reacquainted. Once again, they were what they'd been meant to be. Sharers of nightmares and dreams. Listeners. First and foremost… friends and lovers.

He didn't plan on quitting The TEAM, but he'd definitely be meeting with Murphy for a career adjustment when he got back home. Not that he blamed Murphy for the way he'd buried himself in his work to forget how much he'd missed London. But now that he had her back, the sky was their limit. The rest of their lives had already begun. Heston intended to get it right this time.

Her hair was turquoise again, and, all by herself, she'd sought counseling for her PTSD. Of all people, she'd hooked up with Shelby Cartwright, Gabe's wife, at her first group session. Turned out Shelby had given up her home-healthcare practice and was now a certified PTSD counselor. London made a new friend and Heston was thrilled, especially since he and Gabe had cars in common. Gabe had restored a beefed-up '69 Nova, then topped off the restoration by replacing the stock engine with an LS engine. The man had built a damned ten-second car.

While London and Shelby talked girl-stuff whenever they got together, Heston and Gabe talked cars, engines, and raceways. Heston had toyed with racing his Challenger at Evergreen Speedway in Washington, but had never taken the time to follow that dream. If London was willing, he would now, but only with her riding shotgun. That was the way the rest of his life would work, with her by his side.

"You ready?" he asked, his hand on the door handle, ready to jump out of the car before his parents burst out of their house.

London giggled. Her tropical eyes were as hot and beautiful as ever. She was the epitome of life again. "I'm ready if you are."

"Then" —He pushed his door open— "let's go!"

She laughed as he ran around the front of the car, opened her door for her, and scooped the woman he adored into his arms. Still giggling, she wrapped both arms around his neck, and together, they faced his parents' home.

He stopped in his tracks, not ready to turn her over to his mother. Not yet. But he would. Heston had a feeling Mama needed London as much as London needed her. Mama could be bossy, but he knew she already considered London part of her family.

She didn't yet know he'd had another ring made, this one as brilliant as the first, but different. The stone wasn't blue-topaz, and it wasn't enhanced by white diamonds. It was simply a brilliant two-carat solitaire diamond, set in a solid gold band. Heston only needed one rare blue-topaz in his life and that was London.

"You ready?" he asked again.

She laid her head on his shoulder. "Whenever you are. Wherever you go, I will go. And whatever you want to do, I will do, too. No matter what happens next, I'm in this with you all the way, Hes."

He pressed a kiss to her forehead. "I know, babe. I know."

"Heston!" his mother called out from her front door. "Bring that girl inside. She needs a hug. Hurry!"

As if Mama couldn't see he was already hugging London? Heston grinned, turned his back on his adorable mother, and kissed the hell out of his woman. Only when London was breathless, did he do as Mama ordered. From now on, the only woman he was taking orders from was... London.

The End

Bonus Epilogue

"They won't let me leave, Boss. They keep giving me drugs. Why won't they let me go? I've got a job. I work for you. Get me out of here!"

Murphy cocked his head, studying the troubled agent fidgeting with the hem of the gray Shady Creek Asylum t-shirt he'd been wearing the past three days. Sitting on the edge of his hospital bed, Grissom had both his gaze and his feet on the floor. Murphy leaned forward from the chair at the foot of the bed, wishing this agent would, just once, make eye contact. "Why do you think you're here?"

Grissom shrugged. "I don't know. Did I take one to the head and don't remember? Is it a TBI? Am I dying? That why they won't let me leave?"

"You're too tough to die, but you're not well. You asked me to find your boys, remember?"

Grissom nodded, then slowly, like every other time Murphy had tried to jog Grissom's memory, the nod changed to head shake. "No. I... ah... don't remember asking... anything." He scrubbed both hands over his bearded face, then up over his shaggy hair as if searching for those elusive memories. "I ... I got shot, recall that clear as a bell... I think. Least, I know I was in a shootout or something... somewhere... But I can't find any point of entry. Was it my head? Did I take one to my skull? Is a bullet still in my brain?"

The tenor of his voice rose even as he avoided looking at Murphy, "Is that what's why I'm here? Who did it? Who shot me?"

"You weren't shot, but—" That happened when Grissom was still active duty Air Force. It had nothing to do with this voluntary confinement.

"Where's my damned kids?" Grissom cut Murphy off, peering around him to the closed and locked door of his room. "If I asked you to find them, they gotta be missing. Where are they?"

Murphy's chest lifted with anguish more than the relief he wished he were feeling. "We're still looking for them. You don't remember, but—"

"Pam took my boys, didn't she? She ran out on me and took Tanner and Luke and—"

That sounded promising, as if Grissom was remembering. "And half The TEAM's looking for them."

"Half? Half's not good enough. Get me out of here. I'll find them. I will, and I'll find Pamela, and when I do—"

"You're not going to find her. Think. Please, just stop and think, remember what I told you."

Grissom's life had become a tragic rerun that wouldn't stop playing. As many times as Murphy'd explained what had happened to his wife and sons, Grissom kept asking. Always the same questions. Always getting the same answers. The truth wasn't kind, and his brain wasn't letting him accept it anyway. It was protecting him and doing a bang-up job at that.

As for Pamela, she'd done Grissom dirty on so many levels. First, by cheating on him whenever he'd been OCONUS, while still active duty. Then, by taking Tanner and

Luke with her when she'd fled to South America with her boyfriend, Mike Estes.

Unfortunately for her, karma was a sneaky bitch. Murphy now knew Estes had made his living providing guided tours in one of the three Cessna's he owned. *Had* being the key word. He was the one flying the plane when it went down off Costa Rica's west coast. Fortunately for Grissom, his boys weren't part of that tour. But Costa Rican navy pulled Pamela, Estes, and four paying tourists out of the ocean.

Murphy still had no idea where Tanner and Luke were. Between him and TEAM One's top dog, Mark Houston, they had a dozen TEAM agents working to locate the boys. From her home, where she was recovering from minor surgery, Agent Leisha Warner had backtracked Pam's activities up to the morning she'd left the States. Pam's neighbors had been just as helpful. The retired couple across the street from Grissom informed Leisha that every time he'd gone OCONUS, Estes had all but lived with Pam and his sons. God, Murphy hoped those boys were still alive. Pam wouldn't have been vindictive enough to have them, would she?

"Oh… Oh, yeah." Oddly, Grissom calmed as quickly as he'd escalated. "Sure. Robin's good. My boys love her. She babysits a lot for us."

His breathing settled, which was great, but Murphy had no idea what or who Grissom was talking about. "Robin who?"

"My neighbor. Robin Dillon. She's a real good girl. My boys love her. She babysits for us." He pursed his lips, as if forcing himself to breathe, like a pregnant woman in labor, would help. "I need to see 'em, Murph. You'll make sure they come see me as soon as they get here. Is Robin bringing them?" Grissom swiped a hand over his hair again, as if he wanted to look good for whoever Robin was.

"You're injured, Gris." Murphy pressed a hand to his sternum. "Here."

Grissom had yet to make direct eye contact, and that was troubling. "You sure? Cuz I gotta tell you, there's no hole in my chest or belly big enough to even stick my little finger into. I checked. I can't find any wounds anywhere. No entries. No exits. Christ sakes, don't you think I'd know if I was dying?" The longer he talked, the higher his voice crept into hysteria.

This visit was going nowhere. It was time for Murphy to back off. Inhaling a gut full of regret, he lifted to his feet.

Grissom jumped up, staring past him to the door. "Don't go. Please. This place is killing me. All they wanna do here is talk, and I'm fucking sick of it. I… I got a wife and kids to get home to… two kids… two little boys… err, don't I? Pamela. That's her na-a-a-m-m-me…" The nervous tone in his voice rapped down low into slow gear, like a vinyl record on a turntable losing power. "Pamela," he whispered, blinking but still not facing Murphy. "It's not me, is it? It's her. It's Pam. She's… she's gone. She's run off and took my boys and she…"

Died. Just say it, Grissom. Remember. That's the only way you're getting out of here.

Grissom's gray eyes went blank. His lips thinned.

Murphy sucked in a breath, knowing what was coming next.

Sure enough. Grissom blinked and yawned, as if his poor brain had just rebooted, and he'd woken up in the middle of the same nightmare. "Well, hey, Murph. You come to win back the cash you lost playing poker last night?"

"Just came for a visit," Murphy replied softly. "How are they treating you here?"

"Here?" Grissom blinked again and once again, his gaze hit the exit door of the room that would be his home for as long as it took for him to remember. Four cream-colored walls and a comfortable bed with a navy-blue comforter, a mostly empty closet, a dresser, and a desk. A private bath and a single picture window framing bullet-proof, unbreakable, polycarbonate glass. No one could get in and Grissom couldn't get out. For now the world was safe.

There were no pens or pencils in the desk. No paper clips, either. The dresser was bolted to the floor and the drawers were painted on. The bed was bolted down, as well, and the blinds on the windows were enclosed inside two panes of that bullet-proof glass. No drawstrings. Nothing anywhere to fashion a weapon with. Which didn't mean squat when the man inside this room was a trained killer.

"Boss?" Grissom asked for what seemed like the hundredth time in the last thirty minutes. "Where am I?"

Murphy sucked in a bellyful of patience and sat back down. Grissom's nerves were shot and his heart had been blown away with them. He just didn't know it yet, and there was no way to help him understand. He'd lost touch with reality, and judging by the way this visit had gone, he wouldn't be coming back anytime soon.

But then...

Grissom did something he hadn't done since becoming a full-time resident of the Shady Creek Asylum. His gaze scrolled from the door and, without blinking, he stared Murphy dead in the eye. "She really left me this time, didn't she?" he asked, his voice a rock in the middle of the shitstorm that was his life. "Pam ran off with that guy who's been hanging around. That's what you've been trying to tell me, isn't it? She took my sons and she dumped them somewhere in" —he closed his eyes and touched two fingertips to his right temple— "fucking Costa Rica."

His nostrils flared as he drew in a deep breath and his belly inflated. Murphy could only guess that the pain and suffering Grissom was under had somehow freed his brain from its trauma. He needed his boys. Good fathers always did. But the stark sadness in his voice was a knockout punch Murphy hadn't seen coming. Neither did he expect Grissom to lift to both feet, plant them like he was ready to fight, and declare, "Help me find my boys or get the hell out of my way, Murph. Like it or not, I'm leaving."

"Now hold on a minute." Murphy put both palms forward, as if placating a man the size of Grissom would stop a father hellbent on finding his children.

Grissom stood a good foot over Murphy. He was as tall as Shane and bulkier than Beau. His eyes were mean for the first time in days, both dark brows narrowed over two pissed off steel-blue death rays. He leaned over Murphy, glared down at him, and hissed, "I said move, old man."

Murphy allowed a faint smile. Sass was another step in the right direction. "Call me old man again, and I won't sign off on them letting you out of here."

"I don't need you signing anything. I'm a man, damn it. Get the hell out of my way."

"You're not going anywhere—"

"The fuck I'm not!" Grissom's roar blistered over the top of Murphy's nearly bald head. But rules were rules.

"Back off, buster!" He could bellow, too. "If you'd shut up and listen for a guldarned minute, you'd understand you can't go—" Damned if this junior agent's hands didn't ball into fists. "—ALONE! You big dummy!" Murphy yelled before Grissom could cock that hammer-of-a-fist and knock him on his ass. "One is none and two is one! Remember? You've got to be smart. Take someone with you. Hell, take everyone. We're all on your side, and you know better!"

Grissom's chest heaved, and God Almighty, Murphy knew his time to reason with this bull of a man was running out. Either he got through to Grissom or he lost him for good. Righteous rage was one thing, but Grissom going rogue could get them both killed.

"Yes, Pam took Tanner and Luke to Costa Rica. We've tracked them that far," Murphy explained hurriedly. "Your mission is to locate your sons without killing anyone else, you understand?"

A grunt was all Murphy got for an answer. He kept talking. "Which agents do you want on your six?"

"Alex."

Murphy shook his head. "No can do. He just retired, this time for good. Who else?" Alex would only remain retired until the shit hit the fan, but Murphy refused to let Grissom punch that ticket.

"Leisha Warner."

"Sorry, she twisted her knee playing volleyball two nights ago and can't walk. Might be looking at surgery. Pick someone else."

"Cassidy Dancer."

Murphy gulped. Okay, not everyone could support Grissom. "She's on maternity leave." He seemed focused on female operators, so Murphy offered, "Phoenix Bond and Jenna Bates are available. So are Everlee Yeager-Hayes, Izza Maher, Camilla Garner, and—"

"Taylor Armstrong, Cord Shepherd, and Walker Judge."

Murphy shrugged fisted knots of tension off his shoulders. "They're yours. Anyone else?"

"Alex," Grissom barked.

Damn it, this was where Murphy drew a hardline. "No," he told his hard-headed agent again.

"Yeah, Murph. Alex'll come if he knows what I'm up against. He'll understand, I know he will."

And he would. Alex was a father and a hard charging son of a gun who always had his agents' backs. Which is why Murphy refused to call him. "Think, Grissom. Kelsey just survived a shot to the head, and she damned near drowned. She needs Alex a helluva lot more than you do." *And I'm in charge of TEAM Two, damn it. Not Alex. Not anymore.*

Grissom's brows furrowed into a dangerous V. Which told Murphy the man in front of him didn't remember how close Kelsey had recently come to death, or that he'd been there the day both TEAMs had taken down the human trafficking ring of then-Secretary of State Tristan Obermeyer and his buddies, Michael Keane, Lancaster and Miles Wirth. It was Lancaster who'd put the hit on Kelsey; his son Miles who'd hired Ryan Malloy, Ireland's best sniper, to do the ugly deed. One of the three main players, no one knew which, had then offed Malloy and hired a couple local tough guys to kidnap London Wilde, Heston's fiancé. Heston had rescued London, and Murphy knew where Obermeyer's body was. But the FBI still dutifully considered both Wirths missing and unaccounted for. Not like Murphy cared what the Bureau thought. Even if he knew where Alex buried the Wirths, he'd never tell.

"Call him," Grissom ordered. "Alex is the best there is."

"If anyone's going with you, it's me. Let me make a few calls—"

"Then step on it! I gotta get gone. My boys need me, Boss!"

At last! Grissom called Murphy *'Boss.'*

"Understood. Grab a shower while I work on getting you released. Then we'll call Mother to line up an Air Force bird out of Joint Base Andrews. Most of TEAM One's already in Costa Rica searching for your boys." All except agents managing permanent workloads: Mark, Harley, Zack, Maverick, Tripp, Jake, and Beckam.

Grissom headed for the head. "Grab me some decent clothes while you're at it. My go-bag and tactical gear. My vest. And I need weapons, Murph. Get me my knife and my pistols."

Murphy watched the bathroom door close on Grissom. With any luck, Grissom's brain was finally on the mend. If not? Murphy blew out a sigh. He was in for one helluva flight to Costa Rica.

**Thank you for reading
Heston and London's story!**

**You are the key to this book's
success!**

Please tell other readers why you liked Heston
by leaving an honest review
at the retail site where you purchased it.

Recommend him to your friends. Lend him.
Most of all, enjoy him!

Other Irish Winters' best-selling series:

In the Company of Snipers

Alex
Mark
Zack
Harley
Connor
Rory
Taylor
Gabe
Maverick
Cassidy
Adam
Lee
Ky
Hunter
Eric
Jake
Seth
Beau
Renner
Beckam
Walker
Jameson
Tripp
Shane

Deuces Wild
King of Hearts
Joker Joker
One-Eyed Jack
Ace

Hearts and Ashes
Smoke
Ash

SOBs Novels
Angel
Assassin
Vaquero
Damned

To keep up with my new releases, giveaways, and actionable intel, sign up for my spam-free newsletter at IrishWinters.com.

About the Author

Irish Winters…

…is a best-selling author who, when she isn't writing, dabbles in poetry, grandchildren, and rarely (as in extremely rarely) the kitchen. More prone to be outdoors than in, she grew up the quintessential tomboy on a dairy farm in rural Wisconsin, spent her teen years in the Pacific Northwest, but calls the Wasatch Mountains of Northern Utah, home. For now.

She believes in making every day count for something, and follows the wise admonition of her mother to, *"Look out the window and see something!"*

Connect with Irish online:
On Facebook: https:/www.facebook.com/author.irishwinters
On Twitter: https://twitter.com/irishwinters1
Or at http://www. IrishWinters.com